To Sarah —

You're stronger than you know.

BURDEN
of
POWER

THE WALLKEEPER TRILOGY
BOOK ONE

CAREN HAHN

Published by Seventy-Second Press

ISBN 978-1-7352272-0-7

Cover and layout design by Andrew Hahn.

carenhahn.com

SEVENTY-SECOND

PRESS

To Crystal,
for convincing me to dust off
my old writing dreams.

The Wallkeeper Trilogy

Burden of Power
Pain of Betrayal
Gleam of Crown

Burden of Power

THE WALLKEEPER TRILOGY

BOOK ONE

SEVENTY-SECOND

PRESS

One

"Are you the king today?"

Ria stood on the terrace and leaned against the doorframe to her father's room. The sun was warm against her back, brightening the pale yellow stones beneath her feet so that she squinted against the light. A fresh breeze teased wisps of hair against her neck, carrying the sweet scent of apple blossoms from the king's private garden.

"Of course I'm the king." Sindal's voice, emerging from the dark recesses of his room, held the beginning of a reproof. "Who else would I be?"

"I wasn't sure." Ria lingered at the threshold. Not because her father wouldn't welcome her, but because she was reticent to enter the shadowed room. This was the first warm day of the season, and she was loath to retreat indoors. Instead she peered into the room, struggling to see Sindal's expression clearly. Bright sunlight spilled onto his desk from the diamond-paned window, but he sat just out of reach in the dimness, made all the darker for the light.

"The king would have been standing at my side when the Khouri ambassador arrived with his retinue," Ria continued. "And yet, I was conspicuously alone."

A sound like the rustling of paper.

"That's not until tomorrow," the king said dismissively.

"No, Far, it was most certainly today."

Sindal's chair creaked, and Ria sensed his bulk shifting.

"Are you sure?"

"Unless I simply imagined the lovely gift ceremony that took place an hour ago. Lord Melo brought a dazzling array of opals. And no, I'm not going to share, so don't ask."

"Why did no one tell me it was today?" Again the creak of wood straining.

"You mean this morning when Galinn came to fetch you and you refused to let him in? You've got to stop doing that to your own steward, Far. I made excuses for you, of course. But really, how did you manage for two years without me?"

"It was far longer for Galinn than for me," Sindal said with dry humor.

Ria laughed and stepped into the room, leaving the warmth behind. As her eyes adjusted to the shadows, she noticed a pile of papers littering the floor near the king's feet. "What are you working on that you lost track of the day?"

Sindal laid down his pen and pulled distractedly at his thick, sandy beard, leaving ink behind. The quill seemed to have leaked more ink onto his hands than the paper. Or maybe at fault was the upended inkwell, its contents spilling onto the discarded papers cascading across his desk and onto the floor.

"I can't remember. I get so close and then it's gone."

"Remember what?"

In answer, Sindal shuffled through the nearest pile of papers and thrust one at her.

Ria gingerly stepped through the mess to take it, lifting her skirt to avoid sweeping the wet ink with her hem. It appeared to be a report of some kind which had now been repurposed to compose music. A roughly written staff spanned both sides, with notes dotting the paper and then crossed out in an angry frenzy.

"You're composing! How lovely!" Ria glanced over the notes and a melody blossomed in her head. Without thinking, she hummed it through until the written music ended abruptly with a heavy ink blot.

"It's beautiful, Far. Is this your creation?"

"No. Yes, maybe." Sindal yawned and stretched his back. "It feels familiar to me, but I can't think of where it comes from. This is the closest I've gotten."

Ria picked up a sheet of paper to examine from the untouched pile at the king's elbow. "Is there a paper crisis I'm unaware of?" It was a personal letter from Merek Strong, her father's First Captain over the Wall Guard. Beneath it lay an official report from Strong regarding the outer regions of Rahm where he and his troops guarded the borders of the land.

"Why are you composing on…" Ria shifted aside the discarded papers on the floor, peering beneath her father's scribbles to discern the signature. Understanding dawned. "Ah, I see." Her smile dimmed. "Far," she said sternly. "These documents are all from Captain Strong."

Sindal grunted. He grabbed the letter out of her hands and began scratching a staff right over the top of it, the hasty lines uneven and shaky. His head bent low over the desk, as if his wide shoulders could repel her accusation.

But she would not be deterred. "Troop reports, wall security, even some personal letters. Every single one of these papers came from Captain Strong, and you're treating them like so much waste."

Sindal stopped writing and glared at her, his blue eyes crackling a warning. "What does it matter to you?"

"He's your oldest friend. I don't know what's really going on between you, but this feels…childish."

"Childish?" Sindal's hand shot out, angrily crumpling the paper and catching the inkwell as he tossed the paper to the floor. Ria gasped as black ink slashed the front of her gown.

"Far! Look what you've done!" She reached for a handkerchief, but it only smeared the ink, staining her fingers black. "Biren will never be able to get this out."

Sindal cringed, and his face reddened. "I'm sorry, Ria. I didn't mean to…I spent all night trying to remember this melody that won't leave me alone, and I thought if I could write it down, maybe I could sleep."

"You didn't sleep all night?" Her irritation faded at his sheepish expression and bloodshot eyes. His momentary flash of ire was gone, replaced with regret.

Sindal yawned and stood, the chair scraping against the polished wood floor as he pushed his girth out of it. He had put on weight in the years she'd been gone, and since her return two months earlier she had yet to see him join the soldiers in training. At first she thought it was the winter chill that kept him indoors, but spring was erupting around the grounds and still he preferred to keep to his quarters. As he moved to stand before the window, the light emphasized heavy pouches under his eyes.

He's gotten old, Ria realized suddenly. Somehow, the playful father of her youth was gone, and she felt an unspeakable loss. She stepped up beside him and took his arm, hoping to reassure him by her presence. He didn't stand as straight as when she'd left Albon two years earlier, and now she was nearly his height. Across the terrace of blinding stones, fruit trees were just beginning to blossom in the king's garden, forming a fragrant haze of white and pink. It was her favorite view in all of Thorodan Hall. Her own rooms had a less romantic view of the courtyard, and she was more likely to wake to the cackling of a rooster than the cheerful twittering of birds.

After a moment, Sindal shook his head. "You're right, Ria. This is childish. I've wasted half my day trying to capture the ghost of a tune instead of tending to my duties. Was Lord Melo very upset?"

"He's a Khouri," Ria said with a wry smile. "Even his anger comes out as apologies and polite smiles. Besides, you can make it up to him this evening at the reception."

Sindal groaned and ran a hand through his thinning hair. "Don't you ever grow tired of it all? Don't you ever wish for a moment's peace?"

"Of course I do. That's why I never learned to hunt, so there's at least one entertainment from which I'm excused. While you and our distinguished guests are up before dawn chasing some poor creature in the damp and the cold, I'll be enjoying a quiet morning alone with my feet warming by the fire."

Sindal chuckled and squeezed her hand on his elbow. "Enjoy such luxuries now, my dear. They will be harder to come by when you're queen."

"I don't know about that. Apparently I can ignore foreign dignitaries and lock myself away composing music anytime I wish."

Her father prodded the papers on the floor with his boot. "I'll have Martin burn these. They're rubbish anyway."

"Oh Far, don't do that!" Ria snatched one off the desk. "Save one and finish it," she commanded. "It really is lovely. It would be even lovelier if it were written up properly instead of scrawled over Captain Strong's letters. I'll ask for a clerk to copy it out on some clean paper and you can perform it for the captain the next time he comes to Albon."

Sindal tensed. "Leave it alone, Ria. That's a private matter."

"Hardly. All of Albon knows that he refused your appointment to general. So he's a fool. Men have been guilty of worse. How long do you intend to punish him?"

"You wouldn't understand." Sindal patted her hand again, but this time Ria felt a flush of annoyance.

I understand more than you think, she thought. Her father's brooding. His troubled sleep. His disagreement with Captain Strong had left him shaken and unsure. But Ria wouldn't say these things to him. For now, she was just pleased that his good humor had returned. If the price was enduring his condescension, her pride would weather it well enough.

It had weathered far worse in recent months and emerged intact.

She felt a tightening in her chest as she always did when she thought of Artem. It had been excruciating seeing him as she passed through Ardania on her return home to Rahm, his new bride on his arm. She'd already heard he'd married, of course.

Even in the mountains of Branvik where she'd spent the summer, the court had talked of little else for weeks. They said the king of Ardania had nearly disowned his son over the unsuitable match.

"I'm sorry, my dear," Sindal said, breaking into her thoughts. "I'm afraid I'm not very good company today."

Ria roused herself and forced a smile, pushing thoughts of Artem away. "Join us for dinner, and all will be forgiven. If you're particularly attentive to Lord Melo, I might even share the opals."

"You know that those gifts are property of the crown and must be duly accounted for, not squirreled away in your room."

"Tch, tch," Ria said dismissively. "Then *you* lead the welcome ceremony next time. At least it's not offensive for you to be taller than your guest. Do you know how uncomfortable it is to have to shrink as much as possible without appearing to slouch? If I were a man, my height wouldn't be a point of insult."

"If you were a man, you would be joining me on the hunt tomorrow." Sindal's smile made him seem years younger.

"Fair point. I suppose we both have our own onerous tasks, but that's one I'll gleefully leave to you."

"You're a strong enough rider. You should join us."

"Far, did you forget who you're talking to?"

He looked confused, and heat rose a little in her cheeks.

"Isn't the point of a hunting expedition to…" she trailed off, hoping he wouldn't make her finish. "Kill an animal?"

"Ah," he nodded. "Yes, I forgot. I suppose you wouldn't have to watch."

Ria wrinkled her nose in distaste. "Forgive me, but I'd rather not embarrass myself in front of our guests."

The words sounded ironic to her own ears as she bade her father goodbye and stepped over the piles of ink-stained paper on her way toward the door. As yet her father's odd moods hadn't become public knowledge, but she worried about the humiliation he would face if they did. Her eye caught Captain Strong's signature and she made a mental note to ask Galinn about what had really happened between her father and his oldest friend.

Two

D anvir's Wall cleaved apart the dense forest. Stefan stood in a
column of golden light cast by the setting sun as he leaned
against the parapet, watching the darkness deepen under the trees.
Familiar trees stood behind him, friendly and welcoming. Deep in
their sheltering arms lay home and family. But before him, on the
Fehr side of the wall, the Dimm Forest felt menacing.

Perhaps that's simply the nature of a soldier, Stefan reflected, *to see
danger where there is none.* Fehr bandits rarely attacked their village
these days. Danvir's Wall had seen to that. But he remembered the
days of his childhood when he had cowered in his bed during the
night, and he didn't trust the forest on the other side of the wall.

"Nice night for patrol," Borth said. "Much better than the soaking
Ryken and I got last week."

Stefan smirked. "It was probably good for Ryken. Give him something new to whine about for a change."

Borth snickered. He was a local man who didn't seem to mind the
feeling that came from spending your days and nights in a wooded
tunnel. Not all soldiers could withstand the mental pressures of wall
duty in the northern forest of Rahm, and Stefan suspected Ryken—a
young soldier fresh from training in Albon—wouldn't last the year.

They walked without aid of torches, so as to not impede their
night vision as the sun set and dusk gave way to darkness. Wall duty
was a relaxed affair. They would likely not see another living soul the

whole of the night. They didn't speak much, but the silence was comfortable, much as if they were tracking animals in the forest.

The wall was marked at intervals to help them keep their bearings, but they had patrolled this area for so many years that Stefan looked for other landmarks: the way the rock changed color where the builders incorporated more local stone rather than that which came from the quarries in the south; the spot where the land fell away sharply in a deep depression; how the wall curved to the north for a time to skirt around a hidden lake.

"Have you heard any word lately from Captain Strong, sir?" Borth interrupted his thoughts.

Stefan frowned. "If you're wondering about the rumors Ryken has been spreading like thistle seeds, no. I don't know any more than you do. Or any more than Ryken's far does, I'd wager, no matter what he claims in his letters."

"That's a shame. I thought that with you and the captain being such close mates and all, maybe you'd know if it's true."

"And if you were embroiled in a scandal that had all of Albon talking, would you hurry to tell your mates all about it?"

"No, sir, I suppose not." Borth was silent for a few minutes, but when he spoke again it was clear he wasn't finished. "But just think of it. Can you imagine our own Captain Strong as general over the whole army? Second in command to King Sindal himself? That would give us all from the north a bit of glory now, I'd say!"

"You want glory, you shouldn't have taken this post," Stefan said. "Merek Strong wouldn't be First Captain over the Wall Guard now if he'd come home first chance he got. You should be in Albon or Endvar if you want to make something more of your career."

"Well, we can't all be Merek Strong, can we?"

"No." Stefan smiled in spite of himself. "No, we cannot."

Borth stiffened just as Stefan caught a glimpse of something in the forest on the Fehr side. A light, but so distant that it was difficult to discern the nature of it.

"What is it? Fire?" he muttered.

"Torch, I think, sir," was Borth's reply. "But I can't be sure, it—"

Borth's cry choked off as a heavy arm grasped his neck from behind. Stefan whirled, drawing his sword. Borth's hooded attacker held a blade to his neck, pinning his other arm uselessly behind him.

"What is your business attacking a soldier of the King's Wall Guard?" Stefan called out, hoping his voice didn't betray his fear.

In answer, the stranger released Borth and raised his head so the hood fell back. "Simply testing his readiness in case his commanding officer drops by."

Stefan gasped. "Merek Strong! What are you…? Excuse me, sir." Relief gave way to laughter. Sheathing his sword, Stefan offered a sharp salute. "Captain Strong, allow me to introduce Corporal Borth."

Borth echoed his salute, a little less sharply, still breathing heavily.

Captain Strong grinned and gripped the young man on the shoulder. "Sorry for startling you, Corporal, but I've recently developed a certain climbing technique and wanted to try it on His Majesty's troops."

"Climbing!" Stefan gaped. "You don't mean to say you climbed the wall!"

"Hmm, you think it's impossible just because it hasn't been done." Strong shrugged. "Until now."

"But how?" The height of the wall didn't normally make Stefan queasy, but the thought of climbing it gave him a distinctly uncomfortable feeling in his belly.

"Details for later. Now, tell me. What grabbed your attention so completely a moment ago that I was able to sneak up on you unawares?"

Still somewhat dazed, Stefan turned back to the forest on the Fehr side and pointed to where they'd seen the light. It was gone.

"We can't be sure what it was; it was so brief. Might have been no more than a hunter's campfire."

Captain Strong frowned. "Not likely if it was extinguished so quickly. If there were nearer scouts who saw our scuffle…"

"Scouts? You mean, bandits, sir?" Borth had finally found his voice.

Captain Strong turned to the young man, and his frown dissolved into a smile. "Borth, you say? Tell me, where do you come from? You look like a man of the forest."

Borth straightened under the captain's attention, forgetting his earlier question. But the unsettling thought of bandits hovered in Stefan's mind all the way back to the guard house.

"And as I'm standing there outside his house made of perfectly cut wall stone, with the royal quarrier's own stamp, he has the gall to say, 'I'm sure I don't know. They just came out of the ground that way.'"

The other soldiers laughed. The small room was filled with a dozen of Stefan's men who had come to see Merek Strong, First Captain of the Wall Guard. The more senior officers claimed the seats around the small wooden table, while the junior ones crowded against whatever section of wall was free.

One called out, "What did you do then?"

"Well, he obviously didn't move all that rock on his own. So I suggested that he and his sheep move in with whichever son or grandson helped him steal the wall stone because he was about to be left homeless. Then I set my men to work disassembling the walls of his house."

More laughter.

Stefan smiled. They lived a quiet enough life in the Dimm Forest that having the great Captain Strong in their midst was reason to celebrate. His men's countenances were lighter than normal. Unfortunately, so were their tongues.

"Excuse me, sir?" young Ryken spoke from the corner. "My father says that King Sindal wanted to promote you to general, but you refused. Why would you refuse, sir?"

Stefan straightened with a nervous glance at Strong. What was the fool boy thinking, asking a question like that? But Merek didn't seem to mind. Instead, he looked curiously at the young man.

"Who might your father be, soldier?"

"Rustov Halworth, sir."

Strong brightened at the name. "I know your father well! He was a fine mentor during the Sondiv Campaigns. How is he?"

The young soldier glowed with pride at the attention. "He's well, sir. I'm the last of his sons to serve, and I expect he'll be reading my letters to every visitor the way he did my brothers'."

Captain Strong scratched at his beard. "Then I suppose I'd better be careful how I answer your question."

A low rumble of chuckles filled the room, followed by an expectant silence.

"I hadn't expected the rumor to travel so fast from Albon, but yes, the king and I did discuss my taking the post. Eventually, we both decided it was a poor match."

Stefan watched his old friend closely. There was more to this story than Strong was telling.

Ryken wasn't satisfied either. "My father says there isn't a finer man in the king's service today, sir. He was angry with the world for a week when he heard the news."

"And I believe it was your father who once told me that promotion has less to do with skill, and more to do with how you look on a horse," Strong returned with good humor. "So you can tell your father that I'm just not pretty enough to be general."

The men laughed.

Lorenz, an older veteran leaning back in his chair with his cup resting on his ample belly, called out. "I think it's a simple case of the wanderlust. All that traveling, never staying put in one place for long. General would have tied him down."

Another voice interjected, "Sounds more like running from a disappointed lover."

"Or her husband!" Lorenz added.

Strong just smiled while the laughter rippled anew.

Stefan stood and stifled a yawn. Time to put a stop to this before the men forgot themselves completely. "All right, let's call it a night. I'm sure Captain Strong is tired from his climb."

The soldiers laughed, standing with a chorus of chairs scraping against the floor and cups hitting the table. They would be telling that particular tale for weeks.

As the last of the men filed out, Stefan refilled both of their cups and watched his friend. Strong did look tired, but now that the men had left, he also looked troubled.

"Sorry about Lorenz and the others. They talk too much."

Strong grunted. "Some people will never think of me as anything but the boy they used to chase out of their gardens."

Stefan shook his head. "Nah, it's not that. They're too familiar, yes, but they have nothing but respect for you. They couldn't be prouder of you if you were one of their own sons. It was good of you to visit with them tonight."

"It was good of so many to come. I suppose a good story and free drink helps."

"Merek, about what Ryken said. I know that I shouldn't ask, but it's had me in knots since I heard. Why *did* you turn down the post? The boy is right. No one could have done it better."

Strong leaned back in his chair and rubbed his beard thoughtfully. He was dressed like a simple forester in layers of earthy browns and greens, the clothing filthy from his climb. At the forearms, it was torn completely through, showing scrapes on the skin underneath.

"I thought very hard about accepting," Strong admitted. "But I just couldn't see myself spending all my time in Albon. I feel…Do you remember how excited we were when the wall crew finally reached Haldin?"

"Of course." They had spent long hours in their boyhood watching the elaborate pulley system that raised the heavy stones into place, feeling as if they shared in the victory when the builders wedged an unruly rock into place.

Strong looked at Stefan's expression and nodded. "You understand, don't you? You know what it meant to our families to bring the wall here. And in that same way, I can't abandon it. That is my place, as surely as if I'd helped build it. To leave it in someone else's care feels wrong somehow."

Stefan did understand. He remembered well the day they'd buried Merek's father. But to refuse the highest military office in the land? "To lead the armies would be a great honor," he said.

"It's not honor I seek," Strong scoffed. "You of all people should know that. It's been years since Rahm faced any serious military threat. Danvir's Wall has done more to secure peace than all the wars we fought together while he was alive."

Stefan grunted. "My children don't even believe the tales I tell them of the Delth. They think it's all a lark when I tell them stories of fighting under King Danvir to drive them out of the southern plains."

"How quickly safety makes us forget." Strong sighed. "But you and I can't forget. And if we keep the wall strong, we keep war at bay. That's more to my liking than the highest honor Sindal can give."

Stefan thought this over. "And did you tell the king this?"

"I tried. He wouldn't listen. He stopped short of stripping me of my rank, but in all these years I've never seen him so angry." Strong glowered at his cup. Then, as if remembering something, he looked up at Stefan and asked, "Have you heard who Sindal appointed instead?"

"I heard a rumor it was Grammel."

"Oh good, then he listened to me. I wasn't sure he would."

Stefan didn't answer right away, unsure of what to say. They had joined the army together at fifteen, but those days seemed like a lifetime away. Their lives had gone such different directions. Merek had formed an unlikely friendship with the older Prince Sindal, and his career had followed a path far beyond what any simple forest boy had a right to dream. But Stefan had returned home to Haldin the first chance he got, content to watch Merek's rise from a distance. At times like this, Stefan felt the difference between their lives gaping wide.

Feeling inadequate, he offered a simple, "I'm sure he'll get over it soon. You've been friends for too long for the king to want you as an enemy."

Strong didn't respond, instead reaching for his cup. After he swallowed, he changed the subject. "Have you seen lights in the forest before tonight?"

"Nothing unusual, no. My men haven't reported anything on recent patrols either. What do you think we saw out there?"

Strong yawned. "I'm not sure. It could be nothing, but it wouldn't hurt to know who was out there and what they were doing."

Stefan rubbed the polished lip of his wooden cup with his forefinger. "I'll send Garth and Hendl tomorrow to check things out. They'll be discreet and stay unseen."

Merek nodded.

"Are you going to tell me what that stunt was all about tonight?" Stefan asked. "I know you weren't just showing off. Though it will certainly fan the flames of the stories being told about our legendary Captain Strong. I wouldn't be surprised if in a month the story goes that you were one-handed and carrying a child on your back!"

His old friend snorted and looked down at his scraped hands.

"There's no way I'll ever be doing that one-handed. I've been practicing for months, just to see if it was possible. But there was once I thought I wouldn't make it, and my back would be broken just like anyone else's if I fell from that height."

"So, what was it all for?"

With a glint in his gray eyes, Strong said, "First, I wanted to see if it could be done. And now that I've proven that it can, I'll be training you and your men."

Stefan felt the color drain from his face. "Merek, there is no way—"

"Not all of them, of course. But looking around the room tonight,

I saw three or four who look strong and fearless enough to learn. It's not just about strength, of course. It also takes patience and an ability to keep your wits under pressure. A certain tolerance for pain doesn't hurt either." He stood and stretched, wincing slightly. "We'll go over the details tomorrow. I'll try it out with your unit first, then move on to all of them once we have the training perfected."

"You're serious about this?"

"Of course. If I can do it, it's only a matter of time before our enemies try it."

"But what good would it do them?" Stefan protested. "An entire army can't climb the wall, and any bandit who tries wouldn't be able to carry anything with him on the return. If he tried to escape through one of the gates, he'd be stopped by guards. What would be the point?"

"And what if he wasn't after sheep or farm tools?" Strong answered grimly. "What if he and a few of his fellows were skilled assassins who removed the guards on patrol first, then attacked the guards at the access doors? Once they had control of one of the gates—even a small door like this one—they would have all night to move in reinforcements unchallenged."

"I don't know, Merek. It still sounds pretty unlikely."

"Which is exactly why it would work. We think the main gates are the ones most likely to be attacked, so we put our greatest strength there and think that they'll keep us safe. But we forget that the most vulnerable parts of the wall are the ones we worry about the least."

"So train the Endvar unit. They're more likely to face a coordinated attack anyway."

"No, it's too big and too public," Merek said, pushing his chair back to stand. "I want a small unit that can train and test quietly. Preferably led by someone I trust as well as myself. I don't want word to get out about what we're up to."

Stefan felt his ego warm at the praise, and hid it by grumbling, "It sounds like asking for nothing but bruised hands and broken backs."

Captain Strong smirked. "Don't be such a coward, Stefan. Besides," he called over his shoulder as he walked out of the room. "*Climbing the wall is just the beginning.*"

Three

"Do you find Albon changed, Biren?" Ria looked up to catch her maid's eye in the looking glass. Biren's fingers paused, suspending Ria's hair mid twist, as she considered the question.

"Changed in what way, my lady?" Biren mumbled around the jeweled hair pins pressed between her lips. Her fingers resumed their work, tightening the strands of hair.

Ria winced against the pulling on her scalp. "I can't say exactly. The people seemed genuinely happy to welcome me home when I first arrived. But now…sometimes I feel like they don't quite know what to do with me."

Biren finished the twist and slipped pins into place to hold the ends. "I think you don't give yourself enough credit, my lady. Whether or not Albon is changed, I can't say. But surely you have. You've experienced things in the past two years that most of the people in this city will never understand. Some of it was wondrous. Some of it was painful. But all of it will make you a better queen someday."

Ria regarded her reflection and the amber gems glinting in the morning light against her brown hair. "You're an inspiration, Biren. Thank you."

But she couldn't speak to Biren of the things which most disturbed her. It felt like betrayal to complain of the king's erratic behavior or admit that he had grown distant in her absence.

Then there were the rumors. The stories circulating about what had happened in Ardania were getting increasingly difficult to ignore. Just the previous night, she had overheard two guests gossiping over a particularly vicious tale that implicated Biren herself, and Ria had to leave the room before she said something she regretted.

As Biren busied herself packing away the pins and combs, Ria thought about what her maid had said about change. "I suppose I must get used to the idea that as much as I longed for Albon while we traveled, there's no going back to the home I left. I'm simply not the same person I was then. The most I can do is move forward."

Biren nodded hesitantly. "Would this be an appropriate time to share news of Lord Sabir?"

"Of course," Ria said, a little too cheerfully. If Biren had good news, she would have spoken with more enthusiasm.

"It seems that he and Lady Polina were wed during the autumn equinox. I understand that she's already expecting their first."

"How productive of her."

"I'm sorry, my lady."

Ria sighed. "Forgive me, Biren. It's too early in the day for bitterness. And really, it's to be expected, isn't it? I gave Sabir and the others no reason to wait for me." *Because I assumed I'd be returning with a husband of my own.*

The thought of Artem made her stomach feel sour. She burned with shame when she thought of how she'd admired him. How naive she'd been! And now she continued to pay a high price for her youthful attachment. With this most recent news, she had to accept that any man who might have once earned her favor had long since bestowed his attention on someone more willing. The fickle princess who left them all to chase a foreign prince had missed her chance to claim the best that Rahm had to offer.

Ria pressed her lips against a frown and turned her back on her reflection.

She must stop thinking such things. Already she'd wasted too much time running away from Artem and her broken future. She was Honoria Thorodan. Daughter of kings. First woman heir to the throne of Rahm. And she would act like it.

Beginning with her father.

Ria straightened her shoulders and affected a smile before going in search of the king. Her silk slippers padded softly on polished wood floors as she passed through the family's private quarters into the more public part of the house. The wood paneled walls of Thorodan Hall were dark and comforting, but at times like these she longed for the bright sunlight of Khourin or the open spaces of Ardania's eastern plains. Maybe she would speak to Galinn about whitewashing her bedchamber walls.

But when she found her father's steward, all frivolous thoughts of improving her room disappeared at the sight of his anxious frown.

"Princess Honoria, I'm glad I found you," Galinn said, his breath coming quickly. "The king is to pronounce judgment today on a particularly sensitive land dispute, but Martin says he is unwell. The lords from Yaneth have already arrived. Would you consider welcoming them so they don't feel slighted?"

Ria's smile drained of feeling, but she kept it firmly in place. "Of course. Thank you, Galinn. I'm sure it's little more than excitement from the party last night."

"I thought the king retired early."

"Yes. He did. But the dancing was especially energetic and he didn't rest until long after the guests went home," Ria lied smoothly. How long would she have to make excuses for her father's behavior? First the Khouri Ambassador and now the lords from Yaneth. Ria wasn't above shirking her responsibilities on occasion, but never anything of real significance. And always with Sindal's voice in her head reminding her that to avoid her duties was to incur a debt that could only be repaid at a higher cost.

Now it was the king himself accumulating debts that she seemed destined to fulfill.

She affected a smile as she passed through the gallery overlooking the entrance hall. Golden sunlight spilled through windows of stained glass set above the doors, sending shafts of light that illuminated the floor below in fractured patterns. There two country lords stood, their ill-dressed attendants looking around their surroundings with open appreciation. Ria felt a surge of generosity as she skimmed swiftly down the stairs. She would do her best to welcome her guests as her father would have. It wasn't their fault that he was distracted and ill-tempered of late. But someday soon there would have to be an accounting of Sindal's mounting debts to her.

Night had already fallen when Merek returned to Endvar. The soft rain that had been his companion since he left Haldin grew into a steady downpour, soaking him through despite his heavily oiled traveling cloak. Exhausted and cold, Merek still felt pleased. He had spent a week with Stefan's unit, and the training was going better than expected. The four young men Stefan selected were taking their new assignment seriously, and two showed particular promise. As the hulking outline of Endvar's city wall rose before him, Merek's mind drifted to planning an assault on the stronghold to test the readiness of his men.

With the building of Danvir's Wall, three eastern roads had been diverted through Endvar, funneling the majority of traffic through the border city, which had grown in size and wealth to rival the capital city of Albon. Now Endvar spilled beyond its walls, with settlements clustered on the outskirts so that the city gates stayed open all night to allow easy passage.

As Merek passed through the western gate, the dark streets of the city proper lay quiet and still under the steady rain. Few people braved the cold and the wet after nightfall, and the clipped sound of his horse's hooves echoed against the stone walls and down the empty alleys. A light gray with veins of red and green that caught the light during the day, the stones of Endvar turned a deep black when wet, making shadows deeper and unsettling. But after six years, Merek knew these streets well. In a career that had long required a transient lifestyle, Endvar was the closest thing he had to home.

A muffled cry roused him from his drowsiness. Merek pulled hard on the reins, listening carefully above the stamping and snorting of his horse. There—a fleeting shadow of movement caught his eye. Drearily, he considered the wet clothing clinging to his skin and the dry bed that waited for him in his small rented room above the draper's shop. Sighing inwardly, he dismounted. If someone was in distress, sleep and warmth could wait.

Leaving his sword secured to his saddle, Merek followed down the street with one hand on his knife, stepping over a sleeping tramp who smelled like ale and urine. He paused at a narrow alley, listening above the rain, until a low grunt and a heavy thump drew him into the close darkness. In the feeble light of a torch, a man stood threateningly over a shapeless form on the ground. Merek stepped forward in alarm, but was immediately seized by two strong pairs of hands.

"Lost, mate?"

The voice in his ear was coarse and tense.

"Do I look like the kind of man who would be lost this time of night?" Merek asked impatiently.

There was a pause.

"So you have business here?"

"If I do, it doesn't concern you."

"Wrong. No one sees the master without being invited, and I don't recall ever seeing you before."

Merek turned his head to see if he could catch a glimpse of the man speaking to him, but was stopped with a stinging blow to the side of his head. His hood fell back and rain coursed down his face. Annoyed, he pulled against the hands which held him, testing their strength.

The man standing over the unmoving shape turned, and the smoking torchlight fell over his face. Merek froze, the fight within him suddenly quelled.

"So I ask you again, are you lost?" the gruff voice behind him asked.

"Yes," Merek said, eyes on the man in the torchlight as he turned his back to him. "Yes, I think I am."

"Then best get out of here before you find yourself in trouble."

He let the men haul him in the other direction. He didn't resist their roughness or even bother to turn back and catch a glimpse of their faces after they released him. His mind was full of the face he had seen, puzzling over what it meant as he made his way home. He was so distracted that he stripped off his wet clothing and collapsed into bed without even lighting a candle. Exhausted in body but troubled in mind, he tossed in his rough woolen blanket for a long time before sleep finally claimed him.

Four

"When you're finished, there's something I want you to see." Imar, like most Khouri men, was not very expressive by nature. But the glint in his eye told Aiya that her brother was uncharacteristically excited.

She laid aside Imar's waistcoat with the loose stitching. The mending could wait. Instead, Aiya seized upon this promise of something new on a morning that otherwise stretched ahead of her with monotonous predictability. The only distraction in her quiet life typically came from the captain who rented the room above their shop. But he'd been away for nearly three months, and life had slid into a dull routine in his absence.

Aiya followed Imar into the shop where bands of sunlight warmed the polished oak counter. Tidy stacks of fabric sat patiently on shelves, waiting for Endvar's elite to come and wonder about their potential. That's what Aiya liked most about working with textiles. The silks and brocades invited the imagination to dream of what might be. Even the wools were of higher quality than many citizens of Endvar could afford, making a statement that those who wore it were neither simple nor common. Imar would never settle for less than the best.

What he now lifted from a wooden crate made her catch her breath. Of all the fine fabrics that passed through their draper's shop, Aiya had never seen anything quite like it. She ran her hand over the deep green silk, marveling at the subtle design that caressed her fingertips. The sheen reflected the morning light, throwing it back at her as the cloth shifted beneath her hand.

"It's beautiful."

Imar smiled. "It is worth a small fortune. Send a note to Lady Ogmun that we have something special for her."

"For this, I should visit her in person."

Imar frowned, a small tightening around his black eyes. "A note will suffice." He moved to repack the fabric, practiced hands folding it with precision.

"I don't mind. It's no trouble."

Imar looked at Aiya over his spectacles. She knew that he didn't need them, but it lent him an air of docility that the Rahmish people appreciated. She rarely saw her brother without them, even when it was only the two of them alone.

"In truth, Aiya, it's not Lady Ogmun I am thinking of. I have decided it is time to look toward Albon."

Aiya started as he slammed the lid of the crate shut. "Albon? What do you mean?"

"We've made a good life here, but Endvar has not the opportunities of Albon. Think of the success we could have with a whole city full of Lady Ogmuns!"

"You want to leave Endvar?" The words felt strange on her tongue, and as she said them, the thought of leaving the captain filled her with a dull sense of regret.

"It would not be so difficult. I'm sure Lord Ogmun would give us a fine introduction, and it would not take so long to establish ourselves there as it did here."

"We would have more competition," Aiya protested.

Imar dismissed this with a flick of his fingers. "Competition is merely the whetstone to sharpen the knife. Do not trouble yourself about that. It is a little warmer, they tell me. You would like that."

He turned his back with finality and moved to the door that separated their shop from their living quarters. As he did so, he reached for a pile of letters sitting on the end of the counter. It took a full minute for the significance of the letters to penetrate the haze of shock in Aiya's mind. When it did, she roused herself and followed.

"Why do you lie to me, Imar?" she accused.

Imar looked up from where he sat poring over a sheet of vellum. His dark eyes registered surprise but not confusion, affirming her suspicion.

Indignation gave Aiya strength. "This lie about Albon, where did it come from? You do not wish to move there. For months you have been negotiating with suppliers in Branvik. You will be the first draper in Endvar to carry Branvik wool. That's what you have said."

Imar's eyes narrowed. "So I will be the first draper in Albon to carry Branvik wool instead. There is little difference."

"Except that Albon was never a thought in your mind, but now it is. Something has changed. Something that you are hiding from me. What is it?"

Imar glared at her, but she held his gaze defiantly. At last, he shrank a little. "You ask too many questions, Aiya. It's for your own good that I keep these things from you."

"Tell me."

Imar removed his spectacles. "It's not safe for us any longer. Behni has come to Endvar."

"Behni!" Aiya felt a sudden chill despite the warm spring morning. "Why did you not tell me sooner?"

"I didn't want to upset you."

Aiya's mouth felt dry. She licked her lips. "Does he know?"

"Did he come for us, you mean? No, I don't believe so. I'm working very hard to learn his business, but as you can imagine, it's difficult to make inquiries when one is supposed to be dead."

"What should we do?" Aiya held very still, leaning against the doorframe for support. She feared to move lest her legs collapse beneath her.

"*You* shall do nothing. You shall keep your movements close to home and stay indoors as much as possible."

"I don't want to leave," she said softly.

Imar sighed. "I don't wish it either. But it may come to that. I'm making inquiries, and will try to keep Behni and Hala at a distance—"

"Hala is here too?"

"And the children."

"Oh. Then he cannot intend—"

"I don't know what he intends, except that his stay will be lengthy. They have taken a home in the northeast quarter with a full staff."

But Aiya refused to despair so easily. "We can avoid them if we choose. Endvar is a large city."

"Not as large as Albon. We would be safer there."

The thought of starting over again in a strange city made Aiya feel weak. It would not be like the last time, when they came to Endvar ten years before. They would not be penniless and half-starved. Instead, they could travel in comfort and would already know the language and ways of the people. But still, thinking of running from Behni again made the air in the small room feel too close.

Aiya reached for a basin and cloth.

"Where are you going?" Imar asked sharply as she moved toward the outer door.

"Upstairs."

Imar frowned, but he relaxed. "I've never known a room to need so much cleaning when its occupant is absent," he chided.

"It gives me something to do." *And someone else's company, even if it is just my own,* she did not say.

It felt like Merek had been asleep mere minutes before waking to the sound of breaking pottery and a biting oath in a foreign tongue. Instantly he sat up, grasping his dagger while his mind sluggishly tried to place where he was.

Sunlight streaming through the window announced that morning was several hours old and the storm from the previous night had rained itself out. Aiya knelt on the floor, her head of jet black hair bowed as she gathered the remains of the shattered crockery.

"I'm sorry, my lord—"

"Captain," he corrected out of long habit, leaning back onto an elbow. Now that he realized there was no danger, the heavy weight of sleep threatened him again.

"I'm sorry, my captain. You startled me. I didn't know that you had returned, and I didn't recognize you at first. If I had known that you were here—"

"It's all right." He closed his eyes, trying to chase away the desire to collapse back onto the mattress. "I came in during the night and didn't want to wake you."

Aiya finished gathering the broken pieces into her apron and stood with her head still bowed. "Would you like breakfast, sir?"

Merek noticed the flush in her dark cheeks and was suddenly conscious of his half-dressed state. He swallowed a smile. In the years he had rented this room, this was the closest he had ever seen her come to losing her careful Khouri composure. But it seemed cruel to let her see his amusement, so he tried not to let even a hint of humor into his voice when he spoke.

"Thank you, Aiya. A good washing is in order, I think, and I'll be needing your skill with the scissors."

"Of course, my lord—captain," she corrected herself, turning toward the door. It had taken years to convince Aiya that he was no nobleman and still she struggled to remember.

Aiya returned a few minutes later with breakfast, and Imar accompanied her with a large basin filled with cool water. Aiya glanced at Merek only once, then immediately blushed and left the room without speaking. But Imar was loquacious, inquiring after Merek's health and travels, and delicately mentioning how many months they had held his room without payment in his absence. Merek thanked him and paid what was due, and at last Imar left him with a gentle bow.

When most of the grit of travel was washed away, Merek trimmed his beard close and Aiya returned with her shears. Now that he was dressed in clean clothes, she seemed to have recovered from her earlier embarrassment.

"If I may say, my captain, you smell much better now, and soon you will be fit to go out in the streets again," she said good-naturedly as she trimmed his hair. Her light accent made his own language sound uncharacteristically musical.

"Thank you. And let me pay for your bowl. I didn't mean to alarm you."

"It is already forgotten," Aiya tsked and made a dismissive gesture with the shears.

Instinctively he flinched, and then felt sheepish.

She laughed warmly. "I know how to keep the blades, my captain. Now, what do you think?"

Aiya stepped in front of him and held out a small looking glass.

"You have transformed me yet again, Aiya. Thank you."

She nodded graciously. "Is there anything more you need?"

Merek paused. "There is something. But I fear to offend, which I would never want to do. Please, will you sit?"

Aiya looked at him sharply, and the warmth between them immediately cooled as she sat stiffly in the proffered chair.

"I know that you don't like to talk about the family that you left in Khourin," Merek began. "Remember that I am not a peacekeeper. I'm not trying to get anyone in trouble. But I must know if Imar is involved in any sort of…questionable activity here in Endvar."

"What a strange question. Why would you ask such a thing?"

Merek hesitated. Her tense posture made him think she already knew. "That is not an answer."

Aiya regarded him with her dark eyes, so black that the pupils were indistinguishable. "What do you know of our history?"

"I understand that you fled Khourin because there were threats on your life. That your grandfather is the leader of a band of criminals there, and something went wrong and you were caught in the middle. Imar said he brought you here because to stay would have been certain death."

"Imar told you this? And yet you ask these questions?" Her voice was cold. "Why would a man who lost everything once risk it all again?"

"I realize it sounds mad—"

"Has Imar ever given you any reason to think he would be involved in something unsavory in your city? Any dishonesty or sedition that—"

"No, of course not. And I wouldn't even ask if I hadn't seen him last night."

Aiya started. "What's this?"

Merek rubbed distractedly at his elbow. "On my way through the city last night, something suspicious drew my attention and I stopped to investigate. Imar was there."

"That's impossible."

"I know what I saw. It was certainly Imar. He didn't see me because his men wouldn't let me get close enough. Whatever was going on, they didn't welcome prying eyes."

Aiya shook her head dismissively. "Imar was home all night with me. You are mistaken. There are other Khouris in this city. It must have been one of them."

"Other Khouris who look just like your brother?" Merek asked in disbelief.

Aiya blinked slowly. In that brief instant, something flickered in her dark eyes. But when she spoke, her voice was flat. "You are mistaken, sir. And now, I have lingered too long. Imar will wonder where I am." She stood as if to go.

"I'm sorry I bothered you, Aiya. I will speak to Imar about it, and you needn't—"

"No! You must not speak to Imar!" Aiya stepped toward him. "Promise me you will not speak to Imar!" She broke off the Rahmish and a stream of rapid Khouri poured forth. She was so much shorter than Merek that even with him sitting she was just barely at his eye level. She searched his face as she spoke, and Merek wondered if in her earnestness she even realized that she had switched tongues, and he couldn't understand a single word.

Merek returned her gaze unflinchingly. He didn't know what she saw in his eyes, but after a long, tense silence, she sank back into the chair.

"What did this Khouri man look like?" she asked resignedly. "Like Imar, yes, but did he wear Rahmish clothes? Or clothes like my countrymen wear?"

Merek hadn't paid much attention to the man's clothing, but now he tried to remember what he had seen in the torchlight.

"He was not dressed for the rain. Yes, I think he must have been in Khouri robes. That's odd because—"

"—Imar hasn't worn Khouri garments in years," Aiya finished. "That's because it wasn't Imar. It was my cousin, recently come to Endvar."

She spoke heavily, as if the words took something from her. But to Merek, they brought relief.

"Oh! That explains it then. And this cousin is part of your grandfather's business?"

"Undoubtedly. But their networks have never reached as far as Rahm in the past."

"Very well, then. I will make inquiries elsewhere and leave you and Imar out of it."

"No, you mustn't. Behni is a very dangerous man."

"Is that why you didn't speak of him before?"

Aiya bowed her head. "Forgive me. But my family cannot know where I am. We are both dead to them. We must stay dead to them."

"I understand. I will be very discreet. Thank you for your help, Aiya."

She nodded once. "Please, be careful. Whatever Behni is doing in your city, it is bad for your people. Don't let it be bad for you too."

Merek bent over the large map of Rahm spanning his desk. His clerk sat opposite, comparing the notations on the map with a stack of reports in his hand.

"I think the damage extends further, sir," Rorden said. "Captain Torgrim said the flood waters rose all the way to the road, which means that this section of wall should have been affected too."

Merek made another notation, then leaned back and stretched. "Is that the last of them?"

"It's the last of the reports from the outposts, sir, but I'm afraid that's not all that needs your attention." Rorden indicated another pile of letters.

Merek sighed and looked out the window at the courtyard below where members of the Wall Guard trained in the waning light. Endvar's guard complex was far larger and busier than any other city's in the kingdom, rivaling only the army complex in Albon itself. All new members of the Wall Guard were stationed in Endvar first, and Merek's duties included their training before assigning them to other posts around Rahm. He wished he could be out there with them now instead of going through tedious paperwork.

"Give me the news from Albon first," Merek said, turning back to his clerk and sitting behind the desk.

"Yes, sir." Rorden thumbed through the notices. "I assume that you heard about the appointment of General Grammel. Here's the official notice as well as an invitation to attend the ceremony. And speaking of invitations, you missed the celebration for Princess Honoria's return."

"Oh?" Merek hadn't heard this piece of news. "When was this?"

Rorden paused to think. "Two months ago? I'm not sure, but you were invited. Of course, we got to see her when she passed through the city on her way from Ardania. Such an entourage! There was an entire wagon just to carry all the trunks for her gowns!"

"Knowing her father, I believe it."

"It was incredible! *She* was incredible! It was a cold, cloudy day, but the streets were crowded with people trying to get a glimpse of the princess. She waved out the window of the carriage, but the people on the other side couldn't see her. So she stopped the carriage, climbed up next to the driver, and rode the rest of the way sitting up there in the cold where everyone could see her!" Rorden couldn't finish his story without laughing. "You should have seen the driver's face!"

Merek smiled. "I'll bet the crowd loved that."

"Oh, they whooped and cheered and threw ribbons. And then, like it was planned," Rorden said, gesturing in the air, "at that precise moment, the clouds parted and the sun came out. It was as though the heavens themselves were celebrating to have our princess home! Oh, it was a sight!" He laughed again. "You were invited to the celebration in Albon. I'm sorry that you missed it. I heard it went on for days!"

"You mean you're sorry that *you* missed it. Did you send my regrets?"

"Yes, sir." Rorden grinned. "I wouldn't have minded taking another look at the princess. I've never seen anyone so lovely."

Merek glanced at his young clerk. The princess couldn't possibly be old enough to attract the attention of a man like Rorden, could she? Just how old was she now?

"Is there any news from the king?" Merek asked, bringing his clerk's attention back to the moment.

"I'm afraid no private letters, sir."

"Very well. Thank you, Sergeant. I think we're just about finished here for the night. Tomorrow, I'd like you to begin making two more copies of this map, together with a detailed list of the damage to the wall. I'll want to show them to the king the next time I'm in Albon."

"Yes, sir."

"I also want to see estimates on how long the repairs will take, with approximate manpower and cost. Prioritize the sections from most to least critical, and triple check your numbers. I want to be certain before I see the king."

"Yes, sir. Will that be all?" Rorden stifled a yawn.

"Almost. There's one other thing that I need your help with, but it must stay between us."

Rorden perked up.

"While I was away, I spent some time training one of the northern units on how to climb the wall. Don't—" He waved away Rorden's interruption. "I've already heard the objections. But I tell you, it can be done. I've done it, and I've been teaching a handful of other soldiers how to do it. I expect reports from Captain Stefan Falbrook about their progress, but these should be delivered straight to me and not recorded anywhere else."

"Yes, sir."

"I don't want anyone in Endvar to know about this."

"Yes, sir." Rorden paused. "May I ask why?"

Merek hesitated. Stefan had thought it was a foolish idea, and he didn't relish the idea of justifying himself to Rorden. "My goal is that they will eventually become skilled enough to stage an attack on Endvar."

Rorden mulled this over and nodded. "You plan to test the readiness of Wott's men?"

"Yes. I want to know our weaknesses, but it won't work if even a single stable boy gets the slightest whisper of what we're up to."

"I understand, sir."

This is why Merek had chosen Rorden as his clerk, despite his youth and inexperience. He had a quick mind which minimized the need for lengthy explanations, and he knew how to be discreet.

"Thank you. I think that will be all for tonight."

"I'm sorry, sir, there is one more thing." Rorden looked apologetically back at the papers on the desk. "You have some outstanding dinner invitations that need responses."

Merek frowned. Socializing with the upper classes was the most distasteful part of his position. There was still a part of his forest boy heart that felt uncomfortable with their fine manners, and years of experience had taught him to be suspicious of their overtures of friendship. As a longtime friend of the king, he received an increased measure of interest from every aspiring nobleman and greedy merchant who did business in Endvar.

"I would have thought the invitations would have dropped off after news spread about how I rejected the king's promotion," he grumbled, sifting through the pile.

"On the contrary, sir. It seems that your company is in even higher demand than usual." Rorden tried not to smile. "I believe I've seen something similar with seagulls swarming after the boats bring in the day's kill."

Merek grunted. "Very well. Arrange the appointments that seem most urgent. But that can wait until tomorrow. I'm sure Freida will be wondering where you are."

"Not Freida." Rorden said mournfully as he stood to leave. "One day she was hanging on my arm and talking of a future together, and the next she shut the door in my face and told me she never wanted to see me again."

Merek snorted. "What did you do this time?"

"She wouldn't say! But I think she means it. I haven't seen her in weeks."

"Well, I'm sure it won't take long to find someone else even prettier and more fickle than Frieda."

"Your comforting words are truly inspiring, sir," Rorden replied drily.

Merek laughed. "Go, Sergeant. You're dismissed."

After Rorden left, Merek picked up the royal invitation celebrating the princess's return. It was difficult to know how to interpret the gesture. It might be a good sign that Sindal wasn't angry with him anymore. Or it may just mean that Honoria had insisted. The king hadn't sent any private letters, which was unusual. But with his daughter freshly returned from two years out of the country, surely he'd been busy with more important things.

There was nothing for it. Merek would have to schedule his next trip to Albon soon, but not until he had a firm plan for the wall repairs. After the heated words of their last meeting, he couldn't afford to stand on weak ground when he saw the king again.

Aiya stood at the upstairs window, looking down onto the street. The morning sun was warm through the glass, and she itched to go out into the city again. But Imar continued to keep her close to home, and over the past two weeks she hadn't ventured beyond the milliner at the end of the row.

Imar's quiet inquiries into Behni's business had not yielded much, and the more frustrated he became, the more tightly wound he seemed. Aiya sometimes felt like she was caged with a wounded lion, the way he held his tension so dangerously. She did not fear Imar, never that. But there were times—dared she admit it?—that she resented their closely guarded life. Aside from Imar, she had no true friends in this place, and Imar was becoming increasingly difficult to live with the longer that Behni remained in the city.

There was another way, Aiya knew. But she didn't dare mention it to Imar. If he suspected the thoughts which occupied her, he would take her from the city before the next day dawned.

The outer door opened, and Aiya jumped.

"Forgive me, my lord—"

"Captain," Strong corrected as he shut the door.

"Captain. I was just finishing up," she said, making a show of grabbing the broom despite having already finished the sweeping.

"No matter. I'll be gone again in a moment." Captain Strong moved to a small bureau and thumbed through a pile of papers.

Suddenly, an idea seized Aiya. Maybe there was another way. "Pardon me, my captain. Have you learned anything useful in your inquiries about my cousin?"

Captain Strong looked at her curiously. "I thought you wished to be kept out of it all."

"I do. But anything you learn could be useful to Imar. He wishes only to keep us safe."

Strong found the document he was looking for and slipped it into a folio. "At this point, there's not much to tell. He claims to be here trading fine teas from Khourin. All of his business seems to be in order."

"Which means only that he is very skilled."

Strong nodded. "From what my clerk tells me, establishing new trade in this city is a messy business even when everything goes right. But your cousin seems to be making all the right connections with ease."

"And that is all?"

"For now. I'm afraid my mind has been somewhat occupied with other things of late. But when I return—"

"You are leaving again?"

"I must," he sighed. "This time for Albon. But I hope to learn more about your cousin's business when I return. Do you want to be kept informed?"

"Please," she said gratefully, but felt a keen sense of disappointment. With the captain gone, it could be weeks or even months before he learned anything valuable. And Imar wasn't faring much better.

All the while, Aiya would be pacing in her cage.

Unless…

"Aiya?"

She realized that she was again gazing out the window, momentarily forgetting Captain Strong.

"Forgive me," she said. "I am easily distracted today. Is there anything more I can do for you?"

"If it isn't too much trouble, I do have a small favor to ask," he said apologetically.

She paused. "What is it, my captain?"

Strong grimaced. "A peace offering fit for a king."

Five

Ria found Sindal in the library, dozing quietly on a settee.

"Far! Here you are!" she said loudly, earning a panicked look from his attending servant.

"His Majesty is weary, my lady," Martin said in a soothing tone. "Perhaps you could let him rest, and I'll send word as soon as he awakens."

Ria ignored Martin and sat on the end of the settee, patting her father's knee. "What is it, Far? You spent all night wandering the halls again? If you'd stay in bed you might actually get some sleep, you know."

Sindal stirred awake. "What strident shrew disturbs my slumber?" He cracked open one eye. "Oh, Ria, I should have known."

Ria laughed. "I think you meant to say, 'What are these angelic tones? It's my precious Ria, who brings joy and rapture wherever she goes.'"

"Isn't that what I said?" Sindal's smile twitched his beard.

"Not quite. Far, I have news for you."

Her father yawned and pushed himself into a seated position. "A moment, please. Martin, will you get us some refreshment? If my daughter has news, I fear I need fortifications."

"As well you may," Ria said brightly. "Tonight we have a special guest joining us for dinner."

"Oh?"

"Yes, and I've already sent the invitation so you can't refuse."

"Oh dear. Who is it?"

"None other than your most faithful of first captains, recently arrived from Endvar."

Sindal groaned. "Ah, Ria, you can't be serious."

"Indeed I am. You might not want to see Captain Strong, but I do. And I'm sure he wishes to see me, else why come to Albon now?"

"Not tonight," her father said heavily. "I can't do this tonight."

Ria raised an eyebrow. "As you say most nights. If I must wait until you are ready to entertain, we might as well bar the gates and close the kitchens. Don't worry about Strong. I will handle him."

Sindal shot her a dark look. "This isn't a matter for you, Ria. This is between the two of us. It's not up to you to sort it out."

"Well I don't see you doing much to sort it out yourself, and it's wearing you down," Ria said. "You aren't able to sleep at night, and you seem intent on shutting out the world. If I can help you two reconcile, then I'll be doing all of us a great service."

"It's not your place," Sindal said firmly. "Strong is not the man you think you know. Believe me when I say that it's best if you leave this matter alone."

"Nonsense." Ria stood as Martin entered the room with a flask of wine and two goblets of hammered gold. She poured a small amount into a cup and handed it to her father. "You vilify the captain, but you refuse to give me particulars. So I've been asking questions and have come to the conclusion that he is not as guilty as you make him seem. I think he deserves another chance."

Sindal glowered. "You suggest that I've embellished his faults for my own aims?"

"I didn't say that," Ria said, keeping her tone light. "But one thing I learned in my travels is that every story has another version, which varies depending on who is telling it. I can't hope to know the truth if I only listen to one side."

"Ah," Sindal nodded. "You're not speaking of Prince Artem, are you?"

Ria stopped. Curse her father's perceptiveness.

Sindal regarded her and said pointedly, "It seems we both have matters we wish to keep from each other."

"Very well, Far. You keep your secrets and I'll keep mine. But Captain Strong is coming to dinner tonight by my invitation. Please try to be civil to him. I won't force you to reconcile until you're ready, but for my sake, at least consider it?"

"I make no promises," Sindal grumbled into his cup. "But I will welcome him tonight, for your sake."

"Thank you."

"And while you're being so generous with your invitations, why not issue one to the young Hegrin?"

Ria recoiled. "Ugh. I was hoping to enjoy this evening, Far."

Sindal only chuckled.

"It's easy enough for you to laugh," Ria said. "The entire court isn't trying to pressure *you* into wedding him."

"They only see that he has an extensive fortune and knows that if he has half the sense of his father, he will make the most of it. But they will respect your choice."

"Will they?" Ria asked doubtfully. "And what if it is my choice not to marry?"

Sindal frowned. "That's out of the question, as you well know. If you refuse to do your duty to secure the Thorodan line of succession, then you'll create a storm of contention regarding which line has right to the throne. You would never risk that kind of conflict simply for the sake of your vanity."

"Vanity?" Ria grimaced. "Sanity is more like it. I know, Far. You're right. But I'll wager you didn't suffer this much scrutiny when you were considering your bride."

"Didn't I?" Sindal barked a short laugh. "You are sorely mistaken, my dear! And then I had scarcely laid your mother in the ground before they started pressuring me to marry again."

"And yet, you didn't." Ria cocked her head, considering. "Why not?"

Sindal's smile faded. "It didn't seem fair to give my broken heart to another woman and expect her to mend it. I thought I might, in time, but the older you grew, the more I knew that you were as capable as any son. I didn't dare risk your chance of assuming the throne someday."

"Are you saying that if you'd had a son with another wife that he would have been named heir instead?" Ria asked, both amused and offended.

Sindal sipped at his wine. "I didn't want to risk it. There are those who would have been all too eager to promote a younger brother if you'd had one."

Ria was struck by her father's disclosure. She'd never suspected his reticence to marry again pertained to securing her future as his rightful heir. With a smirk, she said, "Although, then I would have been free to marry or not according to my pleasure. Some days that seems a fair trade."

Sindal smiled. "Some woes are timeless, I assure you. The sooner you can make your choice, the better."

"I have a better idea," Ria said, swilling her wine thoughtfully. "What do you know about pig farmers?"

Aiya twisted her hair into a knot at the base of her neck and slipped the pale yellow veil over her head. She had chosen her clothing carefully, deciding on a gown and veil in the Khouri style. The yellow wouldn't be out of place in Endvar, and although she worried about the veil marking her as an outsider, she ultimately decided it was worth it to obscure her face.

Imar was busy in the shop with a customer as she quietly slipped out the back. Her plan was dangerous, but Aiya knew something Imar did not. If there was one person who hated Behni more than she did, it was his own wife. In earlier days when Aiya and Hala had been close, Hala had confided how much she despised her husband and found little ways to punish him each time he took a new mistress or lost a fortune in a night's gambling. Aiya was certain—*reasonably* certain—that Hala wouldn't betray her to Behni.

She had chosen the place carefully where she would reveal herself and hoped to limit how exposed she would be. But a small dagger rested in her deep pocket, just in case.

As Aiya passed through the busy streets of Endvar toward a market on the opposite end of the city, she chided herself. Only a fool would risk exposure this way. But she could no longer sit restlessly at home and worry about the forces which could bring down catastrophe upon her head.

Then there had been the matter of the gift. *A peace offering,* Captain Strong had called it. *Something to impress even the finest of tastes.* Aiya had immediately thought of the green Ardanian silk.

But Imar had resisted. "This was meant for Lady Ogmun, not some common soldier with no lands or title."

Aiya bristled. "He's not a common soldier. He has great honor in their army, and is said to be a friend to the king himself."

"We don't need connections with the army. Lord Ogmun's influence in this city does far more for our success than Captain Strong's, no matter who his friends are. And how could he afford such a purchase?"

"I don't know, but he assures me that he has the coin."

"Well, he had better be prepared to pay double."

"Double!"

"To compensate for disappointing Lady Ogmun."

At this point, Captain Strong had entered the shop, and Aiya was so incensed that she left her brother to handle the transaction. Stewing alone in her small room, she began planning how to contact Hala.

Aiya slowed as she approached the marketplace. Hala would likely have a servant with her, and perhaps a guard or two, so the more people to provide distraction, the better.

Aiya purchased a large basket from a weaver, and slowly moved through the street, trying to calm her racing heart. The day was warm and the crowd thick and relentless. While passing a particularly fragrant produce stand, her heart leaped as she saw another woman conspicuous in Khouri dress standing only three stalls away.

Aiya stayed where she was. Better to let Hala come to her. She made a show of examining the spring cherries, the red and yellow fruit bursting with promise. In her periphery, she sensed Hala approach. Only one servant attended her, though there were likely guards not far away.

The servant would be a problem. Hala might keep her secret, but Aiya knew better than to trust the servant. Aiya turned her back as Hala approached, grateful for the veil which hid her features.

In halting Rahmish, Hala's servant asked the fruit seller about his cherries. Her accent was so thick, Aiya wondered that the seller could understand her at all. But he knew money when he saw it and nodded deferentially, asking a price triple what he had asked from a Rahmish woman not long before.

Aiya leaned close to Hala. "He robs you," she said quietly in Khouri.

Hala looked at her in surprise.

"He will take half that price if you tell him you'll be back next week for more," Aiya explained.

Hala's expression sharpened. She murmured instructions to her servant.

The fruit seller wasn't pleased to lose his inflated profit, but the reassurance that they would return to his stall mollified him.

"How can I thank you?" Hala said to Aiya as her servant completed the exchange. "It's a comfort to find a fellow countryman in this foreign land. My husband and I have recently come to Endvar—"

"I know who you are," Aiya interrupted. "I have information for you if you will hear it."

Hala narrowed her eyes suspiciously. "What sort of information?"

"About someone from your past. If you wish to know, send your servant away and meet me behind the potter's stall. Alone."

"And if I don't?"

"Then I will not bother you again."

"Who are you?"

"A friend of your cousin Aiya."

Hala stiffened, and Aiya slipped away before she could say anything more.

It took all of Aiya's self control not to bolt away from the market in a panic. She had risked everything in giving Hala her name. But she had to give her something to earn her trust. Aiya's breath came quick and shallow as she skirted around the outside of the fruit seller's stall and darted down an alley, ducking to avoid a line of hanging wash and stopping only when she was in view of the potter's stall.

Hidden in shadow, Aiya wondered what must be going through Hala's mind. How much did she know of what happened all those years before? She'd been visibly shaken by Aiya's words. But was that because she assumed Aiya was dead all this time? Or because she knew of her own husband's role in her disappearance?

Apparently Hala's curiosity was as strong as it had ever been. Hesitantly, she appeared alone at the edge of the stall.

Aiya stepped out of the shadows.

"How much time do you have?"

"A few minutes at most." Hala's voice was hard. "What do you know about Aiya?"

In answer, Aiya unfastened one side of her veil and let it fall, uncovering her face.

Hala's face drained of color. "Aiya! It *is* you! Your voice—I thought—but how?"

"I will tell you what I can, but you must promise not to tell Behni you have seen me. He must not know that I'm alive. Promise me that you will not tell him."

Hala's face darkened briefly at the mention of her husband. "Behni can rot; I don't care. But Aiya—"

She rushed forward, her hands outstretched. She took Aiya's

arms in her own, grasping them at the elbows and leaning her forehead against Aiya's in the intimate Khouri gesture reserved for family. She muttered a Khouri prayer of thanks. "God's smile is my smile this day! His tears are my tears!"

Hala pulled away, gazing at Aiya with eyes bright with emotion. "I thought you were dead! We all did! I was heartbroken to hear about Tupin and Mara. There was talk that maybe you had survived the fire, but when there was no word for so long, we gave up hope. Even Behni, dog that he is, searched for you for weeks before he gave up."

I'm sure he did, Aiya thought darkly. Could Hala truly not know the truth behind her husband's deeds?

"And what of you? What brings you to Endvar?" Aiya asked.

But Hala didn't seem to have heard. "Is Imar here with you?"

She glanced over Aiya's shoulder, as if expecting Imar to step out of the shadows and join them.

"Imar died of fever two winters ago. I'm alone now, but it's all right. He provided for me well before he died." It was amazing how easily the lies came after so many years.

"I'm sorry about Imar, but I am so happy to see you! I must go or Leina will be suspicious. Can we meet again?"

"It's dangerous for us both now that you know I am here. But I must know, Hala, what is Behni doing in this city?"

Hala frowned. "Nothing to do with you. Your secret is safe with me, I swear it."

"Thank you, Hala. Trust me, it is for the best. Will you be in Endvar long?"

"Some months more, I think. Please, can I see you again?"

"I don't think that would be wise. But I am happy that you are well and—"

"Please, Aiya!" Hala's voice broke with emotion. "It has been so hard to be here in this foreign place. You know how Behni is."

Aiya's heart went out to her friend. Her desperate plea seemed sincere. "I will think about it. I'll send word if I can find a safe place.

But you must come alone."

"Of course. Please try, Aiya. I have missed you so!"

Hala embraced her again, then disappeared. It took Aiya twice as long to get home since she doubled back three times to make sure she wasn't being followed. The meeting had taken half of her day, and required more lying to Imar when she got home. By evening, she retired to bed early with a headache from worry and deception. As she lay on her cot that night, she wondered if she shouldn't just flee to Albon as Imar wanted to do from the beginning.

No. This was her home now, and she was tired of running.

Six

Dining with the king was not a privilege to be taken lightly. Merek and Rorden had arrived in Albon only that afternoon, and to be already issued an invitation to court gave him hope. Merek bathed and shaved, eliminating all trace of travel, then changed into his clean dress uniform that he kept in his Albon rooms strictly for the purpose of such formal occasions. The long coat of deep navy was accented with silver buttons and insignias indicating his rank.

Rorden entered the room just as Merek was pulling on shiny black boots that had never seen a day on horseback.

"Will I be joining you this evening, sir?"

"Not this time. I need you to find Jes the cobbler about the special boot we discussed."

Rorden's face fell. "Yes sir."

Merek passed him a coin purse. "Give half of this to Jes, but let him see the whole of it so he knows I'm in earnest. And here are a few silvers for you when you're finished. I expect I'll be out late, so no need to report back until tomorrow."

Anticipation sparked in Rorden's eyes. In a large city like Albon, an unscheduled evening on someone else's coin was rife with possibilities.

Thorodan Hall was built on the royal family's ancestral lands. What had once been a modest estate had grown into a sprawling complex larger than most villages, with multiple stables, army barracks and training grounds, a separate lodge for visitors to the court, and far more servants than ever would have been housed under the first king's rule. But the original house where the royal family lived had been largely preserved untouched. More manor house than fortress, the age of her timbers was comforting to Merek. It reminded him of the solemnity of the forest and that something more lasting than any man was watching over the kings and queens of Rahm.

Merek didn't recognize the servant who greeted him at the door. There had been a time when he had known all the servants' names, but now his duties rarely brought him to the capital more than once or twice in a year. He felt more like a stranger than a friend as he was led to the door of the dining hall.

Nearly two dozen people stood about, mingling politely as they waited for the king. Merek recognized Grammel immediately—*General* Grammel, he reminded himself. The general was talking to a nobleman whose wife—or daughter?—hung on his arm in layers of bright pink that made her look comically like a pastry. A handful of other noblemen were in attendance with their wives, and the foreign gentleman in the tight waistcoat must have been a visiting ambassador from Khourin, with an aide at his side.

"Oi, Strong!"

Merek turned. Captain Talen, the First Captain who commanded the peacekeeping forces, hurried toward him across the room, his curly black hair bouncing as he stepped around an elegant woman who frowned at him in irritation.

"Talen! It's been too long." Merek gripped his shoulder affectionately. "Maybe the evening won't be as dull as I feared."

Talen grinned. "I've been here for two weeks, and it hasn't been dull yet. Now that you're here, it can only get better."

"I hope you mean that as a compliment."

Talen only laughed.

"Captain Strong," General Grammel greeted, stepping forward. The burly man wore the crimson uniform of the army. It didn't complement his ruddy complexion, but his deep voice commanded respect, and the people nearest them shifted away out of deference.

"General. I trust you are settling into your new post well," Merek said amiably.

"Yes, thank you," Grammel said, but his smile did not reach his eyes. He indicated the woman at his side. "Do you remember my wife?"

This began the introductions. As they moved around the room, Merek was only half listening. He didn't care whose title the man with the long nose had inherited, or why the pastry woman had only recently come to court (she was a daughter after all, not a wife). But he smiled and nodded and tried not to neglect his end of the conversation.

Finally, a door opened at the far end of the hall, and King Sindal entered with a lovely young woman on his arm. Merek started, thinking momentarily that Sindal's wife had returned from the grave. The woman was as tall as Sindal, with fair skin and brown hair arranged in intricate looping braids. She wore a wine colored gown adorned simply, but her curving figure and poise gave it an air of regal elegance.

It wasn't until she smiled that Merek realized who this young beauty must be. He hoped his face didn't betray the shock he felt as he tried to recognize the girl he remembered. Just how many years had it been since he had last seen Princess Honoria? The revelation that somehow in that time she'd grown into a woman made him feel uncharacteristically old.

Sindal was also altered from their last meeting. He'd always been a sturdy man, and it was clear from the softening in his face and neck that he had put on weight. Merek watched him closely, feeling a tightening in his gut as he wondered how he would be received.

Sindal circled the room with Honoria at his side, greeting his guests warmly. But when he reached Merek, he said simply, "Captain Strong." There was no warmth in his voice, and he didn't even meet Merek's eyes.

Merek bowed, but Sindal pointedly turned his back and moved on to greet Captain Talen.

Tension crept up the back of Merek's neck. He was aware of General Grammel watching him and tried to keep his expression neutral. Apparently Sindal was not yet ready to forgive him.

"Dear Captain Strong," Honoria said. Merek realized that she had not moved on with her father, but was standing nearby and waited for his attention.

In a quick movement, she reached up to kiss him on the cheek. "Now I truly feel like I've come home. I was so distressed not to see you at my homecoming celebration."

"I apologize, my lady. I was away in the north and only recently learned that you had returned."

"Of course. Although, I would have thought even the furthest reaches of the kingdom received the news eventually. Certainly in weeks rather than months. You're long overdue to pay your respects."

Merek smiled politely. "I'm sorry that I missed your celebration. I trust your father is delighted to have you home."

"At first I felt slighted," she continued, as though he hadn't spoken. "But then I realized that it probably wasn't about me at all. I heard all about how angry my father was the last time you were here in Albon. All that silly general business, you know." She waved her hand dismissively.

Merek blinked. Around the room, conversations stilled to better hear the princess. A few people turned toward them. Even the king's rigid posture showed that he too was listening.

"Oh, I forgot!" she laughed. "This must be the first time you've seen him since then! How very awkward. I'm so sorry for bringing it up. How thoughtless of me."

She didn't look the least bit apologetic. A few people nearby laughed nervously.

Merek hoped the flush rising in his face wasn't noticeable in the candlelight. "There's nothing to apologize for, my lady. Now, if you'll excuse me—"

Honoria wasn't finished. She fixed her dark eyes on him. "But really, Captain. Skulking in the north for months at a time? I would have expected better from a man with your distinguished reputation. Maybe you're not as brave as you'd like everyone to think."

"My lady," Talen interjected hesitantly. "I'm afraid you do Captain Strong a dishonor. No one in this room doubts his character or his courage. If he says that he only just learned of your return, then you can trust that it's the truth."

Honoria smiled at Talen. "Perhaps. Or perhaps you give him too much credit. Perhaps there was more to his absence than you think." She turned and looked at Merek, sizing him up. All conversations in the room had stopped, and the only sound was the gentle music of a quartet playing in the far corner of the room.

Talen shifted uncomfortably. "I would never want to disagree with Your Highness, but I have never known Captain Strong to shrink from duty or danger. I can only assume you have been...misinformed," he ended lamely.

Merek wished Talen would be quiet. He didn't know what game Honoria was playing, but Talen wasn't helping.

"In truth," she directed this to Talen but still spoke loudly enough for the whole room to hear, "I don't know why my father wanted to promote him in the first place. He must have a weakness for his old friend. Now, General Grammel on the other hand, I could never imagine him running away to hide whenever he disagreed with my father."

At this, King Sindal finally spoke. "That's enough, Ria." His tone was firm, but there was a hint of a smile as he turned toward his daughter. "I think the captain has suffered enough. My apologies, Strong. My daughter's tongue has only grown sharper in her time away, I'm afraid."

With his pronouncement, the tension in the room eased, and the knot in Merek's stomach loosened enough for him to find his voice.

"It's a delight to see you again, Your Highness," he said to Honoria without feeling it.

"Honoria, escort the captain to his seat," Sindal said. "And Ria, I trust that you will refrain from insulting his honor again. I would hate to have to take up arms against him on your behalf."

Some of the nearest guests laughed politely. Honoria took Merek's arm as they walked to the table, as if granting him a great honor. But Merek stiffened at her touch, wishing only to keep his distance.

Through the shuffling of the guests, Honoria leaned toward him and said quietly, "I'm sorry, but that's the best I could do. That's the closest you'll ever get to an apology from him. I hope it helps."

Merek looked at her in surprise, but she released his arm and sat without another word. As Merek sat across from her on the king's left, she glanced up and caught his eye. A hidden smile teased her lips before she looked away, engaging the Khouri ambassador in an animated conversation in his native tongue.

Merek's head swam. The evening was just beginning, and already he felt out of his depth. The nobleman with the long nose was seated to Merek's left. He began talking about trade tariffs against their old enemy, the kingdom of Dell, and Merek sighed inwardly. Not a landowner, then. Most likely a merchant family that had been granted a title after performing some civic service.

Merek knew little about trade and felt too unsettled to pretend otherwise. Soon the nobleman gave up and turned his attention to his companion on the other side.

"How goes your vigil on the wall?" King Sindal asked stiffly, drawing Merek's attention.

Merek felt the tension of two opponents sizzle between them at his formal tone.

"Actually, Your Majesty, there have been some developments which bring me to Albon. If I might be granted an audience, I'd like to talk to you about them privately."

"What sort of developments?"

"Repairs, mostly. The flooding of the Nardin caused substantial damage in the south and—"

"Not now," Sindal grunted. "Come tomorrow morning, and I'll make time for you."

"Thank you, sire," Merek said gratefully. Perhaps they could reconcile after all.

He waited while servants refilled the king's glass before nodding toward the other end of the table where the general sat. "I see that you promoted Grammel. Are you pleased with him?"

Sindal shrugged. "He performs his duties well enough."

"Grammel is very capable. I served with him in several campaigns. He has a sharp mind and the loyalty of his men."

"But not as sharp as yours. No, don't be modest." The king cut short Merek's objection. "Enough of Danvir's blood runs in my veins to recognize a brilliant leader when I see one, and Grammel is no Merek Strong. Besides..." He leaned in, his blue eyes twinkling. "Grammel has those unfortunate eyebrows that look like a fox has burrowed into his brain."

Merek snorted into his cup. "I seriously doubt that his eyebrows impede his military abilities, my lord."

"Perhaps not. But I find them so distracting anytime I have a conversation with him. Are you satisfied, Strong? You've doomed me to never be able to look my general in the eye without feeling a distinct itch to laugh."

Merek tried to cover his own laugh by wiping his mouth with his napkin. "Truly I can't fathom the burdens you must bear."

Sindal chuckled freely, and Merek noticed Honoria watching them from across the table. She smiled at him and gave the briefest of conspiratorial nods.

"I didn't know that you were fluent in Khouri," Merek said to her.

"Hardly fluent, but Lord Melo is very patient with me." She smiled at the ambassador. "I spent six months in his beautiful country, but I'm afraid I can't do his musical language justice."

The dark man smiled back. "Not at all, my lady. You honor our language with your sweet tongue."

"Did you spend much time with the prince?" the young lady in pink chirped. "Was he as handsome as they say he is?"

"Ah, the true question is whether he is as handsome as *he* thinks he is. I'm afraid it was difficult to fully appreciate his talents with such a large ego getting in the way."

Honoria turned to the ambassador, who was receiving clarification from his interpreter. "I mean no disrespect, of course. Prince Lahri is all that is good and noble about Khourin."

Merek expected the ambassador to be offended, but he merely chuckled. "The women of my country do not mind the...what did you say?...ego. But I can see it would not please you. You shine so brilliant, why need the sun?"

Merek had never imagined a Khouri could offer such lavish flattery. Either this man was an incredible diplomat, or Honoria had completely won him over.

"Still, it's got to be awfully lonely to always outshine everyone else," the pink young lady said pointedly. "I would rather bask in the warmth of a man more beautiful and talented than I, than spend my life alone because I could never be pleased."

Honoria's smile lost some of its warmth. "Then it is fortunate that with standards like that, you will never have to worry about being alone."

The young lady didn't seem to realize she'd been insulted.

"I just don't understand it," she said to Captain Talen, who sat next to her. "After two years visiting other courts, we all expected that she would come home with half a dozen promises of intent. I'm sure I would have!" She ended with a laugh, but no one at the table joined her.

Maybe she *did* realize she'd been insulted after all.

The king put a hand over Honoria's resting on the table. "Your concern for my daughter's marriage state is notable. But I'm assured that her travels were successful even if they didn't lead to a betrothal."

Honoria's smile dissolved completely. "Thank you, Far. In truth, they were successful precisely *because* they didn't lead to a betrothal."

The young lady tittered her disbelief. "You mean to say that you didn't spend nearly a year in Ardania because you were seeking—"

"This is neither the time nor the place to discuss my preferences for marriage," Honoria said hotly.

The table grew quiet.

Honoria's eyes sparkled as she seemed to reconsider her audience. "But there is some truth to what you say. Yes, I spent the last two years touring Fehr, Branvik, Ardania, and Khourin, but it was not in pursuit of a husband. I lived as a guest in their courts. I visited their villages and saw how their people lived, while befriending their noble houses to learn how their governments are run. It was a most instructive opportunity, and I credit my father's keen understanding for bringing it about."

She smiled at her father, who tipped his cup toward her in return.

When she continued, her voice was confident. Even determined. Only her left hand straying to brush a wisp of hair from her temple suggested that she was uncomfortable.

"If a suitable match had arisen during that time, it was understood that an agreement of marriage would be made. Since I returned home, the gossip has been fierce about why no betrothal took place. I've been alternately glorified, victimized, and vilified. I can guess which of the tales you have been listening to," she said pointedly at the other young woman, who dropped her eyes. There was no trace of the light-hearted, playful spirit Honoria had shown earlier, and Merek realized that she had been gentle with him by comparison.

"The truth, however, is far less exciting. Quite simply, the more I learned about these other countries and the more that I loved their people, the more certain I became that none of these men belonged on the throne of Rahm. In Rahm, our women are treated with dignity. Our noblemen are subject to the same laws as a common worker. Even the king himself is not above the law. But this is not the case in these other lands. I've seen poverty, slavery, and injustice ignored by the monarchs at best and encouraged by them at worst. Our good people deserve better."

The nobleman with the long nose cleared his throat. "Surely a man who married into the royal line with the intent to one day become king could be taught to adopt our ways. Perhaps his unique perspective would even be beneficial."

"Doubtful," Honoria said firmly. "In my travels I've never met a man with the character you describe. It seems that humility does not come easily to the noble class."

King Sindal chuckled appreciatively.

"So there you have it, ladies and gentlemen," Honoria concluded. "I'm sorry that it's not the sordid tale that you were hoping for. But it *is* the truth."

In the heavy silence that followed, Merek offered, "I'm sure I speak for all of us here tonight when I say that you have an uncommon amount of wisdom for a young woman your age."

Honoria turned on him. "Is that meant to be a compliment, Captain?" she challenged, her eyes flashing.

Merek was taken aback. "Well, I—"

"Because in the very compliment where you praise my wisdom, you imply that my youth precludes me from such wisdom. And that prejudice against me for something I cannot control—my age—has insult at its heart."

King Sindal snorted and leaned toward Merek. "I just stop talking when she gets like this," he whispered.

Honoria glanced at her father in irritation, but said nothing more.

Merek caught Talen's eye. His old friend shrugged apologetically with an expression that seemed to say, *You see?*

Not dull indeed.

"Forgive me for my bluntness, Your Highness," an older noblewoman said, "but though your intent may be worthy, the end result is that you are left without a husband, Rahm without a king, and the throne without an heir. And *you* are not getting any younger."

Instead of challenging the old woman, Honoria merely smiled. "Yes, it is a puzzle, isn't it? My duty and love for our people demands both great urgency and great caution. How to decide which is most important?"

King Sindal smiled. Did he know where this was leading?

"I think that the answer," Honoria paused dramatically, "is to eliminate the king altogether. Allow me to rule as Rahm's unmarried queen, and choose my own heir as I think best."

The reaction at the table was immediate. Gasps, coughs, and a flurry of muttered side conversations erupted.

"Unmarried!"

"Abandon the Thorodan line?"

"That's outrageous!"

"But how would you choose?"

"Perhaps I'll have a tournament," Honoria declared. "Or a contest of wits! I expect that I could choose our next king—or queen, for that matter—at least as well as I could give birth to her. Or him. After bringing her to court and teaching her all she needs to know, maybe I could marry for love in my old age and retire to the country."

Honoria affected a wistful expression as she sipped her wine, but Merek saw the glimmer of humor in her eyes. She was enjoying the reaction from the rest of the table.

She saw him watching her and asked, "What do you think of my plan, Captain?"

Merek thought it was all a farce, but didn't dare provoke her further. Instead, he said, "I'm just sitting here trying to find some sign of the girl I knew as a child who rode on my shoulders and called me 'Uncle Merek.' When did she become a mature woman who publicly chastises military commanders, converses freely with foreign politicians, and gives impassioned speeches that are revolutionary in nature, but almost make a degree of sense?"

Honoria set down her cup with a smile. "Thank you. *That,* my dear captain, was a compliment."

The king chuckled. "You haven't even heard the best part. Tell him, Ria. Tell him about the pig farmer."

The princess hesitated. "I think I've given them quite enough to talk about tonight, Far."

"Oh, but this is the best part! You must tell!"

The nearer conversations paused expectantly, and soon the whole table grew still. "I'm afraid my father doesn't like my idea much. He seems to think that there are too many uncertainties and opportunities for contention." There were a few relieved laughs. The king grinned in anticipation. "So I told him I would be willing to agree to a compromise."

"A pig farmer!" Sindal interjected, laughing.

"Well, it doesn't have to be a pig farmer, but they seem to embody the essence of good, hard-working, humble Rahmish life. Really, it could be anyone so long as he was far removed from ever having any political ambitions or desires. That way, I can be free to make all the decisions without an interfering husband trying to play king, but I will still marry and have babies and preserve the Thorodan line. Everyone is happy."

"A pig farmer!" the young woman in pink said in disbelief. "You would invite a commoner—a pig farmer!—to your bed?"

Her father shushed a warning from across the table.

Honoria leaned forward, the jewels in her hair catching the light. "A commoner can wash up just as well as you or I. Though I suppose he might need to have several washings before the wedding night." This brought another peal of laughter from the king.

The older noblewoman spoke up again. "What about keeping you company on cold winter nights? What could you possibly talk about when it's just the two of you?"

"Well, he would have to be educated and well-read, of course. And it might help for him to travel and see something of the world."

Merek laughed. "And just where are you going to find a well-educated, worldly-wise pig farmer who can match you in conversation but not have any political ambitions?"

"I'm sure he's out there somewhere." Honoria looked at Merek appraisingly. "It's too bad that you didn't marry and have a son, Captain Strong. You don't have any younger brothers, do you?"

"No." He paused. "But I do have a nephew."

"A nephew! Excellent! Tell me about him."

"His name is Otten, and he even owns pigs."

"Perfect!"

"He's twelve."

Sindal guffawed so hard that he choked. Crumbs dribbled onto his sandy beard as he struggled for breath, the laughter driving him to tears.

"I suppose that won't do, then," Honoria said in mock disappointment. "But I shall persevere. Someday, I will have my pig farmer. And Rahm will have her king."

Seven

Merek rose early to meet Rorden on the practice field. He'd been careful with his wine, but his head still needed clearing from the previous night's dizzying conversation. He wasn't sure what to make of the princess and her games, but at least the king had been more relaxed in her presence. For most of the evening, Sindal had seemed more like himself than he had in months. Maybe even years. Merek hoped that their meeting later that morning would secure the reconciliation between them.

An otherworldly mist rose from the river in the woods that bordered the practice field, smelling moist and cool. In the pre-dawn light, only a few other soldiers were out on the field, and they kept their distance. Merek and Rorden ran through some warm-up exercises while chatting about the evening's activities before settling into more serious swordplay.

The conversation stopped as they turned their full attention to fighting. It felt good to use his muscles for something besides riding a horse and lifting a fork, and soon Merek broke out in a light sweat.

The day brightened around them as they fought, and Merek was vaguely aware of the practice field filling with other soldiers. By the time he and Rorden finished, the mist had cleared and the sun shone warm and bright, promising a hot day ahead.

Merek wiped the sweat out of his eyes with his sleeve.

"Captain Strong, I was hoping to find you here!" The deep voice of General Grammel boomed out over the sounds of clashing swords and shouting men.

"Good morning, General. You're up early for such a late night."

"But not as early as you, I see. Care to join me in a little skirmish?"

Merek eyed the general. As it had the previous night, Grammel's manner lacked genuine warmth. "Had you been an hour earlier, I would gladly consider it, but Sergeant Rorden and I just finished."

Grammel smirked. "Come, Strong. The sergeant here couldn't even give you a respectable fight."

"We were both holding back," Merek responded as Rorden went pink.

"Good. Then you'll still be fresh when I give you a real challenge."

Merek turned to Rorden. "Unless the general has learned a few things in the years since Durr's End, this shouldn't take long. See to my bath, will you?"

Grammel smiled, but there was an intent look in his eyes. "I think you'll be surprised how much I've learned, Strong."

Merek didn't know what Grammel's purpose was, but he had no intention of holding back. It would be unfortunate to embarrass Grammel in front of his own troops, but since Grammel had insisted, he would have to live with it.

"You shouldn't be so hard on Rorden," Merek said as they circled each other cautiously, each watching how the other moved and held his weapon before making a first strike. "He's a good soldier, and for-tunately for me, an even better clerk."

"I don't care about your clerk," Grammel said. "I want to talk about you."

He made a couple of tentative thrusts that Merek parried easily.

"Because one of the things I've learned since our time together at Durr's End is that no one turns down a promotion like this without having their eye on a better prize. So that makes me wonder—"

From one breath to the next, Grammel dropped the hesitancy and came at him with a fierceness Merek had never before seen in the older man. His skill had indeed improved in the years since they'd fought together. Merek recovered swiftly, countering his heavy blows and quickly shifting his weight to use the force of Grammel's attack to destabilize him. Off-centered now, Grammel's attack lost force, and Merek got in a sound blow before pulling away.

"—what is the prize you have your eye on?" Grammel finished as he swung back around and raised his sword for another attack.

Their swords screamed as blade scraped against blade. It had been a long time since Merek had faced such a skilled opponent. It was invigorating.

And also mildly unsettling.

He met each strike, but had little time to shift from defensive to offensive before Grammel put him back on the defensive again. He tried to settle into a rhythm, to get a sense of Grammel's next move. But Grammel was fast and unpredictable, and Merek barely kept up. The day's heat was catching up to him as well, and he was already thirsty from his earlier skirmish with Rorden. He tried to put his thirst out of his mind, but that just made his throat beg for water.

"I've heard the tales about you, of course." Grammel's forceful attack was becoming harder to sustain. He breathed heavily and sweat ran down his brow. "The great Captain Strong, whose feats are as unbelievable as they are prolific. Clearly you don't plan to sit quietly in the shadows forever."

Grammel jabbed, and Merek deflected. This time, Grammel was an instant too slow to recover, and Merek pounced. He swung Grammel's blade out of the way and attacked while Grammel was still off-balance. Grammel met him stroke for stroke, but struggled to get his feet firmly under him again.

With that, Merek found the rhythm he'd been seeking. He was used to keeping his strength in check when working with Rorden or new recruits, so it felt good to unleash as he attacked Grammel over and over again. Breathing hard and sweating freely now through the layers of his loose clothing, he didn't let up as strike after strike he sent Grammel on the defensive. And Grammel's defenses were sub-tly weakening.

"You give me too much credit for cleverness," Merek grunted. "I only want to serve our king and people the best way I can." This he punctuated with a blow to Grammel's hip. The practice swords were not sharp, but Grammel winced and staggered slightly.

Collecting himself, Grammel responded with an increased burst of power, and for a moment Merek found himself countering his heavy blows again. Briefly, the fatigue from Merek's earlier fight crept at the edges of his mind. He pushed it aside and returned Grammel's blows with a surge of intensity. He couldn't sustain it for long, but if he could only gain the upper hand—

That was all he needed. Grammel's eyes hardened as he recognized the impending defeat. He shrank back and stumbled, coming to his knees with Merek's sword at his chest.

A spontaneous burst of applause sounded across the field. Merek looked around, startled to realize that there was a much larger crowd of soldiers gathered than when the fight had begun. He lowered his sword and bowed his head briefly to the crowd, who whooped and clapped with greater enthusiasm. Then he reached his hand to the kneeling general.

General Grammel took his hand and stood. Still gripping his hand, he leaned toward Merek and spoke fiercely. "I don't know what your game is, Strong. But I warn you, I'm watching. You'll regret it if you try to interfere with me."

Grammel turned and walked away proudly, Merek's feeling of victory souring under his threat. What was that all about? Did he know that Merek himself had encouraged the king to offer him the post? How could he think that Merek would pose any kind of threat?

Merek shook his head. The sooner he finished his business in Albon, the better.

As he walked across the field toward the barracks, the crowd closed in around him. Soldiers shook his hand and patted him on the back.

Some faces he recognized. Others were new. Everyone seemed to want to congratulate him. He smiled and accepted their good will, but wished that he could enjoy it as a simple skirmish the way they did. The general's portentous warning seemed too menacing to dismiss.

At the edge of the practice field, the packed dirt gave way to a stone courtyard. The crowd in the courtyard was even more dense than on the field, and when Merek reached it, they parted to reveal the very last person he expected to see.

Honoria sat on a chair with a table before her and a ring of smiling soldiers around her. One of them was Rorden, Merek noticed with irritation.

Dozens of rebukes and inquiries came to mind, but to his chagrin the one that escaped was, "Are you going to drink that, Your Highness?"

He gestured to the cup that sat beside the remains of her breakfast.

"It doesn't matter if I was, you need it more than I. Please." She picked up the cup. "A victory cup to the winner!" she called dramatically. The soldiers laughed.

That answered the question of how long she'd been sitting there.

The tart juice was cold and welcome on his parched throat. "Thank you, my lady. I apologize for disturbing your breakfast."

She received the cup from him solemnly. "It is my honor. I will never wash this cup again, and it will stand in tribute as the cup from which the valiant Captain Strong drank after defeating the noble General Grammel."

Merek couldn't tell if she enjoyed mocking him specifically, or if it was just her way to make fun of the world at large. Either way, it made him squirm.

"Is there anything I can do for you, my lady? I expect you didn't wander down here this morning by accident."

Honoria smiled at Rorden. "Mmm, I only wish I had wandered down here long ago. I have such a weakness for a man in uniform. Then again, what woman doesn't? To have so many handsome young men showing off their strength and skill, it's enough to make me positively swoon."

Rorden grinned.

Merek grimaced. "We're honored by your visit, my lady, but I would hate to see what effect repeated occurrences would have on the men."

"Very well, gentlemen. Your commander has spoken—"

"I'm not actually their commander."

"—and we wouldn't want to argue with him after he just triumphed over our own dear general—"

"It was only a simple skirmish."

"—so I'm afraid this is farewell for now." She stood, and the soldiers saluted Merek. Or were they saluting the princess? All their eyes were on her, and she waved at them with one last smile over her shoulder before joining Merek.

She moved to take his arm, then seemed to think better of it. Merek was suddenly aware of his sweat-soaked clothing and the grit of the practice field sticking to his skin. As they crossed the courtyard to the barracks, the princess didn't comment on his appearance, but kept her distance nonetheless.

"In fact, Strong, I didn't wander down here by accident," she said. "My father sent me to see if you could meet with him this afternoon. Seeing as how you've been otherwise engaged, I assume you won't mind."

"Thank you. I doubt your father would appreciate my current attire." He glanced down at the simple shirt and breeches he wore.

"Or the smell." Honoria smiled, her dark eyes shining with mirth.

Merek's face reddened. Why couldn't the breeze be blowing the opposite direction, sending the stench of his cooling sweat away from her? It seemed he was doomed to play the fool in front of beautiful women. With a start, he realized that after only one meeting, he'd left behind the image of the youthful Honoria of memory, and had instead accepted the woman she had become.

"Would you like me to accompany you back to the Hall?" he offered, hoping she would decline.

She laughed. "Such manners! I'm sure that's the last thing you want to do right now. I'll manage, thank you."

They reached the side door to the barracks, and Honoria turned to him. Her loose hair—the color of the hazelnuts he had gathered as a boy—was tossed playfully by the breeze, and she held it with one hand to keep it from her face.

"Also, Captain, I wanted to apologize for last night." For once Merek could detect no trace of mockery. "It wasn't fair of me to tease you so mercilessly. You handled it magnificently, though, for which I'm grateful."

Merek wasn't sure how to respond to this frank apology. "You certainly gave the gossips at the table plenty to chew on."

"Oh, they would have gone away with sensational tales either way, but at least we had a say in what those tales will be."

"Did we?" Merek felt like he was the last person with any control over the evening's events.

"Of course. In the end, what they saw was my father and his oldest friend laughing together as though there had never been any harsh words between them. That will go far in settling the rumors that have flown about you these past months."

"I don't care about rumors. They don't keep me from my duty. At least, not when I'm far away from Albon."

"Well, they keep me from mine." Honoria's voice was firm. "And my father as well. There has been a great tension over the Hall since I returned home, and it took me some time before I realized why. But now, thanks to both of us sacrificing a little pride last night, I already feel it lifting."

Merek appreciated her honesty, but was anxious to end the conversation. The air was more still on this side of the building, and his skin itched uncomfortably from the drying sweat. He resisted the urge to vigorously scratch his scalp.

"I'm glad I could be of service, my lady. And now, if you'll excuse me, I really hope that there's a bath waiting for me upstairs. If there isn't, I place the blame squarely on you."

Honoria frowned. "That is a heavy crime, indeed. Very well, Captain. I swear to you that I will not return to the army practice fields and risk distracting your soldiers." She turned to leave and then paused. Sunlight glinted hints of fire in her hair as she turned back and smirked. "Or, at least, not until you return to Endvar and leave them all to me."

Eight

That afternoon, Merek and Rorden were shown into the king's private garden. Despite Merek's additional insignias, the crisp newness of Rorden's coat put Merek's to shame. Of course, Rorden was always more concerned about image than Merek was. Away from Albon, officers were allowed a neatly trimmed beard. But even in Endvar, Rorden preferred to be clean shaven. Merek suspected it was out of vanity, because the women found Rorden so handsome without it. Merek preferred the familiar feel of a close beard, and it rankled him that he had to shave whenever he came to Albon, especially since Sindal himself wore his own beard thick.

The king's private garden was the one place where the openness of Thorodan Hall's sprawling acreage didn't extend. The garden was tucked off a corner of the main house, situated at the crest of a small promontory that offered a breathtaking view of Albon below. At only three feet high, its surrounding wall was more symbolic than functional, but all who had business at the court respected its boundary, giving one small sanctuary where the king could retreat for personal respite.

The afternoon air was warm and thick with the buzzing of insects. Fruit trees and ornamental plants provided welcome shade and layers of privacy between the house and the garden wall. A servant led Merek and Rorden to where the king rested beneath the shade of a pear tree, his eyes closed as he reclined. A small table sat at his elbow with a platter of fruit and cheese. Honoria sat by his side, reading a book and absentmindedly picking at the platter.

The gravel path crunched under their boots, and Honoria raised her head as they drew near.

"Oh joy!" she sang out. "Our hero approaches! With his faithful comrade-in-arms too!"

Merek groaned inwardly. He wasn't sure how much more he could take of Honoria's flirting and games.

Sindal opened his eyes and sat up. "Strong, come and sit! Take some refreshment! Have I met your clerk?"

"This is Sergeant Rorden, sire. He joined my unit about six months ago."

Rorden bowed and the king looked thoughtful. "Rorden...I know some Rordens on the coast. A large fishing family. Are you related?"

"Yes, Your Majesty."

"Excellent! I believe I stayed with them the last time I was in the area. Such a grand view of the ocean! I took my breakfast out on the edge of the cliff each morning, where I could watch the waves pound the rocks and feel the spray on the air. Such power. It was beautiful and terrifying at the same time."

Rorden brightened at the mention of home. "Indeed, sire, that is one of my favorite places as well. And if I may say so, your visits are an honor that we've missed in recent years."

Sindal waved them to sit. "I'm afraid I don't have the energy to travel the way I used to. But when I do, that will definitely be one of my first destinations."

Rorden beamed.

"Do you double as a packhorse, Sergeant?" Honoria asked casually without looking away from her book. "Why are you carrying so many packages?"

Merek took the largest package from Rorden and handed it to the king. "This is for you. From one of the finest textile merchants in all of Endvar. They assured me it was the only one of its kind in all of Rahm."

Honoria looked up. "Oh, lovely! I adore presents!" She sat forward eagerly to watch her father unwrap the brown paper. When he carefully brought the green fabric out into the light, she gasped. "You found this in Endvar? I've seen this silk in Ardania, but even there it was hard to get. You are a lucky man, Far."

The king fingered the fabric appreciatively. "What do you think, Ria? Would this be a good choice for my twentieth anniversary celebration?"

The princess clapped her hands with delight. "Oh yes! You would look very handsome. And so regal!"

Sindal grinned. "Just so! A very hearty thank you, Strong!"

Merek smiled. He would have to thank Imar. It had cost a small fortune, particularly since he'd bought the entire length of fabric to ensure that it was indeed the only one of its kind. But it was a small price to pay to solidify Sindal's newly awakened favor.

"And where is my gift, Strong?" Honoria asked. "Surely you didn't forget me."

Merek hesitated. He *had* forgotten her in Endvar, thinking only of appeasing the king.

Before he could reply, Rorden spoke up. "That is my fault, my lady. I saw how many trunks of fine clothing you brought home when your entourage passed through Endvar, and I convinced the captain that nothing he could bring would measure up. Forgive me if I was mistaken."

Honoria laughed brightly and reached again for her book. "One can never have too many fine clothes, Sergeant, but I accept your apology anyway."

The king placed the fabric on an empty chair and leaned back. "So tell me, Strong, what troubles you about your precious wall?"

Merek nodded to Rorden, who unrolled a map and handed it to the king. Sindal moved the platter of fruit and cheese aside so he could examine it closely on the table. "We've been seeing increasing damage to the wall," Merek said. "Some of it is natural forces, and some of it's intentional."

"Intentional?"

"This section here." He leaned forward and pointed to the map. "The villagers are plundering its stone, using it to build their homes and pen in their animals."

"Really?" Sindal said with a laugh. "How resourceful of them."

Merek paused. "It's not something we want to encourage, sir."

"Maybe not, but when you consider that there is very little timber there, and no local quarries, I can hardly blame them for taking advantage of a storehouse of perfectly cut stone right in their backyard... so to speak." Sindal chuckled drily.

Merek buried a twinge of irritation. If Sindal wasn't in the mood to take his concerns seriously, this meeting would be a waste of time. He tried again. "In addition to that section, there's a portion here that has been damaged by flooding. Here, here, and here, the earth has shifted underneath and the wall has become dangerously unsound. My men can't safely perform their patrols until the foundation stones are reset."

The king looked closely at the areas he indicated, then looked up and spoke to Rorden. "According to this map, the coastal areas all appear sound."

"Yes, Your Majesty," Rorden replied. "We don't wait for soldiers to fix the wall for us. We tend to it ourselves."

"Hmm. Interesting. While one village is out tearing down the wall to use for its own purposes, another is strengthening it all on their own...without waiting for my help."

"Perhaps they don't have the memory of pirates stealing their children the way we do, my lord."

"Well spoken, Sergeant." The king leaned back in his chair. "Very well, Strong. I see your map. What do you need from me?"

Rorden handed him the list of proposed expenses needed to complete the repairs.

"If you approve the materials and extra men," Merek said, "as well as authorize additional stone from the quarries, we can begin repairs at the most critical locations before the summer is over."

Sindal nodded thoughtfully. "Money and stone I can get you. But for men, you'll have to talk to Grammel."

Merek paused.

"Oh, that's right! You just humiliated him in front of his troops today. I doubt he'll be feeling particularly generous."

"That was not my intention, sir."

"And yet, you did. So unwise when he's already smarting from not being my first choice as general." Sindal reclined again, and his eyes glinted mischievously. "I'm afraid you'll have a difficult time getting what you want from him now."

Honoria turned a page in her book and interjected lazily, "Grammel is far too self-important for his own good. He needs a good humbling now and then. I applaud Captain Strong for being bold enough to do it."

Merek thought about Grammel's final threat. "Why must the request come from me, my lord? You are the king. You command the troops *and* the wall."

"Yes, but this is your project. If you want the men, you'll need to convince him." Sindal closed his eyes with an air of finality.

A project? Is that what Sindal thought this was? Merek hesitated, choosing his words carefully. "This is not a project, my lord. It's a stewardship. The wall is yours. The people it protects are yours. It's my job to ensure that it remains strong, but it's your people that I'm trying to protect."

"Hmm." Sindal kept his eyes closed, his face a picture of serene relaxation. "And yet, some would just as soon use the stone to keep out the chill of winter as an imaginary enemy. Perhaps you don't know as much about what the people need as they do."

Merek was dumbfounded. Was Sindal just toying with him? Or was he still bitter over Merek's refusal to serve as his general?

In the uncomfortable silence, Honoria rose from her chair. "Sergeant, would you care to join me in touring the garden? There are some lovely views that not every visitor to court gets to see."

"It would be my pleasure, my lady." Rorden stood and bowed to the king, then followed the princess out of sight down the nearest path. The sound of their idle chatter faded.

Insects droned in the heat. Merek watched his old friend closely. "You're still angry with me."

Sindal opened his eyes and regarded him. After a moment, he shook his head sadly. "It was meant to be a great honor, you know. Who else would be fit to lead my armies except my oldest friend? The man whom I've trusted over a lifetime to fight by my side."

"I *was* honored," Merek admitted. "It was not a light thing to decline. There are times I still question if I made the right decision."

"Well there's no going back now. Grammel has accepted the post, and I'm afraid I'm stuck with him."

"His manner can be difficult, but he will serve you well." Merek thought back to the skirmish earlier that morning and hoped he was right.

"I just wish I understood why you refused."

"I explained myself before."

"Indulge me."

Merek looked out at the garden's collage of verdant color, searching for words that would not offend. He settled on self-effacing. "You know me, Sindal. I'm no nobleman. Give me a quiet post in a small town with simple people instead of the intrigues of court life, and I will count myself blessed."

"Sometimes doing our duty requires uncomfortable sacrifices."

"I assure you, there is much to keep me uncomfortable. Or do you forget how the sewers of Berseth smell in the summer, causing the whole city to stink like Harr's own latrine?"

Sindal's beard twitched. "That I shall never forget. But don't think you can fool me. You love to be out there roaming the land, never staying in one place too long, never putting down roots or growing too attached." A hint of envy tinged his words.

"I confess it's served me well, but there's more than that. My service means something out on the wall. There the dangers are real. Not simply political intrigue over which landowner is trying to grab power from another. When these people face a threat, they are fighting for survival. For their very lives."

"You exaggerate. We have faced no serious threat to our borders since Danvir's Wall was built." Sindal plucked a grape from the platter and tossed it into his mouth. Merek sensed the tension in his deliberateness. Sindal was like a bowstring strung too tightly. A silent tautness, ready to snap.

"With all due respect, sir, the threats are always there. No one understands that better than those who live with it just beyond the wall."

"Nonsense. We're at peace with our neighbors and suffer no threat from the marauders of the past. My father could never have foreseen these days of peace and prosperity. Who would have ever believed that someday we would trade freely with our old enemies, Fehr and Ardania? Or that the great wars between Khourin and Branvik would end peaceably? This is a new world, and we're all prospering. There's no room for the old aggression and violence. I confess, most days I feel that Danvir's Wall is a blight on our peace. A reminder of violence and imagined fears."

Into Merek's mind flashed a memory of silhouettes against a bonfire—the sickening sound of crushed bone that Merek felt deep in his gut as his father crumpled to the earth.

"You heard Rorden," he objected. "They are not imagined fears for the people who lived them!"

"Yes." Sindal's blue eyes snapped up to meet Merek's, and his tone sharpened. "And so what do they do? They maintain the wall because it keeps them safe. But their threat isn't shared by the rest of Rahm. So let them keep the wall, and let anyone else who thinks it helps them sleep at night. But I need you here, not wasting your life there chasing shadows."

"These aren't mere shadows. Just last week I discovered a criminal element newly established in Endvar that gives me considerable alarm."

"That sounds like a concern for the peacekeepers. I suggest you speak to Talen about it."

"That's not the point," Merek said with exasperation. "The truth is that no matter how many treaties we have, there are some things that will never change. As long as there is a kingdom such as ours with so many resources and prosperous people, there will always be those who want to strip her bare and take her riches for themselves. Where there is wealth, there will always be greed. And where there is greed, there will always be bandits lurking in the dark. You would know this if you roused yourself enough to care about something other than your own comfort."

Sindal glared. "That's not fair!"

"No?" The heat of frustration gave fire to his words. "Danvir toured the wall every two years without fail. Have you ever toured it even once? Your life of ease has seduced you into apathy. You haven't even left Albon in years. Come and see the wall for yourself. If nothing else, it would do you good just to get out among the people!"

"How dare you speak to me like—"

"Do you want to know why I refused to be your general? Because it only separates you from your troops and your people. *You* are the one who should be leading your armies. Protecting your people is at the very heart of what it means to be a king."

"In my father's day, perhaps. But the old wars died with him. These are not the battles we fight today. A wise king knows when it's time to put away weapons and promote peace."

"A wise king knows that his weapons must always be close at hand or his peace will not last."

"You think I don't know that? That's why I wanted *you* to take charge of my armies!" Sindal slammed his hand down on the table, and the platter shook, spilling food.

"But I'm not the king!" Merek insisted. "You are! And yet you are withdrawing more and more into your life of comfort with each passing year. You have a duty to your people that should not be shouldered by any other!"

Sindal gripped the edges of his chair. "What do you know of it? You presume to pass judgment when you know nothing of what it means to rule."

"Of course I don't. I'll never be in your place. But I do know what it means to fight and bleed for your people, and I can tell you that a king who refuses to risk his own life to save his people is a waste of flesh."

"I'm weary of your self-righteous certainty, Strong," Sindal said hotly, spittle collecting at the corners of his mouth. "You think that you could do better? You who could scarcely pen a coherent sentence when we first met? I've been too generous with you. You've risen so high that you've forgotten that you were nothing before I gave you status."

"Are we resorting to insults then?" Merek shot back. "What happened to the Sindal I once knew, who said he was proud to call me friend? He never would have demeaned another just to make himself feel superior. Sometimes, I swear I don't even recognize you anymore!"

Sindal stood, red-faced and breathing heavily as he loomed over Merek. "But I see you all too clearly. Your ambition and drive. Always maneuvering yourself into the most favored positions. Just as when we were young and you manipulated my father into paying special attention to you. You played on his sympathies so that he became the father you never had."

With that accusation, the last of Merek's restraint broke. He stood to his full height, towering over the king. "Your father was a wise and kind man who took notice of a poor, ignorant boy from the forest and gave him a chance to prove himself. I will always be grateful to him, but I never looked to him to replace my own father. If you had seen past your own jealousy, you would have known that. Instead you see nothing but suspicion from one who has shown only love and loyalty. If Danvir could see you now, he would be disgusted."

He regretted the words as soon as he said them. Sindal reeled back, knocking over his chair. The raw pain in his eyes made him seem small and helpless, and Merek's anger leaked away under the force of his shame.

Horrified as his words hung in the air between them, Merek struggled to find the words to bring them back. "Sindal, forgive me—"

"Don't!" Sindal breathed. "You will not call me by my name. I am your king."

Merek nodded. "Of course, sire. I mean no disrespect."

Sindal straightened, his posture stiff with anger. "Go. Get out of my house. Go back to your wall, and leave me in peace. I'm finished with you."

"My lady. My lady, the king needs you."

Ria woke in the darkness to find Biren shaking her gently. She rubbed her eyes and tried to gather her wits. "Again? This is getting ridiculous."

"I'm sorry, my lady. But the king—"

"No, you did right." The night air coming through the open window in her room was cool. She wrapped a dressing gown around her loose nightdress and stepped into light slippers before following Biren out into the hallway.

Moonlight shining through the windows of the corridor made patterns of silver light on the floor, rendering Biren's candle superfluous.

She heard her father's voice raised in anger long before she reached his room. Servants gathering at a distance melted back into the shadows as she approached.

Ria pushed the door open and stormed into the room. "Far, you had better not be—"

She stopped mid-sentence as she took in the scene.

Her father's servant, Martin, stood against a far wall, one arm clutching the other protectively. Dark blood dribbled down his sleeve and onto his nightdress. Sindal himself stood nearby, a dagger in his hand, and two guards at his side.

Ria froze. "Martin!"

Martin turned to her, stricken. "My lady, I tried—"

"Ria!" Sindal bellowed. He turned his thunderous gaze on her. "Confound you, meddlesome girl! Get out of here! This is no place for you!"

Biren tugged at her sleeve. "Come, my lady," she urged.

Ria allowed her maid to pull her out of the room and down the corridor. She collapsed onto a bench under a high arched window, her ears ringing, only vaguely aware of Biren at her side pressing a goblet into her hands.

"I'm sorry, my lady. I didn't know...Drink. You're as pale as a spirit."

Cool water slipped down her throat, giving her the strength to attempt words. "Martin. My father—"

"Martin will be well, Your Highness," said a man's voice. "The wound is not serious."

A shape resolved in the moonlight before them. It was one of the guards who had been in her father's chamber; a young man with an earnest expression.

"My father had a knife," Ria protested.

"Martin tried to wrest the dagger from him, but your father is very strong," he said.

"What do you mean? He was wounded in the struggle?"

"My lady, you don't look well. Perhaps you should rest."

Ria sat up straighter, wishing her ears would stop ringing. "What happened, soldier?"

The guard bowed his head briefly, and Ria glimpsed his thinning scalp in the gray light. "Martin heard your father shout and found him out of bed with a knife. He thinks he was having one of his nightmares, but he didn't recognize Martin and attacked him when

Martin tried to help—"

"Brandel," a firm voice called from the king's room. "Take Martin back to his room. He needs rest."

The guard turned away. "Excuse me, my lady."

Ria leaned her head against the window behind her and listened to the sounds coming from her father's bedchamber. His shouting had diminished to a low grumble, and on occasion was punctuated by the firm sounds of the physician's chiding voice.

When the physician emerged, Ria stood. Her head felt clear at last.

"I wish to see my father," she demanded.

Erland looked her over and nodded. "Of course, Your Highness. You'll have a few minutes before the sleeping draught takes effect."

Ria pulled her dressing gown tighter and pushed past him into the room. Two maids hurried out of the room with arms full of soiled cloth, while a third scrubbed at the floor. The king lay on his bed, his eyes closed, but he did not look restful.

"How do you feel, Far?" she asked gently, sitting at his bedside.

He opened his eyes, but took a moment to focus on her. "If you've come to scold me, you're too late. Erland was quite thorough. Fortunately, such accidents do little harm—"

"Accidents?"

"Yes." Sindal looked at her steadily. "Of course it was an accident. I couldn't sleep and decided to sharpen my knife. The movement is soothing to me. Unfortunately my hands were more weary than I thought and Martin startled me."

Knowing her father didn't trust her enough to be honest disturbed Ria almost as much as the thought that he was capable of such violence. "You must be more careful, Far. Perhaps I should tell Martin to remove all weapons from your room. Just to be safe."

Sindal frowned. "You speak as if I were a child. I don't need your meddling. If you want to help, play something for me. Your music is far more soothing than your questions."

"Hmm. You make demands like a child," Ria noted.

Her father harrumphed and closed his eyes.

"But since I'm in a forgiving mood tonight, I will indulge you." Ria nodded wearily to Biren, who quietly slipped out of the room. In the silence that followed, she ventured, "While we wait for my harp, tell me what upset you so much this afternoon. What happened after I left you and Strong in the garden?"

Sindal's brows creased together. "There's nothing to speak of."

"Nonsense. When I left, you were chatting amiably together. By the time I returned, it looked as if you'd nearly come to blows. A chair overturned and food spilling to the ground, with not a sign of you or the captain to explain it." She thought it best not to mention the raised voices she'd heard, or her father's agitated manner at dinner.

"You're meddling again," Sindal said, the edges of his speech becoming slurred as the sleeping draught dulled his senses. "I didn't ask you here, and I don't want you pestering me. These are matters that you can't understand and have no right to question me about."

His tone stung more than his words. He'd been short-tempered with her before, but this was different. There was an edge of hostility that made her feel small and uncertain. *He's just tired,* she told herself. *He doesn't mean what he says.* But she was relieved when Biren entered the room with her lap harp, sparing her the necessity of answering. In her weary and anxious state, any response she gave probably would have incited an argument. But that was nothing compared to the words fomenting in her mind for the next time she saw Captain Strong.

Nine

The entrance to the cobbler's shop was tended by a gangly youth sitting on a stool near the front window, his head bowed intently over a woman's shoe in his lap. The stitching emerging under his steady fingers was even and fine, as if a man three times his age had done it. Merek didn't know the boy, but Rorden greeted him as they entered.

"Hello, Finn. Is your father here?"

"Far!" Finn yelled, not raising his head. "The captain's here!"

From a back room came a hacking cough. Jes appeared in the doorway, a handkerchief to his mouth and one hand on his chest.

"Captain Strong, forgive me. I've had a touch of the summer fever, but I'm on the mend. Come on back. Finn, mind the shop."

Merek and Rorden followed Jes into the back room dominated by a large worktable. Shelves lining the walls housed various tools and boxes of supplies, and the floor was littered with scraps.

"A boot like a second skin, what kind of instruction is that?" Jes grumbled.

"I'm sorry that I couldn't be more specific, Jes. The less you know about this assignment, the better."

"Better for who? Not for me. Come, see what I've got." He motioned to the worktable, then paused as another fit of coughing struck. "The problem with a second skin is, how do you remove it? Feet aren't like hands that can slip in and out of a glove. The heel and ankle become a serious sticking point." He picked up an object from the table, the wisps of remaining hair on his head waving as he moved.

The shoe he held was unlike anything Merek had ever seen. Made of thin, supple leather on top, it wrapped around the foot in sections, tightening above the ankle with embedded laces. But the sole was stiff, encasing the toes like a layered glove.

"This was a tricky one," Jes said with a hint of pride. "Getting the laces just right was quite the puzzle."

"I helped him figure it out," piped up Finn from the doorway.

Jes shot him a look. "I thought I told you to stay out front," he growled, but Finn ignored him, hopping up to sit on a corner of the table.

Merek took the strange shoe from Jes and examined it. The sole was grooved for gripping and more flexible than it appeared at first glance. It would take some getting used to, but the protection would be supreme. Far better than going barefoot, which Stefan's last letter mentioned his men were trying because climbing was too difficult with their boots.

"It wouldn't be comfortable for long use," Jes said. "And the leather is too soft to hold up for very long. You'll be needing new ones more often than you'd like. But it's the closest thing to a glove for your foot that you're ever going to find."

"Sewing the laces onto the inside makes it fit more snug," Finn said. "I can show you if you'd like." Without waiting for an answer, he took it from Merek's hand and strapped it on his own foot. Once it was on, Merek saw how it was contoured to fit the shape of his foot perfectly.

"Remarkable," he muttered.

"Far made it to fit me," Finn announced proudly.

"And that there is the problem," Jes said. "Each boot needs to be fit to the foot that will wear it."

"That's not possible," Merek said immediately. "We could send you measurements. What would you need?"

"Everything. Foot length, width, arch, even the thickness of the ankle…"

Merek turned to Rorden, who was scratching his nose and shaking his head. "What is it?"

"That will never work, sir. Too many variables. Too much information to get wrong. Not to mention the length of time waiting for the post."

"You're right, it won't work." Merek frowned, thinking this over. He noticed Finn, who was still sitting on the table and idly swinging his legs. "What if we take the boy?"

Finn started. "Me?"

"Sir?" Rorden blurted out in surprise.

"He helped you with this one, correct? Could he construct one on his own?"

Jes snorted. "The boy has skill enough if he holds still long enough to use it. But you'd have better luck teaching a rabbit to stand on its head."

"I can do it, Far. I know I can!" Finn jumped off the table, his eyes bright. "Please, let me go?"

Jes answered with a series of wracking coughs into his handkerchief. He wiped his mouth and fixed the boy with a soft look that belied the gruff sound of his voice. "What will I do without you if you go running off, eh? Who will help me here?"

"I'll compensate you, of course," Merek offered. "Perhaps an apprentice's wage?"

"There, see?" Finn said hopefully.

"That's worth a lot more than this fool boy is. Are you sure?" Jes asked, ruffling his son's hair.

"I'd need you to be discreet," Merek warned. "Tell your neighbors he's gone to visit family and will be back before the summer is over." He turned to the boy. "Do you know how to keep your mouth shut? Where we're going you can't talk freely about what you're doing for me."

Jes erupted into a peal of wheezing laughter. "Talking freely is what he does best!"

Finn blushed, but to his credit, he looked Merek straight in the eye. "I can keep quiet about the right things, sir, but I can't promise the wrong things won't come out sometimes."

Jes laughed again and Merek looked at Rorden. He offered an *I don't like it, but I don't have any better ideas* shrug.

That would have to do.

"Well, Finn, you'd best get yourself packed. We leave for Endvar at first light tomorrow."

The stifling heat almost made Ria wish for the shade of a carriage. But she had spent so much time enclosed in carriages while traveling in foreign lands that she'd sworn to walk wherever she could when she returned to the safe streets of Albon.

Ria stayed on the shady side of the broad street, greeting shopkeepers and other pedestrians as she passed. The first few times she had ventured out like this, she'd been fairly mobbed by the curious crowd. Now, however, they were used to seeing their princess out among them, and she enjoyed a little more polite distance. Her destination was a bakery not far from Thorodan Hall where her former nursemaid lived with her husband. Ria had been a small child when her mother had died, her illness as unexpected as it was unrelenting. In her grief, the queen's maid had made it her personal duty to tend to the motherless princess. Soon the bond was fixed, and Lotta was the only mother Ria could remember.

Lotta had never had children, devoting herself instead to raising the princess. But when Ria was sixteen, Lotta had left the Hall to marry Pedr, one of the king's bakers. Ria knew that Lotta should be allowed to pursue her own happiness, and she was happy for her to have found love late in life. But a part of her had sulked to learn that she wasn't the central feature in that happiness.

The street sloped upward, and as Ria climbed, her breathing grew heavy in the heat. The angle of the rise gave her a good view of the busy street, and suddenly she became aware of a familiar profile not far ahead: short dark hair—so much darker than her own that it reminded her of the Fehr people in the far north—the prominent nose that wasn't perfectly straight, and an erect posture that spoke of effortless authority.

Hot annoyance rushed over her. How dare Captain Strong smile and enjoy himself after causing her father such distress? Ria quickened her pace. Here was the opportunity she'd been looking for. Captain Strong hadn't been seen at the Hall since that garden meeting, and he owed her an explanation.

She brushed against a man pulling a handcart up the road, stepping to the side to approach the captain from behind. Without warning, she slipped her arm through his and latched on as though it was the most natural thing in the world.

He tensed in surprise, then relaxed when he saw who held his arm.

"Princess. You have a knack for turning up in unexpected places. In another life, I could have trained you as a border spy."

"Captain Strong, you've been avoiding me."

"Have I?"

"Yes. These past three nights I've not seen you at our table."

"I believe Rorden sent my regrets."

"Oh yes, he's been very conscientious." Ria flashed a smile at Rorden, who grinned in return. For a brief moment, she was pleased that she had chosen her light blue gown. Its wide neck was very flattering, and Captain Strong's young aide was very handsome. "But it's your presence I asked for, not your regrets."

"I'm afraid we've been very busy," the captain said, "with little time for diversions."

Diversions? "I should hardly call reconciliation with your sovereign a mere diversion," Ria said sourly.

"I agree. But I cannot force a reconciliation where it's not welcome."

"Then walk with me now. I'm on my way to see Lotta. You remember her?" She squeezed his arm to pull him up the street, marveling at how firm his taut muscles were beneath the thin shirt. So different from her father's softness. It wasn't good for the king to spend so much time resting during the day instead of being outside working his body.

"I do remember Lotta. How is she?"

"She is well. And married, did you know?"

"I'm glad. She was always very kind. Wish her well for me."

"I will." Ria said, then returned to her original concern. "Come to the Hall tonight. I'll make excuses to our other guests, and you may have a private audience with my father."

He glanced down at her, his gray eyes suspicious. "At the king's invitation?"

"At *my* invitation, and for the good of the king."

"That won't do. The king has made it clear that he'll be happier the sooner I return to Endvar, and I'm eager to oblige."

"You leave soon?"

"In the morning, in fact."

"So you come to Albon just long enough to stir up trouble and then flee before things have been sorted out?" she accused.

"Believe me, my lady, this is not what I wished for," he said with a hint of irritation. "But there's nothing more I can do here. Best not to intrude upon your father's favor any longer."

"Tell me what went on after I left you in the garden," Ria demanded, turning squarely to look at him. Their abrupt stop caused a few exclamations from pedestrians, until they saw who it was and ducked their heads. Soon the flow of traffic moved around them, the bustling noise providing a mask of privacy.

Captain Strong raised an eyebrow at her bluntness. "You'll have to speak with your father about that. It's not my place." *And not your place to inquire,* his tone suggested.

"My father won't speak of it. I know that he refused the men you asked for, but there must have been something more. Did you argue with him about this whole Grammel business?"

"No. Well, yes, but not—" He caught himself, his voice growing firm. "Princess, I really shouldn't be discussing this with you. Talk to your father. I don't feel comfortable sharing what he wants to keep private."

Usually Ria didn't mind the captain's reserved self-control. It just made it that much more fun to tease him. There were even times, if she were honest, that she admired him for it. Right now, it was infuriating.

"Captain," Ria said sternly. "I don't ask out of idle curiosity. There may come a day when it is *I* whom you will petition for men and supplies. The more I can learn of your needs regarding maintaining the wall, the better support I can give you when that day comes."

The captain seemed to consider this for a moment. Standing this close to him, she noticed the faint line of an old scar on his jaw: a sign of an age of war long past.

When he looked at her, he seemed to really see her for the first time.

Yes, she thought with satisfaction. *Remember that one day I will be your queen, and not so easily dismissed.*

"Of course, Your Highness," he said submissively. "Forgive my reticence."

Captain Strong turned and began walking up the street again. "The only thing of relevance I can tell you is that I attempted to persuade the king to come and tour the wall, to see the damaged sections for himself."

"And he refused?"

"Decidedly."

"And?"

Captain Strong hesitated. "You have to understand that your father and I have known each other for a very long time. Sometimes with old friends you say things—"

"You lost your temper?" she guessed. "Never mind, Captain, I understand." And she did. What would have seemed a reasonable request to the captain would have been very upsetting to her father. Travel was out of the question in his current state, and being reminded of his inability to fulfill his kingly duties would have created a crushing weight of failure.

Had the circumstances been different, she might have confided this to Captain Strong. But as it was, he was preparing to leave the city and it would probably be many months before he returned. This was a problem she had to solve on her own.

"My lady?"

Ria's thoughts came back to the present and she realized they had almost reached the bakery. "Oh, I see that we've arrived. Thank you for escorting me, Captain. I'll let you return to your duties. And Sergeant Rorden," she said, flashing the young man her most dazzling smile. "I hope to see you in Albon again soon."

Rorden offered her a dimpled grin as he bowed. "It has been a great pleasure, my lady."

Ria turned to Captain Strong. "Goodbye, Captain. Safe journey. And please," she said softly, putting her hand on his arm, "don't be too hard on my father. If there's anything you can do to make amends, I beg you to try."

Then, swallowing the sinking feeling that she had said both too much and far too little, she turned her back on the captain and the unasked question in his eyes.

Ten

Ria found Lotta and Pedr cleaning up after the day's baking. The large brick ovens were cool, and Lotta was washing bowls when Ria entered.

"Ria, my dear! I'm almost finished here. Come in! Give me a hug!"

Ria hugged the plump woman, her skin sticky with the sweat of a long day's work. She stooped to kiss Pedr on the cheek where he was preparing tomorrow's starter dough. His blush reached past his ears, which had sprouted tufts of white hair in the two years Ria had been gone.

"Will you be a dear and bring me that stack of pans?" Lotta asked.

Ria obeyed, and then dried the clean pans against Pedr's objections.

"It's not right that the Crown Princess should be working in my kitchen," he complained.

"I don't mind. Besides, Lotta never likes to see me idle, do you, Lotta?"

"It's true. There's far too much work to do in the world to sit around and wait for someone else to do it. Even a princess needs to learn that. It will make her a better queen, someday."

Ria smiled. She'd heard it before, countless times. Lotta chattered on about the day as they worked, while Ria listened without saying much. It was soothing to hear Lotta's gossip, but her mind was heavy with worry, and she couldn't bring herself to respond as she normally would. When the pans were washed and the floor swept, Lotta kissed Pedr and murmured in his ear before steering Ria to the back door.

The small courtyard behind the house boasted a thriving kitchen garden, with herbs growing in boxes and fragrant roses climbing the wall. At this time of day, the house shaded the garden, and a slight breeze cooled them pleasantly as they settled onto a rough wooden bench.

Lotta sighed and smoothed the hair away from Ria's face, tucking it behind her ear like she was a little girl again. "Tell me, why is my chirping bird so silent today? You look as though you're carrying the weight of the world."

Ria had rehearsed what to say, but now was torn about how to begin. "Lotta, how well do you know my father?"

"Oh, what a question! I suppose I know him better than most, though not as well as some." Lotta paused thoughtfully. "Your father has a great gift for making people feel at ease around him. I think this leads to many people thinking they know him well, when really they just enjoy being in his presence. He's actually a very private person who doesn't let many people get very close to him. Your mother was fond of him, though. After she died, I saw a side of him that very few did."

"How is that?"

Lotta smiled. "I saw him as a father. If there's any way to get a true sense of who a man is, it's to see how he is as a father. I suppose in that way, I know him better than most. Certainly not as well as Merek Strong, of course. Those two were thick as thieves when they were young. It's a pity that Merek doesn't visit very often anymore."

"He's in Albon now. In fact, I saw him on my way here. I forgot to tell you that he sends his regards."

"Does he, then?" Lotta beamed. "Isn't that just like him? He's always been so thoughtful. When I came here with your mother so long ago, I was terrified of making a mistake and disgracing the new queen in front of all the household. I remember one night I took her linens to the laundry in a panic because I'd forgotten to wash some garments she needed for an outing the following afternoon. All the other servants had gone to bed, and I was alone in the back room, almost in tears. Merek was a regular fixture at the Hall in those days and happened to pass by on his way back to the barracks. He looked in and gave me such a fright! But when he saw my distress, he rolled up his sleeves and jumped right in to help!"

"He didn't!" Ria laughed at the thought.

"Can you imagine?" Lotta chuckled with her. "Of course, he was just a young soldier then. No fancy titles or medals."

"But a soldier washing the queen's undergarments? How did he endure the teasing?"

"Oh, I didn't tell a soul! For the sake of his honor, mine, and most of all, my lady's! But he didn't even ask it of me. It was as if he were above such humiliation. With his help, I finished the job in half the time, and everything was dry before your mother needed it the next day."

Ria shook her head at the ridiculous image of a young Merek Strong up to his elbows in royal laundry. "Have you never thought his friendship with my father is a bit odd? They are such opposites."

"No, not truly opposites." Lotta wiped the sweat from her face with a handkerchief. "Not in what matters. Yes, your father is charming and knows how to delight a crowd, whereas Merek doesn't seek attention. But they're both loyal to the people of Rahm and take their duties very seriously. Trustworthy, courageous, it just comes out in different ways. I've always thought Merek's steadying influence was a great strength to your father, especially in those early years when he first assumed the throne. Their friendship is a gift, and they are both better men for it."

Somehow this didn't make Ria feel better. "I'm afraid their friendship may be a thing of the past. It seemed that it was on the mend when Captain Strong first came to the city, but now it's even more deeply damaged than before. And it's affecting my father very sorely."

"How so?"

"He is not…himself lately. When it's just the two of us, he's some-times surly and cross, and I find myself looking for ways to get away from him. He doesn't sleep. And when he does sleep, his dreams are frightful and leave him more exhausted than he was before. The phy-sician can do nothing to help him. Far tries to carry on during the day as though nothing is wrong, but it's taking its toll." She stopped short of telling her about the knife incident. Her grim suspicions were too disturbing to share even with Lotta.

Lotta frowned. "You think this is related to a strain in his rela-tionship with Captain Strong?"

"It must be. As near as I can tell, it started when Captain Strong refused to serve as general. I can find no other reason for it."

"I see. Have you considered that instead of their conflict causing your father's troubles, it might be the other way around?"

Ria thought about this. "I suppose I haven't."

Lotta took Ria's hand in hers and stroked it in her lap. "There have been times I've wondered if your father wouldn't have done bet-ter to be a second or third son, rather than the only child in line for the throne."

Ria prickled at the criticism. "My father is a good king, and he's much beloved—"

"Hush dearest," Lotta shushed her. "That's not what I said. Yes, your father has done many great things for our country. I don't mean to suggest that he's not a good king. Rather that being king has not been good for *him*."

Ria bit off a retort as she turned these words over in her mind.

"Your father is a kind and generous king, and for that we're all grateful. But not all men have the stamina it takes to rule. With his temperament he may have been much happier as a rich scholar on a remote estate than he is now bearing the weight of the crown."

Ria could hear the truth in her words, even as she hated it. In-stead of arguing, she asked meekly, "What is to be done?"

Lotta patted her hand. "Well, first, you must think of yourself. No, don't argue. You can't spend so many hours tending him at night, or your own health will suffer."

"How do you know I—"

"Because I know you, Ria. I don't just say this because I worry about you. I also say it because it's your duty."

"My duty is to my father. If he needs me, I should be there for him."

"No, it isn't. As Crown Princess, your first duty is to Rahm."

"My father *is* Rahm."

"Today he is, but not forever. Someday, perhaps soon, *you* will assume the throne. It's not too early to prepare for that day. When your father was your age, Danvir was already declining in illness, and Sindal was not much older than you when he became king."

Ria felt as if the world shifted underneath her. "But I'm not ready. There's so much I need to learn, and Far—"

"I suspect your father didn't feel any more prepared than you do now. You will learn just as he did."

"I feel so lost sometimes. I don't even know how to begin."

"First, you need to get help with your father. I'm sure you're trying to be discreet, but you shouldn't be caring for him alone. Find a few people you trust who can share your burden. Then, do what you can to fulfill the duties he can't."

"But he doesn't want people to know that he's unwell," Ria protested.

"They needn't know. It won't seem strange for you to take on some of his responsibilities. It's natural at this stage in your life. And speaking of this stage in your life," Lotta said pointedly, "one of the most important things you should be doing is looking for a husband to secure the royal line."

Ria scoffed. "I would sooner be successful in finding a cure for my father's troubles."

"Ah. I had heard, of course—"

"It was *I* who refused Artem, not the other way around. No matter what you may have heard," Ria said bitterly.

Lotta paused as if waiting for more. When Ria didn't continue, she asked kindly, "What really happened between you? When you left for Ardania two years ago, you had visions of wedding lace in your eyes."

"Please, don't remind me. It was a childish romance that we both outgrew."

"Childish?" Lotta looked at her hard. "No, my dear. I used to watch you together and marvel at how you brightened like a sun lily whenever he was around. He, for his part, never seemed perfectly at ease without you near. You were well-matched, the two of you."

Heat crept up Ria's neck. "And that's why we could never be truly compatible. He is too like me. Too charming and insists on being adored. Fortunately, we recognized our folly in time to save us both the embarrassment of regret."

"And yet, you have pain. Deep pain, if your efforts to conceal it are any indication."

Her words cut Ria, and she replied sharply, "Nonsense. We parted on well enough terms. What more is there to tell?"

"Nothing more if you wish me not to know it," Lotta responded mildly.

Ria sighed. Lotta didn't deserve such dishonesty. "Artem is… complicated. One moment he would be the carefree, spontaneous companion I remember from my youth. The next he would be conniving and manipulative and—must we speak of him?"

"Not if it upsets you, dear."

Ria's stomach twisted in memory. "It shouldn't upset me so. It's been so long, and now he's wed. I should be able to forget, shouldn't I? But seeing him again when I passed through Rellana on my way home made everything fresh. I just felt so betrayed when I learned of his true nature. I was hurt and angry, but mostly angry at myself that I didn't see earlier who he really was."

"And what is his true nature?"

"Cruel. Heartless. Incapable of seeing people as anything but means to an end."

"Artem? I have a hard time believing it. The way he doted on you…"

Instantly, Ria regretted her words. "This is why I haven't spoken of it," she snapped. "No one can believe the golden princeling is really a wolf in sheep's clothing."

Lotta shrank a little. "Forgive me. Of course I trust your judgment. It's just hard to imagine! I always had a soft spot for him."

"Didn't we all?" Ria said mournfully. She reached for a sprig of mint and crushed a leaf, breathing in its scent. "Perhaps he wasn't always that way. I'd like to think that our friendship wasn't a lie. He was never cruel to me, you understand, but there were things that gave me pause. Servants who looked at me with pity when they thought I didn't notice. Pretty maids who disappeared after he paid them special attention. I'd never seen it before because my visits had always been so brief. But living there for nearly six months…" She shuddered. No, she wouldn't speak of what she'd seen. Perhaps if her father's health improved then she might bear to tell him, but for now she couldn't speak the words to anyone.

If Lotta sensed her resistance, she said nothing. She simply listened, her brow creased with concern.

"In all that time," Ria continued, "Tollana became like a sister to me. I suspect that's why she couldn't bear to keep the truth from me any longer, even though she must have known her brother would be furious. I was so shaken by what I learned that I could scarcely see straight, so I left immediately for Khourin. When I next returned, Tollana had been married to a distant duke and sent far away."

"You think Artem arranged Tollana's marriage out of spite?"

"I don't know. Maybe it was her own form of escape."

Lotta squeezed Ria's hand. "These are dark thoughts indeed. I'm sorry you've faced such disappointment, but I'm not sorry you didn't wed him if this is his true nature. You know I want you to be happy."

"I'm happy to know he's wed and I no longer have to think of him."

"Of course. I won't speak of him again if you wish."

There was a long moment of silence in which Ria steeled herself for what she knew would follow.

"However," Lotta said at last, "Ardania is not the only place to find a husband. Surely there are many eligible young men right here in Rahm that would suit your fancy. Perhaps even here in Albon."

"Experience has proven otherwise," Ria said darkly.

"Come now, Ria. You've only been home a few months."

"Yes, and Thorodan Hall has seen a steady stream of noblemen with their eligible sons since I returned. Either they grovel and sicken me with suffocating flattery, or they expect me to sit quietly and never say anything more interesting than comment on their good sense of fashion. The letters I receive are either inane or insulting. I humor them or rebuke them, depending on my mood, but I can't bring myself to encourage them."

"I see. You're still grieving."

"Grieving? I told you that *I* refused *him*," Ria said indignantly.

Lotta smoothed her graying hair away from her face where the breeze had tugged it loose. It seemed that Lotta had always been old and wise, but Ria was startled to realize that when her mother died, Lotta must have been no older than Ria was now. How strange that the person she had trusted most in her tender years was, in fact, so young and inexperienced herself.

"It's not the man you grieve," Lotta explained, "but what you once had: a certain future that filled you with hope. Now you face gossip, uncertainty, and the unhappy challenge of choosing a husband among those whom you previously rejected. But it's still grief all the same."

For a moment, Lotta's keen assessment took Ria's breath away. Her throat felt very dry, and she wished for a cup of sweet wine.

Watching her expression, Lotta nodded sadly. "Your heart needs time to heal. But with your father's health failing, Rahm cannot afford to wait."

"Then I am trapped," Ria said, the words heavy on her tongue.

"No! Not trapped! You have many fine options to choose from."

Ria grimaced. "I have many *insipid* options to choose from. I do not exaggerate, Lotta! It seems the more eager they are, the more unbearably dull. I actually told the young Hegrin that if I was ever in need of a faithful dog, he would be the first one I asked. He didn't even have enough wit to realize he was being insulted."

Lotta laughed. "Just remember, Ria, it's not always the most charming or dazzling of men who make the best companions."

"Would you see me married to a man I can't respect?"

"Of course not. That would bring nothing but misery for you both. But not all worthy men will shine as dinner guests at Thorodan Hall, surrounded by competition. Perhaps it's time to consider other ways of getting to know them. Give it time and you may find your opinions changing. Affection comes in many forms, and one sour experience doesn't mean the hope of it is lost forever."

Ria groaned and stood. The shadows were long against the far wall of the garden, and she needed to return. "Affection is the last thing I want right now. Between Artem's deception and the sycophants at court, I can't trust that I would know honest affection if I saw it. Except between you and Pedr, of course."

Lotta smiled. "Don't be too hasty to judge those young men. There may be deeper layers you haven't uncovered yet." Lotta's words did make some sense, and wasn't that essentially what Ria had just asked Captain Strong to do for her father? But how could she become more familiar with any of her potential suitors in a way that didn't create false expectations?

"I'll think about it. Thank you, Lotta. Your advice is always appreciated."

Lotta grinned, the wrinkles around her eyes deepening. "Maybe not appreciated, but at least tolerated." She wrapped one arm around Ria and squeezed affectionately. "It's so good to have you home. I enjoyed your letters, but it's not like having you with me. Come and see me again soon."

"I will." Ria turned and hugged her back. "Thank you. I really will think on what you've said."

As Ria walked back in the brightness of the evening sun, her mind was full of many things. She thought about her conversation with Lotta, and the unexpected one with Captain Strong. At the edge of her mind, the beginning of a plan was taking shape.

"Did someone fetch my harp?"

"Yes, my lady. It should be waiting for you."

Ria yawned as she followed Biren to her father's bedroom. Martin waited just inside, illuminated by only a small candle. Ria was relieved to see no signs of violence. Her father sat at the window, silhouetted against the moonlight. Wrapped in blankets, his shape was more bear than man.

"Has Erland been here?" Ria asked Martin softly.

"No. The king won't see him. He says the sleeping draughts don't work. They only make the dreams more vivid and harder to wake from," Martin whispered. He was only a little older than her father, but these past months had aged him. His shoulders hunched and his wrinkles were more pronounced, as though he was slowly deflating under the strain of caring for his master.

Ria took a deep breath and turned to her father. Making her tone bright, she called, "Hello, Far! What suits your fancy tonight? Music or some dazzling conversation?"

He didn't respond. Not even a twitch to show he knew she was there.

"Music it is, then. You're in luck. There are still a few melodies that you haven't heard. I've been saving them for something special. Where should we start?"

She sat on a padded chair, holding her small harp on a wooden stool. She had a large harp in her own chambers, but the size of her lap harp made it more useful for calming her father during his fits.

After warming up with a few arpeggios, Ria began a somber melody that she'd learned from a minstrel in Branvik. As she played, she almost imagined that she was back in those treacherous mountains with the snow blowing around her.

Inevitably, her fingers turned to the familiar patterns of an Ardanian love song. But where her fingers went, her thoughts soon followed.

Bare feet.

In the dark stillness of her father's bedchamber, memories teased Ria's exhausted mind.

Bare feet pale against the pavers, drained of color in the cool pre-dawn light. She stared at them, her eyes fixed on the hair that sprinkled the tops of his toes. Better that than looking at his face.

She'd tried to leave early to avoid this scene. But somehow there he was, trying to stop her from boarding the waiting carriage. He'd clearly dressed in a hurry, his shirt open at the neck, and stubble on his jaw. She'd never seen him with so much as a hair out of place, and his unkempt earnestness somehow filled her with longing and regret.

No. She wouldn't think of this tonight. Not when she already felt so frayed with worry over her father. It was much easier to think of the cold, calculating Artem she saw upon her return to Ardania. It reassured her to believe that he'd never truly cared for her, and that she had narrowly avoided the unhappy fate she saw on the face of his distant bride.

She could convince herself of that as long as she didn't think about the morning she left. But if she dared remember the pain in his eyes, or the agony in his voice as he begged her not to leave, then she felt an unraveling deep in her bones that frightened her.

So she took a deep breath and pushed the memory away. Sick with loneliness and tired of the silence, Ria switched to a lighter tune that reminded her of baking in the heat in Khourin.

Still, her father sat motionless.

In a deep voice, she broke the stillness.

"Your playing is so lovely, Ria," she said.

She responded in her normal voice. "Thank you, Far. My musical abilities may never approach yours, but I am happy to please you."

She transitioned to a new melody, her fingers plucking out the notes her father had written earlier in the spring. It was a lovely tune, and she'd added her own touches to it, finishing the piece. She waited, but there was still no response from the window.

"I am feeling much more myself now," she said again in the deep voice, mimicking her father.

"Oh good. I'm so sorry that you had such a troubling day."

"It's that blasted Captain Strong. I wish he had stayed far away at his troublesome wall and not come back to Albon," she said, continuing the one-sided dialogue.

"Surely you don't mean that, Far. Captain Strong has always been a loyal friend to you, and I know that you enjoy his company very much. You would feel much better if you made amends."

"I will never make amends. He is rude and outspoken and bossy." Ria thought back to the day he bested General Grammel. "And sweaty."

"You know what I think it is, Far?" she said in her own voice. "I have had a good deal of time to think about this since I returned. Ewan was not the most inspiring of travel companions, but I did learn a lot from him about my grandfather. As his steward, Ewan had some very interesting perspectives to share about Danvir. And you."

She paused, considering whether to continue her provocation. Sindal had not yet reacted to either the words or the music. "I've decided that you are jealous of Captain Strong. Somehow, despite all your gifts and opportunities, you look at him and fear you do not measure up."

Ria watched her father's silhouette carefully for any sign that he was listening. He was far away indeed to not respond to her accusation. Had he fallen asleep? Or was he so caught up in whatever darkness he battled in his dreams that he wasn't even aware of her in the room?

Ria stopped playing abruptly. Her last notes faded into the stillness.

"You are a brilliant king, Far. And Strong is a fine First Captain. Let him serve you as he does best. Trust him as you used to."

Finally, her father turned from the window. His face was pale in the moonlight, his eyes lost in dark shadows. "I think," he said slowly, "I will sleep now."

Martin jumped forward from where he had been dozing against the wall. He helped Sindal into bed, arranging the blankets around him. Martin nodded vigorously to Ria and she began playing again, a soft, slow Rahmish tune. She didn't speak, letting the traditional melody tell its own story of joy in the face of loss, peace in spite of doubt, and hope overcoming fear.

Eleven

"These Rahmish don't understand subtlety," Hala complained. "I spent an hour this morning trying to explain to my cook that drowning vegetables in pepper masks their natural flavor. I would have had more success talking to a brick wall."

"You get much further with them if you just say what you want. The louder the better," Aiya advised.

"I had a headache when I was done. I don't know how they can live like that."

"They're not all so bad. Some have very fine manners indeed." Aiya stopped herself before sharing a story of Lady Ogmun. Hala did not know her true history in this city, and speaking of her connections would only invite questions.

They sat in her rented room as they had done weekly since the day that Aiya revealed herself in the market. It had cost more than half of Aiya's savings to secure and furnish the room, making it appear as if she lived here. She'd offered to pay for three months' rent up front in exchange for the landlord's silence, and he—with a greedy look in his eye—had demanded six in return. But the location kept her far from the textile district and Imar, so the added expense was worth it.

The summer sun streamed through the window, glinting off the silver ornaments on Hala's red silk headdress that held back her dark curls. She looked much the same as she always had, with only a few lines near her eyes to show the passing years. But she smiled less than

Aiya remembered, and her pronounced cheekbones lent her an air of severity.

"How do you find the tea?" Hala asked.

Aiya sighed appreciatively. "It's like a breath of Khouri air. Thank you. How are Behni's attempts at selling Khouri tea here? Do these Rahmish with their love of strong wine have any appreciation for such things?"

"It is going well enough, I suppose. I don't see him much, so I don't complain. I know you will ask now if I know what he is doing here besides selling tea, and I will tell you as I have said before, that I don't know any more than he wishes me to know."

"But you agree that his main interest is not tea."

Hala eyed her as she sipped. "I can't imagine why you are so interested in his business. I assure you that it has nothing to do with you. Behni thinks you long dead."

This was reassuring, but still Aiya had to ask. "You are certain he doesn't know about these visits?"

Hala frowned. "Aiya, do you think I could have survived fifteen years of marriage to that putrid cur if I didn't know how to keep secrets? I would never betray you. You have been my salvation since coming to this city. When I am with you, it seems like Khourin isn't so far away."

"Do you miss it very much?"

Hala closed her eyes and turned her face to the sun. "It isn't so bad now, but I thought I would go mad with all the rain when we first arrived."

Aiya smiled. "After ten years, I don't mind it so much. But I still love summer the most."

Hala opened her eyes and watched the people passing on the street. "These Rahmish all look the same. The women have no refinement and the men are all hair."

Aiya laughed. "I used to think so too. It was very hard when Imar was starting his business. I once deeply offended a wealthy customer because I thought it was the man who collected our refuse."

"How awful! Behni would never forgive me!" Hala's laugh was light and airy, and when it subsided she seemed years younger. "Now, tell me, what was Imar's business? You never speak of it."

Aiya chided herself for her carelessness. "He was a wheelwright," she lied smoothly. "It did not fit his true talents, but it was steady work, and he was good at it."

"I miss Imar," Hala said wistfully. "He was the only man of sense that Behni ever listened to."

"I miss him too," Aiya said uncomfortably, thinking of the story she had told Imar that morning when she left to meet Hala. If he knew the truth behind these long errands that took her away from home every week, he would be furious.

Hala reached across the table for Aiya's hand. The polished wood was warm against Aiya's skin, even warmer than Hala's touch. "You have had so much sorrow in your young life," Hala said. "Would you consider coming back to Khourin and starting over? You cannot yet be thirty. I hate to think of you languishing here alone in this dreary country."

"No," Aiya said quickly. "Thank you, but my life is here. There is nothing for me in Khourin."

Hala narrowed her eyes, and Aiya felt a searching in her gaze that made her anxious to move the conversation in a new direction.

"Forgive me if I speak out of turn," Hala said. "But I must ask. Has one of these hairy Rahmish men stolen your heart?"

Aiya started inwardly, thinking immediately of the captain, but hid her discomfort by patting Hala's hand affectionately. "Would it please you if I said yes?"

"Well, I wouldn't understand your taste, but I would feel better knowing that you might have a chance for happiness," Hala teased.

"You were always a great romantic, Hala. Now, you must be getting along or Leina will start to wonder."

"You only say that because I speak too near the truth!"

Aiya merely laughed as she embraced Hala in farewell, watching from the window until she entered her carriage. As soon as the carriage disappeared, Aiya stripped off her gown and threw on a shirt and trousers. The shirt was baggy, and the extra layers of a waistcoat and short jacket obscured her gender even further. With her hair tucked into a cap, and dirt applied liberally to her neck, face, and hands, she looked enough like a street urchin to be easily lost in a crowd.

Aiya had worn variations of this disguise hundreds of times in her youth. With her small frame, it was the easiest way to achieve anonymity: going wherever she wanted without attracting attention. She and Tupin had carried off more elaborate schemes that required complicated disguises, but these many years later she only felt confident assuming this simple one.

Her visits with Hala had not revealed much beyond what Imar had already learned. Hala didn't know much about what Behni did, nor his true business in Endvar, so one day Aiya had followed her home. Every visit afterward, Aiya had donned these clothes, and—using side streets and back alleys where a carriage couldn't go—arrived in time to watch the house before Hala returned.

Not only was Behni hiding something, he was clearly hiding it from Hala. He used her absence as a time to host an assortment of visitors that Aiya quickly determined were not in any way connected to his tea trade. Some were unsavory characters that Imar had learned long ago to avoid doing business with. Others she didn't know personally, but something about them made her suspicious. These she followed until she could determine where they lived or worked. She just hoped that Captain Strong would be able to use the information when he returned to Endvar. She didn't dare share it with Imar and risk revealing her duplicity.

As Aiya slouched down the back alley—hunching her shoulders and changing her gait to look more boyish—a part of her stirred with glee. She used to think there wasn't anything she missed about her old life, but this new intrigue excited her. Long-buried memories surfaced again: racing in the dark with Tupin along the clay tile roofs of Khourin; easily outdistancing a guard or officer after making a particularly notable theft; laughing and kissing passionately in the flush of victory as they made it to safety. Aiya had never worried that they were hurting anyone. They were thieves, not assassins. It was a glorious game, each job a challenging new puzzle to solve.

Until Tupin robbed the wrong man, and her world had burned.

Pushing these thoughts away, Aiya turned onto Behni's street. The thatched roofs of Rahm didn't lend themselves to climbing, but trees lined many of the streets and it was common in warm weather to see children hanging from their branches. One particular tree near a tavern gave her a good view of Behni's house, its rough bark easy to hang onto as she shimmied up the trunk and into the lower branches.

There she sat, patiently biding her time. Behni's rented house wasn't as grand as she'd expected, but on consideration she realized it was further proof of his deception. If he'd really been trying to establish a trade here, he would have rented a home in the wealthier sections of the city. A prosperous image would have been necessary to establish alliances with Endvar's elite. As it was, this was little more than a cottage. It was well maintained, with flowers planted in boxes and a sturdy oak door, but not like the wealth Behni and Hala would have been used to at home. Comfortable, but not in danger of attracting too much attention.

After a time, Hala's carriage approached down the street and Aiya felt a pull of disappointment that there would be no extra scouting today. Then a door opened off the back of Benhi's house and a figure emerged. Aiya felt a jolt of recognition.

At last.

His fair hair and clean-shaven face made him easy to identify. Not many men in this country preferred to go without a beard. She had seen him at Behni's several times, but still didn't know who he was. The man was dressed simply, but held himself as one used to giving orders rather than receiving them.

Aiya lowered herself carefully out of the tree, jumping the last distance to the street. The man disappeared down a side street out of her view, but she knew an alternate route that would bring her onto a connecting street. With any luck, she would be able to beat him to the intersection, making it less obvious that *she* was following *him*.

Aiya shuffled quickly down the street, keeping her cap low. This street wasn't as crowded, so she slowed her pace, letting him get further away. She followed him like this for several more blocks and two turns until coming to a part of the city that she was unfamiliar with. She didn't worry about getting lost, but she was increasingly concerned that the homes were becoming larger and grander, set off from each other by high walled gardens. This was a wealthy area where someone like her—or the young street urchin she was pretending to be—wouldn't be tolerated.

When the stranger turned and went through a wide gate, Aiya followed cautiously. She approached the gate, glimpsing a fine house on the other side of a stone courtyard shielded from view by trees and heavy shrubbery. The light-haired man wasn't immediately visible, and she scanned the grounds wondering which direction he had gone.

Her hesitation cost her.

A heavy weight crashed down on her right shoulder, streaking pain down her back. She stumbled, but quickly caught herself and ducked out of the way of the open carriage before the heavy cane could strike again.

"Loiter at someone else's gate, you filthy rat," a man's voice growled.

Aiya scampered away, catching sight of a fleshy man in violet robes settling back into his seat as he passed through the gates. She didn't know him, but would remember his smug face if she saw him again.

An hour later, clean and dressed as a woman again, Aiya returned home. Imar wasn't there, and didn't return until after she'd finished preparing their evening meal.

"Good evening, brother," she greeted when she heard his step on the threshold. "I trust you're well."

Imar didn't respond. Aiya looked up. He stood in the doorway, leaning against the wooden frame with an inscrutable expression.

"Is something wrong?" She carried a bowl of greens to the table and paused, waiting.

"I know that you've been meeting Hala," he said quietly.

Aiya tensed. She looked at his stony expression and then down at the floor, heat rising to her cheeks. How had she been discovered? How long had he known? *What* did he know?

But all she said was, "She's told Behni nothing of us, but I won't ask you not to be angry."

"I *am* angry," he admitted. "But I'm also sad. I didn't see that you were unhappy. I see now that I am your only friend in this city. You do not seek out any other company besides my own all these years. It's natural that you would want to seek out a familiar face."

Aiya felt a twinge of relief. So he must not know about the other activities: dressing in disguise and spying on Behni's house. At the same time, she ached to hear his compassion, knowing that it was misplaced. She wanted to reassure him that she didn't turn to Hala because she was bored with his company. She wanted to tell him that she would never risk their safety unless it was for something more important than idle friendship. But she remained silent, knowing that it was best if he didn't know the whole truth.

Imar finally came to the table and sat down with a sigh. "It isn't safe to continue to meet Behni's wife. He is…ruthless. I don't know what has brought him to our city, but I will not rest easy until he leaves."

Imar removed his spectacles and rubbed his face in exhaustion. He looked so small and vulnerable. Was this shrunken little man her older brother who had protected her all these years? Was his burden so heavy that he had dwindled as he had aged? Or was it her own perspective that had changed?

Imar met her eyes. "I don't think it is safe," he repeated. "But you have proven to be quite resourceful in doing what you want no matter what I think. I do not know whether to forbid you, or help you."

Aiya's breath caught in her throat. This was more than she could have hoped. Quietly, she said, "I have told her that you are dead. She knows nothing of my true life here. I will end it if you wish, but I fear it would only arouse suspicion if I do. If she discovers that I've been lying to her, she may tell Behni."

Imar considered this for a long moment. He nodded. "I see. For now, then, you should continue your visits as scheduled. But I will accompany you to ensure that you are safe."

Aiya started to protest, but he raised a finger to still her.

"She won't see me unless I think you are in danger. And if you are in danger, it will do no good to pretend I do not exist."

Aiya nodded in surrender, and brought the last dishes for their meal to the table. Under the circumstances, she knew that she should just be grateful that it was all he was asking of her. But she still felt disappointed knowing her days of spying on Behni's companions were done.

They settled into a quiet meal. Aiya didn't feel much like talking, and Imar seemed lost in his own thoughts. When a sudden knock came at the door, she was so startled that her knife clattered to the table.

Imar answered the door and Aiya listened with interest when she heard her own name. She couldn't see who stood outside, but Imar responded genially in Rahmish, "I am glad to hear the captain has returned safely. Dinner might take some time. Is there anything more he needs while he waits?"

Aiya felt a rush of excitement. Captain Strong was back.

And asking for her.

She kept her face neutral as Imar closed the door.

"The captain has returned and would like you to bring him a meal. A meal for two, the soldier said. I told him that it would be a while. You can finish your meal first."

Hoping that she didn't betray her eagerness, Aiya stood and began gathering the food. "I'm not very hungry tonight, and if I bring it now, it will still be warm. Wouldn't you rather have a warm meal when you have just returned from traveling?"

Imar grunted, but didn't object. With the dishes gathered onto a large platter, Aiya left through the back door to the outside staircase that accessed the upstairs room. Her shoulder was very sore, and even the simple act of knocking on the heavy wooden door pained her. While she waited, she imagined a suitable curse for the fat man who'd struck her.

A handsome young soldier opened the door and ushered her in. His eyes brightened as he looked her over, and she saw the hint of dimples as he held in a smile.

Captain Strong sat at the small table, rubbing the early growth of a new beard as he studied a sheet of paper intently. He scarcely glanced up when she placed the platter on the table.

"Thank you, Aiya. Finn! Your food is here!"

A boy sat in front of the window, his forehead pressed against the glass as he watched the busy street below. At Captain Strong's invitation, he jumped up and ran to the table.

"At last!" he sighed. "I thought I would die!"

Aiya heard a chuckle from the young soldier behind her. Captain Strong pushed the platter closer to the boy.

"You act as though we've starved you," he said. "How does your mother keep you fed?"

The boy placed a large helping of spiced meat on a slice of bread and took a bite. "She doesn't. I'm hungry all the time," he said through a mouthful of food.

Aiya was glad she had brought enough for two men. As it was, she wasn't sure the boy would leave any for the captain.

"Will you eat, my captain?"

"Later. When he's finished." He turned back to the paper he had been examining before.

"If I may ask, sir, who is the boy?"

Captain Strong glanced up distractedly. "This is Finn."

It wasn't much of an answer. The boy looked at the captain, at Aiya, and then back at his food. Aiya wanted to ask why he was there, but when she looked at the captain, he was watching her thoughtfully.

"Aiya, would you and Imar be willing to let the boy stay with you for a few days? I have a new group of soldiers waiting for training, so I won't be around much. I'm sure he would be happier staying with you than idling his time alone in my empty room."

Aiya felt a spark of irritation. He wouldn't tell her who this boy was, but he wanted to burden her with him for several days?

"Imar will want to know why."

"Tell him that I am doing a service for a friend. I'll pay him for the inconvenience."

That would please Imar. "I suppose he won't be too much trouble."

"He's pleasant enough, but I won't tell you that you won't notice he's there."

"No," the young soldier scoffed from the corner. "He'll talk you to an early grave. Unless he's eating, that is."

"Hey!" Finn protested.

"Then I will keep him well fed," Aiya said, smiling at the boy. She stepped closer to the captain and lowered her voice. "When you have time, my captain, I have news."

Captain Strong looked at her with interest. "What is it?"

"Not now." She glanced guardedly at the other soldier. "Another time."

Captain Strong nodded to the soldier. "Aiya, this is my clerk, Sergeant Rorden. He can be trusted. Please, sit." He gestured to a chair near him. "Tell me what you've learned."

Aiya sat at the table, and Rorden joined them on the opposite side, attentive with interest. Finn ignored them, rolling a single green pea off the edge of the table and crouching down to watch at eye level as it fell onto the floor. He seemed to have finally had his fill.

Aiya withdrew a note and placed it before the captain. Even the small movement was painful. "I have tracked these men coming and going from my cousin's house. They are not the sort of men someone of character would associate with. I believe they are part of his true business in this city."

Captain Strong looked over the list. "I know some of these names. Have you learned what his business is?"

She shook her head. "I still don't know. But when I lived in Khourin, he ran—" She paused, trying to think of the word. "Hiding, moving objects? Illegal things."

"Smuggling?" Sergeant Rorden offered.

"Smuggling, yes. It could be the oim leaf. My uncle made much money that way. Or his business might be people."

"People? You mean slaves?" Captain Strong asked.

"There was some of that before I left." She lowered her voice, but Finn had returned to the window and seemed oblivious to their conversation. "Not just adults. Young ones too."

"That is grim news indeed, if that is your cousin's business here in Rahm. I'll have some men look into this and see what connections we can discover."

"Sir, if she's right," Rorden said, leaning forward on his elbows, "this is a problem for the peacekeepers. Should we turn the matter over to Captain Wott?"

"Maybe. But I'm not ready to let it go yet. There's something about it…" The captain rubbed at his cheek thoughtfully. "Like when you're tracking a doe in the forest and you suddenly sense that something's not right. You've wandered onto some predator's territory—a bear or a big cat—and even though you haven't yet noticed all the subtle signs, your mind has made sense of it and is shouting at you to run before you even know why."

The room was silent as he finished.

Rorden winked at Aiya across the table. "This is the moment, sir, when you realize that no one else in the room has had that experience."

Aiya suppressed a smile. She was surprised by the soldier's blunt humor, but the captain didn't seem to mind.

"Of course not. I forget that you don't have proper forests on the coast," he grumbled good-naturedly.

"My captain," Aiya interjected. "There's another man not on this list because I do not know his name. I followed him today to this address." She handed him a scrap of paper. "Like your forest tale, I do not know why he seems important, but he does. Perhaps more than the rest."

"Did you get a good look at him?"

"From a distance. He's not as tall as you. Thin. Light hair, longer past his ears. No beard. He dresses like a rich servant or poor nobleman. Simple, but good quality."

The captain grunted, adding notes to the paper and handing it to Rorden. "Let's start with him. That address puts him in the wealthier part of the city. Whatever his connections, they'll be important."

Rorden nodded.

"There is one more thing," Aiya said. She produced a leather strap with writing scratched into the surface. "I found this last week when following one of these men. He discarded it in a refuse bin."

She waited with anticipation as Captain Strong examined the writing. He then passed it to the younger soldier, who looked at her perplexed. It was a senseless grouping of letters, interspersed with numbers. Some of them were altered slightly: either carelessly or deliberately, it was difficult to tell at first glance.

They didn't see it.

"This is a smuggler's code," Aiya said excitedly.

Captain Strong raised an eyebrow. "You're sure?"

"Yes, my captain. It could be thieves, but I think it's smugglers. They imprint everyday objects that won't draw suspicion. If it falls into the wrong hands, without the key it is meaningless."

"How can we learn the key?"

"It's difficult to say. The key could be anything. I would like to keep working on it to see if I can make sense of it."

Captain Strong nodded to Rorden, who copied the code out carefully on another sheet of paper. "Thank you, Aiya. This is very helpful."

Aiya simply bowed her head, basking in the warm glow of his praise.

Rorden stood and called to the boy. "Finn! Where is your pack? You're going to stay with this lovely lady tonight."

"I'm not staying with the captain?" The boy turned from the window, his forehead red from where he had pressed it against the glass.

"Aiya will take good care of you," Captain Strong said.

"Will I still get to see the big gates?" Finn asked.

Rorden gathered the boy's pack and slung it over his shoulder. Finn staggered under the sudden weight. "You be good for Aiya, and I will take you to see the big gates tomorrow. Does that sound good, Finny-boy?"

"Just Finn," he growled. Rorden tousled his hair playfully as he steered him toward the door where Aiya was waiting.

"It was a pleasure to meet you, Aiya. If he gives you any trouble, just tell him you'll put a snake in his blankets. He'll straighten right up."

Finn's face reddened. "That wasn't funny. I'm going to get you back, I promise."

Aiya fought a smile. "Come Finn. Let's go and get you comfortable."

When the door closed behind Aiya and the boy, Rorden leaned against it and folded his arms. "Remind me not to ever face you in cards, sir. You can keep a secret better than I would have guessed."

"What secret?" Merek said without looking up.

"*My* captain?" Rorden said pointedly.

"What? That? That's nothing. It's a language…confusion."

"Mmm-hmm." Rorden strode to Aiya's vacated chair and strad-dled it backwards. "With all due respect, sir, I think you are the only one confused. I think Aiya means exactly what she says."

"That's ridiculous," Merek scoffed.

"Is it? Have you considered why she's so willing to help you?"

"Why wouldn't she? She's a good person. A—" Here he paused, trying to explain why he trusted Aiya without divulging the truth about her past. That was not his secret to share.

"A patriot?" Rorden said ironically. "A soldier? She's not one of your men, sir."

"Of course not. But some people just like to do the right thing. I've known her for years, and she isn't that way."

Rorden grinned. "I'm sorry, sir, but I know women, and I can promise that there's only one reason a beautiful woman like that would be so eager to please a man to whom she owes nothing. If she's not in love with you, then I am a boneless soup head."

"A boneless—what? Your fishing expressions don't make any sense," Merek said dismissively, but his face warmed from Rorden's words. He chafed at the younger man's confidence and knowing smile. "If you're quite finished, I want to talk to you about the boy. Eldar has a new group of soldiers waiting for training, so I won't be around much. Can I trust that you'll look out for him and not tease him mercilessly as you have since we left Albon?"

Rorden's arrogant smile slipped. "I'll do my best, sir. But I know that he likes it, no matter what he says."

"I'm glad to see you becoming so attached, because it looks like you'll be taking him to Haldin for me."

"Sir?"

"I want to learn more about these men and discover all I can about their connections to Behni. But Stefan's men have waited long enough for the boots, so you'll take the boy to Haldin in my place."

Rorden cursed mildly to let Merek know he'd found his mark. "You're sure this isn't punishment for teasing you about Aiya?" he complained.

"You'll have lots of time on your journey to contemplate that, won't you?"

Rorden laughed heartily. "Understood, sir. Though I meant it as a compliment. If I can figure out how you did it, maybe I can win Freida back."

Merek chuckled in spite of himself, but Rorden's suspicions about Aiya sat uncomfortably in the back of his mind long after his clerk left.

Twelve

"How do you find them, Captain?" Merek asked. He stood atop Danvir's Wall, shading his eyes against the sun. Below him, two dozen armored soldiers stood at attention.

Captain Eldar, a seasoned soldier with three fingers missing, shrugged. "Some of them were trained by Praki, so we've been tightening up the basics. But they're quick to learn. And they work together better than any group we've seen in awhile."

"Good. Let's begin."

Eldar bellowed to the men standing on the grass below. "I hope you've saved your strength on your march from the city, because you're going to need it today. We're running the same drill we've been doing, but with an important change. When you reach the top of the stairs, you've got a quarter mile run back to this position where you will stand off against Captain Strong, First Captain of the Wall Guard. And then, your real training begins."

There was an excited stirring among the men.

"You'll notice that Captain Strong's not wearing armor. That's for two reasons. When you fight an enemy on the wall, you can't expect that he'll be weighed down with armor like you. Your armor protects you, but it also makes you slow. Compensate and make every movement count. The first man to Captain Strong will earn a pint of ale from me at The Seven Moons tonight. The last man will be polishing the captain's boots. Understood?"

"Yes, sir!' a chorus of deep voices answered.

One soldier cupped his hands and called out, "What's the second reason, sir? You said there were two reasons Captain Strong isn't wearing armor, but you only told us one."

Eldar barked out a short laugh. "Oh, you'll soon see."

The men below jostled for position as Eldar called out a countdown. At his signal, they set off at a sprint for the stairs, a few of them whooping as they left.

"I'm betting it's Dan or Nils first," Eldar said as they waited. "Dan's quick. But Nils is stronger, so if the armor slows Dan too much, Nils might beat him."

Merek knew how hard it was to run the stairs to the top of the wall in full armor. The men would be hot and tired before they reached him, while he stood in his loose shirtsleeves, enjoying the breeze at the top of the wall.

The narrow stairs channeled the men into a single line, and as they ran they spread out further. At most, Merek might have to face two at a time, but more than that was unlikely.

The first of the soldiers approached at a run.

"It looks like Sergeant Dan is getting a drink from me tonight!" Eldar called out.

The soldier was short, but fast. He raised his sword and rushed at Merek, yelling out as their blades met, sweat streaming down his temples. Merek parried with him for a few moments, testing his strength and reflexes, before disarming him so that he could turn his attention to the next arrival.

"Against the wall, soldier," Merek ordered. The man stepped back and slumped against the parapet, pulling off his helmet and gulping air.

Eldar grinned. "Do you still wonder why Captain Strong didn't need armor when he faced you lot?"

One after another, the soldiers came, each one more weary than the last. Some approached in pairs, but in the small space it was difficult to coordinate an attack. Each time, Merek disarmed them before they could do much more than take a couple of swings.

When the last of the soldiers had collapsed against the wall, Merek sheathed his sword and addressed them.

"That was a good effort. No, don't get up," he said as some of the soldiers gathered their feet beneath them. "Rest. The purpose of that exercise was twofold. First, to show me your weaknesses. Nothing is as effective for that as exhaustion. Now I know what I'm dealing with, and I like what I saw.

"The second," he said, gesturing to indicate the length of the wall, "was to show *you* some of the unique challenges that come with service in the King's Wall Guard. As you've seen today, it doesn't require a large force to either defend or conquer the wall. One man can hold off two dozen skilled soldiers if he's fresh and they're tired, and if he knows how to use the small space to his advantage and they do not. You're all experienced soldiers, but much of what you've learned in your army service will not help you here."

A few of the soldiers exchanged glances with each other. The first man up the wall had already recovered, his fair hair drying in springy patches. He sat in a half crouch, like a cat waiting to pounce.

Merek continued, "The terrain is unforgiving. A false step in a fight could send you to your death. The height twists your perspective and makes shooting an enemy on the ground harder than you think, particularly if he is under cover of trees. The limited access makes coordination with your fellow soldiers absolutely critical. But Captain Eldar tells me you learn fast. That's what I want to see. No bravado. No games. Just hard work and honest sweat, and you'll be the best of the king's men by the time I'm through with you."

Some of the soldiers nodded and grinned to each other. Merek was glad to see that there was already a sense of camaraderie between these men. That would make training them more enjoyable.

"Eldar tells me you've been training one on one. Today, we'll start two on two. You'll find that this gets complicated in such a restricted space. Pay close attention to your footwork. Keep your feet firmly planted and your movements small." He demonstrated a thrust and slice, shifting his weight while moving his feet very little. "It will feel awkward at first, but you'll be able to control the fight if you know where you are and where you are going."

He nodded to Eldar, who stepped forward.

"On your feet!" Eldar called. He paired them off and the groups of four spread out along the wall. The sun was relentless overhead with no shade to give them rest. Merek and Eldar moved among the groups, observing and making corrections as they saw fit.

Most of the men were deliberate and focused in their movements, even hesitant as they adjusted to the new situation. But in one foursome, a soldier fought with a ferocity that drove his redheaded companion back. The redheaded man faltered as he checked behind him to make sure he wasn't getting too close to the parapet. Merek recognized the aggressive soldier as the first one who had made it up the wall. He watched him, trying to determine whether his aggression was arrogance or earnestness. There was one way to find out.

He approached the soldier from behind and waited until he shifted his weight from front to back. At that moment, Merek swept the soldier's foot out from underneath him, stepping out of the way as the man lost his balance and fell backwards, sword clanging on the stone. The man grunted as he hit the ground hard. Merek knelt on the stone and leaned over him.

"Feet firmly planted. Small movements. And once in a while, look behind you."

The soldier grimaced as his companions chuckled. But he looked chagrined, not angry. Not arrogance, then. Good.

"Come. On your feet." Merek stood and gripped the soldier's hand, raising him to stand. "What's your name, son?"

"Sergeant Ennoth, sir," the soldier said, at the same time that Eldar said, "This is Sergeant Dan."

Merek raised an eyebrow.

The soldier clarified. "They call me Dan, sir. It's supposed to be a joke." He hesitated as the redheaded man snickered. "My given name is Danvir."

"Ah, I see." Merek fought a smile as he eyed the diminutive man. "That would be a big name to live up to."

"Enormous, sir," the soldier replied. "I...just go by Dan."

"And what made you want to join the Wall Guard, Sergeant Dan?"

The man thought about this. He was older than Merek had first assumed, his height giving the impression that he was younger than he really was. "Well, sir, I guess you could say I wanted to do some good."

"You don't think you were doing good at your previous post?"

"Nah. If you'll pardon me, sir, the army doesn't do anything useful these days." Dan wiped the sweat from his brow with his sleeve. "Not like the campaigns of before, driving out the enemies within our borders."

"You don't much care for peace, I gather."

"No, sir, peace is what I want to fight for. But the only soldiers who get to defend Rahm are those who serve with you on the wall. I want to be a part of it."

Merek noticed the redheaded man nodding. "You feel the same way, Corporal—"

"Jax, sir. Yes, I do. We could spend a lifetime doing nothing more than building roads and mucking out villages when the Nardin floods."

This triggered something in Merek's memory. "You came from Lorin?"

"Berseth. But Lorin before that."

"I see. Who was your commander in Berseth?"

"Alvard, sir," Jax replied.

Merek thought on this. "Well, I'm glad to have you with us. But let's pray that you never have to see the kind of warfare that ravaged our land in your namesake's generation," he said to Dan. "Now, let's see your attack again with more restraint in your footwork."

The sun had begun its slow descent toward the horizon before

Eldar called the men to stop. They lined up on the wall and Merek addressed them again.

"Well done, today. I think you're ready to be introduced to the final piece that makes wall service a unique challenge. Unlike the battle-field, when you face an enemy on the wall, it will most often be in the dark. This is the end of your daylight training. From here on out, all of your wall training will be done at night. Rest well tonight, and meet here tomorrow before sunset."

A few of them murmured appreciatively. Merek added, "I realize it will be twenty-four hours before I see you again. But I warn you: any of you who arrive tomorrow drunk or otherwise impaired will be volunteering as targets for our archery drill."

Aiya entered the shop to find Imar talking to a customer and the boy Finn wrapping a package in brown paper. She went to Finn, placing her hand on his shoulder in greeting.

"Have you behaved for Imar?" she asked him.

Finn nodded, his mousy brown hair flopping into his eyes. She wondered if it would be too presumptuous of her to offer to cut it. "This is easy. I help my far make boots, and it's much harder than what Imar does all day."

"Your father is lucky to have your help, then." Aiya was curious about this boy who had traveled with the captain. So far he hadn't divulged much, but Aiya had long since learned that all secrets have a way of working their way to the surface eventually.

Finn finished the package and placed it with others that were already wrapped. "I'm hungry. Is it time to eat?"

"Come, you can talk to me while I prepare our meal. I'm sure Imar won't mind."

Finn followed her back into their living quarters behind the shop. The main room served as both kitchen and sitting area, with bedrooms to the side.

"I wish the captain was coming with us," Finn complained. "Sergeant Rorden is mean to me."

Aiya smoothed his hair affectionately. "He likes to tease. It is the way of brothers," she said. "I have seen it many times."

Finn wasn't convinced.

"Do you have brothers?" she asked as she unwrapped a package of dried fish. She was keeping the meal simple to avoid starting a fire in the heat of the day.

"One. His name is Devn and he's younger than me. I had two sisters once, but they died when they were babies."

He said this so matter-of-factly, Aiya didn't know whether to be disturbed or envious at his lack of grief.

"I'm so sorry," she said. "That must be so hard for your mother."

"They were too small. Twins," he explained. "My mor still cries when she talks about them. So I don't talk about them."

"No, I suppose you wouldn't."

"Far says that God missed them too much and wanted them back home with him. Mor says no one could miss them as much as she does. Not even God." After a pause, Finn asked, "Do you have any children, Aiya?"

It would be so easy to lie.

"I had a daughter once," she found herself saying. "She would have been about your age."

Finn looked at her with interest. "What happened to her?"

Aiya's throat felt constricted. "She died as a small child."

"Oh. What was her name?"

"Marasel. We called her Mara," she said softly.

Unexpectedly, Finn stood and hugged her. Aiya froze in surprise, then relaxed and stroked his head against her shoulder, breathing in his smell and enjoying the feel of his bony arms around her.

"Thank you, Finn." She blinked wetness from her eyes. "Would you like to start on the peas?" she asked, gesturing to the bowl on the table.

As Finn eased the peas out of their green husks, he chanted a little poem. It had a sing-songy feel and Aiya felt the rhythm of it settle into her mind as she chopped vegetables. She hadn't heard the song before, but something about it tugged at her memory. She slipped her hand into her pocket and withdrew a piece of paper, the one with the smuggler's code written on it.

"Finn, what is that little rhyme? Can you say it again from the beginning?"

Finn stopped, surprised. "You don't know it? Everyone knows it." He started over from the beginning.

> *Kiss your fair ones, swallow fear.*
> *Take your sword and shield and spear.*
> *Bit and bridle, bell and horn,*
> *Stamp the mighty beasts of war.*
> *Grind your axe and string your bow*
> *Lay the mighty conquerors low.*

Aiya's breath quickened as she read the code. "Finn, can you write it out for me? Captain Strong will want to see this."

Thirteen

When the church bells tolled two in the morning, Merek sent his men back to the barracks, then stayed behind to climb the wall alone. There hadn't been time in recent weeks to practice, and it was slow going in the dark. But he was in no hurry. He had all night, and he needed to think.

For days he had puzzled over the smuggler's code, but to no avail. Rorden had been working on it too, and although he had identified some potential patterns, nothing had been a clear connection. Merek knew that it might not lead to anything more than illegal trade goods, but it gnawed at him.

Climbing the wall forced him to empty his mind of everything. His muscles strained with the effort, and soon he was breathing hard. It *had* been too long, he thought, reaching for another handhold. Strips of fabric wrapped around his hands and feet helped to protect his skin from abrasions, but they wouldn't be much protection in the colder months. His mind wandered to Finn's special boot and idly wondered if he should set him to work making a pair for himself before the boy left Endvar.

The moon had risen by the time Merek finished, and he had lost track of the hour completely. It was dark and still when he entered the courtyard of the guard complex. All was quiet, the few soldiers on guard duty motionless at their stations. So he was surprised when another set of footsteps sounded across the stones. He turned to find

Rorden hurrying toward him.

"What is it?" Merek spoke quietly, but his voice sounded loud in the stillness.

"Sir, Aiya came tonight. She's in your office. You're going to want to see what she found."

When Merek opened the door to his office, a single candle burned on his desk. In the dimness, Aiya sat against the wall. She jumped forward when he entered, a piece of paper in her hand.

"Do you know this, my captain? These words?" she asked eagerly.

Merek stepped toward the candle to examine it in the light. On the paper was written familiar lines of verse. "Yes," he said. "It's a children's rhyme. It tells of when Albon drove out the Delth invaders. All Rahmish children know it."

Aiya nodded. "Now, see. Ignore the numbers for now." She handed Merek a copy of the smuggler's code. As he scanned the familiar lines of letters and numbers, she began reciting. Between her foreign accent and the candlelight, the familiar words sounded lonesome and eerie.

Kiss your fair ones, swallow fear.
Take your sword and shield and spear.

By the time she reached *Bit and bridle,* Merek was saying the rhyme along with her, quickly scanning through the rest of the code.

"It's incredible. How did you figure it out?"

"Finn sang it to me tonight. I do not know these Rahmish nursery rhymes. But you agree it matches, my captain?"

"It must. It's too close. And the numbers…?"

Rorden stepped forward eagerly. "Aiya and I think that the numbers indicate the part of the rhyme where the message is hidden. We've spent most of the night pulling out the words from the text and working and reworking them with various numeric connections."

"And?"

He shrugged. "We have a few ideas, but it'll take some time."

Merek sat at the desk and examined the code again. Now that

he knew the key, it seemed obvious. "Why a children's rhyme?" he muttered.

"We've talked about that too," Rorden said, looking at Aiya.

"You say all Rahmish know it," she said. "I don't know who Behni is working for, but a simple nursery rhyme means he probably doesn't know his crew well. They might even change frequently."

"Which means that the message probably won't be hard to decipher if he has to keep things as simple as possible," Rorden added.

"And his crew is most likely all native Rahmish," Merek realized. "This is good work," he said to them both. "Really, well done. Aiya, do you need an escort home tonight?"

Aiya shook her head. "Imar doesn't know I left. If I return before he wakes, he will never suspect."

"And you?" he asked Rorden.

"I can't sleep yet. I want to look over these combinations again and see if I can make sense of anything."

"Well, then," Merek said, feeling a stirring of wakeful anticipation. "We'd better light some more candles."

Ria stood and excused herself from her guests. It was a small dinner party this evening, but she didn't have the heart for conversation. Her father had not come to dinner at all, and she couldn't shake the feeling of dread that something was wrong.

The air was warm and sticky, and she longed for a fresh breeze as she walked through the upstairs gallery to the corridor that led to her father's room. His door was open and when she looked in, the evening sun warmed everything with a golden glow.

Her father's bed was made, and everything was tidy. There was no sign of him.

Well, that was a relief. Whatever had kept him, at least it hadn't been one of his fits.

As Ria approached her father's study, she heard voices and paused outside the door. It wasn't latched completely, and in the quiet hallway she recognized the grating voice of General Grammel. She leaned against the wall to listen.

"Alvard. Korth. Garreth. I don't even know how many more he's contacted that didn't think to tell me."

"And you're telling me this because…?" Her father sounded distracted.

"Call him off. He's subverting my authority and distracting my men."

"Then it sounds like you have a problem with your men."

"Of course I've told them to deny his request. But he's the one who needs to be reined in. Yet I have no authority over him."

Sindal sighed. "Would it have killed you to just give him the men he asked for?"

The strain was evident in Grammel's voice. "If you order me, sire, I will give him the men."

Ria's father spoke so low she had to lean closer to the door to hear him. "I'm not going to do that. I told you that I wouldn't meddle with your decisions, and I meant it."

"I wish the same were true of Strong," Grammel growled. "He can't seem to resist meddling where he has no right. He's put himself above any authority but himself. If you do not want to rein him in, put him under my command. Let him answer to me."

A chair creaked as the king shifted his weight. Ria assumed it was the king. Grammel couldn't possibly be sitting, as agitated as he sounded. Sindal's voice was calm when he spoke.

"You are giving this matter more weight than it deserves. Don't rise to his provocation, and it will all blow over."

"Will it?" Grammel said hotly. "Think about it, sire. Have you ever considered what a dangerous adversary he could be if he ever meant to do you harm?"

"That's enough, Grammel."

"He reports to no one but you, and that only loosely. He has the loyalty of most of your troops, and many of the people too. If he so desired, it wouldn't take much to unite people and soldiers against you. No one would suspect anything until it was too late."

Ria felt hot indignation at the general's words. It was all she could do not to walk through the door and tell him what a fool he was. Instead, she held still and listened for her father's reply.

"Grammel," Sindal said wearily, and Ria could hear the underlying tension in his voice. "The same could just as easily be said of you."

Grammel started to speak, but Sindal cut him off. Ria wondered if Grammel knew her father well enough to know how far he was pushing him.

"I will consider your words as no more than idle speculation. I don't always agree with Merek Strong, but I have no doubt of his loyalty. Don't make the mistake of making him your enemy."

Ria waited for the general's reply. Instead, the door opened, and Grammel stormed out, flushed and with a line of sweat along his brow. He stopped abruptly when he saw Ria standing at the door.

"Good evening, General," she said calmly.

The burly man glanced back at the door to the king's study. "I'm sorry, my lady. I didn't know you were here."

"Of course you didn't. That's the whole point of eavesdropping."

His face flushed darker and his eyes narrowed under his heavy brow. She dismissed him with a nod, and he had no choice but to bow and turn on his heel.

Ria made sure the door latched behind her when she entered her father's study. He looked up, his eyes bloodshot and distant.

"Such a pleasant man, that General Grammel," she said, leaning over Sindal's desk to kiss him on the head. "Always good for some stimulating conversation, don't you think?"

Her father just groaned. He rubbed his face with both hands, then clasped them behind his neck in a posture of defeated exhaustion.

"What was he so upset about? I gather it has to do with Captain Strong, but I didn't catch the details." Ria moved to sit on the sill of the long window. It was open to the evening air, but the breeze was faint and warm. Not adequate to cool the room.

Sindal looked up. "Apparently when he could get nowhere with General Grammel, Strong contacted some of Grammel's captains directly to ask if they could spare some men. Claims he has reports from some recent trainees that some of the units are wasting in idleness and might appreciate the chance to do some work."

"How clever!" She bit back a laugh when she saw her father's expression. "I'm sorry, I know that's not the way things are done in the army. But you have to admire his tenacity."

"Don't let Grammel hear you say that. He thinks Strong is on the verge of anarchy."

Ria turned toward the window where the light was fading over the garden. "You and I both know that's as likely as saying the moon will shine green tonight," she scoffed. Sindal didn't answer her right away, and she looked back at her father. He was gazing thoughtfully but without focus. "Far? You don't really think that Captain Strong is capable of treachery, do you?"

He shook himself. "It's just that, when you think about it, Grammel is right. I'm not saying that Strong would ever commit treason, but if he did, he would be in a unique position to be highly effective at it. It does make one think."

"It makes *me* think Grammel is a petty man blinded by pride. You were right to put him in his place. I can't help but think that a man who is so eager to accuse another of treachery cannot be fully trustworthy himself."

"Grammel is proud, yes, but he serves me well. To be honest, I can hardly blame him. Strong has made himself an annoyance over this wall. He's written me every other day since he left the city, pleading the same cause over and over again. I don't even open his letters anymore." He indicated a pile on a nearby table.

Underneath the letters, Ria recognized the maps that Captain Strong had left. She pulled out the topmost map, carefully sliding the letters back into place. An idea that had been forming for days fully blossomed as she examined the areas needing inspection and repair.

"Far, I have a proposition for you. It may solve your problems with both Captain Strong and General Grammel, and possibly help me with one of my own." She picked up the map and laid it before him, sitting on the edge of his desk.

"I'm listening," he said guardedly.

"I saw Captain Strong in the city the day before he left. He told me that he asked you to tour the wall as Danvir used to do. You don't have to explain to me why you turned him down," she said hastily. "But I was thinking, what if I went in your place?"

Sindal frowned. "You? Tour the wall?"

"I would send detailed reports home to you, so that you could decide what to do. Captain Strong would be appeased because he gets what he wants—or close enough—and General Grammel would be appeased because he doesn't have to give up his men. At least not until you have firm evidence that it's the best thing to do."

Sindal looked dismayed. "But you know nothing about the wall!"

"I know as much as you do. 'Oh, look at that stone that fell down. Let's pick it up and put it back.' How hard can it be?"

"The travel alone would be difficult. There would be no carriages. It would be long days of riding for weeks. Many of the areas near the wall are remote and wild. You wouldn't be sleeping in inns and noble houses, I'm afraid."

A part of Ria recoiled at the thought, but she buried it and spoke resolutely. "I promise that I will not write to you of the saddle blisters. But Lotta mentioned something when I last visited her that has me thinking." Here she hesitated. It was so much easier to publicly spurn the idea of marriage. It was much harder to speak openly and honestly about it. She felt so vulnerable when she did. And she hated feeling vulnerable. "Lotta suggested that I might have more success finding a suitable marriage companion if I saw some of the nobles in their home territory, as it were. Gave them a chance to shine at their own estates rather than trying to impress me here. We might have to alter the tour slightly to make this happen, but I think it could be done without making it seem too…obvious."

Her father considered this, looking over the map before him. "I suppose that makes sense. And I won't deny that it's an enticing prospect to get Strong and Grammel off my back."

"Excellent!" Ria hopped off the desk. "With your permission, I want to leave next week. I want to take advantage of as much good weather as I can before autumn."

Sindal sighed. "I can't believe we're discussing you leaving again after you just got home."

"I'll be back before you know it!" she said excitedly. She hadn't realized how much she needed this until verbalizing it to her father. A chance to do something useful and not just sit around waiting for something to happen. Or worse, watching helplessly as her father withdrew further and further into himself.

"Far," she said hesitantly. "I will speak to Erland about staying close during the night. You will be in good hands while I am gone."

"Bah!" he said gruffly. "I don't need a physician. Martin will suffice."

"Nevertheless, I'm sure he'll be happy to do it, and I will feel better about it while I'm gone. For my sake, please let him?"

He grunted noncommittally.

"Now, please come away from this hot room and walk with me in the garden. The moon is rising and we will not have many more of these fine nights together."

Fourteen

Merek lay flat against the ground, trying to ignore the thorns pressing into his skin.

"Couldn't you have picked a better place?" he whispered to Sergeant Dan. "I can't squeeze through these briars as easily as you."

"You're not suggesting my size is an advantage, are you, sir?" Dan said, his smirk barely visible in the darkness. He didn't smile much, this man who carried the weight of a king's name, but his dry wit compensated for his seriousness.

They were outside the city gates, deep enough in the surrounding forest that the lights of Endvar were obscured by trees. Jax and Lom were hidden a short distance away, with two other men from Sergeant Dan's squad planted farther up the road.

The Vifar River lay in the empty darkness behind them, and before them sat a dilapidated house and barn. The structures had appeared empty and abandoned, but as they watched, a wagon approached from the direction of the city, and two men exited the barn to greet it. The three men, working by meager lantern light, loaded long boxes from the barn into the wagon.

Rorden and Aiya had worked tirelessly to interpret the message hidden in the smuggler's code. Aiya had confided to Merek that "the sergeant is a big tease, but he has a sharp eye for patterns." But since Rorden left for Haldin, Aiya had worked more slowly on her own. Eventually, she'd produced half a dozen plausible dates and locations.

It had been up to Merek to pursue the ones that seemed most promising, and for this, he'd enlisted the help of Sergeant Dan and his squad. The first two attempts had taken them to a silversmith's home and one of Endvar's common schools for children, neither of which showed any sign of suspicious activity. But this time, watching the men work under cover of darkness, Merek was hopeful they had unraveled the meaning of the code at last.

When the crates were loaded onto the wagon, one of the men from the barn climbed up to sit next to the driver, holding something bulky that looked suspiciously like a crossbow. The other moved to the rear.

"Do we follow, sir?" Dan whispered.

"Yes. If it appears they're returning to the city, stop them before they get near the gates. Otherwise, give them space to see where they go."

Dan gave a curt nod, then sidled out of the briars to go find his squad. He moved so smoothly that the briars barely shifted, no more than what a stiff breeze from the river would cause. Merek was wedged in so tightly that he didn't so much as twitch until the wagon rolled slowly away.

Vague shapes moved in the underbrush, following the wagon from a safe distance. The lantern light would work to the soldiers' advantage, making it easy to follow the wagon while restricting the vision of the men driving it.

With the wagon on its way and Dan and his men safely following, Merek eased backward out of the briars. The barbs were wickedly long, and Merek wished he'd changed out of his uniform before leaving the guard complex. As the fabric tore, he thought of some choice words to say to Dan when he saw him again.

A shout sounded in the direction of the wagon. The rhythmic creaking of the wheels accelerated. Merek cursed, yanking himself free and cringing at the sharp pain of tearing skin. He ran toward the glow of lantern light.

What had spooked them? The faint shouts of the driver drifted toward him over the beating of the horses' hooves. Merek leaped out into the road. It curved in a wide arc toward the river before turning back to approach the city. If he cut through the forest he might be able to intercept the wagon before it rounded that final bend, but he would have to be fast. Very fast.

Merek ran down the rutted road, stretching his legs out and breathing hard. It was dangerous in the dark. More than once he narrowly avoided a large hole, and he couldn't maintain a full sprint. But he tracked the glow of the lanterns through the trees and thought he had a good chance of beating them. If, that is, he could remember at which point he would need to leave the road.

There. The wagon turned into the final bend. He jumped off the road, crashing into the undergrowth. Blessedly, there were no briars here, and he burst through the foliage and out onto the road mere seconds before the wagon reached him.

The horses reared in fear. They shied away from him, plunging off the road and nearly overturning the wagon. The driver cursed and pulled hard on the reins, standing in case he had to jump free of the wagon. His companion grabbed the sides of the wagon to keep from pitching over into the darkness beneath the wheels.

The wagon slowed quickly once its wheels dug into the soft loam on the shoulder. Merek reached for his bow and held his ground as the wagon came to a stop, trying to slow his breathing with an arrow nocked and at the ready. The two men watched him warily.

"In the name of the king," Merek called out clearly in the night, "I order you to stand down." One of the lanterns had gone out in the chase, but the other remained lit, and Merek knew that its light should be enough to illuminate his uniform.

Neither of the men spoke. Nor did they do as Merek commanded. They merely stood there, shifting nervously. One leaned toward the fallen crossbow.

"You don't want to do that." Sergeant Dan's voice sounded from behind the wagon as he approached with a crossbow of his own. Fickle weapons. Merek didn't trust them as much as a well-used bow. But they were widely used in the army as many men didn't have the training necessary to take advantage of the bow's finesse. Brute force was sometimes preferable to reliable accuracy.

Jax and Lom emerged from the darkness, crossbows trained on the men in the wagon. Seeing themselves outnumbered and surrounded, the two men climbed down from the wagon. Jax and Lom grabbed them as they reached the ground, taking their weapons while Dan stood guard.

"Where is the third man?" Merek asked as he approached the wagon, slinging his bow onto his back to free his hands.

"Jumped off the back when they started running, sir," Dan said. "Sagnar and Regin went after him."

Merek reached out to stroke the jittery horses, muttering soothing noises to calm them.

"How did you get here before us, sir?" Dan asked incredulously over his shoulder, not taking his eyes off the two men as Jax and Lom tied their hands behind their backs and pushed them to a seated position on the ground.

"Oh, it wasn't too hard, thanks to your short legs."

Dan huffed.

"How did they know you were there?"

"It was Sagnar," Dan said. "Tripped and fell."

Merek lifted the lantern from the wagon and crouched down before the two men, removing their hats to examine their faces. With such heavy beards, they could have been anyone. His own brother—if he'd had one—would have been unrecognizable. Their eyes followed him cautiously.

"I see that you are both clever. You didn't fight when you knew there was nothing to be gained from it. So this is what we're going to do," Merek said calmly. "I will ask questions. You will answer them.

There's nothing to be gained by lying or refusing to cooperate. But I may be able to do some good for you if you answer honestly."

The two men glanced at each other, but said nothing.

"What are your names?" Merek asked.

They didn't reply.

"Where were you taking this wagon? For what purpose?"

Still no answer.

"And I don't suppose there is any point in asking you who you work for?" Merek sighed.

Again, the men looked at each other, but didn't respond. Merek watched them to see which one seemed the most jumpy. It was difficult to tell. They both regarded him dispassionately. But the older man's eyes flickered back to the wagon occasionally, while the younger man only had eyes for Merek. It wasn't much, but he decided to take a chance.

In a flash, Merek slammed a fist into the younger man's nose. The man yelled in surprise and rolled over onto the ground, cursing. Jax grabbed him, pulling him back up to sit. Blood trickled down his face unchecked, and his eyes streamed with tears.

Merek ignored him and turned to the older man.

"Let's try this again. Who do you work for? Or do you want a taste of your own blood tonight?" he said mildly.

The older man glanced at his companion. "It ain't like that," he began.

"Shut up, Alf!" the younger man growled.

"I'm not saying nothing!" the older man snapped. He turned to Merek. "That is, I don't *know* nothing. None of us do! They don't exactly share details with men like us, do they?"

"Who are 'they?'" Merek demanded. "You must know something. Who hired you? What were your instructions?"

The younger man glared resentfully at his companion, whose eyes flitted nervously toward the wagon. He definitely knew more than he implied. Merek would have to question them separately after they returned to the city.

For now, he left them under guard and gestured to Dan to follow him to the wagon bed. The lantern's pale light illuminated half a dozen barrels, two of them knocked over from the jostling. The rest of the bed was empty.

"Where are the...what happened to the boxes?" Dan exclaimed.

"How well could you see the wagon after they picked up speed?" Merek asked.

"Well enough to know that they didn't throw anything off the back, sir," Dan answered firmly.

Merek looked at him pointedly and Dan faltered.

"The bed was hidden in shadow, and we didn't always have a good view through the brush," he admitted. "But there's no way that they could have dumped half a dozen long crates. I'm certain of it, sir."

Merek inspected the wagon itself. "Your men probably lost the third man, or they would have returned by now."

Dan nodded, abashed. "Yes, sir."

Crouching down, Merek raised the lantern to illuminate the darkness beneath the wagon. Horizontal planks skirted the bed below the wagon's sides. Not an uncommon construction, but something about it caught his notice. He moved to the rear of the wagon, inspecting the closed tailgate. Setting the lantern on the ground, he slid his hands along the wooden planks, calloused fingers questing gingerly in the darkness.

Dan watched him curiously. "Is there something I can—"

"Ah!" Merek said with satisfaction. A piece of cool metal behind the lowest plank was attached to a length of coiled wire. He reached further, trying to determine how to release the latch. A pin slid partway out of a sleeve, but nothing happened. "Dan, check the other side. See if you can find a lever or pin or...anything."

Dan jumped to his side, reaching behind the other end of the plank. Merek heard a click, then slid the pin out again. The plank fell toward him, revealing a compartment hidden beneath the wagon bed. It was not large, but appeared to fill the entire area of the bed. The short end of a wooden crate was just visible in the low light.

"False floor," Dan said, impressed. "Well done, sir."

Merek lifted the lantern close to the interior to inspect it. All at once, a foot shot out of the darkness, kicking the lantern from his hand. The light clattered to the ground and went out, plunging them into sudden darkness as a weight pushed against him, knocking him backward. Merek stumbled to the ground with the dark hulk of a man on top of him. He raised his arms instinctively and felt the hot sting of a knife slice into his forearm, deflecting the blow aimed for his neck. Merek cried out and drew his own knife, but the man leaped lightly off his chest and jumped toward Dan.

Dan, stunned, was slow to draw his sword. He grunted as the small figure attacked, kicking him in a move that Merek could barely make out in the darkness as he pushed to his feet. The lithe man moved in a part leap, part thrust, almost as though performing a dance. Merek paused. He'd heard tales of Khouri warriors who could defeat dozens of soldiers to a man, with little or no weapon. He'd never seen one, but as he eyed the fighter in dark clothing—a black scarf wrapped around his head that obscured his features and made him seem less than human—Merek felt a sense of dread.

The dark fighter ran out of sight around the wagon, leaving Dan doubled over, gulping for air.

"Jax, he's heading for you!" Merek called, drawing his sword and following the stranger.

Shouts and scuffling came from the other side of the wagon. A crossbow bolt zipped in front of Merek and lodged in the wagon mere inches from his face.

"Hold your bow, soldier!" he shouted.

"I'm sorry, sir." Lom's voice sounded muffled. "He got my crossbow from me."

Merek ran to the soldiers on the ground. Lom was on his face in the dirt, holding his head. He rose to his knees, but wobbled and fell again when he tried to stand. Jax lay on the ground, groaning and holding a hand to his side.

A short distance away, the dark Khouri fighter bent over the two prisoners, knife gleaming as he raised it to cut their bonds. No, not freeing them. Slitting their throats. First one man, then another fell under the dark man's knife.

Merek cursed, leaping over Jax and plowing into the small man. He fell to the ground with a grunt, kicking and trying to scramble out from underneath Merek's weight. He twisted awkwardly, and Merek drove his right knee into the side of the man's bent leg beneath him. The man panted with pain, but he didn't cry out. His dark eyes visible through the slit in the scarf showed pain, but no fear.

Merek grabbed the hand that held the knife and twisted it behind his back, while bringing his other fist hard against the man's head. The Khouri fighter lay still at last.

"Dan!" he called.

"Here, sir."

"See to the prisoners."

"They're both dead," Dan said gravely.

Merek stood, hauling the smaller man to his feet roughly. The Khouri man was still reeling from the blow to his head, and didn't struggle as Merek pinned his arms behind him.

"Rope," Merek demanded.

"I have it, sir," Jax groaned, standing. Merek glanced at him briefly, noting the dark stain of blood on his uniform.

"Put pressure on that, soldier," he ordered, nodding to Dan to help.

The distraction was only for a moment, but a moment was all the dark man needed.

The Khouri fighter sprang to life, kicking back toward Merek and connecting with his shin. Merek gritted his teeth against the pain, dropping the rope but tightening his grip on his prisoner. The man twisted and writhed like a snake. Merek's hold slipped, and he kicked out at the man's injured knee. But he was too close to get any real strength behind the kick, and in a moment the slippery man had twisted free.

The Khouri man leaped, performing another graceful high kick, this time aimed at Merek. Merek grabbed his attacker's foot as it connected, twisting and yanking to knock him off balance. But the small man recovered quickly. He dropped to the ground on his hands, bringing his free foot to connect with Merek's jaw. He was surprisingly strong for a man so small, and Merek's skull rattled, his vision wavering.

The fighter jumped up and spun. He and Merek watched each other, tense. To the side, Merek vaguely noticed Dan with his sword drawn. The man looked back and forth between him and Dan warily.

From out of the darkness behind the stranger, two more uniformed soldiers appeared, swords drawn. *Bless them for finally returning,* Merek thought grimly. Sagnar and Regin stepped forward, joining Merek and Dan. The four of them closed in around the black fighter. He danced lightly in a circle, favoring his injured leg while eyeing them, a long knife in one hand and a smaller one in the other.

Merek knew from the postures of the other soldiers that they were hesitant to engage this unpredictable creature. Although they all towered over him—even Dan was a good head taller than he—they were as cautious as if they were outnumbered. And maybe they were.

Hoping the foreign man didn't speak Rahmish, Merek called out. "We want to take him alive. He's left us no other choice," he said, thinking of the dead men lying not far away. "On my count. Three... two...one!"

All four soldiers rushed the enemy at once. He threw the knives at Merek and Dan, drawing two more from his belt and flinging them at Sagnar and Regin. The soldiers dodged, but didn't break stride. Sagnar approached him from behind, swinging in a wide arc.

The instant before Sagnar reached him, the man leaped and Sagnar's blade sliced harmlessly through the air. The smaller man twisted in the air, grabbing Sagnar's sword arm and neck to leverage a powerful kick in the chest to Regin. Regin grunted, staggering back, while Sagnar dropped his sword and tried to pry the stranger off him. In a flash, the smaller man scurried up to Sagnar's shoulders, jumped over him, and landed on the ground behind. The force of his leap pushed Sagnar to the ground, and Merek caught only a glimpse of the shadowy figure as he disappeared into the forest.

The other soldiers watched his escape in astonishment.

"What was that?" Regin asked, bewildered.

Sagnar came to his feet, letting out a string of curses. Dan growled in frustration as he sheathed his sword.

"Dan, see to the wagon," Merek commanded. "You two," he nodded to Sagnar and Regin. "Keep watch in case our slippery friend returns."

Merek crouched over the two dead men. Their neck wounds were black where the blood ran in the dim light. Merek felt a wave of disgust. With the prisoners dead, he had lost his hope for getting answers.

Next, he moved to his own two men. Jax lay on the ground, with Lom kneeling next to him, holding his coat against Jax's side.

"How is he?" he asked Lom.

"I'm fine, sir," Jax said, weakly.

"The bleeding is slowing, but he'll need a surgeon," Lom said. He looked up at Merek. "I'm sorry I wasn't any help, sir. I feel a fool for letting him get my crossbow. And then he bashed me senseless with it." He shook his head ruefully.

Merek laid a hand on his shoulder. "He made a fool of all of us."

"I've never seen anything like it," Lom said, dismayed.

"Nor I," Merek said. "But I sense that we're lucky it didn't end worse. Do you think he's safe to move?" He nodded to Jax.

Jax muttered a curse under his breath. "I said I'm fine! Stop talking about me like I've got one foot in the grave." He slapped a hand at Lom, but then slumped back against the ground.

Merek didn't respond to Jax. "Get him into the wagon. If he gives you too much trouble, I hear a crossbow to the skull works well."

Jax glared at this, but Lom just chuckled.

Merek joined Dan at the wagon. He'd retrieved one of the lanterns and was working to light it again. It cast a warm yellow light over his solemn features, throwing the forest behind him into deeper darkness.

"I want to bring the bodies back," Merek told Dan. "Chances are, they won't have anything to identify them, but it's worth trying."

They rounded the wagon to the rear. The hidden door still hung open where it had been abandoned, the compartment behind it gaping black. Dan placed the lantern on the wagon bed, and he and Merek grasped the visible crate, sliding it forward. It was heavy, and Merek felt the pain in his right arm flare anew at the exertion. *He* should probably plan to see the surgeon before the night was over.

But for now, nothing was more important than seeing what was hidden in this wagon. With their two prisoners dead, this was the last connection to finding out what intrigue had brought a criminal network to their city.

They placed the long crate on the ground and pried opened the lid. The lantern revealed a large collection of swords, knives, a few maces and an assortment of axes stowed inside. Most of them appeared to be of Rahmish make, but there were some that had an unfamiliar style. Perhaps Khouri, but it was difficult to tell in the dark.

Dan let out a low whistle, his eyes gleaming. He looked at Merek with anticipation.

Merek just grunted. "Load it up, and get Jax and the others in the wagon."

"Yes, sir," Dan said, not without disappointment.

Merek knew Dan had questions, but he couldn't offer any answers when he had none himself.

Fifteen

"Ack!" Aiya licked her fingers where they'd grazed the iron pan. She was cooking flatbread in the morning to avoid building a fire later when the sun baked their little rooms. She should have used tongs, but she was distracted and couldn't be bothered. Besides, her mother had taught her to make flatbread this way, testing the doneness by the way the dough felt when she pinched it.

Impatiently, she checked the timepiece on the shelf again. When the captain was training at night, he asked not to be disturbed until afternoon. She would need distraction for at least another hour. She tried to convince herself that it would probably be another false lead and nothing would come of it, but the old flare of excitement had been increasing lately, and she greeted each day with more enjoyment than she had in years.

Dull footsteps sounded overhead, and Aiya's heart jumped. She quickly stored the flatbread in its cinnamon-colored crockery and grabbed a tray of cold meal and fresh fruit, trying to calm the agitation in her fingers. It was thrilling to be a part of something important again, something that went beyond the walls of the shop.

Puzzles to be solved and secrets to be discovered.

As she prepared to leave, Imar appeared in the doorway.

"Are you taking breakfast to the captain?" he asked. "I think I'll come with you today."

Aiya's heart sank. She tried not to show her irritation, but merely paused and waited for Imar to place his spectacles on the table and join her. He hummed a little tune, and she smiled at him.

"You seem pleased with yourself," she said.

Imar looked slightly embarrassed, but beamed all the same. "The merchant in Branvik is confident that only a few details remain to finalize the contract. We may need to travel there before the summer is out to formalize the agreement in person."

We? Aiya thought in dismay.

Upstairs, Captain Strong ushered them in and greeted Imar amicably. His white shirtsleeves were rolled up, and as he took the tray from Aiya, she noticed that his right forearm was bandaged. She met his eyes questioningly and he gave the briefest of nods, causing her stomach to flutter with excitement. Oh, if only they could be alone to speak freely!

"Your training did not go so well last night, I see," Imar noted with a small chuckle.

Captain Strong shrugged. "Not at all. It's always a good sign when my men can best me."

"Of course, of course," Imar said.

The bell rang downstairs, signaling that someone had entered the shop. Imar bowed slightly to the captain. "Come Aiya, let us leave the captain to his meal."

"Actually," Captain Strong said, picking up a uniform coat from the back of a chair. "I'd like to speak with Aiya about some repairs to my uniform."

Imar looked back and forth between Aiya and Captain Strong. Aiya held his gaze unflinchingly, keeping her expression calm. She could see Imar struggling between tending to the customer and not wanting to leave the two of them alone.

With one last meaningful look at Aiya, Imar relented. "I will be downstairs if you need me."

When the door closed, Aiya relaxed. "He is getting suspicious. I must not stay long."

Captain Strong handed her the coat, together with one of his white shirts. The right sleeves on both were torn and stained stiff with dried blood. "I do need these repaired, if you will."

"What happened, my captain?" she asked, taking the clothing from him. "This was no training accident?"

"No." His gray eyes were bright with excitement. "We intercepted a wagon outside the city last night, but it didn't go well. I believe your cousin brought a Khouri warrior with him to Endvar."

Aiya swore softly. "You are sure?"

"I've never fought one before, but he fought like the earth couldn't hold him."

"Your men, they are...?"

"They'll be fine. But he killed the drivers of the wagon before we could question them."

"This is disturbing news." Aiya frowned. "I've heard the tales your people tell of Khouri soldiers, but most of them are no more gifted than your own people. Only a select few are ever trained in the art of Manari. If Behni has brought a Manari warrior, then whoever has hired him must be very dangerous."

Captain Strong sighed and pulled on his dark blue coat. Aiya didn't envy him the extra layers in the summer heat. Suddenly aware of how long she had lingered, Aiya moved toward the door.

"I must go before Imar worries. But I meet my cousin's wife tomorrow. Perhaps I will learn something then."

"Is Imar still accompanying you on your visits?" Captain Strong asked, buttoning the silver buttons of his coat.

Aiya nodded. "He means well but makes it very difficult."

The captain looked at her thoughtfully. "You've been very helpful, Aiya. We couldn't have done what we did last night without you. For that, I'm grateful. But I don't want to put you in unnecessary danger. Maybe it's time to stop these meetings. Rorden will be back from the north soon. There's no need for you to risk yourself any longer."

Aiya felt a wave of intense disappointment. The thought that this all might end—the secret meetings with Hala, sharing in the captain's confidences, helping him unravel the smuggler's code—filled her with panic. How could she return to her colorless life as though none of this had happened?

"There is no danger," she insisted, if not completely truthfully. "I know how to stay safe."

Captain Strong fidgeted with the cuff of his sleeve. "I'm sure you do. It's just that I fear I've taken advantage of our…personal connection by asking for your help. It doesn't seem right for you to risk so much on my behalf."

Aiya's cheeks grew warm. What was he trying to say? Did he share her feelings of attachment? Or was this his way of keeping her at a distance? It was maddening. But if there was one thing she knew how to do, it was to keep the turmoil hidden. So she said simply, "I know well the risks I take. You needn't worry. I will tell you if I learn anything from Hala."

Captain Strong nodded and moved to the door. He paused before opening it, standing close enough to Aiya that her heart skipped a beat. She held a hand out against the wall behind her to steady her.

"I'll be dining this evening with Lord Ogmun," he said. "If anything comes up that can't wait until tomorrow, ask for Sergeant Dan. He proved himself to be quite capable last night."

"Very well, my captain." Aiya smiled. She would not be excluded. Not yet. She felt a little dazed to realize how much she needed it.

Merek took a deep breath and entered the stone hall at Lord Ogmun's grand estate. The floor was polished smooth and black, and light from dozens of candelabra shimmered in its reflective surface.

The last light of the evening sky illuminated stained glass windows set along one wall, their colors a faint glow that drew attention to their beauty without actually lighting the room. Beneath them, a row of doors stood open to balconies festooned with flowers and greenery.

Dozens of people milled about the large room, the men wearing long coats and the women in voluminous dresses. It seemed that all of Endvar's elite were here, together with attendants and aides close at hand. The low hum of conversation provided a steady backdrop to the strains of music emanating from a group of musicians in the corner.

Nothing made Merek feel more like he'd wandered far from his forest home. He liked Lord Ogmun well enough. The man was sincere and never put on airs despite being the king's agent in Endvar. Unfortunately, his position also meant he was always surrounded by sycophants and opportunists, and these made Merek's skin crawl.

As he walked into the room, he wished that Rorden had already returned from Haldin. Merek relied on the young man's talent for natural conversation. Few things were more distasteful than trying to come up with things to say to interest people with whom he had nothing in common, and who would just as likely use his words against him if given the chance.

As he moved through the room, a tall woman dressed in a rust-colored gown disengaged from her conversation and approached.

"Good evening, Lady Ogmun." He bowed respectfully. The tall woman could have been statuesque, but she lacked the poise needed to put her great height to advantage.

Her smile was warm as she greeted him, and she held out a long arm. "My husband will be so glad to see you, Captain Strong. It's been too long since we've enjoyed your company."

"My apologies. We recently began a new round of training, and it has kept me very busy."

"It must be ghastly in this heat. Do you enjoy training or is it a necessary nuisance?"

"I do enjoy it. The men who are assigned to me come because they want to be here. It's much more fulfilling than training raw recruits for the army. Of course," he added, "there is always the odd man who finds he can't stomach heights."

"That would be a handicap indeed!"

"I've seen men who fight like lions on the battlefield wilt like yesterday's greens when they first look out from the top of the wall. A few years ago, we had one man so terrified that we had to pry him away from the parapet and bodily haul him down to safety."

Lady Ogmun laughed appreciatively, revealing small dimples near her eyes that hinted at the beguiling beauty she was rumored to have been in her youth. She took his arm and steered him further into the room to find her husband, her head bobbing on her long neck as she moved.

Lord Ogmun was short and round, in marked contrast to his wife. But he shared her genial temperament and grinned warmly at Merek as he approached.

"Ah, we finally got you away for an evening, Captain!" Lord Ogmun beamed. "Come! I want you to meet someone. My niece is visiting for a time, and I was hoping you might look after her tonight. Where did that girl get off to?" Lord Ogmun's eyes swept over the crowd.

Merek sighed inwardly. It wasn't the first time that he'd been enlisted to entertain a female relative of Lord or Lady Ogmun's. As the highest ranking unmarried officer in Endvar, it was often his duty to pay special attention to whichever cousin or niece or sister-in-law was visiting Ogmun at the time. It wasn't a role he played well, though it was a little easier when Rorden was there to support him. Rorden took to charming women like a fish to water.

Merek was suddenly struck with the skin-prickling sensation of being watched. He glanced around the room, eyes immediately drawn to a thick man dressed in deep scarlet with a ridiculous hat that was so full of cascading feathers it looked as though an exotic bird had met an untimely end under a carriage wheel.

Lord Bolen was a minor nobleman who was notorious for spreading inflammatory gossip and was barely tolerated by those of higher rank. He sat against the wall, talking animatedly to a tall man dressed in green. Neither of them could have been watching Merek, as engrossed as they were in conversation.

But that pale man dressed in dark blue standing next to Bolen... something about him caught Merek's attention, though he couldn't think why. The man's hair was so fair it was almost white, and he held himself with an air of command, despite being dressed as some kind of attendant.

"Excuse me, my lord. Who is that man with Lord Bolen?" Merek asked.

Lord Ogmun glanced at the pale man distractedly. "His new steward, I believe. You know Bolen, can't seem to keep them for long. Where is that child? If she's hiding up in the attic again..."

"She doesn't enjoy parties?" Merek asked, feeling a sudden kinship with the girl.

Ogmun snorted. "Enjoy? She comes from a modest trading family in Cillith. My wife's sister's family, you see. We're hoping to teach her how to move in society and increase her connections, but she seems more comfortable associating with the serving staff than our distinguished guests." He wiped his brow with a handkerchief and sighed.

Merek was only half listening, instead looking around the room again for the fair-haired man. He still stood next to Lord Bolen, but did Merek just imagine he'd been looking his direction moments before?

Lady Ogmun interrupted his thoughts. "I do hope you'll be staying after dinner, Captain. We'll be dancing later this evening."

"I'm sorry, my lady, but I'm useless when it comes to dancing."

"Nonsense! This isn't Albon. We aren't so refined as all that. Just a little after-dinner exercise to get the blood moving. We have several unmarried ladies visiting tonight who would be delighted to serve as your partner."

Merek spoke as firmly as he dared. "I'm expected on the wall to-night, my lady. Forgive me."

Lady Ogmun's eyes twinkled with good humor. "What a shame. Perhaps next time, then?"

Merek opened his mouth to give a noncommittal reply, but Lord Ogmun interrupted him with a rap on his arm.

"Why have you never married, Captain?" he asked, cocking his head as if the question had just occurred to him. "It seems a man of your station and with the king's favor would have plenty of prospects."

Merek suppressed a groan. The older he got, the less he was asked this question, but on occasion it still reared its ugly head. Before he could formulate an answer, Lady Ogmun came to his rescue.

"Don't be impertinent, dear," she chided, but her eyes shone with curiosity. "I'm sure Captain Strong has a good reason for not marry-ing. After all, it must be difficult to start a family when your duties require you to travel all over the kingdom."

Lord Ogmun nodded sagely. "Of course, you're right. Either that or Strong has left a trail of broken hearts all over Rahm!" He guf-fawed loudly, and Merek smiled in spite of himself.

"You do me too much credit, my lord. I'm afraid I've never been very good at courtship. There was almost a young woman once," he remembered fondly. "I met her in Lorin soon after joining the Wall Guard. Her father was a dairyman, and she had hair the color of autumn pumpkins. I even thought we had an understanding before I was assigned away to the west."

"Indeed!"

"What happened to her?"

"Apparently she didn't share the same understanding because she married another before I returned. The next time I saw her she was swollen as big as a melon with her firstborn."

"Oh dear!" Lady Ogmun's cheeks flushed in sympathy.

"What did you do?" Lord Ogmun demanded.

"I did what any man would do," Merek answered with a grin. "I turned right around and rode straight out of town. Spent the next week licking my wounds and never told a soul."

As his companions burst into a fit of laughter, Merek looked across the room to where Lord Bolen sat grumbling to the fair-haired man on his right. Yes, this time he hadn't been mistaking it. The man was watching Merek steadily. His face was impassive, but his eyes were sharp and hard, and Merek's pulse quickened in challenge. The man didn't have a warrior's build, and he wore no weapon that Merek could see. Whatever threat he had to offer—and Merek could feel the threat as surely as if he'd spoken it—it wouldn't be something Merek was accustomed to fighting.

"—Captain?"

"Forgive me. What did you ask?" With great effort, he turned his attention back to Lady Ogmun.

"Her name. What was the name of this lost love of yours?"

"You know, I don't remember. Strange, isn't it? I was ready to spend my life with her, and now I can't even remember her name. It makes me wonder if one day I would have regretted my choice."

"No. Marriage isn't like that," Lady Ogmun said, looking fondly at her husband. "You grow together until you can't imagine having ever been apart."

"I couldn't have said it better myself," Lord Ogmun said with an indulgent smile. "Shall we go greet our other guests, dear?"

As the couple moved away, something clicked into place in Merek's mind. Suddenly he knew why he should have known the pale man. The address Aiya had given him—where she had followed the mysterious stranger from Behni's house—was Lord Bolen's. Could this be the same man? Suddenly alert, he scanned the room, and nearly jumped in surprise when he found the man at his elbow.

"Captain Strong, I believe?" he asked.

"Yes," Merek answered, right hand sliding casually to the dagger at his side.

"My lord wishes to speak with you, if you are not otherwise engaged, sir," he said. Merek thought he caught the faintest trace of an accent, but couldn't be sure. The man barely looked at him and showed no hint of the threatening expression Merek had seen earlier.

Well, he certainly had the humble servant act down. It might be worth Merek's time to listen to Bolen bluster if he could get an idea of who this man was. He followed him to where Lord Bolen stood against the far wall near one of the open balconies. When they approached, Bolen nodded curtly to the fair-haired man, who bowed and withdrew, leaving them alone.

"Captain Strong," Lord Bolen said, his thick voice matching his thick neck. "It is still Captain, is it not? I've heard that the king was considering demoting you after your last encounter."

Merek pressed his lips together in annoyance. "Clearly you heard wrong, my lord. Is there something you needed?"

"I've recently come into some information that you may find useful."

"If it's more rumors about the king, you can save your breath," Merek said, eyes following after the white-haired man. "I'm not interested."

"Well, then. I don't wish to keep you," Bolen said haughtily. "I just thought you might wish to know that I have reason to believe that there will be an attempt on the princess's life."

Merek stifled a yawned. "Very well. I suggest you write to the king and let him know."

"Write to the king?" Bolen looked confused. "Why would I...?" Then his eyes sparkled with delight. "Oh, so you don't know!"

"Know what, my lord?"

"You really don't know!" Bolen looked like a fat toad that had caught a particularly tasty fly. "The First Captain of the Wall Guard and you don't know!" He let out a peal of laughter.

"Please, enlighten me."

Bolen's eyes narrowed. "No, I don't think I will. I've spoken to you tonight out of loyalty to the crown, and you've treated me like I'm something smelly on the bottom of your boot."

"Apologies, my lord. It has been a long day. Your warning is appreciated, of course."

"Well, I should hope so," Bolen snapped. "Now, run along. I know you can't stand the sight of me, so get!" He made a shooing motion with his hand.

Merek started to turn away, then paused. "I do have one question."

"Oh, you'll soon have more than one, I'll wager!" Bolen sneered.

Merek kept his tone polite. "Who is that man with you tonight?"

"Domar? He's my new steward. He's only been with me a few months, and already I wonder why I put up with Falk for so long. Why do you ask?"

"I thought I recognized him. Do you know where he comes from?"

"The north, I think," Bolen said dismissively, then turned his back.

Was Bolen lying? Or had he been lied to? Either way, Merek knew this Domar was not from the north. Whatever hint of accent Merek had picked up, it was not native to the northern lands. The fair hair placed him more from the south. Or perhaps not even Rahmish altogether.

Sixteen

When Aiya opened the door of her rented room, she nearly dropped the vase of flowers in her hand. Hala stood in the doorway, her face uncharacteristically veiled. Only her eyes were visible, the left one swollen and ringed by a dark bruise tinged with green.

"*Shenasti*, Hala!" Aiya cursed. "What happened to you?"

Hala looked at her sharply as she limped into the room and removed her veil. "Such language, Aiya."

With the veil gone, Aiya's anger grew. Hala's lip was split and swollen, and she had an oozing abrasion along her cheekbone. As she lifted her hand, her sleeve fell back and Aiya caught a glimpse of bruises on her arm.

There was a time when Aiya would have ignored such violence against another woman. It was not spoken of in Khourin.

But ten years in Rahm had changed her.

"Oh, Hala! Sit." Aiya hurried to a cupboard nearby to search through the plants and herbs she had stocked there. She wished for her greater stores at home. This lot was just for show, so that it looked as though she truly lived here. She found a small jar filled with a white paste, opened it and sniffed, then nodded.

"It's still good. Let me see." She turned back to Hala.

Hala sat perfectly still on the padded bench, her face a mixture of embarrassment and relief. "Aiya, it's nothing."

"No," Aiya said angrily, dipping her finger into the salve. "This is not 'nothing.' Did Behni do this to you? Of course he did, you don't have to answer. This will sting at first, but it will help."

Hala flinched as Aiya gently applied a thick layer to the angry cut on her cheekbone. "I didn't have any melna leaves, and Leina couldn't find any at the market," Hala said.

"You won't find any melna here. It doesn't grow in this climate, but this will work almost as well."

Hala smiled a little, but it looked grotesque with her swollen lip and she winced with the pain. "Thank you, Nurse Aiya," she said with a hint of gentle reproof. "I'm not as incompetent as you think."

Aiya smiled in return, but she was still troubled, a dreadful suspicion rising in her mind. "What happened? Does Behni do this often?"

"Oh no. Usually Behni just ignores me. He almost never lays a hand on me. This was very…" Hala paused. "Well, I suppose it won't hurt to tell you. One of his shipments was disrupted two nights ago. Robbed, if you can believe it. I thought Endvar was supposed to be safer than that."

Aiya felt ill. "Two nights ago?"

"It's not just the money he lost in goods that worries him. He has contracts to keep and men he's made promises to. This won't look good for him and may make it difficult for us in this city."

Aiya knew exactly who had disrupted Behni's shipment. And she was responsible. Her anger against Behni increased, fueled by her guilt.

"Behni's troubles do not excuse his behavior," she said sharply. "There are laws against this here. It's not like Khourin where a man can do whatever he wants to his wife and children. I will go with you now and speak to the peacekeepers, if you wish."

Hala looked at her as though she had sprouted a second head. "Why would I do that? Behni may be a worthless louse who comes home each night smelling of death and mud, but he is still my husband. The peacekeepers can't change that. Let's talk of other things. Tell me what this lovely ointment is and where you found it. The pain is already lessening."

Aiya dutifully answered Hala's questions, but she was raging
on the inside with fury at Behni, and fury at herself for not considering that this might happen. She'd been too long in Rahm and
had forgotten the ways of her people. Tupin had never beat her.
He'd been a conniving trickster, but not a violent man. She hadn't
even considered the effect giving aid to Captain Strong might
have on this innocent woman.

The mood in the room was grim, and Hala ended her visit early.
She moved stiffly and Aiya wondered how many more injuries she
couldn't see. Again the guilt and rage flared, and it was several minutes before Aiya felt composed enough to join Imar in the back alley.

"You seem troubled," Imar noted as they started walking. "Is something wrong?"

Aiya considered whether or not to tell Imar about Hala's beating.
The knowledge of it burned within her, but she was so enraged that
she didn't think she could speak of it without sharing her own role in
Hala's suffering.

"Hala was not feeling well today. I'm worried about her, that is all."

"Soon you won't need to worry about Hala or Behni," Imar said
cheerfully. "There's reason to believe he plans to leave before winter. It
will take some time to complete my business in Branvik, so I'm sure I
can contrive reasons for us to stay there until Behni is gone."

In that moment, still filled with outrage, Aiya made her decision.

"I'm not going with you to Branvik," she said.

"Excuse me?"

"You go if you wish, but I'm staying here." Aiya felt Imar's eyes on
her, but she looked only at the street, her pace quickening with her
agitation.

"Don't be a fool, Aiya," Imar said flatly. "You cannot stay here
alone."

Aiya rounded on him. "Can I not? Do you believe me so incapable?"

"Why do you speak to me this way?" Imar said defensively.

"Why do you not consider what I want?" Aiya fired back. "Always it is Imar who decides. Imar who knows what is best. When do I get to choose what I want?"

"And what do you want?"

"I want to stay here. I do not want to go to Albon or to Branvik. I want to stay in Endvar. I want to stay in my home."

His black eyes narrowed. "You're a fool. You would stay here alone and unprotected?"

"I wish to decide for myself. I am not helpless, Imar."

"Have I said otherwise?" Imar hissed. "Where is this great ire coming from?"

"It comes from knowing that I have no voice in my own life. Always I am overshadowed by you. Ten years you have protected me, but when will you let me live?" Aiya knew she was being unfair, but the words came before she could stop them.

Imar did not answer right away. His shoulders sank and he resumed walking, but his step was slower. The silence was heavy between them, and Aiya's words rang in her own ears. When they turned onto their own street, Imar finally spoke.

"If you stay," he said, "then I insist upon one thing. These visits with Hala cease while I'm gone. I don't want you to have anything else to do with that woman."

Aiya didn't object, feeling the first hint of victory and not wanting to spoil it. But thinking of Hala renewed her guilt, and when they walked into the house, she grabbed a package sitting on a small table near her sewing chair. It was the captain's uniform, clean and mended.

"I'm going to the guard complex to return Captain Strong's uniform. He said he needed it before tonight."

It was a lie, but a convenient one, and Aiya slipped out the back door before Imar could object.

Merek was crossing the inner courtyard of the guard complex when he noticed Dan sparring with Regin nearby. Most of the men in wall training wouldn't be on the practice fields until late afternoon or evening. But Dan was not like most men. Merek recognized the intensity of a leader who thought he'd failed his men. Until Jax was fully healed from that wicked knife wound given him by the Khouri warrior, Dan would continue to take his injury personally.

Waves of heat rose from the courtyard stones. Merek stood in the shade, leaning against the wall of the nearest barracks. Dan grunted with emphasis each time he struck, and Merek marveled at how much power was packed into the short man.

Merek stepped casually out of the way as Dan drove Regin back against the wall of the barracks. Regin stumbled and hit the wall with a thump, his sword clattering noisily to the ground.

"I said I wasn't ready!" Regin yelled, spitting out a stream of curses.

"Don't say anything that you'll regret, son," Merek said, cutting off Regin's tirade. "Both of you go cool off. This sun is a beast today. If we're not careful, we'll all be at each other's throats."

"Yes, sir," Regin said, but he glared at Dan as he stalked off. Dan shrugged sheepishly before jogging toward the water barrels after his friend.

A door opened nearby and Rorden stepped out of the barracks, freshly shaved and straightening his crisp blue coat.

"You could always just knock next time, sir," he drawled.

Merek grinned. "These boys were up all night training, yet here they are. What's your excuse?"

Rorden smiled with a glint in his eye. "For starters, the first proper bed I've had in days. I'm so tired of sleeping on the ground. I don't know how you do it, sir."

"Don't you know? A hard backside is one of the requirements for a man in my position."

Rorden snorted. "I guess that explains a lot. So, no chance to rest and recover my city legs?"

"City legs?"

"Like a sailor has to get his sea legs back when he's been on land for too long. I've just spent the last several weeks trapped in a tiny village with no more excitement than wondering whose sow will farrow first."

"Watch it. That's my homeland you're talking about."

"It's not that it's bad to be dull," Rorden said amiably. "And the girls were sweet and pretty in their own way. But I'm glad to be back where I don't know the name of everyone I meet on the street. And their life story. And what they ate for breakfast."

Merek clapped a hand on his back. "Well, I'm glad you're tired of being idle because we have work to do. I attended a party at Lord Ogmun's last night, and it was surprisingly illuminating."

"Really?" Rorden perked up. "Anybody interesting there?"

"Yes, but not in the way you mean."

As they exited the shade of the barracks, a small figure entered the courtyard. She was dressed in pale green and clutched a brown package tightly to her chest.

"Is that…?" Rorden began to ask, but Merek was already moving toward her.

"Aiya? What is it?"

"I'm sorry, my lord—captain," she said, breathing quickly from her hurried walk.

"Is everything all right? Is Imar in trouble?"

"Imar is fine. I'm sorry, you might think me a fool, but I needed to talk…" Her voice trailed off and she looked uncomfortably at Rorden. "This is likely a small thing to you, but very troubling to me."

Merek took her elbow and gently guided her around to the shady side of a building where they would not be overheard by the other soldiers.

"It's all right, Aiya. What happened?"

She looked up at him, her dark eyes wide.

"I met with my cousin's wife. Just now. Two nights ago, after you—

after what happened—he beat her. Behni was so angry after the...he beat her."

"How bad is it?"

"I've seen worse," she said darkly. "But it will be weeks before she fully heals."

Merek cursed grimly. "Would you like me to report it to the peacekeepers?"

"What I would like," Aiya said fiercely, "is to scratch his eyes out with my fingernails and feed them to a street dog." She spat on the ground, speaking something hateful in her native tongue.

Rorden laughed warmly. "I like that, Aiya. I'll have to remember that one."

Aiya's expression softened. "Please forgive me. These are not things a lady should say."

"No really, I don't mind," Rorden insisted. Merek silently agreed. Who knew that docile Aiya could feel this strongly about anything?

"How can I help?" Merek asked. "Does she need protection?"

Aiya shook her head mournfully. "She would never agree. It's not the way of Khouri women. What good would it do? Someday she will go back to Khourin with him. But I should have foreseen this. His father always had a great temper."

Rorden looked back and forth between the two of them and said excitedly, "I'm sorry to be a step behind, but are you saying that the code worked?"

Merek nodded. "We intercepted a wagon full of weapons two nights ago."

"Really? Weapons! What does it mean?"

"I'm not sure yet. Two men escaped, and the others were killed, so we didn't learn much."

Aiya laid a hand on Merek's arm, suddenly intent. "Hala said something today. It may not help, but I thought it strange. She said that when Behni comes home, he smells of death and mud. Those were her words."

Merek looked at Rorden, who shrugged.

"It's strange because it hasn't rained in weeks," she said, as if surprised they hadn't realized it.

Merek considered this. "Yes. You're right. The weapons were stored near the river—"

"No, not the river. She said 'death.' The river does not have this stench. It's not normal mud, maybe?"

Merek scratched at his beard, thinking. "Let's go to my office and talk this over. I think I met your elusive pale friend last night as well."

Aiya blinked in surprise. "The beardless man? Who is he?"

"Not here." Merek glanced around guardedly. "Inside."

As they walked, Rorden leaned over and said to Aiya. "Tell me which one it was."

This time, Aiya smiled broadly. "You won't believe it. It was the vowel segments."

"No way!" Rorden laughed.

Aiya nodded, and her eyes shone with amusement. "I think you owe me an apology. I was right after all."

Merek smiled as he listened to Rorden and Aiya banter with each other. He had watched Aiya carefully in recent weeks for any sign of Rorden's suspicions, and had decided that Rorden was imagining things. If anything, she seemed more relaxed and affectionate toward Rorden than she ever did with Merek.

"Captain Strong!" A soldier hurried toward him and saluted. "Captain Eldar sent me—"

Merek cut him off with a wave of the hand. "Is Eldar in his office?"

"Yes sir, but—"

"Tell him I will see him shortly," Merek said, ignoring his protests and mounting the stairs. The wood creaked under his weight as he moved through the upstairs corridor to his office.

When Merek opened the door, he stopped short, his attention arrested by the woman sitting in his chair. Princess Honoria leaned against the wall, balancing on the back legs of his chair in a decidedly unladylike posture. Her bare feet rested on his desk, crossed ankles visible beneath the hem of her shapely gown. In one hand, she held a book. In the other, she fanned herself with a delicate fan, tendrils of brown hair waving in the breeze where they had loosened from the pile of hair swept away from her brow.

Merek was vaguely aware of a young woman sitting in the corner and a man in the king's livery at the window. Chagrined, he remembered the earnest young man downstairs and the urgent message he'd tried to deliver. Honoria looked up as he entered and smiled languidly.

"It's about time, Captain Strong. How rude of you to keep me waiting."

Seventeen

Ria watched, amused, as the emotions flashed across the captain's face. Surprise first, followed by confusion, until settling into restrained annoyance. That was fine with her. It had been difficult keeping her arrival a surprise, and all her efforts would have been wasted if he hadn't been at least a little put out. She thought the gesture with her feet on his desk was a nice touch.

Ria almost didn't recognize Captain Strong. She'd never seen him with a beard before, as all soldiers were clean-shaven in Albon. His dark beard was short and neatly trimmed, drawing attention to his gray eyes. If his great height filling the doorway hadn't assured her of his identity, those thoughtful gray eyes would have.

Captain Strong stepped into the room, followed by two others whose conversation had cut off at the sight of her. One of them was the captain's handsome young clerk. What was his name again? Rory? No, Rorden. She would have to call him Rory sometime as a lark. The other was a lovely Khouri woman with perfect posture and the flawless skin that made the women of her race beautiful at all ages. Her curtsy was as graceful as any Ria had seen at court.

"I'm surprised to see you, Princess," Captain Strong said. "I wasn't informed that you'd come to Endvar." His eyes flickered to the hallway.

"I stashed Captain Drenall and my guards in the office next door. The one with the nice captain who offered me bread and cheese while I waited. I assured him that I would be dining with you this afternoon, but if I'd known I would be waiting so long," Ria said, stifling a yawn, "I would have accepted. As it is, I was almost ready to give up." She closed her book with a snap and stood.

"If I'd known you were coming, I would have made arrangements to meet you." He sounded dazed.

"But that would have taken all the fun out of the surprise!" Ria rounded the corner of the desk, handing her book to Biren and holding out a hand to the captain. "I must say the beard is quite dashing. Adds an air of rugged mystery," she added with a wink, and was rewarded with a faint flush in the captain's cheeks.

At this, the exotic Khouri woman turned to Captain Strong. "I think I should leave now, my captain," she said quietly, her low voice like soft music.

My captain? Ria raised an eyebrow. Who was this woman? She wasn't dressed like a servant. What business did she have with Captain Strong? And, more importantly, how could Ria use it to tease him?

Captain Strong barely acknowledged the other woman with a curt nod. "Thank you, Aiya."

Rorden followed the other woman out, and the low hum of their voices sounded as soon as the door closed behind them. There was a story here; she sensed it. How delightful. Already she was glad she had come.

"I hope you don't mind, but I sent word to The Flying Goose this morning. They'll be bringing dinner in an hour or two."

"Bringing dinner?"

"Yes, did you know that they do that? Deliver a meal anywhere in the city? Well, maybe they just do it for me, but it's very convenient. Much better than being interrupted."

"I'm sorry, my lady. Have I missed something?"

"I'm glad you asked. We'll need more chairs, unless you prefer to stand." Ria returned to the chair behind the desk and sat again, frowning. "A cushion would be nice too, since your chair is a bit hard for my taste. And I expect we'll need somewhere to put the food since your desk will hardly do for that."

Captain Strong shot a desperate glance at Edvin and Biren. Edvin shuffled his feet, and Biren struggled to hide a smile. Oh really, he almost made it too easy.

"What are we working on, exactly?" Captain Strong said, stepping to the desk where she had arranged various maps. He glanced at a pile of papers on a stool in the corner and his lips tightened in annoyance. Those had been the desk's previous occupants before she'd asked Edvin to clear them away to make room for her things.

Ria smiled and produced a letter. He frowned as he recognized it as one of his own. "For weeks now you've petitioned my father for repairs to the wall. He's decided to listen to your suggestion—" this was a generous understatement, since 'badgering' and 'demands' were the words her father had used, "— and investigate the need for repairs. Through me."

"Through you, my lady?" he asked warily.

"Yes. I'm going to tour the wall in my father's place and send him detailed reports. If all goes well, you will soon have the men and stone you need, and I will have had a grand time seeing the country and learning all there is to know about the fascinating subject of stone deterioration."

Captain Strong took a closer look at the papers arrayed on the desk: copies of the maps he'd left with the king, with additional notations in Ria's own hand. He looked at her. "Are you serious?"

"Absolutely." She sat back, picking up her fan again. With the sun glaring through the open window, the room was getting hotter by the minute.

Captain Strong placed his hands on the desk, still holding her gaze. His voice was calm and careful. "Princess, I can't guess what your intentions are, and I don't really care. I will not waste your time explaining that this would not be a pleasure trip and detailing the hardships that come with sleeping on the road and riding hard day after day. I'm sure you already know this. So I don't know what your game is, but I'm not going to play. I'm sorry you wasted your time coming here, but I will ask you now to leave as I have real work to do."

Biren gasped in the corner. Ria's cheeks grew hot. Standing and drawing herself up to her full height—which, unfortunately still meant that the captain towered over her, it was horribly unfair that he was so tall—she placed her hands on the desk and leaned toward him, mimicking his own stance. She doubted it was quite as intimidating when she did it, but she tried to put as much fire as possible into her words.

"It is not up to you to decide when I leave, Captain Strong. Thank you for skipping your speech about why I'm ill-equipped for the rigors that this trip will demand. Believe me, I have no interest in playing games, and have wasted more time than I care to explaining myself to you. Now, shall we move on to the real business at hand? I wish to leave in two days' time."

Ria fought the urge to look away from his penetrating gaze. Let him back down first. She stoked her anger a little to give her courage.

Eventually he leaned back, folding his arms. "Two days?" he asked flatly.

Did he practice that glare or did it just come naturally to a man in uniform?

Ria relaxed slightly at the capitulation. "Yes. Edvin has procured the necessary supplies. I've already determined the route, for the most part. There are a few things that we still need to discuss, but I see no reason not to leave as soon as possible."

She gestured to one of the maps, inviting him to view it.

He didn't.

"Is something the matter, Strong?" she asked. That's what her father would have called him, right? It felt presumptuous not to use his title, but it was time to start acting like his superior.

There was no hint of challenge in his voice when he spoke. Only an expectation that he was accustomed to being obeyed. "There are important matters I need to attend to here. I won't be able to leave for at least a week. Possibly two. If you had sent word in advance, I could have made arrangements. As it is, I need more time."

Ria nodded. "I see. And if my father were here today instead of me, would you say the same thing to him?"

Captain Strong hesitated.

Ria smiled. "From now on, Strong, I am my father. The sooner you accept that, the easier this will be. I will be leaving in two days, with or without you. But it will be better for us both if you are there." She was not above threatening if she had to.

After a moment Captain Strong nodded sharply, but hostility leaked from him as he leaned forward to inspect the map. Now that her own anger had passed, she found it amusing. She knew him well enough to know that he wouldn't stay angry for long.

At least, she hoped he wouldn't.

"How long would you say that a full wall tour takes?" Ria asked.

"Depending on how large our party is, three or four months," Captain Strong guessed.

Ria nodded. "That's what Edvin said too. I'm only interested in seeing the damaged sections that you indicated on this map, so I expect it won't take longer than six or eight weeks. Smile, Captain. You'll be rid of me before you know it."

Captain Strong relaxed a little. "What of these other areas?" he asked, pointing to one of the cities with Ria's notations.

"Oh, yes. Well, I thought we could plan our tour to visit those cities along the way. It seems too good of an opportunity to pass up, since we'll be so close and I haven't visited in so long." Ria tried to sound casual. She hoped that he wouldn't notice that these were also cities that housed unmarried young noblemen.

The captain's eyes narrowed. "Some of these cities are nowhere near the wall."

"They're close enough. It won't take us that much out of the way, and you can't blame me for wanting a warm bed and fresh meal whenever it's available, can you?"

To his credit, he didn't point out the contradiction. Hadn't she just insisted that she was up to the challenges of rough travel?

Instead, the captain simply shrugged. "Well then, Your Highness. Let's plan your first wall tour, shall we?"

Hours later, the sun had finally sunk to the horizon, but the small room was still hot and sticky despite the open window. The remains of their meal sat forgotten on a small side table as Merek, Rorden, and the princess's clerk pored over the maps and ledgers, trying to determine how to meet Honoria's strict timeline while not cutting out any of the extra cities she expected to visit. Infuriatingly, she didn't just seem to want a bed for a night, but she planned to stay at least a full day resting in each location.

As the evening dragged on, Honoria had left the haggling to resume her relaxed posture in Merek's chair, her bare feet resting on a stool. Her face shone with perspiration, despite her persistent fanning, and she'd even given up on reading, sitting with her eyes closed as though any extra effort would create too much heat.

It probably would. Merek and Rorden had long since removed their coats, rolling up their sleeves and loosening the collars of their shirts beneath. Still, it made little difference, and they frequently wiped their brows to keep the sweat from dripping onto the maps.

"I curse the scratching of your quills," Honoria said, eyes still closed. "All that muttering and scratching with nothing to show for it. If you aim to torture me, Captain, you're doing a marvelous job."

Merek merely grunted before turning back to Edvin and responding to his query about why a certain city needed to be approached from the south rather than the west. "These marshlands are marked incorrectly. This road is only used during winter when the ground is frozen. Certainly not this time of year. We'd be better off approaching from this direction."

Edvin, a bespectacled man who stuttered when he got upset, protested. "B-but that takes us too f-far out of the way. Surely there's a b-better alternative."

"There is," Merek said, shooting a glance at the reclining princess. "We forget Berseth and save ourselves at least three days."

"I already told you, Strong." Honoria's voice was heavy with exhaustion. "That is not an option."

With a sigh, the three men turned back to the map.

Honoria opened her eyes and watched them. "Edvin, why don't you see if you can find us some chilled wine. I think we could all use some refreshment."

"No." Merek held out a hand to stop him. "Just water for us."

Edvin nodded and left obediently.

"No wine, Captain?" Honoria eyed him. "It seems like you could use it more than most. Loosen up that scowl you've worn all evening."

"Not while we're on duty, my lady," Merek responded, taking advantage of the pause to stretch his back.

Honoria cocked her head. "Are you on duty? I didn't realize uniformed officers were allowed such a state of casual undress while on duty."

She was right, of course. Without another word, Merek began unrolling his shirtsleeves.

"Oh stop," the princess scolded. "I don't want you in full uniform. It's immoral in this heat. My point is that surely allowances can be made under the circumstances."

Merek shook his head. "It's a sore offense that we even removed our coats. If the king had been here, we wouldn't have been so presumptuous except under his invitation. I beg your pardon."

"Well I won't give it," she snapped. "Not unless you take some wine."

In response, Merek reached for his coat.

Honoria laughed, a short burst of amusement that sounded like a fresh breeze in the stuffy room. "Fine. Captain Strong, I order you to remove your coat and whatever else is making you uncomfortable in this heat. If you add even a single button to your person beyond what is strictly necessary, I'm afraid I will burst into flame by association."

Merek snorted, but he gratefully removed his coat again.

Rorden began unlacing a boot. "You did say 'whatever else,' right, my lady?"

This time, her laugh was even more free, primed now after hours of disuse. "I did, yes, Sergeant. Perhaps I should have clarified. This room is far too small, and my nose far too delicate."

Soon, Edvin returned with the chilled wine and water. Honoria sipped it appreciatively, licking her lips with a sigh. The beads of condensation on her cup's rim teased Merek's thirst. The water wasn't chilled and fell short of being truly refreshing.

The room grew silent as they drank. Merek's mind wandered to the stranger he'd met the previous night, the fair-haired man named Domar, and Aiya's puzzling revelation from earlier in the day. How could he possibly take time to investigate it all when he was trapped into this foolish errand with the princess? Though, in fairness, he *had* requested this of Sindal. If it had been Sindal who appeared without warning in his office, he would not have hesitated in his duty.

Honoria sat up, gulped down the last of her wine, and slammed her cup on the desk. Her maid, who'd been dozing in the corner, jumped at the sound. "I think we've done enough for tonight. Let's work out the details on the road. You're certain about the first part of the journey?"

"Yes, my lady. We all agree that Lorin is where we need to start," Merek said.

The princess nodded, decision overriding exhaustion in the moment. "That will do for now. Let's not delay our departure. You have one day to get your affairs in order, Captain."

Merek wanted to object. There were so many details still unresolved. But she'd been like a stone wall, refusing to give way no matter how persuasive his arguments. Instead, he turned to Edvin. "Let's meet again tomorrow. We still have much to discuss."

Edvin nodded, then gathered up his papers and notified the guards waiting in the hallway. The maid collected the princess's stockings and shoes, smiling shyly at Rorden when she caught his eye.

Honoria seemed oblivious to it all, eyes distant as she looked out the window at the darkening sky. The faint evening breeze teased her loosening hair, and she idly twirled a strand of it around her finger. She had her mother's beauty, the kind that drew covert glances of appreciation from passersby, and her features were soft and feminine. But her dark eyes held an intensity that Merek had never seen in the kindly queen. That intensity—that sense of purpose—was all Sindal. A fierce strength hidden beneath a playful exterior. It pleased Merek to see it.

Honoria turned to see him watching her. Suddenly, he felt self-conscious and fought the urge to look away like a boy caught stealing a candy stick. Instead, he stepped forward and her expression softened into a smile.

"You've done good work tonight, Captain," she said. "I just might be glad to have you join me after all."

Merek didn't know how to respond. Should he thank her? "I hope we can both say that by the time we're finished," he said.

Her dark eyes glinted with humor. "Indeed."

After the door closed behind the princess and her maid, Rorden let out a heavy sigh. "I pity the man who becomes our next king."

"Sergeant!" Merek said, shocked at Rorden's rudeness.

"I'm sorry, sir. I know she's like family to you, but after tonight I'm no longer surprised she's still unmarried."

Merek, too, was not surprised, but for different reasons. What he'd seen in the princess that night was not a spoiled child who wanted her way. It was the unapologetic confidence of an emerging leader. She was in that period of transition that comes with assuming leadership for the first time. A princess might expect to be obeyed because she felt entitled. A leader would expect to be obeyed because her greater purpose demanded it. There were bound to be some growing pains as those around her resisted the change.

But he didn't know how to explain this to Rorden. Instead, he said, "She's still your future queen. Be careful how you speak of her. Besides, you were following her around like a lovesick pup in Albon not too long ago."

"I was not!" Rorden's face reddened. "Well, maybe I did. But that's before I knew how bossy she could be. Before, she was a vision of loveliness, like ripe fruit bursting with sweetness."

"I'm not sure how I feel about that metaphor, Rorden," Merek warned.

"I mean no disrespect, sir. Women like being compared to something edible. It makes them feel irresistible."

"I'm trusting your judgment on women less and less by the moment." Merek gathered up the remaining maps and stored them carefully away in a cupboard. "It would probably be best if you follow the princess's advice and stop thinking of her as a woman. Think of her as her father, instead."

"That…" Rorden shook his head. "That would be like trying to convince a drowning man he's only splashing in a puddle."

Merek smiled. "Then it's fortunate for you that you won't be joining us. I need you to see to some things here while I'm gone. Eldar's men have almost finished their training, but I'm going to keep Sergeant Dan's squad here in the city. You can use them as necessary for your investigations."

Merek then shared with Rorden the events of the past few days, with a detailed account of the weapons and the Khouri warrior he and Dan's men had faced. Rorden leaned forward in eagerness, asking questions about the way the man was dressed and how he moved. Merek felt frustrated that he had very few answers. It had happened so fast, and the man had beaten them all too soundly.

Afterward, Rorden gave a more detailed report from his time in

Haldin. Finn had indeed been successful at reproducing the specially fitted boot. After seeing how the men were using it and hearing their suggestions, he'd even improved on it.

"I hope you don't mind that I allowed him to watch the men. It seemed best to allow him to see firsthand what they're doing. Although," Rorden added, chagrined, "I'm afraid it may have given him some ideas of his own. Captain Falbrook had to put a little fire into his blood to keep Finn from climbing the wall himself."

"Hmm, yes, I should have thought of that. Stefan should be able to keep him in line, though. He has plenty of practice with his own children." Merek sighed. This tour could not have come at a worse time. "Perhaps I'll go to Haldin on our return to see their progress, and you can join me there."

"It's very impressive, sir," Rorden said. "They're getting better at climbing with weapons and are strong enough that they aren't too tired to fight when they get to the top."

"Good, very good." Merek ran his hand through his hair and stood. "I'm going out to the wall. I want to spend one last night with these men, since they'll be reassigned before I return. As for you, I'd like you to spend some time working up preliminary scenarios for Stefan's men."

"Scenarios, sir?"

"Yes. To plan their assault on Endvar."

Eighteen

Ria woke to muted light diffused by her canvas tent. And pain. Oh, the pain. Her body protested as she moved, hips and shoulders aching from pressing against the ground. For all her confident words, Ria had been woefully unprepared for so many hours of riding day after day.

The morning they departed Endvar, Captain Strong had taken one look at her—perched elegantly on her woman's saddle and wearing a lovely riding frock of yellow linen trimmed in green—and ordered a new saddle and a pair of trousers brought so that she could ride astride her mount.

Like a man.

"We're not going on parade, Princess," he'd said.

At first she'd been annoyed, suspecting that he was just being difficult. But eventually she realized he was right. Sidesaddles created an image of equine femininity, but they weren't practical for long distances over rough terrain.

To be honest, Ria rather liked the trousers. They were coarse and didn't accentuate her curves like a well-made gown, but they also gave her a daring sense of freedom. As long as it was only temporary, she decided she would enjoy it. Ria was determined to be optimistic and prove to her father and Captain Strong that she could do this, and do it gracefully.

That was before the soreness had set in. Apparently riding this way worked a different set of muscles in her legs and back. By the end of the first day, Ria was exhausted and struggled to speak civilly to anyone. The following morning, she could barely walk.

Biren was a lifesaver. As daughter to the king's horsemaster, Biren had grown up as comfortable in a saddle as on her two feet. She patiently showed Ria helpful stretches and insisted that she take time to do them at each stop. At first, Ria had resisted, thinking it only added to her humiliation. But by the second day, she had humbly submitted. No indignity could be worse than the pain.

Ria stretched now in the privacy of her tent. An unpleasant stench rose from her clothing. Five days without a bath was not long when you had clean clothes and spent your time avoiding physical exertion. But as it was, Ria was wearing the same loose shirt and trousers she'd adopted in Endvar, and they smelled of horse and sweat.

When Biren entered a few minutes later, Ria had finished stretching and was buttoning her waistcoat. Not even a full week on the road and already she was dressing herself. Would Lotta be proud of her resourcefulness? Or disappointed that she wasn't holding to a higher standard of refinement?

"Oh, you're already awake!" Biren said. "I was hoping to let you sleep, my lady. Captain Strong said that we are less than a day from Lorin and won't need to start so early this morning."

"No matter. I couldn't have lasted another minute on that hard ground anyway," Ria said, fighting a surge of irritation at Biren's words. Was she the last one in camp to have received the word? She sat cross-legged—one benefit of trousers that she quite appreciated—so that Biren could more easily work out the snarls in her hair. Despite beginning each day with a tight braid, it always seemed to be a tangled mess after the wind worked at it hour after hour.

Ria gritted her teeth as Biren tugged, listening to the sounds of the soldiers breaking camp around her. They were a small group; the princess and her maid, her clerk Edvin, Captain Strong, and a dozen additional soldiers of the Royal Guard under the command of Captain Drenall. Ria was the only one with a tent, the soldiers sleeping instead under the stars in the warm summer air. Even Edvin had been required to sleep outside, as Captain Strong had explained that one tent would be burden enough.

Listening to the activity, Ria said, "I thought we didn't need an early start."

"I believe the late start was to give you a chance to rest, my lady," Biren replied, laying aside the brush and separating six strands of hair for braiding. "I suspect that it's not the disposition of soldiers to sleep in."

Ria felt irritation rising again. "I see."

"What is it, my lady?"

"How is it that he has so firmly seized control of this expedition?" Ria complained. "At home, when I was planning this trip, I was in command. But here? I've been relegated to the role of a useless child who needs to be kept out of the way while the adults do the real work."

"Hmm." Biren's reply was noncommittal, but Ria knew her too well to leave it alone.

"You disagree?"

"I'm sorry, my lady, but I don't believe Captain Strong has seized anything that wasn't already his. He's a natural leader, and the men look to him without question. Even you defer to him, whether you realize it or not."

"Well, not anymore," Ria said, scrambling to her feet and ignoring Biren's cry of protest as the unfinished braid slipped out of her fingers.

They were camped near a stand of trees next to the Nardin River. It took only a moment for Ria to spot the captain, sitting on a fallen log cleaning his gear. Another soldier sat nearby, laughing at something the smiling captain had said.

The air this close to the river was cool and humid, and a breeze made Ria wish for her light jacket. Soldiers turned and nodded to her as she stalked toward the captain, her resolve threatening to leak away in the open air.

"Captain Strong," she said firmly as she neared him.

He stood at her approach, the oilcloth still in his hands. "Good morning, Princess. I trust you slept well."

"I wish to discuss our schedule for the day."

"Of course. I'm nearly finished here and will be with you shortly." He turned back to his work.

"Good. Then it will be that much easier to return to it *after* I am finished." She didn't even try to keep the impatience from her voice. There was a part of her that wisely pointed out that she was tired and hungry and sore and was likely to say something she would regret later, but this part of her was shouted down by the tired and hungry and sore part that wanted to say exactly what she thought.

Strong paused, then handed his oilcloth to the other soldier.

"I'm at your service, my lady," he said with a hint of amusement in his eyes. In the morning light they looked almost blue, a startling contrast to his dark hair and beard. It wasn't like him to be so cheeky in public, but she supposed the other soldier might not have noticed the nuances of his tone the way she had.

Ria walked a few paces closer to the stand of trees, and he followed obediently.

"Tell me, Princess, are you always this irritable first thing in the morning?"

"Only when I'm being ignored," Ria snapped.

"I don't understand. How have you been ignored? Is there something I've missed?" He glanced over her and she was suddenly aware of her rumpled clothing and unraveling hair. What right did he have to look so…*together* so early in the morning? His uniform must have been made of sturdier stuff than her own clothing, as it didn't show the same signs of abuse. He looked very authoritative towering over her with his many insignias and perfect posture and…

Oh, this was going to be hard.

Be regal, she told herself. *Take command.* She folded her arms, hoping she seemed stern and not petulant.

"I'm tired of getting information from my maid, as though I'm merely a passenger in a caravan."

"I'm afraid I still don't see a problem. I'm following the plan that you approved. Am I to understand that you want me to run every last decision by you? When we stop for meals? Where we camp?"

Ria's hair blew forward into her face on a gust of wind, and she tossed it back impatiently. "And if my father were here? Wouldn't he be making those decisions?"

Infuriatingly, Captain Strong just grinned, the skin around his eyes crinkling pleasantly. He leaned toward her and said softly, "Honoria," and it startled her to hear him use her given name. "I understand what you're trying to do. Really, I do. But you need to be patient. If your father were here, he wouldn't end each day by collapsing off his horse, then crawling to bed in an exhausted stupor. Come to think of it, did you get anything to eat last night?"

Ria felt foolish, which in turn made her angry. "That's none of your concern."

Captain Strong nodded as though that were answer enough. "An oversight. We'll have to make sure that doesn't happen again." He placed a patronizing hand on her shoulder. "May I suggest that in the future, you make sure that you have a full stomach before deciding whether or not you've been wronged? You need your strength, which includes rest and food. If you can't handle the rigors of this expedition, you'll soon find yourself in forced convalescence. So it *is* very much my concern. Do you understand?" He held her gaze, and she found herself nodding in spite of herself.

When she opened her mouth to speak, he stopped her. "The rest will come. Be patient. You're new at this, but it will come."

"Your Highness!"

Ria turned to see Edvin hurrying toward her. She was perversely satisfied to see that he looked as rumpled as she felt, his hair askew from fitful sleep. Captain Strong released her, and she stepped forward to greet her clerk. But her eyes followed the captain and she had a hard time listening to Edvin.

She'd come to air her grievances about being marginalized and had been treated with respectful condescension that made her feel even more insignificant than before. This angered her, but a part of her knew that his words made sense. Which in turn just made her more annoyed.

But talking of food made her realize how drained she was. In truth, the previous evening was such a blur that she couldn't remember whether or not she had eaten before lying down. Now she felt so ravenous that she wondered how she even had the strength to stand upright.

Holding up a hand, she stopped Edvin. "We'll discuss this later. I need some breakfast."

The Nardin River lay calm and placid, its surface reflecting the sunlight in shifting patterns of broken light. Ria had a hard time imagining the torrential floodwaters that had caused so much damage to the town of Lorin a few months earlier. She saw the debris line in the trees and foliage high on the bank but couldn't envision the amount of water that would have brought the river to that level.

Biren rode on one side of her with Edvin on the other. Ria listened as her father's clerk detailed the damage done by the floods. The Nardin had flooded its banks three times over the course of the spring, the last time extending past the town to damage the wall.

But Ria wasn't focusing on Edvin's words, her mind wandering instead to her earlier conversation with Captain Strong. She hadn't spoken to him since, but her temper had cooled in the fresh morning air and—she grudgingly admitted—after a filling breakfast. It annoyed her that he'd been right, but that wasn't what distracted her from Edvin's monologue. No, it was his curious words about knowing what she was about that troubled her.

Just what had he meant by it? There was a chance he might guess that she hoped this expedition would be a bridge in bringing the king and the captain together again, but it seemed unlikely. Even less likely was the thought that Captain Strong suspected that her father was unwell and Ria was taking her first steps toward assuming his responsibilities.

As for the other matter…well, it was completely laughable that he could have guessed the truth about her visits to the noble houses. Yet. She knew she wouldn't be able to hide the truth from him forever. He was too clever not to figure it out. But it made her squirm to think about having *that* conversation with him. No matter how she looked at it, she couldn't shake the feeling that it was an act of pitiful desperation.

Besides, the last person she wanted to discuss her love life with was Captain Strong.

Presently, the captain turned his horse and rode toward her. She fought a rising blush and raised her chin confidently. She wore a wide brimmed hat to shade her from the sun, but so many hours of exposure were hard to combat and she cringed to think of how freckled her skin would be before their travels were ended.

"Yes, Strong?" she greeted as he approached.

"If we continue on this road, we'll reach Lorin in four or five hours," he said. "Or we can leave the road and view the damaged section of the wall first before continuing on to the city."

"How close is it?" Ria asked. In the distance, portions of the wall rose over the gently rolling hills like the spine of an enormous slumbering beast.

"An hour, maybe less."

"Let's do it," Ria said. "We'll stop and eat then as well, before our final push to the town."

Captain Strong nodded. "Yes, my lady."

Was it her imagination or did she catch the twitch of a smile? Ria wouldn't allow herself to sink into petty irritation again today.

She finally had something to look forward to besides endless hours of riding. Soon she would see her first section of damaged wall and would have something useful to do. That evening, she would enjoy a real meal and a soft bed.

Lord Renick was a minor nobleman with no sons, so they would only stay one night. But it would be a blessed relief from sleeping on the ground and eating the same dried traveling food meal after meal; stringy meat, fruit that was shriveled beyond recognition, and crumbly biscuits that could only be swallowed with a mouthful of water washing them down.

Yes, there was much to keep her spirits up.

Captain Strong led them over a bridge and off the road. With the river behind them, the terrain became much steeper, and once again Ria was grateful to have left her sidesaddle behind as her legs gripped harder to keep her in place. At last, they crested a rise and the captain halted. Ria rode up alongside him to view the scene below. The Nardin curved through the valley like a wide, glimmering ribbon of light. The wall formed a narrower gray ribbon, its curves more gentle and contrived. Where they came closest to meeting, the wall was replaced by rubble and debris.

Ria breathed in sharply. It was difficult to imagine the force that could have reduced the wall to a pile of stones. She moved her horse forward, picking a path down toward the destruction. As she neared it, she was amazed at its enormity.

The wall was an impressive structure, casting a large shadow over her as she rode near its base. She stopped at the foot of the debris pile and waited for Captain Drenall to help her dismount. Broken stones mixed with fallen tree limbs, mud, and large tangles of roots to form a massive pile that towered over her. She walked around its footprint, leaving the group behind.

Then, she began to climb.

Ria stepped on a tree trunk and bounced slightly to ensure that it was wedged in tightly, then pulled herself up onto a near boulder. It was large and felt secure beneath her feet, so she crawled to another.

"I would advise against that, Princess," Captain Strong's voice sounded from below.

"No surprise there," she called back, scrambling further up the pile. It felt good to use her arms and legs in such a way, though she was glad for her riding gloves that protected her hands from splinters and scrapes.

At one point, a boulder shifted when she put her weight on it. She backed off of it, but the shifting set off a chain reaction of movement with dozens of rocks tumbling further down the pile.

"Oops," Ria said. She heard the captain complaining below and grinned to herself. "This is what you get for giving me a pair of trousers, Strong!"

When she reached the top, Ria stood and caught her breath. She felt exhilarated by the exertion and stood triumphantly with her hands on her hips, taking deep breaths of the warm air.

Looking out from the top of the wall, she saw what must be the northern edge of Dell. There were no signs of farms or villages, just more rolling hills with pockets of trees showing where streams and rivers fed the grasslands.

Turning, she surveyed her homeland. Her kingdom. It looked much the same as the country behind her, but there were lumps of debris in the flood zone that surely must have once been houses, barns, fences, and other structures.

How curious that this fertile land which supported her people on one side of the wall was left untended on the other. Ria turned around again to view the country on the other side of the wall. Why didn't the Dell people make their homes here? She knew they had once been fierce conquerors, but beyond that she didn't know much about them. Rahm wasn't on friendly terms with Dell, and she regretted being so uneducated about their aggressive neighbor to the south.

Without warning, the stones beneath her feet shifted. Her stomach lurched, and she fell forward onto her knees. She scrambled higher to escape the rock slide, but the grinding force of moving rock was relentless. Everything under her was moving, opening pockets that threatened to swallow a foot or a leg, and it was only with panicking effort that she kept free.

Then a large pair of hands grabbed her and hoisted her out of the moving rock pile, setting her safely onto solid footing. Fear gave way to relief, and through the heightened sense of adrenalin she was aware of Captain Strong's arms holding her. He held her just long enough for her to regain her balance, then released her.

"I believe I advised against that." His voice sounded as relieved as she felt.

"I know how much you like to be right, Strong. But really, triggering a rock slide just to prove a point?" Her voice was shakier than she wished. For that matter, *she* felt shakier than she wished, and she grabbed his arm to steady herself.

It was a sign of his worry that he didn't respond to her goading him. "Are you all right?" he asked.

"A little bruised, perhaps, but thanks to your timely arrival, nothing broken." Ria took a deep breath to calm her nerves. She was standing higher on the rock pile than he was, which brought them almost to eye level. He was less imposing this way. Maybe she should insist on standing on a box every time they had a conversation. "I must say, I *am* glad you were feeling overprotective just now. I hate to think what would have happened if you'd been sitting with the others enjoying your meal."

Captain Strong snorted. "I know you better than they do. I would ask you not to do things that put you in danger, but you would see it only as an invitation. So don't be too surprised if I don't stray too far from you while you're in my care."

"That sounds temptingly like a challenge." She grinned mischievously, feeling remarkably lighthearted now that the danger had passed. "Is that Lorin right there?" she asked, pointing to a cluster of rooftops in the distance.

The captain carefully climbed up next to her, and she reached a
hand out reflexively as his weight moved the rock. He grabbed her
elbow, steadying her, until the rock settled.

"Yes. We'll have to work our way around the Nardin and back
onto the road. Probably another three hours. If you're finished risking
your life for today, I suggest you get something to eat so we can get
started." He must be feeling better if his sarcasm had returned.

"But it can't be more than an hour away if we just cut across. Look,
there's even a door in the wall."

"Of course there is, but it's not a true gate. No traffic passes between Rahm and Dell. It's merely an access door for maintenance
that will be kept locked, barred, and heavily guarded."

"If it's guarded, that means someone can let us in." Ria began picking her way down the other side of the pile of rubble.

"Honoria!" His voice was filled with concern, and she could hear
in it the urge to grab her again. "You're going into Delth territory. I
strongly urge you to reconsider."

Ria scanned the countryside again. "I see no sign of anyone, but if
you're worried, you'd better come along."

She sensed his hesitation. If he waited too long, she would get
too far ahead. But if he went back for reinforcements, then he gave
up any hope of talking her out of it. Ria didn't bother to look back at
him to see what he was going to do. She was too focused on trying
not to start another slide with her descent.

Finally, she heard an exasperated sigh that brought a smile to her
lips. "You do realize this means we have to leave the horses behind,"
he said. "We can't get them over this pile of debris, so we'll be walking
the entire way."

At this, she paused. She was almost at the bottom, perched in a
crouch on the edge of a rock, preparing to lower herself over the edge.
She felt very much like a frog—a funny feeling that she dimly recognized from childhood play. She looked up at the captain, squinting
against the brightness of the sky behind him.

"If you were hoping to change my mind with that statement, then you don't know me as well as you think. I would crawl all the way if it meant I didn't have to spend three more hours on that lovely beast." Flashing him a wide smile, she dropped to the ground below.

Nineteen

"Don't say it."

"Excuse me?"

"Just…don't."

"I don't know—"

"I know you're thinking it. I can hear it churning in your mind clear across the room."

Ria sat against the dirty wooden floor of the guard house, knees pulled up to her chest. Captain Strong stood across the room, leaning against the wall.

He raised an eyebrow. "You mean, that I warned you this was a bad idea?"

Ria growled and covered her head with her arms. "I said not to say it." She glared at him. "Don't you ever get tired of being right all the time?"

Strong didn't answer her. He just folded his arms and looked out the small window at the street. He'd been in a sour mood since they reached Lorin.

"What is it? I can see the retort behind your eyes."

He just shook his head.

"Let me guess. Your witty response would be, 'Don't you ever get tired of acting like a fool?'"

He frowned. "I would never say such a thing, Your Highness."

"Far would say it if he were here," Ria grumbled. "And he would be right." She laid her head on her knees despondently.

They'd made it across the Delth territory without incident. Captain Strong had thought to bring water, for which Ria was grateful. The exertion of walking such a distance under the hot summer sun had fueled an unquenchable thirst.

That had been the easy part. Gaining entrance back into Rahm had proven to be more difficult. Captain Strong had hollered for a quarter of an hour before a portly soldier had finally responded and let them in. Ria had found the irony of the Crown Princess being locked outside her own kingdom highly amusing, but Captain Strong had been incensed. After some sharp words to the soldier for neglecting his post, he turned his ire on the supervising captain.

Captain Torgrim was all red-faced apologies, particularly when Strong confirmed Ria's identity. It annoyed her that none of the soldiers had believed she was whom she claimed to be. But on reflection, not only did she appear in the last place they would have expected—on foot outside a little used access door on the Delth side of the wall—she supposed she also didn't look anything like a princess; filthy, dressed in trousers and with hair grimy and dull from traveling. When she saw their expressions, Ria began to doubt her spontaneous decision. The one bright spot in her day was the easing of her soreness. Though she was tired from the long walk, it had done her muscles good.

Just how far away did Lord Renick live? It shouldn't take that long to send a carriage for her. Ria was becoming less and less impressed with Lorin with each passing minute. She was about to say so when Captain Strong spoke softly.

"That's like asking if the wind tires of blowing or the autumn leaves tire of falling. How does one argue with a force of nature?"

Ria cocked her head at him, confused.

He smiled slightly. "That's the retort I was thinking of. Earlier."

She thought this through and managed a tired laugh. "Very good. More clever than I expected, though you lose points for arrogance."

"That's what would have delighted your father the most." He straightened up and moved to the window. "Excuse me, I see Captain Torgrim returning."

Strong left Ria alone, and she stood, brushing off her clothing. When he entered again a few moments later, his expression was grim.

A well-dressed nobleman entered behind him, followed by the chastened captain. Lord Renick stood a little taller than she did, with graying hair that curled tightly around his head. His jowls hung low and waggled when he moved, but his eyes were keen and carried a considerable weight.

"Your Highness," he greeted, taking her hand respectfully. "I'm so sorry that you haven't been received the way you deserve."

Ria felt chagrined for putting this man in such an impossible position. "Don't apologize, Lord Renick. You could not have expected that I would arrive in the manner I did. I'm sure that all will be made right when I dine with you in your lovely home this evening."

Lord Renick looked uncomfortable. "Yes, well, I'm afraid that things might not be what you expect." He glanced nervously at Captain Strong, who stood silently with an inscrutable expression. Ria's mood dimmed. "My home is not…well, we're not really fit for such distinguished guests. I'm sorry, Your Highness. I did try to write when I learned that you would be visiting, but you must not have received…" He trailed off, and Ria noticed beads of sweat forming on his brow.

When Captain Strong spoke, his voice was tinged with something Ria didn't immediately recognize. Respect. "Nearly half of Lorin's population were left homeless from the flooding. Lord Renick has opened his home to the sick, the wounded, and elderly, while others are sheltering on his grounds until such time as they can replace their homes. I've assured Lord Renick that we're perfectly capable of making camp on his estate and won't inconvenience him or his people."

Ria's dreams of a soft bed and warm meal dissolved in an instant. With enormous effort, she smiled. "Of course," she said, hoping her words didn't sound as forced to him as they did to her. "It will be no trouble. Shall we?" She couldn't stay in the tiny hot room any longer and pushed past the men into the street. She paused, looking for the waiting carriage. The small street was empty.

Lord Renick followed after her. "I'm afraid I have no carriage either. Mine are being used for clean up and construction. We're trying to get as many homes rebuilt before the weather turns as we can. But my home is not far, if you don't mind walking."

"Mind? Of course not," Ria said wearily. She walked toward the end of the street where it opened onto a larger road, and Lord Renick fell into step beside her. At least Captain Strong remained behind at the guardhouse in conversation with Captain Torgrim. It would be easier to pretend she was content with the arrangements if he wasn't listening.

"Have you received sufficient aid from the king?" she asked Lord Renick as they walked.

"Ah…well, I'm sure the king has been as generous as he can."

Ria frowned. "Is the aid not sufficient?"

"I do not mean to complain. But with an effort like this, we could always use more soldiers and supplies."

Lord Renick led her in a generally downhill course sloping toward the river. Most of the two- and three-story structures were made of wood and sported fine carved detailing on their gables and over the doorways. They would have been quite charming if they hadn't had such an air of emptiness about them. There were few people out on the streets, and most of the shops were closed. It was an unsettling feeling. This was a place that should have been bustling with cheerful activity.

Then they emerged onto a large intersection and Ria gasped. The buildings on this street looked as though they'd been tossed about by a giant throwing a tantrum. Some were leaning dangerously toward their neighbors, walls straining precariously and roofs in various stages of collapse. Others had been lifted entirely off their foundations and dumped into the street.

Although much of the mud and flood debris had been cleared out
of the street, the water line was still visible on the affected buildings.
The smell was dank and musty—the stink of life left to rot in a putrid
bath of river water and human filth.

Here, in the midst of it all, were Lorin's people. But they weren't
selling wares or conducting the business of life. Instead, men, women,
and children alike shoveled muck out of buildings, searched through
rubble, and worked to disassemble the buildings whose timbers were
still worth saving.

Ria stopped in the middle of the street, taking it all in. Surprisingly, above the horror and pity she felt, the emotion that nearly over-
whelmed her was shame. Had she really, just moments before, felt
sorry for herself because there wasn't a hot bath and a soft bed waiting for her at Lord Renick's home? Looking at the exhausted faces
of the people of Lorin, she felt appalled over her earlier resentment
at having to sleep on the ground another night. These people looked
like they hadn't had proper beds in months and likely were underfed
for the amount of effort they were putting in day after day.

It was one of the most disheartening things she'd ever seen.
She watched Lord Renick move among them, smiling and calling
them by name. They responded with tired smiles of gratitude for
their lord, but barely spared Ria a glance, even though she too
tried to engage them. Of course, why should they? Who was she
to them? This strange woman dressed as a man—sunburned and
disheveled without even a proper horse—could be no one of con-
sequence.

Suddenly Ria realized she had made a huge mistake. These people—*her* people—didn't need an impetuous princess who came to
view their suffering as an impassive observer, who thought more on
her own aches and pains than she did their welfare. They needed
someone with dignity and compassion who could show them that all
was not lost and give them hope of a brighter tomorrow.

They needed a queen.

Eventually the road turned uphill toward a modest estate. This must be Lord Renick's home, but it was unrecognizable as such. The grounds were so crowded with makeshift tents and lean-tos made from salvaged lumber that it looked more like the slums she had seen in Khourin.

Ria paused at the gate to Renick's estate. "Lord Renick, I have a request."

He bowed his head obediently, jowls quivering. "How may I be of service?"

"I need a bath."

Lord Renick paused uncertainly. "Your Highness, I'm afraid every available room in my home is being used to care for the sick and wounded. Lady Renick and I are staying in the carriage house. Such luxuries—"

Ria cut him off with a raised hand. "I'm not trying to appease my vanity, though I admit it can be a rather powerful force to reckon with at times."

A familiar snort sounded behind her, and she turned to find Captain Strong approaching.

Of course, now *he returns.* She shot him a dark look and continued.

"I will bathe in one of your livestock watering troughs if I must, but I'm quite insistent. My own maid won't arrive for some time with the rest of our party, so I'll also need the assistance of your most trusted lady's maid if you can spare her. If not, I suppose a scullery maid will do as she'll have lots of practice with the kind of scouring I will need. Then, if I might borrow one of your wife's dresses?"

Lord Renick looked confused, but acquiesced. "I'll see what I can do, my lady."

Captain Strong raised a questioning eyebrow at her, but she merely nodded curtly at him—ignoring his unasked question—and followed Lord Renick through the gates.

⟫————◇

In the end, Ria didn't have to endure the cold humiliation of a watering trough. Lord Renick wasn't exaggerating when he said that every room in his house had been turned into an infirmary. Even the library housed a dozen makeshift beds on the floor, the chairs and tables pushed aside. But Renick ordered his own bath filled for the princess, and guided her through the maze of sick and wounded to the small room next to his bedchamber.

The water wasn't as hot as she would have liked, but as Ria sank into its depths, she sighed in contentment. Never had she felt such luxury. Lady Renick's maid had been commissioned to help her, and she washed her hair three times before Ria declared it sufficient. Ria would have loved to stay and soak in the cooling water, but there were only a few hours of daylight left, and she didn't have time to waste.

Dressing proved to be a little more difficult. Lady Renick was apparently a slender woman, and Ria could barely get the dress over her hips. Fastening it was out of the question.

"This won't do at all," she said, frowning.

Lady Renick's shy maid didn't respond.

Ria eyed her. She wasn't as tall as Ria—few women Ria had met were—but she had a similar build. "Perhaps I could try one of your dresses instead."

The girl jumped, startled. "Mine, my lady?"

"Yes." Ria smiled kindly. "Your nicest dress. One you wear to church for worship, perhaps. You and I are close to the same size, I think."

The girl blushed and ducked her head. "It's not so fine, my lady, but if you insist."

It was quite possibly the ugliest thing Ria had ever worn. Well, aside from the shirt and trousers that lay discarded in a filthy heap on the floor of the bathing chamber. But the way the girl presented it to her proved that it was a cherished possession.

The dress was a pale cream linen, almost white, with no embroidery or other adornments. It was cut simply with a loose bodice and skirt, only a slight gathering at the waist hinting at much shape. The weave was coarse compared to the soft textiles Ria was accustomed to. But it fit, and there was no question that it would be far more appropriate than the elaborate gowns packed in Ria's saddlebags.

As the maid combed through her wet hair, Biren burst through the door. She stopped, gaping in horror.

"My lady, what are you wearing?"

"Hello, Biren. Your timing is impeccable. This lovely young lady has loaned me her dress, but says that she isn't quite comfortable attempting my hair. Will you please?"

Biren eyed the maid suspiciously and snatched the comb out of her hand. She glanced at Ria's dress again. "I'm not sure what hairstyle would be fitting this particular…style."

"Something simple, yet elegant. To match the dress."

Lady Renick's maid beamed.

When Biren finished, Ria braved her reflection in the looking glass. Her brown hair was braided into a lovely crown around her head, a simple design which looked surprisingly natural with the maid's dress. Rustic, perhaps, but with an earthy grace. And, she cringed to admit, more suitable to the sunburned and windblown state of her complexion.

Lord Renick's eyes widened in surprise at the sight of her.

"I wish to meet your people," she told him. "As many as possible."

"Of course! Yes, yes, I shall be happy to oblige." He smiled with approval. Whatever he'd expected from the princess, it wasn't this.

"Renick." She lowered her voice so that only he could hear. "If we might keep the visits…" She blushed, trying to think of a delicate way to state it. There really was no delicate way. "You're going to think me very foolish, I'm sure. But I'm afraid I find the sight of blood rather…disagreeable. It may be best to avoid any injuries that are particularly gruesome."

Whatever Lord Renick thought of this request, he was well-mannered enough not to show it. Instead, he gladly escorted her through his home to meet victims of the Nardin's flood. Some were reticent to speak with her, or couldn't because their injuries were too severe. But others were anxious to tell her their stories. Though she entered each room standing, it wasn't long before she found herself kneeling by their pallets on the floor, or—in the rare instances when one was available—sitting next to them in a chair.

Some tales were almost too harrowing to listen to, like the father whose young daughter was torn from his grasp when they tried to escape to higher ground. Or the woman who watched helpless as her betrothed drowned, pinned by a large tree limb that she couldn't move.

But with these painful stories were also the ones of miraculous rescue. Strangers who risked their lives to save a man's aged mother trapped in an upstairs room while the waters rose around her. A woman who dropped the last of her possessions as she fled the torrent in order to carry another woman's child to safety.

As Ria traveled from room to room, word of her visit spread and soon the people were sitting up anxiously or standing when she entered a room, waiting for the princess.

By the time she left the manor, the sun was setting in the west and the heat of the day had finally broken. The camp outside was even more full of activity than before, as people returned from their labors of the day. They too had heard she was there, and many of them eagerly gathered to greet her as she descended the steps.

Ria tried to meet them all and walked through the camp to see those who couldn't come to her. She felt their pain, but she also felt something else she didn't expect. She'd seen suffering before in her travels. Great poverty, disease, and tyranny. In many of those instances she'd felt angry. Angry at the waste of human life and dignity. Angry at the way it turned people into animals who employed any form of barbarism in their fight for survival.

But here, she saw nobility. She saw the people of Lorin reaching out to help each other, to ease another's suffering even when they didn't have enough. She saw compassionate generosity in the way

Lord Renick knew their names and gave openly to all. It made her proud to be Rahmish.

It wasn't until Captain Strong pressed a bowl of hot stew into her hands and commanded her to rest that she realized it was so late. Darkness had fallen, and small cookfires dotted the grounds. She didn't protest as he led her to their own camp farthest from the manor. Sitting by the campfire and eating the hot vegetables and spicy meat, she realized just how exhausted she was. She wasn't sure she could even muster the energy to go to bed.

But instead of retiring, she sat up by the fire, penning a long letter to her father about the events of the day. She knew that he would already be getting reports from Lord Renick about the destruction and rebuilding efforts, so she focused instead on telling the stories of the people she had met.

Then she paused, remembering the reason she had come. It would be easy to describe the destruction to the wall, but part of her purpose was to judge for herself the threat to the people. That wasn't going to be easy. She simply didn't know enough about these people and their lands.

"Captain Strong?" she asked. He and Captain Drenall were the only others who remained at the fire, conversing in low tones. Everyone else had retired for the night. "How much of a threat are the Delth to these people? Why have they not been attacked in their vulnerable state?"

Captain Strong frowned into the fire, his profile exaggerated by the flickering light. "The Delth have long been a menace to the people living in the border lands. This was one of the last areas where they put up resistance when your grandfather was still alive. It took us years to finally drive them out."

"I'm not interested in history," Ria said impatiently. "I want to know about today. Are they still a threat?"

He blinked slowly and she saw weariness in his eyes. "I don't know," he said simply. "There's been little or no activity on this border in recent years. Some worry that they're amassing for a larger attack. Others speak of a great plague in Dell that ravaged their population. But with no eye witness accounts, I can't speak for what's true and what's folklore."

"Either scenario would be devastating for these people," Ria mused darkly. "Perhaps it's time we consider sending emissaries to Dell."

"Emissaries to whom? They have no central government. They're splintered into tribal groups who fight amongst themselves almost as readily as they make war with their neighbors."

Ria brushed her quill against her chin thoughtfully. "What about their holy man? Isn't there a shaman who rules over them all?"

"Rules?" Strong spat with contempt. "Not the way you think. They commit unspeakable atrocities in his name, but answer to no law. They're bloodthirsty savages who can't be governed or reasoned with. Your emissaries would be just as likely to end up with their heads on a stake."

Ria sighed and began writing again. Strong's words had more than a little flavor of prejudice to them, but with their borders closed to the Delth, it was impossible to know the truth.

After a few minutes, a thought occurred to her and she looked up. "Where were you all afternoon, Captain?"

Captain Strong looked at her a little sheepishly. "I hope you don't mind, Princess. It seemed you were in good hands, so Drenall and I took some of the men to see if we could be useful."

Captain Drenall yawned. The captain of the Royal Guard was considerably older, with age spots that shadowed his face in the semi-darkness. "I wish we had a hundred fresh men to help us," he added. "We could really get something done then."

Ria noticed for the first time that their boots were caked with mud and their once neat uniforms were filthy. She'd been so absorbed in her own thoughts, that she hadn't noticed the obvious. These men were exhausted, and she was keeping them from their beds. She hastily wrote the last few lines to her father, then stood and yawned, stretching her back. The captains stood with her.

Captain Strong nodded at her respectfully. "You did good work today, Princess."

Ria scoffed. "It would have been better if I had the strength of an ox like you two and not just a clean dress and a kind word."

"No." Strong shook his head. "They needed this. They needed you to remind them of the life they will have again someday. It's good sometimes to be reminded of what you are working for, especially when the labor is long and relentless."

Ria smiled. It was the first sincere praise he'd ever given her. As a woman who was accustomed to flattery and adoration, it was strange to realize how much it meant to her.

Twenty

Rorden whittled near the servant's gate, taking note of the people coming and going across the courtyard. After two weeks, he was familiar with the routines of Lord Bolen's staff and had traded his uniform for the humble dress of a common tradesman; heavy breeches worn loose, a light shirt with sleeves rolled up to the elbows, and a loose waistcoat over the top.

A familiar handcart rounded the corner near the gate and Rorden called out, "Oi, Oskel! Fancy earning a little extra today?"

The man pulling the cart stopped and set its back wheels down. Scratching his head, he looked Rorden up and down.

"Again? You must really have it bad. Which one is it, then?"

"Why, Oskel? You jealous? Wish you had a bit more flair for the ladies?" In truth, Rorden hadn't yet decided. He had to choose a maid who would be interested enough to want him coming around, but not so interested that things would get sticky and require a hasty exit.

Oskel just shook his head and continued pushing his cart toward the servant gate.

"Come on, Osk, just a joke." Rorden fell into step beside him, keeping his voice low and pleading. "Don't send me away empty-handed. I had to work all night just to get some time off this morning. It'll be three days before I have another chance."

Oskel paused and shot him a suspicious look. "I can't decide if you're an honest fellow who needs a fair chance at happiness, or a lying wretch who's about to break a sweet girl's heart. Just don't make me regret this."

Rorden grinned as he entered the gate moments later carrying the crate of groceries Oskel had handed over in exchange for a few coins. He didn't mind letting it show that he was pleased with himself. It fit his image of the smitten young man off to do some courting.

Now if he could only decide which of the kitchen maids he was supposed to be smitten with…

Miranda, with her long eyelashes and full lips, always seemed happy to see him. But curvy Bellak was the one who contrived reasons to keep him there a few minutes longer. He'd been careful to flirt with each of them equally, testing the waters as it were. Well, except for Yulda, the scullery maid. She was so quiet that he barely noticed she was there, and she didn't respond to his teasing the way the other girls did.

"Cookie!" Rorden greeted cheerfully as he entered the back door to Lord Bolen's kitchen. "The sun has risen without me once again, I see, basking its warmth on your fair countenance."

Cook snorted. "You again, eh? Come to torment me with your nonsense and distract my maids so's they can barely keep a thought in their heads?" She frowned into a pot, her biting tone matching her expression as she thrust it at Yulda, who accepted it without a word. "Go on, I got no time for you today, and she's not here so don't waste time asking."

Rorden set the heavy crate of groceries down on the massive table where Cook was rolling out biscuit dough. "Who's that, Cookie, my love?"

"I'm not daft, boy. Miranda has captured more hearts than she has a right to, with her soft brain and slow hands."

Ah, so Miranda it was. If that was what the kitchen maids had decided, it was best if he acted the part.

"Maybe I just fancied a chat with you, Cookie." He hoisted himself up on the table to sit next to where she was working.

"If you fancy your kneecaps, you'll get off my table," Cook said gruffly, raising her heavy rolling pin with big beefy arms. This close, he could see faint whiskers on her upper lip. She was as ill-tempered as any drill sergeant he'd known, and no amount of charm had softened her up.

Begrudgingly, he slid off the table. "Where are the girls this morning?" He wandered casually to the other end of the table and joined Yulda in peeling a large bowl of apples. She frowned at him, but said nothing.

"Why should I tell you?" Cook grunted. "They're doing their work, which is more than I can say for you. Does Oskel know how you annoy your customers when you make your deliveries?"

"I only annoy my favorites," he said with a wink at Yulda. She pressed her lips into a tight line.

"I have no time for your nonsense today, Prestin," Cook growled. "Lord Bolen has planned a picnic for his guests. They leave within the hour, and if those two girls don't have everything packed as instructed, it will all be a disaster!"

"Oh, I love a picnic! Let me help," he offered. "I'm sure Master Domar wouldn't mind one more helping hand, eh?"

Yulda stiffened next to him at the mention of Domar's name and attacked the next apple with vigor.

Cook glowered at Rorden. "You'll stay far away from Master Domar, you hear me? You upset him and you'll get all of us dumped out on the street!"

"I don't mean any harm, Cookie. Is Master Domar so ill-tempered, then? That's a shame. Master Falk always seemed so kind-hearted, as I remember." He'd never known Domar's predecessor, but a few discreet questions had revealed that Falk was universally liked.

Surprisingly, it was shy Yulda who answered. "Master Falk was the best of men. It's a shame his father died so suddenly and he had to leave us."

"What do you know of it, girl?" Cook slapped a baking sheet on the table, making Yulda jump. "People die all the time, who are you to say when it's sudden or not? What, did Master Falk confide in you?"

Rorden's patience with the woman was growing thin. He would have to leave soon or risk saying something out of character that would guarantee he'd never be welcome in Cook's kitchen again.

Fortunately, raised voices sounded in the hall, distracting Cook from her insults. Two girls burst into the room, flushed with excitement. The golden-haired Miranda smiled brightly when she saw him, but before she could say anything, Bellak spoke to Cook in a rush.

"The basket you said to use for the sweet meats," she began. "Mice—"

"They must have chewed through the bottom—" Miranda interrupted.

"We didn't know until we lifted the basket—"

She didn't need to finish. Cook threw her hands in the air and cursed loudly at them both. They cringed, but Miranda still managed to sneak a smile at Rorden before following Cook and her virulent tirade out the door.

The kitchen grew still in their absence. Rorden was pleased with this unexpected opportunity alone with the quiet Yulda. Knowing it wouldn't last long, he tried to resurrect the earlier conversation.

"So," he began. "I gather you don't much like Master Domar?"

She shrugged. "It's not my place to like him or not like him. Just to do what he says."

"That sounds like something Cook would say," he said with humor.

She frowned. "Maybe it is. What's it to you?"

He winced dramatically. "And that is definitely like Cook. Though you need a little more vinegar in your tone to get it just right. Keep practicing, though, and I'm sure you'll get it." He winked at her again, and this time her mouth twitched.

Yulda turned away from him to the bowl of peeled apples and began cutting them into thin slices.

"I always thought all stewards were haughty and ill-tempered," Rorden tried again. "I expect Master Domar is just like the rest, and it's Master Falk who was the rare breed."

Yulda shook her head. "No, Master Domar is something different. He's not just proud. The way he watches you, it's like he's got a secret. But it's not just any secret. It's a secret to do with you, and if you ever find out what it is, it'll make you weep." Her knife punctuated her words aggressively.

Rorden was taken aback by this description from the quiet scullery maid. "But surely you don't have many dealings with him, do you? I wouldn't think the steward would pay attention to the kitchen maids as long as Cook keeps her kitchen in order."

She glanced at him warily, then resumed her work without an answer.

"What is it?"

Yulda looked at him suspiciously. "I shouldn't be talking to you like this, Prestin. Cook wouldn't like it, and I don't even know—" She clamped her mouth shut, shaking her head.

Rorden sat on the table facing her, refusing to be ignored. If it had been Miranda or Bellak, he would have reached out a hand to hers, but he didn't think such a gesture would be appreciated by the young Yulda. "Please, Yulda. What's troubling you? You can trust me."

She narrowed her eyes at him. "Trust you? If there's one thing I know, it's that I can't trust you. You show up here, pretending to be lovestruck, but there's something about you that doesn't fit. The other boys would be asking me questions about the other girls right now, trying to find out how to win their affection. But you only have questions about Master Domar. He makes my skin crawl when he's around, but I can't say I trust you any more than I do him. Is Prestin even your real name?"

Rorden was at a loss for words. How had this girl seen so much in so short a time? He supposed that being the most easily ignored person in Bolen's entire household gave ample opportunity to be the most observant as well.

Instead of denying her claims, he said simply, "Does your skin crawl when I'm around?"

"No," she admitted. "But I still don't know what you're about, and I don't think I should be talking to you."

"Perhaps you're right," he agreed, and was rewarded with a surprised look. "I can see that you have good instincts about people. If those instincts warn you to stay away from me, then I suppose you'd better trust them."

Yulda paused, considering what he'd said. "I wouldn't say that exactly. But I won't listen to any more lies. Is your name really Prestin?"

He shrugged. "It works as well as any name I've been given."

"Well then, our conversation is over. Please leave now. And I would suggest that whatever your business is, you take it elsewhere or I'll tell Cook what I suspect about you." She picked up her bowl of apples and moved it to the other end of the table.

Rorden was surprised at the confidence with which she spoke. Perhaps he'd misunderstood her earlier silence. He had assumed she was timid when really she was…what? Disinterested? Mistrusting? If others underestimated her as he did, she could be a valuable ally. But first, he needed to earn her trust.

"All right, so it's not my real name, but that's not so unusual. How many people in this house know Cook's real name? Yet you trust her well enough."

"Because she isn't pretending to be anything other than what she is. I can't say the same for you. Something that you and Master Domar share."

Again, he saw a flicker in her eyes when she said his name. Was it fear? Whatever it was, just speaking of him made her uncomfortable.

"What makes you say that? Why are you so sure he isn't who he says he is?"

Yulda shrugged. "I don't know. He says he's from the lake country, but his accent seems off. My family lived there when I was a child, so I asked him about it one day, just trying to be friendly. He acted too high and mighty to respond, but I think he was lying. I think he's from somewhere else and didn't know any of the people or places I mentioned."

"Why would he lie about where he's from?"

Yulda looked at him pointedly. "You would know better than I."

Her tone was acerbic, but he took it as a good sign that she was even talking to him. He saw the interest in her eyes even as she tried to bury it. She was torn between the thought of what she should do—throw him out—and the desire to satisfy her curiosity by letting him stay.

"There's something more, though, isn't there? I see the way you look when I mention his name. What is it that you're not saying?"

Yulda barked a short laugh. "What, you think you can come in here and talk sweetly with your big, brown eyes and I'll just tell you all my secrets?"

Rorden reddened, and she laughed again.

"I don't know what sort of girls you're used to, but they must be sorry types to be so desperate to please you."

"Fine," he said exasperatedly. "Then will you just tell me what I can say to get you to trust me?"

She cocked her head at him. "A bit of sincerity, that's a start. Now, how about you tell me your real name?"

He sighed. "Rorden."

She raised one eyebrow expectantly, waiting for more.

"I'm a soldier in the Wall Guard, but beyond that I really can't say."

She nodded. "Very well, then. In return, I'll tell you about the time Master Domar nearly caused me to die of fright. I can barely stand the sight of him now, and when I told Cook about it she told me not to say anything to anyone, so I know it gave her the shivers too."

Yulda stepped closer and lowered her voice, glancing at the door to the hallway. "One night I was up late. Last one to bed every night, you know. Well, I left the kitchen for a moment, and when I came back, he was coming right out of the larder there!" She brandished her knife at a door behind Rorden.

"He was in the larder?"

"I'm not making it up," she said defensively. "I know what I saw.

Just about scared me out of my skin. But he just looked at me in his eerie way, the kind that makes me feel like he's peeling all the hair off my scalp, and said he was checking on my work. Can you imagine? Hiding in the larder late at night just to check on my work? It's given me the shivers more times than I can count ever since."

"Might I take a look?"

But just then Cook's voice sounded down the hall.

"You'd best not be here when she gets back. Go!"

Rorden jumped off the table. "When I come back, though—"

"Just go!" Yulda interrupted, her eyes widening in alarm, and she shut the door on him before he could finish.

Twenty-One

I questioned Lord Bolen as you requested. Behind the bluster, I was unable to glean anything of significance. But I agree that it's curious that he should know of Princess Honoria's plans to tour the wall when you yourself hadn't been informed. While I'm pursuing the other matter, I'll watch for anything that might shed light on his claims.

Merek read through Rorden's postscript again, then folded the letter and placed it in an inner pocket of his uniform coat. He drummed his fingers idly on the bench next to him. The alcove where he sat looked out on Lord Hegrin's brightly lit ballroom, borrowing just enough light to read the letters waiting for him when their company arrived in Berseth.

The ballroom was enormous, with a vaulted ceiling soaring high overhead and stone pillars lining either side of the long room. This was the third evening of dining and dancing Merek had endured in the past week as their little touring party worked their way west. Despite the princess's insistence that she was only visiting as a courtesy while she was in the area, the nobles who hosted them in each city insisted on throwing lavish parties in her honor, inviting dozens of guests and feasting into the late hours of the night.

Merek thought about Rorden's letter and itched to be back in Endvar. Reading between the lines, he assumed that Rorden was positioning himself close to one of Lord Bolen's staff, most likely a young woman. There was such a delay in the post that Rorden may have already discovered something useful about Master Domar. Or he may have been discovered himself. It was impossible to know, and Merek yearned to be there instead of wasting another evening in idle entertainment.

At least there had always been young men in attendance to occupy the princess's attention. Merek watched Honoria dancing with the young Hegrin, a thin man with a dimpled chin who moved almost as gracefully as she did. She was dressed in an exquisite gown of deep burgundy, which looked almost black in the candlelight and made her skin luminescent by contrast. Her hair was piled high on her head, accented with glittering silver pins that caught the light.

She was radiant. There was no other word for it. Rested from her travels and dressed in the finery that fit her as naturally as Merek's sword hilt fit his hand, she couldn't have been more beautiful. Yet, as she laughed at something her partner said, Merek felt a bitter twinge of disappointment. There was something about this woman who charmed a room as easily as she moved that felt...hollow.

He had seen something more when they were in Lorin. He remembered well returning to the camp after spending the day knee-deep in the Nardin's refuse. He'd expected to find the princess resting from the arduous day, but instead discovered her ministering to the refugees in the makeshift camp. Her simple white dress was so plain it looked like a flour sack in comparison to the sumptuous gown she now wore. But in the fading light, the pale dress had almost glowed. The fierce look in her eyes had given her an air of regal pride as though she would defend her people by sheer willpower alone. In his own tired state—his mind burdened by the destruction he had seen and the overwhelming work yet to be done—she had appeared as a beacon of hope. And it was the most beautiful sight he'd ever seen.

But once they left Lorin and turned west, it seemed that her mind was only full of food and dancing and amusement. It was hard to reconcile the image of the fierce protector dressed in humble clothing with the dazzling princess in all her finery who seemed to care only for her own comfort.

In truth, there was another reason Merek was eager to leave Berseth. Although he had seen nothing but gentlemanly civility from the son, he felt great unease being under the elder Lord Hegrin's roof. The man had a reputation for cruelty and deceit that made Merek anxious to put distance between them. Even now, Hegrin watched Honoria greedily as his son escorted her off the ballroom floor. Whatever plans might be forming in that corrupt mind of his, they would not serve her well.

Merek watched him for a few minutes more, considering whether he should intervene. Did Honoria know of Lord Hegrin's reputation? Should Merek tell her of the whispers of underhanded dealings he'd heard over the years? Merek glanced back at the banquet table, but the princess was no longer there.

"I suspected I might find you in the library, but this is equally reclusive so I guess it will do."

Honoria stepped out of the shadows of the alcove and sidled up to Merek, reaching to take the wine glass out of his hand and replace it with her own.

She took a sip from his glass, then cringed. "It's no wonder you never have any fun at these parties. Is this how you always drink?"

"My father always said that strong wine makes a wise man a fool, and a fool more likely to get a knife in his back."

She arched an eyebrow. "I find that strong wine is the best way to endure a night of boorish company. The stronger the better."

"I don't like the way it dulls my senses."

"Which is exactly what it's supposed to do, especially if you are spending your evening with the future Lord Hegrin." She took another sip, and eyed the glass suspiciously.

"You aren't enjoying yourself, Your Highness?" For some reason, this gratified him.

"Oh, I'm enjoying myself. Enjoying coming up with ways of expressing how I feel without letting him know that he's been insulted. It's quite a clever exercise."

Merek chuckled. "So you won't be disappointed to leave tomorrow?"

He expected another clever quip, but instead she looked thoughtful. "Disappointed? No, not in the way you mean."

She saw him watching her and the thoughtful expression passed. She smiled, her dark eyes twinkling mischievously. "But come. I can't bear to see you skulking in dark corners. Come dance with me, Strong."

She slipped her arm through his and pulled him toward the light of the ballroom.

Merek didn't move.

"I'm sorry, Princess, but I'm afraid I would make a very poor partner. For your sake, I must refuse."

"Refuse me?" she laughed. "You know I won't accept that."

Feeling suddenly quite warm, Merek struggled to meet her eyes. "I am…in earnest. Please Honoria, it would be humiliating for us both. You have many partners to choose from, all who are far more skilled than I."

She regarded him for a moment. Her eyes were such a dark brown that in the low light they looked deep black. "Surely you haven't always worn this uniform. Weren't you ever young once?"

"Of course I was young once. But where I come from, we don't do…this." He gestured toward the handsome couples moving in flowing rhythm.

"You don't dance?" she asked incredulously.

"No, we dance. But it's not like this. It's not an art. It's more…lively. Energetic. Whirling motion that drives away your troubles. Not a graceful performance meant to be admired."

"Hmm. I think I should like to see this kind of dancing," the princess said, taking another sip of wine.

Relieved that she was not pushing the matter further, Merek drank his own wine, swallowing half the cup in an effort to relieve his dry throat.

Except he forgot it wasn't his wine.

The wine burned, but it was the taste that caused him to gag. He choked, trying to swallow instead of spitting it all over himself. He barely got it down, but it left him coughing and struggling for breath.

Honoria, stunned at first, realized what had happened and dissolved into a fit of uncontrollable giggles. Not the measured, musical laughter she'd been using all evening. But gasping, face-reddening, unrestrained mirth.

"What *is* that?" Merek demanded when he could speak.

"It's awful, isn't it? But you're not supposed to guzzle it all at once!" She burst into another fit of giggles, pressing her face into his arm and shaking with laughter.

"Wine is not supposed to taste like that. If that's what they are drinking," he said, nodding to the dancing couples, "how can they even stand to look at each other? The smell of their partner's breath must be revolting!" Still, the sight of the princess laughing pleased him.

Honoria took a deep breath to calm herself, but her eyes still danced with amusement. "Hegrin is quite proud of it. He says it's a special family recipe that is generations old, but I suspect that someone must have recorded the method wrong somewhere along the line. Either that or they develop an immunity to it in the womb. It's supposed to be quite intoxicating, but who could ever stomach enough of it to know?"

Merek pointedly switched glasses with her again and downed the rest of his own watered down drink. As he did so, he noticed Lord Hegrin watching them steadily, a dark expression on his face. His son chatted amiably with another young woman, but his smile faltered when he glanced their direction.

"Your Highness, I think it's time that you rejoin your party."

"I would rather stay here with you and guess what wretched ingredients Lord Hegrin uses in his wine. Perhaps the horn of a wild boar, soaked until the marrow is drinkable?"

Merek removed Honoria's hand from his arm, pulling away to put distance between them.

"Forgive me, Your Highness, but it's not appropriate for us to be so publicly familiar."

"Familiar?" she laughed. "You're practically an uncle to me, Strong. No one could suspect you of any impropriety."

An unpleasant sensation churned in his stomach. Blasted wine.

"But I suppose it is rude to linger too long," Honoria said, her smile fading. "Thank you for the diversion. I never suspected that hiding in dark corners could be so amusing. Now I'll know where to go when my companions become too dull."

The thought of her returning to Hegrin's side tugged at him. "Careful, Princess," Merek warned. "There's a fine line between enjoying humor at your companions' expense and showing contempt for them."

She stifled a yawn. "Wise words for a skulker. But I'm afraid I crossed that line somewhere in the middle of dinner."

Merek lowered his voice. "Then why are we wasting our time here? I understand that you don't want to offend your subjects, but must we really prolong our journey just so that you can spend your evenings dancing with men who bore…"

He trailed off as something connected in his mind. The evenings of dining and dancing with the noble houses. Going so far out of their way to visit Lord Hegrin. It wasn't merely a coincidence that each evening had included an unmarried son or heir to keep her company.

It was intended.

The wine must have indeed been strong to cause the heat of anger that suddenly boiled inside of him. He looked sharply at the princess. She watched him warily, a guilty flush creeping into her cheeks.

"I have no tolerance for deception, Honoria. Answer me honestly. Did you manipulate me into bringing you on this tour so that you could...*go courting?*"

"Keep your voice down, Strong," Honoria begged, blushing furiously.

Shame washed over him, stoking his anger. "I've been a fool. A trusting, idiotic fool. What else have you kept from me?"

"Calm down, it's not as bad as that. But this isn't the place to have this conversation, especially while you're angry."

Merek didn't care about the room full of people. All he could think of was Rorden and Aiya and the danger they were putting themselves in without his help. All because he'd been sent on a foolish errand for a careless girl who thought she could use him with no thought of the consequences. He felt sick with fury and didn't trust himself to speak.

"We'll speak of this later," Honoria said curtly, then turned to walk away.

Merek grabbed her arm.

She gasped. "What do you—"

"You lied to me. You owe me an explanation. Now." He kept his voice even, but she shrank a little under his glare.

After a moment's pause, she nodded and walked to the nearest set of doors opening onto a small balcony.

A late summer rainstorm had blown through earlier in the evening, leaving the outside air cool and moist. The breeze gusted about them, warning of additional storms before the night was over. The wind felt soothing against Merek's skin, but his anger still simmered dangerously.

So did Honoria's.

As soon as they were outside, she whirled on him. "You will not handle me in such a manner, Strong. My own father doesn't treat me that way. You certainly don't have the right."

"Save your indignation for someone who deserves it," Merek growled. "You have no right to take me away from my duty on false pretenses, endangering people that I care about. If you were a soldier under my command, you would be facing serious disciplinary measures for such deception."

"But I'm not, am I?" she spat. "And you will never treat me like that again. Is that understood?"

Unexpectedly, Merek found himself taking a step back. She spoke with the force of an experienced captain twice her age, despite standing more than a full head shorter than he and having to crane her neck to stare him down.

"I apologize for the disrespect, *Princess*." He poured all the disgust he felt into the word. She flinched visibly.

He turned his back on her and strode to the balcony's edge. The light from the open doors illuminated the stone balustrade, but all was black beyond it. Merek gripped the railing and breathed deeply, willing himself to calm down. He'd been made a fool, but all was not lost. He was only five days from Endvar if he made an early start in the morning and cut across country. The sooner he could put distance between himself and this woman, the better.

But a part of him knew he couldn't leave. Captain Drenall would see the princess safely home, but to abandon her would do irreparable harm to his relationship with Sindal. He would have to stay, at least for the time being.

He rubbed his forehead in frustration, trying to see a way out of his predicament. She had trapped him too well.

Silently, Honoria stepped up beside him. He braced himself for more angry words, but she stood quietly.

"I'm sorry that I deceived you." Her voice was quiet and she appeared to speak with great effort. "I knew that you would figure it out eventually, but oh how I wished you wouldn't!"

Merek said nothing. He wasn't ready to let go of his anger, no matter how sincere her apology. But he listened.

"No one knows but my father. We thought it might seem more... natural this way."

"Why me?" Merek asked flatly. "Why not just travel around Rahm with Captain Drenall? Why the ruse of touring the wall?"

Honoria looked at him, her eyes wide and pleading. "It isn't a ruse. I truly want to see the damage to the wall. Everything I've said about that is true. I'm committed to doing what's best for my people and serving in my father's stead. I'm sorry that I deceived you about the nature of the other...visits." She grimaced.

"You say that as though you aren't enjoying yourself," he scoffed.

She just shook her head and turned her face away into the wind. He caught a faint flowery scent on the breeze, and something that made him feel unaccountably strange. Almost homesick. Inwardly he cursed the wine that had toyed with his emotions so much that night.

"Your Highness?" a voice asked hesitantly from the open door.

Merek groaned softly. He didn't trust himself to be civil to Hegrin or anyone else at the moment.

Honoria turned to the young man and smiled weakly. "Forgive me for my bad manners. An urgent matter has come up that demands my attention. The captain is helping me sort it out."

"Is there anything I can do to help?" A few tentative footsteps sounded as he stepped onto the balcony.

"We're almost finished. Thank you for giving us a little privacy."

The footsteps retreated reluctantly and Honoria returned to stand beside Merek, placing her hands on the railing.

She sighed softly. "This is not what I desire," she said in a near whisper. "What you said earlier about contempt is true. Trying to choose a husband among those whom I don't respect—" Her voice caught and she paused. Clearing her throat, she continued with resolution. "But it's my duty, just as it was my father's before me, and I will do what my kingdom demands of me."

"You're not the only one who has a duty to perform," Merek said, but some of the hostility had leaked from his tone.

"I know. Please forgive me for being inconsiderate of you and the sacrifices you have made."

"I received word tonight that makes me anxious to return to End-var. Would you consider allowing Captain Drenall to complete the tour in my absence?"

"Please, don't leave me to do this alone." Honoria touched his hand, and he reflexively pulled it away. Stricken, she took a step back. Gone was the mask of dazzling charm. She looked at him with desperate uncertainty.

He was reminded again of that night in Lorin and felt his resolve weakening. For as much as his duty pulled him back to Endvar, he also had a duty to her.

Honoria breathed deeply and lifted her chin, meeting his eyes. "Captain Strong, it was wrong of me to be dishonest with you. I would be grateful if you would continue to accompany me on my journey, but if you are needed elsewhere, I will release you with gratitude for the honorable service you have performed."

Merek saw how it pained her to say the words. Hearing her say them anyway washed away the last of his resistance. He sighed heavily. "I warned you that nothing good comes from strong wine."

She didn't speak, waiting breathlessly for his decision.

"If you ask it of me, I will finish the tour."

She exhaled in relief. "Oh yes, please!" She moved as though to reach for him again, but thought better of it and clasped her hands.

He held out a finger. "But I have one request. Now that I know your added purpose, I insist on reviewing our itinerary and making changes as I see fit."

"You want to advise me on my marriage prospects?" she sputtered.

"Not particularly, except as they unnecessarily impede our progress. Although," he added, eyeing the ballroom. "It seems you could use some sound advice."

She flushed. "I suppose it wouldn't hurt to have another opinion. But please, be kind. I'm not sure I can take any more of your wicked tongue lashings."

Merek snorted. "*My* tongue lashings? It's been years since I've been rebuked so soundly. If you weren't my superior, I would have been tempted to draw my sword and put you in your place."

Honoria laughed a little, shyly, but relieved. And although he still worried about Rorden and the danger brewing in Endvar, Merek was glad that he would be able to hear the sound of her laugh for a few more weeks.

Twenty-Two

Aiya awoke while it was yet dark. The night had been hot and humid, and she'd had trouble sleeping, so it was a relief to hear the soothing sound of rain on the city streets. A cool breeze blew through her open window, and she lay for a few minutes enjoying the feeling of it against her skin.

As she lay there, she grew drowsy and considered going back to sleep. But then her eyes snapped open. A noise. Had she just imagined it? She lay still, her senses alert. Yes, there was definitely movement in the next room.

Without making a sound, Aiya slipped from her bed and reached for her knife under the mattress. She slowly opened her door.

The kitchen was lit only by the faint outline of gray visible around the edges of the curtained window, but it was enough light to see that the room was empty. Aiya paused, waiting, ears straining for the source of the sound she had heard.

Suddenly a shape loomed out of the fireplace on her left. She reacted with a swipe of the knife, then moved swiftly toward the outer door.

There was a cry of pain, and Aiya gasped, dropping her knife.

"Imar! What are you doing?" She ran to the window and opened the curtain to let in more light. Imar stood before her in his nightclothes, holding his upper arm.

"Confound you, Aiya! Why couldn't you just light a candle like a normal woman instead of attacking me like some thief in the night?" he growled, hastily stuffing something into his pocket with sooty fingers.

"Let me see your arm," she said, contrite. He removed his hand and allowed her to give the wound a quick look. It was bleeding freely, but wasn't very deep. "It's just a scratch. You should know better than to go sneaking around in the dark," she scolded. "What else did you expect me to do?"

Imar just grunted as Aiya moved to light a candle so that she could dress his wound. She tossed her long braid over her shoulder, then rolled up the sleeve of his night shirt and held a cloth on his arm to staunch the bleeding. There had been a great awkwardness between them since she had refused to go to Branvik, as though neither of them knew quite how to talk to the other anymore. He was set to leave on his journey at dawn, and she regretted not finding a way to reconcile before he left.

"I'm sorry I hurt you," Aiya said. "But you shouldn't have been acting like an intruder. What were you doing, anyway?"

"This is not how I wanted to tell you. I was hoping to make it a grand gift."

Aiya unrolled a length of bandage. "A gift of what?"

Imar didn't answer right away. She glanced at him and was surprised to see him looking at her with tenderness in his eyes.

The sudden emotion unnerved her, and she pulled away. "Imar, what is it? Is something wrong?"

He laid a hand over hers. "I always hoped that you would find love again. I just thought after so many years that I would be more ready to let you go. But if there was ever a man that I could trust to keep you safe, it's Captain Strong."

Aiya froze. Her heart leaped to her throat and she barely choked out the words. "Captain Strong? I don't know what you're saying."

Imar smiled knowingly. "I've suspected for some time that you had feelings for him, but it's only recently that it's become clear that he returns your affection."

Aiya felt sick. She wanted to explain that the captain didn't feel that way for her, but then she would have to come up with another reason to excuse the secret meetings—which surely Imar knew about. So instead, she just protested lamely with, "It's not what you think."

"Perhaps not. Not yet, at least. That's why I've been saving this."

He reached into a pocket and retrieved a small velvet bag.

Aiya gasped. "Imar, you fool!" she hissed. "What are you doing with that? Do you want to get us both killed?"

Imar laid the velvet pouch on the table mournfully. "I'm sorry I didn't tell you. That night…everything happened so fast. Tupin must have dropped them because when I came to the house…" he trailed off, watching Aiya warily.

The memory rose unbidden into Aiya's mind. Two men bursting into the house and cutting down Tupin before he could even cry out in alarm. They'd been preparing to flee, hastily packing a few provisions and hoping to escape before Behni's father discovered the theft. Aiya was too terrified to even be angry with Tupin when he'd revealed what he'd done.

And then Tupin died right in front of her. Her mind shied away from that moment and instead focused on Imar. Her brother had interrupted the attack, giving Aiya time to flee. She grabbed Mara and escaped out a window, holding her daughter tightly against her chest as she jumped to the ground below. It wasn't far, but Mara cried out and alerted a man outside. Soon he was upon them, and Aiya threw herself over her daughter to protect her. But the attack didn't come. Because Imar was there.

If only that was how it had ended. Imar the hero. Mara safe. How different these years would have been if Mara had lived.

And here he sat, holding that cursed bag. The bag which held the stolen jewels that her husband and daughter had died for. A king's fortune, but worth nothing in her eyes.

"How could you?" she whispered, her throat tight with emotion.

"I didn't know what else to do with them. I didn't realize I still had them until several days later, and then I didn't dare tell you. I always thought there would be a right time, but there never was. Then I thought, maybe you could use them someday to start over, if you ever found love again."

"What, like a dowry?" She laughed bitterly. Some dowry. Bought with the blood of her dead family. But she knew that Imar couldn't fully understand. He hadn't left a family behind when they fled. He hadn't held his daughter in his arms as she died.

But he *had* been the one to drag Aiya from the flames when her uncle's men set the house on fire. He had saved her, even when she didn't want to be saved.

"I know you mean well, Imar," she said, trying to swallow the grief that welled anew. "But I will never touch those stones." Aiya tied the bandage roughly around his arm and busied herself cleaning up.

Imar frowned. "I only want to help you find happiness. I'm glad you have found love again—"

"Please!" Aiya interrupted sharply. "Don't speak of things you don't understand."

Imar looked as though he'd been slapped. She hadn't meant to speak so harshly, but if he said anything else about this supposed future she had with Captain Strong, she would no longer be able to hold back the tears. The lies and the disappointment were too great. She took a deep breath and shuddered as she exhaled.

"I do appreciate your kindness," she conceded. "And if there comes a time when your hopes are fulfilled, you will be the first to know."

Aiya let Imar finish his travel preparations alone. She should have fussed over him, making sure he hadn't forgotten anything. Imar had never had a wife to do this for him. They only had each other. But she was still shaken by the sight of that black velvet bag and could barely look him in the eye. She didn't know what he'd done with it, and didn't ask. Just so long as she never had to see it again.

As she embraced him on the doorstep, she did manage to smile a little. "I'm sorry about the arm."

He smiled back grudgingly. "I suppose you think you've proven that you can take care of yourself after all. But I know better. Stay away from Hala and keep the captain close. But not too close." He smirked.

Aiya's insides twisted with the deception. Someday she would have to explain. Or contrive a more convincing lie.

Dearest Lotta,

Your letters have finally caught up with me in Cillith, and I have enjoyed a pleasant afternoon perusing them at my leisure. As always, it's been rejuvenating to my soul to hear your voice. I didn't even care when you scolded me about wearing trousers because it brought your face to mind very clearly. I must admit that I've grown quite accustomed to them, though I shall not admit such to Captain Strong. My pride would suffer if he learned that the practical nature of the garments holds a certain appeal for me. He insists that women's riding attire is poorly suited to the equine sports. I told him that is precisely the point, as we women care less for sport than we do for fashion. He simply looked at me as if I was mad. I suppose that a man who wears the same uniform day after day can't be expected to appreciate the sublime joys of refined fashion.

We're staying at an inn tonight, so I have no parties or balls to distract me. That's not a complaint, as I will be able to devote my full attention to penning a letter to you. I'll pretend that I'm sitting by your side in your kitchen, eating Pedr's fresh cinnamon bread as I relate the tales of these past days, instead of sitting in a stuffy upper room wedged between a desk and a bed with no proper room to stretch my legs.

You may wonder how I came to be in Cillith. We've altered our route and are cutting across the country on our way to Haldin. There's nothing of interest regarding damage to the wall there, but Captain Strong has business to conduct, and I have a great interest in seeing the north country myself. It's Strong's homeland and I suspect holds unique perspectives on his character, something I feel driven of late to understand. Behind his mild, reserved exterior is a fire that burns hot when kindled, one of many intriguing paradoxes I've discovered in our time together. I fear he finds me frivolous, vain, and lacking in judgment (and I confess that I'm all of those things at times). But, in spite of that, he's a loyal companion whom I would want on my side in a conflict.

Haldin will be our last stop on our tour, and then I'll be on my way home. Edvin expects that we'll be home in as little as ten days. I think he's looking forward to it more than I am. I've learned so much in these past weeks and hope that you will find me improved when you see me again. At every turn it seems I'm being reminded that I don't know as much as I think I do.

Shall I give you an example? Three days ago we were in Yaneth. Captain Strong informed me before we arrived that the damage to the wall in that area was a result of the citizens disassembling the stones and using them to build their homes and corral their animals. (No easy feat, as I've experienced the strength necessary to move even one stone for myself.)

I thought I was prepared for what I would see, expecting to find a few places where stone needed to be replaced. But when we came over a grassy hill and saw the area for the first time, I was shocked. The entire wall was missing! Only the large foundation stones remained, just visible above the earth. Apparently what started as a clandestine raid by a few villagers has become an accepted practice by them all.

I confess it made me angry. Strong has told me stories of the men who sacrificed and died to build the wall during my grandfather's time. To see their labor treated with such selfish contempt made me incensed. I entered the town with half a mind to have them all arrested for stealing from the king.

But then I saw the sod huts many of the people lived in, and heard the tales of years of contention between village leaders that have led to disputations with merchants and inflated timber costs. With no substantial local source of timber (I don't understand why anyone would choose to live in that place of uninspiring prairies and swamplands), I began to understand why the people had turned to the wall. They weren't thieves because they had no honor. They were thieves out of desperation. I felt ashamed of my anger and instead searched for a way to help. It will take some time to untangle that difficult knot, but I've written to my father in hopes that he'll know what to do.

These experiences make me loath to return home to a life of privilege. It inspires me to see the people of Rahm and learn what makes their challenges unique and what they value most in this world. I feel less like an ornament and more like I have a true connection with the people in our kingdom. And yes, I will say it. It saddens me that my father has neglected that connection in recent years.

Still, I won't miss sleeping on the ground, wearing dirty clothing, and eating dried food that is hardly distinguishable as what it once was. I do appreciate your concern about my health and comfort. I've been well cared for, as much as is possible in rough conditions. Biren is very thoughtful, though her duties have included caring for horses and helping with meals as well as tending to me. It may take some adjusting for both of us to remember how I should be properly spoiled when I return, but I will do my best.

Biren has just informed me that my bath is ready, so I must close before my water cools. My room is very well-furnished for an inn, despite how I disparaged the establishment earlier when comparing it to resting at your own hearth. In addition to a private bath, I've been told that they are renowned for their sumptuous dining and evening entertainment.

This is the point where if we were together you would gently remind me that I haven't answered all of your questions. That is because I'm trying to distract you from the disappointment you will feel when I tell you that there is one way in which my situation has not improved. My feelings on the subject of marriage are largely unchanged. My feelings on the individuals we discussed before my departure are also unchanged. (Or, if they have changed, it's for the worse.)

But do not despair. There's reason to be optimistic. An idea has come to mind that I would like to discuss with you when I return. It's still stewing, and I haven't fully committed to it, but when it occurred to me it was such a brilliant solution that I wondered why I had never considered it before.

Ria paused, pressing the quill pen to her lips thoughtfully, considering whether or not to say more. She looked out the large bay window onto the inn yard bordered by a smokehouse and stables. Grooms and maids moved about their evening chores, one lad chasing the chickens and trying to herd them into their coop, their squawks drifting through the open window on the breeze.

Deciding that the matter was too delicate to discuss in writing, Ria left the subject alone and instead asked Lotta if she might look in on her father. She didn't need to tell her why she was concerned. Lotta would understand.

Her father's letters had been few and uncharacteristically brief since Ria had left home. In the beginning, he'd been in a foul mood and alternated between criticizing everyone in his household and begging her to come home. More recently, he had hinted at a project that was occupying much of his time. She was glad he'd found something to capture his interest but was concerned that he hadn't even acknowledged the detailed reports she'd sent. He should have at least received her report from Lorin, and likely the others as well. She'd expected to hear some wise and generous counsel, praising her for her efforts and assuring her that she had his full support. Instead, he'd merely scrawled a few disinterested lines hinting at a big surprise on her return.

Ria sighed and set aside the letter and pen.

Her bedchamber opened directly onto a private bathing room with stone floors and an open hearth for winter months. After settling into the bath, she asked Biren to leave her alone with her thoughts so she could relax uninterrupted.

A small window showed a sky vibrant in pink and orange as the sun set somewhere behind the city. Ria would have loved to have gone out to see more of Cillith and its people, but they planned an early start the following morning, and she wanted to take full advantage of a comfortable bed that night. Although she'd adjusted to sleeping on the ground—it only took her a few minutes each morning to be civil instead of half the day—a bed was a luxury she would not take for granted.

Biren didn't return, but Ria was restless and couldn't fully relax. Instead, she decided to end her bath early and write a letter to her father before retiring. The air coming through the window was cool as Ria dressed in her thin nightdress, a sign that summer was nearing its end and autumn would soon be upon them. This made her feel somewhat mournful as she slipped her linen dressing gown over her shoulders.

A sound in her bedchamber signaled Biren's return. Ria suddenly felt famished. Wise Biren, anticipating her need before she had. She would eat while Biren combed the tangles from her wet hair.

Ria went eagerly to the next room, but was several steps in before she realized that Biren wasn't there. Instead, a man bent over the table before the window, his back turned to her.

"What are you doing?" she demanded.

The man spun around guiltily, holding her letter to Lotta. He was dressed roughly and had stringy hair and a coarse beard.

Enraged that a filthy stranger would dare to handle her things, Ria stomped toward him. "You have no business here! Leave at once!"

The man glanced at the door, but he didn't move. He sized her up and slipped his hand into an inner waistcoat pocket, withdrawing a small blade.

At once Ria felt very exposed, facing this stranger with no weapon and dressed in only her nightclothes. What was she doing? Shouldn't she have been yelling for help? Or better yet, running the other way? With dread, she realized that she was standing between the stranger and the only exit.

Ria turned to flee as the intruder lunged for her. But it was too late. She shrieked—an anemic, pitiful sound that was cut off as he plowed into her from behind. She fell against a small table, knocking it to the floor and shattering a vase of flowers with a terrific crash.

Pain flashed through her hip and side as she fell among the broken glass. Wet hair spilled over her face, and she grasped blindly for something she could use as a weapon. But in an instant, the man bounded up and ran for the door.

Over the sound of her own frantic breathing, Ria heard footsteps running down the hall. She scrambled to her knees, pulling strands of hair out of her mouth. Exclamations of surprise and a few curses piled on top of each other as Biren, Captain Strong, and two other soldiers crowded the doorway.

"Go! Get him!" she yelled urgently, waving them away.

The soldiers ran in opposite directions down the hall. Biren hurried to her side, face pale and eyes wide.

"My lady! What happened? Are you hurt?" She helped Ria to her feet.

"He didn't hurt me. I'm all right," she said, her voice shaking.

Biren pleaded with her to rest, but Ria couldn't sit still. Instead she paced, wishing that the soldiers would return with word of the intruder's capture. Exhaustion had fled, and her senses were heightened magnificently.

"He was right here," she said, standing before the writing table. "I heard a noise and thought it was you, but it was that man." Ria had the sense that she'd said these words before. Might she be babbling? The way her mind was racing, she couldn't be sure.

"Shall I get you some wine to calm your nerves?" Biren offered.

At her words, Ria felt thirsty. "Please."

Left alone, Ria paced in front of the window, watching the gathering night. Suddenly, she was gripped with intense fear at the thought of the oncoming darkness and quickly closed and latched the window. When a booted footstep sounded in the open doorway, she jumped.

It was only Captain Strong.

She hadn't realized she was holding in her breath until it all came out in a rush.

"Did you find him?" she asked, her voice sounding unnaturally high in her ears.

The captain's gray eyes were angry. "Drenall is leading a search with his men, but in an unfamiliar city..." He shook his head in frustration.

"I deeply regret failing to protect you, my lady. There should have been a guard posted to your room. I'll find out why he wasn't at his post, I assure you."

Ria nodded. She still felt jittery, like she didn't belong in her own skin, but it was reassuring to have Captain Strong there.

That is, until he stepped close to her and gently gripped her shoulders. "Are you sure you're all right, Honoria?" he asked, searching her face.

His concern unnerved her. Anger was good. It kept her strong. But this tenderness…it threatened her composure.

She pulled away from his touch, suddenly conscious of the fact that she was wearing no more than a simple nightdress and thin dressing gown, with her hair drying in a tangled mess around her shoulders.

"I'm well enough. Just a little shaken." *A little?* Surely he sensed her quivering. Time for a distraction. "Do you have any idea what he wanted?"

"I can't say. Was it just a common thief? Or someone specifically looking for the princess? We're just lucky that he didn't intend you harm."

An alternate scene flashed through Ria's mind of the intruder coming into her bathing room while she was alone. She shivered and felt suddenly weak. The surge of energy that had sustained her was passing, leaving her drained.

"Have you noticed anything missing?" Captain Strong asked.

"No, I didn't even look." Now that she was safe, Ria felt so tired. As she turned to the table, her vision wavered and she staggered. Strong reached forward to steady her, and as he touched her, pain flared in her side. She gasped.

He pulled away in alarm. "What is it?"

Ria hunched over, cradling her side. This was more than a simple bruise. It felt like her skin was ripping. Carefully, she drew her loose dressing gown aside and gaped at the red stain seeping through a tear in her nightdress.

Captain Strong swore under his breath. He grabbed the sleeve of her dressing gown and yanked it from her shoulders. "Why didn't you tell me you were hurt?" he demanded.

"Obviously I didn't know, did I?" she snapped, and then closed her eyes against the feeling of vertigo that swept over her. All she could see was red.

She felt his hands on her, trying to move her, but she resisted, shrugging him off. If she could just get to the window, the cool air would help. She smelled the blood and felt the tackiness of it on her fingers.

Don't think about it. Just breathe. But her throat was constricted. The air felt suffocating. Why had she closed the window?

She could hear Captain Strong saying her name, but she pushed him away. She couldn't focus on anything except breathing. And then his voice grew muffled. She opened her eyes, stumbling as she desperately tried to find the chair that should have been nearby. A familiar rushing sound filled her head, dampening all other noise. And then all went black.

Twenty-Three

Merek woke with a start. Again. The high-backed chair wasn't conducive to sleep, but the intensity of the previous night had left him unspeakably weary. Biren had refused to leave Honoria's side as well and now slumbered in a plushly padded chair near her lady's bed, wrapped in a woolen blanket.

The long-toothed physician had assured him that the princess was in no danger. Her injuries were not that severe, he'd explained. Apparently she had only minor cuts from broken glass, and the only reason he had sewn the deepest laceration was to help it heal while traveling.

But Merek wouldn't rest until Honoria wakened. The physician had given her a pain draught that left her groggy and disoriented, then followed it up with a sleeping draught due to the trauma of the evening. Since then, she'd been unnaturally still for hours, and Merek was desperate to know for himself that she was well.

Dawn lit the room with a cold light, bringing the muted sound of early morning birds outside. Honoria lay as still as she had all night, looking small and young in comparison to the dynamic fiery woman he knew. She looked so lifeless that more than once during the dark, candlelit hours Merek had approached the bed to make sure she was breathing.

Merek stood and stretched. Drenall had returned empty-handed midway through the night. The grizzled veteran had turned the matter over to the local peacekeepers, but they both knew the best chance for catching the intruder had passed. They would probably never find him or discover his intent.

Merek quietly slipped out the door and downstairs to the inn's common room. It was empty except for a handful of Drenall's soldiers and the physician, who sat at a table alone eating a hot breakfast of eggs fried with tomatoes and summer squash. He waved his fork at Merek, gesturing him over.

"You said she would awaken by morning," Merek said by way of greeting.

The physician just shrugged and swallowed. "It's still morning and will be for some hours more. It's difficult to know how different draughts will affect individuals you've never treated before. But she will wake, Captain, and sooner rather than later."

Merek sat at the table across from the physician. The man ate voraciously, hunched over his plate and smacking his lips, but the very smell of the food turned Merek's stomach. He rested his head in his hands, giving in momentarily to the weight of exhaustion from a sleepless night.

The physician eyed him. "I admire your concern for the young lady, but it might be good for you to get some rest."

Merek just grunted.

"Well, at least get something to eat." The physician motioned to the innkeeper's daughter to bring another plate of food.

The girl produced it in minutes, but Merek just stared at it.

"Go on, you need your strength."

Merek opened his mouth to protest but was interrupted by the sound of hasty footsteps on the stairs. Grasping the balustrade, Biren called out, "She's awake!" before turning and running back the way she had come.

Merek began to stand, but the physician stopped him with a hand on his shoulder. "Let me examine her first," he said. "Eat. She's not going anywhere."

Merek clenched his jaw in frustration, but obeyed. He picked at his food while he waited, bouncing his knee in impatience.

After what seemed like an eternity, the stairs creaked and the physician returned, a pleased expression on his face. "Her Highness is doing very well. She will need to rest another day or so, and it would be best to get a carriage—"

But Merek wasn't listening. He brushed past the physician and raced up the stairs to the princess's room.

Honoria was laying on one side when he entered, looking pale and weak with her brown hair matted from sleep.

"Oh, it's you, Captain," she said, pushing herself up onto one elbow. "I thought it was a herd of horses by the thundering down the hall."

Merek felt suddenly sheepish and paused in the doorway, unsure of whether or not to enter her room. In the anxiety of the night, he'd thought nothing of it, but now that she was awake he felt like it was improper.

"Well, come in, Strong," Honoria said, easing herself up to a seated position as Biren arranged pillows behind her back. "I've already shamed myself in front of you in almost every way imaginable, so I'm sure there can't be any harm in letting you see me in this wretched state."

"Nonsense," he said, stepping further into the room. "You handled the events of last night with great courage. No one would expect beauty too."

She grimaced, and he realized that it didn't sound as much like the compliment he'd intended. "You're not exactly looking your best this morning either, Captain, with your bloodshot eyes and general… dishabille. You look as though you haven't slept all night."

Merek reddened, noticing for the first time his untucked shirt, open waistcoat, and loosened collar. As he hastily tended to his appearance, Biren leaned down and whispered something into the princess's ear. Honoria's eyes widened slightly and flickered to the wooden chair at the foot of her bed where Merek had spent the night.

"Oh," she said, looking chagrined. "I see that I've worried you needlessly. Forgive me, I should have warned you. It wasn't the injury which caused...You see, I don't handle blood well. Particularly my own."

Merek brought the chair closer and sat next to her bed. "I feared the worst at first, but the physician assures me that your wounds are very mild." He meant it reassuringly, but she frowned.

"You're supposed to be making me feel better, not even more foolish."

He grinned, an impish streak rising as his worry dissipated. "Very well, how is this?" He cleared his throat. "You bled for hours and narrowly escaped death. The physician said he'd never seen such grievous wounds. But what truly awed him is how you refused the pain draught and endured his ministrations with nothing but your own regal honor to comfort you." He paused dramatically, then concluded, "That's what I will put in the official report to your father."

Honoria blinked at him. "I really don't like you very much."

"Oh really? That's not what you said last night after taking the pain draught. Let's see, what was it you said about my eyes?" He paused, pretending to remember.

Honoria gasped, her face reddening. "I didn't!" She looked at Biren. "Please tell me I didn't say any such thing!"

Biren shrugged noncommittally and Merek's esteem for the young maid raised considerably.

Honoria buried her face in the quilt. "Tell me when he's gone, Biren," she moaned. "I'm sure I shan't be able to face him again."

Merek laughed, and she looked up, her eyes narrowing suspiciously.

"Merek Strong," she said haughtily. "You're a cruel man with the blackest of hearts. How dare you take advantage of a poor young lady whose wits have been compromised?"

He laughed harder. "Your wits are just as sharp as ever. It seemed an opportunity that I'm not likely to ever have again."

"Well, I suppose that I wouldn't have hesitated to do the same."

She laughed a little, then winced. "But perhaps you might refrain from amusement at my expense for a few days?" She settled back against the pillow and closed her eyes.

Merek immediately felt ashamed for causing her discomfort. What was he doing? Teasing her when she was wounded and should be resting? And to be so relaxed about it, too. It was almost like… something he couldn't name, but seemed distantly familiar. That light feeling in his chest that came as if from a memory of a former life.

And then the horrible realization struck him.

Was he actually *flirting* with the princess?

Instantly his mirth dampened with shame. This was not to be tolerated, and he chided himself for being a fool. He needed rest and food and a little distance to get his composure back before she noticed his lapse. But first, he needed an excuse to leave.

"You must be famished. Might I get you some breakfast, Your Highness?" he asked, standing.

She opened her eyes. "Actually, I was just going to ask Biren to get me something to eat. Just something light, please."

The quiet girl nodded, and Merek followed her toward the door.

"Please stay, Strong," Honoria said. "There's something I want to speak with you about."

Biren paused in the doorway, looking back and forth uncertainly between the two of them.

"Thank you, Biren," the princess said dismissively, and the maid had no choice but to leave the room. "Close the door, Strong."

Merek closed the door reluctantly, then returned to her side, cursing himself for having lost control of his tongue. He needed to leave the room to clear his head, but a part of him was pleased that she'd asked him to stay. Disgusted with himself, he sat.

Honoria's smile faded when they were alone. "Did you mean it when you said you would report this incident to the king?"

Merek paused. That wasn't a question he'd expected. "I'll only report the facts. No embellishment."

"Of course. I just mean—" She looked down at the quilt, tracing a pattern in the stitching with her forefinger. "Have you been sending regular reports to my father?"

"Well, yes. It would be expected in any case, but whereas I had charge of his daughter—" *His daughter!* What would Sindal think of his behavior? "—I thought more frequent reports were in order. I've been writing to him at each stop on our tour."

The princess nodded, as if this was something she should have expected. "Does he respond?" Her hand drifted to her right ear and absently curled a lock of hair behind it.

"What is this about? You seem…concerned."

"It's nothing."

"You're not a very good liar," he accused.

She laughed, one short burst of irony. "Of course I'm a good liar. Weren't you recently angry with me for being dishonest with you?"

"That's not what I meant," he said, shaking his head. "Yes, you're good at telling people what they want to hear. You're skilled at bending the truth. But you're not good at telling an out-and-out lie. That's not a criticism. It's a compliment. It's reassuring that maybe I can trust some of what you say."

She looked at him as though she was measuring something with her gaze. Then she sighed. "I ask these questions because I've heard very little from my father since I left Albon. I thought if he had been writing to you, you might know more of his state of mind."

Merek chuckled bitterly. "I'm afraid ours is a very one-sided conversation."

"I see."

"It wasn't always that way, but this past year has left me in a very different place with your father than I've ever been."

Honoria sat up straighter, wincing as she shifted. "I blamed you at first for the change in his mood. I am sorry for that. I see now that it is outside you, or me, or anyone else."

"You do?"

"I don't understand it, not really. I fear he is fighting a war inside himself that I can't touch. I thought at first I could, and I tried—oh, how I tried! But getting away for a time and seeing things from a distance, I see now that I can't."

Merek leaned forward, resting his forearms on his knees. "Tell me how he's changed."

Honoria hesitated as if uncertain what to say. "I don't know when or how it began. When I came home from my travels, I noticed that he didn't laugh as easily or enjoy life as much as he did before. He was sometimes surly—something he rarely was before—and he would lose his temper over small things. Not with me," she quickly amended, "but with the servants."

"And you assumed it was my fault? Because I refused his appointment to general?"

"My father was still very angry with you, I could see that. But after I'd been home for a time, I learned about the nightmares. Some nights he would be tormented by gripping dreams that made him thrash about in his sleep, yelling and only waking after great effort. The next day he wouldn't speak of them, but would be withdrawn, as though continuing to battle whatever demon he had faced in the night."

"Has he seen the physician?"

A knock sounded on the door, and Biren entered with a tray of fresh bread and sliced summer melons. Honoria's intense expression faded to a pleasant smile. "Thank you, Biren. You may leave the tray. If I need anything more, I'll let you know."

Merek moved a small table closer to the bed—a twin to the one that had been destroyed the previous night—and Biren placed the tray on it, then left the room with a silent curtsy. Honoria reached for the cup and sipped its contents slowly, but ignored the food.

"Sleeping draughts don't help," she continued when they were alone again. "The nightmares still come, and the draughts make it even more difficult to wake. I fear that he's now avoiding sleep entirely, though he won't admit it. It's beginning to color more than just his relationship with you. His first letter to me after I left was full of all manner of accusations against the household staff. Ridiculous things that he would never believe if he were in his right mind."

As troubling as this news was about his old friend, Merek felt oddly relieved to finally have an explanation for Sindal's spiteful behavior.

Honoria leaned back against the pillow and turned away to look out the window. Even with her appearance untended, she was lovely. The daylight was warm and brought life and color to her skin. But it didn't ease the look of consternation on her brow.

"Sometimes I regret leaving him alone," she said quietly. "If he's worsened in my absence, I will never forgive myself."

Wanting to ease her suffering, Merek made a quick decision. "I'll speak with Captain Drenall today about returning home immediately. It may take a day or two to hire a suitable carriage, but we can have you home before the end of the week."

Honoria turned her gaze from the window and fixed it on him, her dark eyes inscrutable. "I'm not going home, Strong," she said, a note of surprise in her voice. "Our tour is not finished."

"But, Honoria," Merek said, frowning in puzzlement. "You need rest and your father needs you. Under the circumstances, it seems prudent to cut your tour short and send you home."

She smirked. "So quick to jump to the wrong conclusion. And please, don't call me Honoria. I always wonder for a moment who you're talking to when you use it. I much prefer Ria."

Merek ignored this last statement. This wasn't the time for discussing the appropriateness of familiar names.

"So, do I understand you correctly that you want to continue your journey to the north?"

"Of course! That's your homeland, is it not?"

"Well, yes, though I can't imagine what difference that makes."

She settled back, satisfied. "I should like very much to see it. This journey has been most instructive, and I'm confident my education is not yet finished. Besides," she added, her eyes twinkling. "I hear that northern village dancing can be quite invigorating, and I fully expect a demonstration if the opportunity arises."

Twenty-Four

"I just don't think it's right that we have to slog through sewers when he's wooing maids and—" Jax cut off as Rorden entered Captain Strong's office. Sergeant Dan and his squad were gathered in the room, waiting for him. They sat in a semicircle around the desk, the captain's chair left conspicuously empty.

Rorden sighed. "Are you going on about that again, Jax?"

Sergeant Dan eyed the redheaded man. "How are you going to woo any fair maid with that face of yours, Jax? Let the pretty boy do what he does best."

Rorden didn't much like being called a "pretty boy," but as he had no real authority over Dan and his men, he let it slide. The truth was, his attempts to learn more from Lord Bolen's household weren't going as well as he would have liked. Miranda was softening to his attentions, but the person he really needed more time with was Yulda. With Cook there, it was impossible to get even a snatch of conversation with her without arousing suspicion.

But he couldn't say any of this to the other soldiers. They spent their days wading through the city's drains and sewers, so they would not be sympathetic.

"What have you got for me, Dan?" he asked, bending over the desk where lay a map of Endvar. Lines sketched over the top of the streets indicated the sewers they had searched while trying to find an explanation for Hala's strange comment about foul-smelling mud.

They had started at the river, looking for caves or caverns, but Aiya had been insistent about looking in the city proper, and her instincts had served them well so far.

"What have we got for you?" Dan asked, his dry voice rumbling deep in his chest. "The same thing we've got for you every day for the past month. A lot of rats and wet boots—"

"Not to mention the fungus I've got that stretches from my feet to my—" Jax jumped in.

"It would be easier if we had some idea of where we should be looking," Dan continued loudly, ignoring Jax's scowl. "With no map to go by, we're just searching blindly."

It was true. If a map of the city's sewers existed, they had yet to find one. They'd been doing their best to sketch out the areas they had searched, but there was much of the city that they hadn't even explored.

Rorden narrowed his eyes at the drawing of Lord Bolen's estate on the map of Endvar. It wasn't large or well-marked, but he knew it well enough by now.

"I wonder," he said brightly, "if any of you wish to join me tonight on a little expedition. I can't promise it will be any more fruitful than your previous searches, but if it is, it might be helpful if I'm not alone."

Dan looked at him with interest. "What do you have in mind?"

Rorden related the experience Yulda had shared about Domar hiding in the larder. "I'm certain that whatever he was doing in that room, he was not spying on Bolen's scullery maid. It seems worth taking a look, don't you think?"

The other men looked to Dan, who shrugged. "It'd be nice to keep our feet dry for once."

"Good," Rorden said. "Let's meet after dark. We'll have to wait until the house is quiet."

As the other soldiers moved to leave, Rorden folded the map and unlocked the nearest cupboard to place it with his plans for Captain Falbrook's climbers. But the plans weren't there. He hastily shuffled through the contents of the cupboard, a sinking feeling settling into his stomach.

"Dan!" he called sharply. Rorden tried not to make it sound like an accusation, but there was really no other way to say it. "Did you get into this cupboard today before I came?"

Dan's eyes flickered briefly with humor. "You mean the cupboard whose sole key you're holding in your hand? Why yes, now that you mention it. I picked the lock and stole the pretty rhymes you've been writing for your kitchen maid. I thought Jax might like to practice."

Jax snorted a laugh behind him, but Dan had given Rorden an idea. He bent to examine the lock. There were scratches there, but they could just as easily have been from fumbling with the key. No reason to assume a thief had been in the captain's office. Was there any chance he'd left those papers somewhere else?

He searched the room, while Dan and Jax watched him with idle curiosity. "What's the matter, Rorden?" Jax called, a smile in his voice.

Rorden cursed under his breath. "Someone's been here," he said with certainty.

"Are you sure?"

Rorden nodded. "There are papers missing from the cupboard. And this stack of letters I haven't touched…look." He showed them two letters buried in the pile whose seals had been broken.

Rorden's mind raced, trying to assess the damage. If the assault plan was discovered, they risked losing the element of surprise, but nothing more. There was still time to rewrite the plans for the climbers before he went to Haldin to meet Captain Strong. All in all, the thieves hadn't done much damage.

The more disturbing question was, why? What did the thieves want?

And if they didn't find what they were looking for, what would they do?

"Aiya," he groaned. "Come with me!" he said urgently, pushing past the other soldiers.

It wouldn't take much to learn where Captain Strong lived. If the thieves were sent by Behni or Domar, Aiya was in great danger.

As Aiya reached to hang a bunch of thyme in the window of her kitchen, a torrent of heavy boots sounded on the wooden stairs leading to Captain Strong's upstairs room. Aiya jumped as her door flew open and a man burst through.

"Aiya!" Rorden gasped in relief. "You're all right! We need the key to the captain's room. Quickly!"

Aiya hesitated only briefly, with a question on her lips, but handed the key over without a word. She followed Rorden out the door and up the stairs, where three other soldiers waited.

"I aired it out yesterday," she said as Rorden unlocked the door. "There was nothing amiss."

"Would you know if someone had been here?"

Aiya looked around the room. All looked as it had before: the simple pallet bed against the far wall near the leaded windows, a small table near the door, the modest wardrobe. The room was sparsely furnished, but clean and neat. There was no sign of any disturbance.

"No one but me has been here. What is this about, Rorden?"

He wiped at his brow with a sleeve. "Someone has been into Captain Strong's office and taken some documents. Nothing critical, but I feared they might come here next."

Aiya started as she realized what this meant. Immediately, she breathed out a prayer of thanks that Imar was away. If any harm came to her, at least he would be safe.

Rorden was speaking to the other soldiers.

"Guard duty instead of wading through the sewers?" the shortest one said. "I thought you'd never ask."

"Guard duty?" Aiya interrupted.

Rorden nodded. "Dan will have two of his men guarding your house day and night."

"Two soldiers? Here?" she asked, incredulously. "That will be like waving a banner for all to see. 'Come see what we're hiding here!' No, this won't work. It would be best to be subtle."

"No, it's best to keep you safe. If anyone comes here and recognizes you, you'll be grateful for the protection."

Aiya shook her head. "Not like this. Not as soldiers. Perhaps dressed like tradesmen, with no uniforms. I can keep them busy, and they will look less suspicious."

Rorden thought about this for a moment and nodded. "Yes, do that. Especially Jax," he said, raising his voice a little. "Keep him busy, and maybe he won't whine so much."

The redheaded man frowned at Rorden, but it was Dan who responded. "It's a good idea, except for at night when no tradesmen would be working. What is our excuse then?"

Aiya thought this over. "Beggars. Drunks. There are many possibilities. But no soldiers."

"That might work," the soldier said with a brief nod.

After the other soldiers left to inspect the lower floor, Aiya sighed. "I thought I might have more freedom with Imar gone. But now…"

Rorden put an arm around her shoulder. She stiffened instinctively, but then realized he meant it to be comforting. Imar was never so carelessly affectionate, and Aiya was surprised by the gesture. She was even more surprised to find that she liked it. A little.

"They won't be so bad," Rorden promised. "They're a little rough, but they're good, solid men. It may be best if you stay close to home for a while. It will be harder to protect you out in the city."

She nodded. "I cannot leave the shop much anyway with Imar gone."

He sighed heavily, and in that sigh she heard the sound of a great weight. "When Captain Strong returns, he'll know what to do."

It was long past midnight when Rorden left the guard complex with Jax and Lom in tow. He wished Dan had come. The gruff man had a dry sense of humor that made him a surprisingly pleasant companion, but Dan had felt it was best to stay with Regin and Sagnar at Aiya's. They all agreed that an attack would most likely come that night, if it came at all.

Rorden tried not to worry about Aiya as they quietly moved through the empty streets of Endvar. He knew Dan was a capable soldier, and it wasn't likely that the warrior in black would be sent out on a simple thieving job. But he didn't like the idea of leaving a friend in danger.

The servant's gate at Lord Bolen's estate was locked for the night, but it was simply a matter of being hoisted over the top, dropping to the other side, and unbarring the door before they were all three safely inside the wall. The kitchen windows were dark. Even Yulda must have retired for the night. One window had been left open to the cool breeze of the late summer night. Lom boosted Rorden up to the sill, and he pulled himself inside, moving carefully to unlatch the door for the other two men.

Rorden lit two of the candles that were sitting out on the work table. They cast only a dim light due to the faint moonlight coming through the windows, but brightened as he entered the darkness of the larder, illuminating its shelves crowded with pottery and baskets.

"Looks like a larder to me," Jax said with a hint of mockery.

Rorden ignored him. "Look for a hidden door or something that doesn't seem to fit."

They started by quietly pulling items off the shelves to check the wall behind, then moved to pulling out barrels and examining floorboards, looking for anything unusual. There was nothing.

Rorden began to feel foolish. Perhaps Domar really was eccentric enough to spy on Yulda late at night. Cringing at the thought of Jax's gibes if nothing turned up, he sat down on a large barrel in the corner to think.

"Giving up already?" A mocking voice sounded in the doorway.

Rorden jumped to his feet. Yulda stood there, illuminated faintly by Jax's small candle, as though an apparition had appeared out of the air. She was dressed in a simple nightdress, with a light shawl wrapped around her shoulders.

"What are you doing here?" Rorden exclaimed in a rough whisper.

He knew it was a daft question as soon as he said it.

"I believe *you* are the ones trespassing." She smirked. "I'm surprised it took you as long as you did. I've been expecting you for days now."

"Expecting us?"

Yulda sighed. "Really, Prestin. Or Rorden, I mean. If you're going to be skulking about in other people's kitchens where you don't belong, you could at least be clever about it."

Jax snorted and Rorden shot him a glare. Yulda stepped into the room and took Rorden's candle from off a nearby shelf, holding it up high.

"How did you know I would come?" he demanded.

The girl shrugged. With her hair loose and the candlelight softening her features, she didn't seem quite as shrewish as usual, though her voice was still acerbic.

"You show up asking questions about Domar, and I tell you a story about him being in the larder late at night. How could you not take a look yourself?"

Rorden shook his head. Once again, her insight astounded him. "I don't understand how someone as clever as you could end up as a scullery maid under Lord Bolen's thumb."

He meant it as a compliment, but Yulda just glowered. "What do you know of it?" she snapped.

Rorden shrugged and returned to his search.

"What exactly are you looking for?" Yulda asked tauntingly.

Rorden ignored her. Talking to her was like trying to befriend an injured dog. Just when he thought she might accept some kindness from him, she'd bite.

After a moment, Yulda sighed heavily and moved toward the barrel he'd been sitting on earlier. But still he ignored her, dropping instead to his hands and knees to peer under a lower shelf.

Lom yelped in surprise.

Rorden turned and saw Yulda standing next to the barrel. The front of the barrel had swung forward as if it were a door, revealing a dark, yawning interior.

Rorden leaped to his feet.

This time, Yulda smiled slyly. "I might have already taken a look myself."

"Yulda, you darling girl!" Rorden cried. "We might have searched all night and not found this."

"That's because you've never been a scullery maid," she scoffed, but her eyes were bright with satisfaction.

Rorden took the candle from her and knelt before the barrel. Where the wall should have been was instead a gaping hole. The barrel itself was embedded in the wall, a permanent fixture whose placement looked so natural that it wouldn't be questioned. If he shifted his shoulders sideways, it was large enough to crawl through. After passing through the wall, the space opened up enough to stand. He stood at the top of a stone staircase, the walls on either side close enough to touch.

Jax and Lom followed behind him, and the sound of their whispered oaths told him they were as excited as he.

Rorden soon wished they had torches or lamps and not mere candles. The light didn't penetrate very far, especially since they had to shield the candles protectively against the draft. What really worried him as they descended deep into the bowels of the earth, however, was the possibility of being discovered and trapped in this narrow passage.

Eventually they reached level ground and the tunnel widened. The damp walls were cut out of the earth. The air smelled dank and although there was no mud underfoot, it wasn't hard to imagine that other areas with more moisture might well smell as Hala had described them.

Feeling satisfied that they were on the right track, Rorden turned to his companions and whispered. "I dare not go further. Not when we don't know where we're going and what might be waiting for us. Let's talk to Dan and come back with torches."

Jax and Lom grunted their approval. To Rorden's surprise, Yulda stepped out from behind them. She was so small and quiet, he hadn't realized she had followed.

"There's nothing dangerous here. It goes on for some time yet before branching off. That's where it gets tricky," she said.

"You've been down here?" Rorden exclaimed.

"Of course! You think I would find the entrance and not see where it leads?"

That was exactly what he'd assumed. "How much have you explored?"

She shrugged. "Lots. This tunnel joins up with a larger one, and then there are dozens that branch off from there. Some are dead ends. Others have been used recently."

"Could you sketch it out for me?" he asked.

"Already did, you big oaf. Been waiting for you to come and get it."

She withdrew a sheet of paper from the deep pocket of her nightdress. It had been folded many times until it was thick and small.

Again, he shook his head. "Yulda, you are a puzzle. How *did* you come to be in Bolen's kitchen? With that head of yours you could be a clerk in a shop or even a lady's maid."

Her expression darkened again, but this time he saw in it sorrow and regret. "It just wouldn't work for me."

Suddenly, Jax grabbed Rorden's arm.

"Look!" he whispered, jabbing a finger toward the darkness of the tunnel. A faint light was glowing just out of sight and growing brighter. The sound of voices drifted toward them from a distance.

Rorden cursed under his breath. "Candles out!" he commanded, immediately dousing his own flame. "Go! Go!"

Jax and Lom were already on the move, stumbling over each other in the darkness. Rorden reached forward and felt for Yulda. He half expected her to slap his hand away, but she clutched it fearfully as together they shuffled back the way they had come. The light behind them wasn't close enough to illuminate their path, so they moved with arms outstretched, every sense straining to find their way.

A stifled grunt up ahead told Rorden that Jax and Lom had found the stairs. Tripped over them, most likely. Judging by the distance, they'd made much faster progress than he and Yulda. He hoped they would have the presence of mind to flee the house as soon as they made it up the stairs.

When Rorden and Yulda reached the staircase, he gently pushed her forward to go first. The steps were not cut uniformly and it was much slower going up in the dark than it had been going down. Yulda's nightdress tripped her several times, and once she fell hard. Rorden reached for her but it was too late. With a cry of pain, she hit the stairs and let out a thick curse. The hum of voices behind them quieted.

"Get up!" Rorden pleaded.

"Get up yourself!" she panted in a harsh whisper, and let out a soft moan.

Rorden grabbed her around the middle and hoisted her to her feet. "I'm sorry you're hurt, but if they find us here a few bruises will be the least of your concerns."

She growled at him, but began climbing again.

A few agonizing minutes later, Yulda breathed out, "We're here," and dropped to her knees. The opening to the larder appeared a muted gray as Rorden followed her. It was a relief to have some light, even if it was only the shadows of filtered moonlight through the kitchen windows. The kitchen was empty, with no sign of Jax and Lom.

Rorden whispered to Yulda. "Can you make it back to your rooms in time?"

She turned to him, her eyes wide. "Don't be a fool. Whoever it is, he's already heard us. If there's no one here when they arrive, it will be far too suspicious."

"It's too dangerous!" Rorden urged. "If you're discovered—"

Suddenly, Yulda burst into tears. She covered her face with her hands and sobbed in huge, gasping gulps.

Rorden watched her in horrified shock. With the noise she was making, she would wake half the household.

"What were you thinking?" she wailed. "I trusted you!"

Rorden stared at her.

Yulda dropped her hands and glared at him. Her eyes were dry. *She's pretending,* he realized. *Trying to explain the cry from earlier when she fell.*

"I don't—" he stammered hesitantly, trying to guess what he was supposed to do. But the pending danger made it hard to think.

"You're pathetic!" she sneered in a low whisper.

"This wasn't my idea," he snarled back.

She sighed and rolled her eyes. "Come here!"

Just as they heard motion in the larder, Yulda grabbed him by the front of his shirt, pulled him toward her and kissed him hard on the mouth.

Rorden was so shocked, he instinctively pulled back, but her grip was surprisingly strong. He had kissed many young women, but this was nothing like he'd ever experienced. It wasn't tender or sweet, nor was it full of promise and desire. It was rough and angry, mimicking passion but fueled by terror. He just prayed that whoever came through that larder door wouldn't see the lie.

"Yulda!" The man's voice was sharp in the quiet room.

They both jumped. Yulda turned, trying to block Rorden behind her.

"Master Domar!" Yulda cried breathlessly, wiping at her mouth.

"What is the meaning of this, girl? How dare you bring shame on this house!" His fair hair and pale skin glowed yellow in the light of the oil lamp he held, but the rest of him was shrouded in black. He spoke with an icy malevolence that made Rorden's spine tingle.

"This is not what it looks like, Master! I swear it! He was just leaving," she said, her tone pleading even as she stood protectively between Domar and Rorden.

Again, Rorden was amazed at how quick her mind worked. His was still reeling from the kiss, and she was already pushing him toward the door.

"Young man," Domar said, stepping forward. Rorden hoped his reticence to meet his eye would be seen as cowardice. He was grateful he'd worn the plain clothes of Prestin's character that night.

"Yes, Master. I'll be going now." He pulled his cap lower over his head and shuffled to the door.

Domar grabbed him by the arm and it took all of Rorden's self-control to relax and not respond to the threat as a soldier.

"If I ever see you again, you will regret it," he said in a low tone. "Is that clear?"

Rorden nodded and hurried out the door, hating himself for leaving Yulda. But the best thing he could do was to play his part and divert any suspicion away from her. He hurried down the back steps and ran across the courtyard, making as much noise as possible to make his escape clear. Then he paused and carefully crept back to the open window.

Yulda was crying, though whether it was genuine or not, he couldn't tell.

"Please, Master, I swear it will never happen again!" she begged.

Domar responded in a low voice, but Rorden couldn't make out the words.

"Yes, Master," Yulda sniffed. "Thank you, sir." She spoke loudly enough that Rorden suspected she knew he was listening.

He breathed a sigh of relief. There would be no more visiting Lord Bolen's house, either as Prestin or Rorden. But with Yulda's hand drawn map tucked safely in his jacket pocket, there was no longer any need.

Twenty-Five

The road to Haldin was unusually crowded with villagers making their way from neighboring settlements. It wasn't until they passed the sixth mule cart with the driver's wife and children freshly scrubbed that Merek realized why.

"It's the Gathering Festival," he said to Captain Drenall. "They're celebrating the end of summer and the bounty of the harvest."

"How opportune," the older man said ironically as his horse shied away from a spirited youth darting past. "The princess will be glad to hear it. She was just lamenting yesterday that there's been a dearth of feasts and festivals on this tour."

"A dearth?" Merek scoffed. "I've been feasted to my death, like a spring hog being fattened for the slaughter. Which we'll probably enjoy while we're here, come to think of it."

"I look forward to it." Drenall smiled, wrinkles lining his pocked face. "I've always found the Dimm Forest to be dreary, so a little gaiety will be a pleasant change. What a grim life it must be living in the shadows," he added, glancing around at the towering trees.

Merek chuckled. It was a common enough complaint from visitors who were used to the abundant farmlands and open pastures that typified the rest of Rahm. Merek, on the other hand, found the deep, muted closeness of the forest sheltering and comfortable.

The very air about them was tinged with deep green. Moss hung copiously from the trees, and large ferns crowded the road on either side, some nearly as tall as his horse's shoulder. Creeping vines winding up trunks were already turning color, making bright splashes of yellow and orange against the many layers of green. He breathed in the scent of moist life and relaxed a little in the saddle.

They rounded the final bend to Haldin, and the village came into view. Through the trees, Merek could just make out tents erected in a large clearing. Festive garland hung from trees, ribbons of color dancing gaily in the breeze. The sound of clapping from the hired carriage made him smile. The princess had seen the decorations too.

The past few days had been much quieter with Ria—no, *Honoria*, he must be careful not to make that slip—riding in the carriage with her maid and clerk. Drenall's company was considerably more dull, but Merek knew the distance from the princess was necessary. He'd been growing too comfortable with her, as evidenced by his behavior in Cillith.

But it would not be repeated. In the days since they left Cillith, he'd made great efforts to resume an appropriate level of formal distance with the princess. If she'd noticed, she said nothing, continuing to treat him with the same mixture of humor and exasperation as she always had.

As they rode into the crowded square full of market booths, the air was thick with the smell of baked goods. Merek smiled. There would be plenty to distract Ria—Honoria—while they were here, giving him time to meet with Stefan and his climbers. If Rorden had come as planned, he would hear firsthand of the intrigues developing in Endvar. But first, he needed to find someone whom he could trust to take charge of the princess in his absence.

Merek dismounted and searched the square on foot. It didn't take long before he found her, standing beneath a canopy chatting with a few older women from the village.

Sigrid's face brightened at the sight of him. "Merek, dear!" she called out in greeting. "What a delightful surprise!"

"Hello, Mor," he replied, stooping to kiss her cheek. "I didn't realize it was the Gathering. What a happy coincidence."

"What brings you here?"

"I have some business with Stefan, but I need to ask you for a favor."

"Of course. What is it?"

"I'm not here alone. Princess Honoria is here as well, with a small entourage. Might you entertain her for a few hours?"

His mother's look of surprise was only surpassed by those of her friends, who began speaking excitedly to each other, craning their necks to see through the crowd.

"The princess is here in Haldin? My my," Sigrid said, patting his cheek. "I suppose that explains why you've tended to your appearance."

The other women tittered as Merek's cheeks grew warm.

Pitching her voice lower, Sigrid asked, "How can I entertain a princess, Merek? What could I possibly say to her?"

"Please, Mor, there's no one else I dare ask. Just show her the booths, make sure she's comfortable, that sort of thing. She's pleasant-tempered and won't be a tedious companion, especially with the festival providing a diversion."

His mother looked at him doubtfully. "I will try. But I'm sure she's used to much finer manners than mine."

Merek grinned, and kissed his mother gratefully. "Thank you, Mor. Don't worry about your manners. She's put up with mine for nearly two months now. I'm sure she will find yours to be a refreshing change."

Sigrid smiled. "That I believe. Come, take me to this princess of yours."

Merek led his mother through the crowd of villagers dressed in the traditional dress of the northern people, which gave him a thrill of nostalgia. These were festival clothes—blue, yellow, violet, and even some red—a stark contrast from the muted earth tones of green and brown they usually wore. The men wore colored waistcoats over white shirts, and the women's skirts and fitted pinafores were bright against their white blouses.

By the time they reached the edge of the square, Drenall had already escorted the princess from her carriage. She stretched her back without any sign of discomfort, Merek was glad to see, evidence that she was indeed healing as well as she claimed. As Ria scanned the square, her eyes alighted on Merek.

"Ah, there he is! Strong, what a delightful party you've managed to drum up for my arrival! I hope you didn't go to too much trouble."

"I am nothing if not solicitous," he replied.

"Overwhelmingly so, I would say," she said, laughing appreciatively.

Sigrid watched this exchange with a mixture of awe and interest.

"Your Highness," he said, addressing Ria. "I must tend to some matters with my men here, but I'm leaving you in very capable hands. Sigrid has agreed to be your guide, and Captain Drenall and his men will be close."

Sigrid gave a stiff curtsy, and it was clear that it wasn't a practiced movement. But Merek wasn't concerned with whether or not she impressed Ria. He was more worried about Ria giving offense. One thing was certain: Whatever his mother thought she knew of the princess would change by the end of the day.

Ria greeted her warmly. "Sigrid, you said? I'm delighted to meet you and enjoy the festival through your eyes—" She broke off, looking back and forth between the two of them. "Strong!' she exclaimed. "Is this your mother?"

Her eyes gleamed with the discovery, and she didn't wait for his reply. "Of course! She must be! The eyes are very similar, although hers are more blue than gray. How perfectly lovely to meet you, Sigrid! Indeed, how fortunate. I'd hoped to meet some of Strong's family while I was here, but his own mother!" She leaned conspiratorially toward the older woman. "To be honest, I wasn't quite sure you existed. There are times I've wondered if our Captain Strong came into this world as a grown man in soldier's uniform."

Sigrid blinked in surprise. With a flash of misgiving, Merek wondered if he had made a mistake.

But she recovered quickly and managed to respond with, "You have it just about right, Your Highness. Except for the uniform. That he had to grow into."

Ria smiled mischievously, and Merek felt a sudden urge to steer his mother away from the scheming woman. She must have sensed this, because she turned to him, hooking her arm through Sigrid's, and said, "Run along then, Captain. We shall not miss you, I'm sure."

He looked one last time at his mother, who still seemed off-balance from her first encounter with the king's daughter, but was at least smiling. She nodded at him reassuringly, and he took this as his dismissal.

Ria spared only a glance for Captain Strong as he left the square before focusing her attention on the woman at her side. Sigrid seemed uncertain how to proceed, so Ria made it easy for her by expressing interest in a woodcarver's stall nearby. As they looked over the carvings and clever toys, Ria only feigned interest. Her real interest was Sigrid herself.

She was nearly as tall as Ria, and in her youth may very well have surpassed Ria's height. Now she stooped a little with her advanced years, a roundness in the shoulders indicating the weight of age echoed in her graying hair and lined skin. Her eyes were very like her son's, but the bright blue made them softer and more gentle. Her delicate features were nothing like her son's strong jaw and proud nose, leading Ria to wonder what Strong's father had looked like.

Ria continued to hold Sigrid's arm as they moved from booth to booth. Everywhere they went, villagers stared. Many of them addressed Sigrid with deference, but seemed afraid to speak directly to the princess. Haldin had no noble families, but it was clear that

Strong's mother was well-respected in the village. Again, Ria wondered about his father. Was it his reputation that continued to grant his widow such respect? Or was it the son who had risen so far in the esteem of the king?

As she considered this, more questions came to mind. Had Captain Strong intentionally selected his mother as her escort because he knew how it would raise her position in the community? He didn't seem the type to engage in such intrigue, so perhaps it was simply a lucky accident.

As Sigrid relaxed, she seemed to abandon her concern for impressing the princess. She didn't have the polished air of a noble lady, but she possessed a quiet strength that felt familiar. Unassuming, yet constant. Steady and trustworthy.

"You must be very proud of your son," Ria said, as they paused for a drink of water from the well in the center of the village.

"Yes, I am," Sigrid answered, her face softening in a smile. "But I was proud of him before he ever left to join the army. He's always been thoughtful and conscientious, almost to a fault. He sacrificed so much to take care of me and his little sister when he was young."

"When your husband died?" Ria guessed.

Sigrid glanced at her and paused. "He didn't die, Your Highness. Well, he did. But that was only a few years ago. No, what I speak of happened when Merek was young. It was before Danvir's Wall was built and bandit attacks were a constant part of our life. One night, when my husband left to frighten off the bandits, Merek followed him in secret. The bandits attacked Leif and beat him. Merek tried to defend him with his bow, but he was just a child, not more than ten or eleven years old. I think he always blamed himself that his father never recovered."

She must have seen Ria's confused look. "Oh, he lived. Lived more than twenty years. But he was never the same. He couldn't speak or care for himself in any way. My husband was lost that night to the bandits; we just didn't bury him until twenty years later."

Ria was speechless. She wanted to reach out to Sigrid in some comforting gesture but wasn't sure it would be welcome. "I'm sorry," she offered lamely.

Sigrid shook her head, and her smile was warm and genuine, with no hint of lingering pain. "Forgive me, Your Highness. It's a time for celebration, not melancholy. But yes, in answer to your question, I am very proud of my son."

Feeling subdued, Ria followed Sigrid to the other side of the square. How very little she knew of Captain Strong. She marveled at what else he might have withheld from her, even as she tried to listen to Sigrid describe the customs surrounding the Gathering Festival and the weeks of hard labor that preceded it. Although the days were still warm with summer, the nights this far north were cooling toward autumn, and the Gathering was the last piece of color in their lives before the long dark night of winter ahead.

In an effort to shake off her pensive mood, Ria picked up a figure made of corn husks and grass with one small bone bead giving the impression of an eye.

"Tell me about this," she said. She'd seen similar figures at nearly every booth, and many children playing with them. At first she had thought there was a bead missing, but eventually she realized that all the figures intentionally only had one eye.

"That is the Gathering Witch. Not a real witch, of course," Sigrid added hastily. "It's only a harmless tradition. We do not follow the old pagan ways."

"Of course." Ria smiled reassuringly. "Tell me, who is she? What does she do?"

"It is said that the Gathering Witch watches over the harvest, ensuring that the elements will smile on us until all is safely gathered into barns and cellars. If anyone catches a view of the Gathering Witch on the night of the Gathering, they will be granted a wish. Their heart's desire will be theirs."

"Why only one eye?"

"Because the other eye is watching over the harvest. Anyone who sees her during the Gathering—the only time when she can be seen—will only see her with one eye."

"Hmm," Ria said doubtfully. "It seems she might be more useful at guarding the harvest if she used both eyes, don't you think?"

Sigrid's blue eyes sparkled in a smile. "Have you never grown weary of a task and found your mind wandering? You can't fault her for being distracted by the lights and laughter of the festival."

Ria laughed. "Indeed, I cannot."

At that moment, she noticed a uniformed young man passing nearby.

Well, well.

"Rory!" she called.

Captain Strong's handsome young clerk turned, a look of confusion on his face. He smiled when he saw the princess and changed his course to approach her.

Sigrid glanced at her uncomfortably. "This is my son's clerk, Sergeant Rorden." She delicately emphasized his name.

"Yes, we've met. Rory, what brings you here? I thought you were in Endvar," Ria said.

His initial confusion passed, and a look of resignation took its place. He recognized her game and was going to ignore it. Good for him. That would make it more fun.

"Good day to you, Your Highness." He bowed to the two women respectfully. "I came two days past, but it seems you were delayed. I trust your journey hasn't been too arduous."

"Arduous, tedious, and some days completely excruciating. But almost all of it was worth it."

"Almost?"

"Yes, which is more than I'd hoped for when I began. Never fear, Rory. I'm sure you'll hear some wonderful tales from your captain. Just don't believe anything that makes me look bad. Those parts are all lies."

With a grin, Rorden took his leave of the two women and disappeared down the road into the forest.

They'd reached an area of the square where tents were still being erected and a temporary fence was being placed for a small pen. The festival proper wouldn't begin until sundown. Sigrid informed Ria that while the market stalls would last for three days, the true celebration would happen that night. Which meant that Ria only had a few hours.

"Sigrid, you've been most attentive. But I mean to do more than casually observe tonight, and so, I'm going to need your help."

"Of course, Your Highness. How may I help?"

"First," Ria said eagerly, "I'm going to need a dress."

"Incredible," Merek said in awe, watching Stefan's climbers scaling the wall. Not only did they move at a faster speed than he could, but they did it with swords and even shields strapped to their backs.

"They need help getting their weapons when they get to the top, of course," Stefan said from beside him. "So they need to stay together in pairs."

Merek nodded. "Have you drilled them on what to do if they get into trouble?" They wouldn't be using lethal force against Eldar's men, but the same couldn't be said for their opponents. If all went according to plan, they would immobilize the Endvar soldiers quickly and identify themselves to eliminate the danger. But if not, they needed to have an alternate plan of escape.

"Yes, sir," Stefan replied. "But they're young and daft and think they won't need it."

As they walked back to the guardhouse, Merek asked, "Did you ever try it yourself?"

"No, sir," Stefan scoffed. "Not in a hundred years. I've got eight kids waiting for me to come home at night. You just tell me, how would I explain it to Veln? She already worries too much."

When they reached the guardhouse, Rorden was waiting for them. He produced a sketch on a sheet of paper that had been folded many times. "This is the drawing from that girl I wrote you about."

"Bolen's kitchen maid?"

"Yes. I haven't been able to verify the accuracy myself, but comparing it against Dan's searches makes it appear credible." He placed a map of Endvar on the table, with a dizzying array of tunnels drawn over the top.

Merek studied the two side by side for a moment. "The tunnels are all in the older part of the city?"

"It makes the most sense. Lord Ogmun didn't know anything about them, and his family has lived in Endvar for generations. So they must date back to when Endvar was just an ancient keep protecting disjointed townships."

Stefan tapped the map thoughtfully. "How do you know that you haven't just uncovered an underground skirmish between noble houses?"

Merek sighed. "We don't. That's why I'm proceeding with caution. If it's just two warring factions anxious to keep their conflict out of the sight of the king, that's a job for Wott's peacekeepers." He leaned back in his chair and scratched his beard thoughtfully. "Stefan, your men may need to wait a little longer before they come to Endvar. I don't feel comfortable bringing them into the city when we don't know what intrigue is brewing in her bowels."

"They'll be disappointed to hear that, sir," Stefan said gruffly. "They've been hoping that your arrival meant it was time for action."

Merek shook his head. "Not yet. But continue their training. The change in seasons will present new challenges, and I'd like them to be ready at a moment's notice."

"Sir, there's one more thing," Rorden said. "Someone broke into your office and stole some early drafts of the wall attack."

"What?" Merek started. "When did this happen?"

"Right before I came, sir. I had no time to write to you."

Merek groaned. "Any idea who took them? Or why?"

Rorden shook his head. "There would be nothing to gain that I can see. But it's still concerning."

"Concerning yes, but not disastrous," Stefan said mildly. "At worst, we may need to delay or change the attack. That will just give us more time to train."

Merek nodded distractedly. Something about it left him unsettled. Harmless or not, he wouldn't feel at ease until he knew who had taken them and why.

Ria frowned at the unrecognizable mass of charred meat. It was wrapped around a long stick, and embedded into it were bits of fruit that looked equally burned.

"How am I supposed to eat this?" she whispered to Biren. Sigrid had left them some minutes before, excusing herself to help her daughter tend to her children. It was nearly evening and lanterns had been lit in the trees; blue, red, and amber.

Biren eyed her own stick doubtfully. "They all seem to be eating it straight off the stick, my lady."

Ria looked around and saw that she was right. The villagers were indeed tearing straight into the meat with their teeth, and appearing to enjoy each bite.

"No forks or fingers?" Gingerly, she brought the stick to her lips and nibbled at the meat. She tasted burned flesh and frowned.

A young girl standing near her giggled.

"You think you can do better?" Ria asked, smiling. "Come, show your princess how to eat it properly." She held out the stick in invitation.

The girl giggled again and ran away behind a nearby tent. Ria sighed and tried again, taking a larger bite. This time she bit past the charred skin and reached some of the inside of the strange meat. She was surprised to find it tender and juicy, with a wonderful flavor that must have only been achieved through days of prior preparation. The bits of fruit added an unexpected burst of tartness that perfectly complemented the meat, though they sometimes slipped away and rolled down her chin before she could get them into her mouth.

When she was finished, she wiped the grease away with satisfaction. "That was probably the least delicate meal I've ever eaten, but I feel quite fortified for the evening's activities. Though," she added ruefully, looking at the grease stains marring her violet gown, "I'm afraid this gown has seen the last of its usefulness."

"It was already looking rather travel-weary, my lady," Biren said. "I'm sure it was not meant to be abused as it has."

A group of boys ran past, and one of them stopped and stared at Ria.

"I know you!" he said. His playmates jostled him, but he held his ground and soon they ran off.

"Do you?" Ria smiled, surprised at his boldness. All the other children had kept their distance.

"Yes. You came into my far's shop."

Ria shook her head in surprise. "I'm sorry, you must be confused. I haven't been here since I was a child."

"Yes, it was you. You came to ask him about a pair of boots with mother-of-pearl buckles."

Ria started. She *had* stopped into a cobbler's shop in Albon a few months earlier, ducking in on a whim to escape the sun. She'd been delighted to find the very cobbler who had recently made a new pair of boots for her, a pair of boots with mother-of-pearl buckles. But how could this boy know about that?

"What is your name, child?" Ria asked with interest.

"Finn."

"And your father is a cobbler? Is he here with you?"

"Nah. He's at home in Albon."

"Then what are you doing so far away from home? Are you with your mother?"

Two of the boys from before returned and called to Finn to join them. "I'm talking to the princess!" he shouted back. Turning back to Ria he explained, "I came with the captain. Well, not the captain exactly. Sergeant Rorden brought me, but it was the captain what asked my far if I could come."

Ria glanced at Biren, who just shrugged. The boy made no more sense to her than to Ria. "Do you mean Captain Strong? He brought you from Albon all the way to Haldin without your parents? Why on earth would he do that?"

Before he could answer, two playmates grabbed him by both arms and tugged him away, leaving Ria with more questions than answers.

"What do you make of that, Biren?"

Biren watched the boys disappearing into the thickening crowd and shook her head. "I think that Captain Strong has secrets, my lady."

Ria raised an eyebrow. "Good secrets or bad secrets?"

Biren smiled. "Does it matter?"

Ria laughed. Her maid knew her very well.

As Ria and Biren moved among the crowd, never far from Captain Drenall and his men, she kept watch for Strong. But it was full dark before he and Rorden appeared on the edge of a ring of firelight, illuminated by the many small bonfires that flared around the perimeter of the square.

The arrival of the captain was timely, as she was beginning to tire of the festival and wanted someone to talk to who wouldn't merely smile mutely in return. She knew these villagers couldn't all be so simple, but the awe they felt in the presence of the princess left them tongue-tied.

"Are you well, my lady?" Strong asked as she approached. "I hope my mother hasn't abandoned you."

"She did, but only after seeing to my every need. And I'll admit it was for a good cause. Of what concern is a princess when children need to be fed?"

Strong smiled briefly but said nothing more. His mood was too serious and contemplative for her liking. That would have to change or the evening was destined to be dull and disappointing.

"But now that you're here," Ria said, taking his arm. "I expect that will change. Come, introduce me to your Gathering Festival." Never mind that she had already seen all there was to see. It was not for her sake but for his that she insisted on seeing it all again. Hopefully something would catch his interest and lighten his heavy expression.

"Rory," she said to the young soldier. "Have you been introduced to my maid, Biren?"

Rorden buried his irritation with a smooth bow, and Biren responded with a lovely curtsy. Biren's calm exterior didn't falter, but Ria knew her well enough to see that she was pleased as she regarded her assigned partner for the evening.

Cheery music drifted over the crowd from a small group of musicians with pipes and drums, feeding the enthusiasm of the villagers as surely as the ale being ladled out generously from nearby barrels. Against the backdrop of darkness, with lanterns in the trees and shifting firelight on the ground, the booths and children's games and savory food all took on a celebratory glow that had been absent during the day. It was the kind of scene that would have energized Artem. He would have thrown himself into the rustic festivities with gusto, pulling Ria along with him until they were both intoxicated with exhaustion.

By comparison, Strong was politely distracted and far too quiet for her taste.

Ria compensated by teasing Rorden at every opportunity, and he continued to ignore the gibe. She knew he was waiting for her to grow bored—and indeed it was getting rather stale—but she pushed on in spite of it. Perhaps tomorrow she would give up the game, but tonight she was determined to get some kind of a reaction or punish him trying.

She never suspected that he would raise the stakes so dramatically.

They were standing outside a makeshift pen, watching as children climbed through the fence and formed a small mob. A man at the end of the corral opened a crate and two squealing piglets rushed out. The children immediately scattered to chase them, shrieking in delight.

The crowd cheered, laughing as the children stumbled over each other in an effort to lay their hands on the slippery piglets. To make matters worse, the ground underfoot was wet and soon became a soup of thick mud up to the children's ankles. Ria stood next to Rorden, laughing at the display, and even Strong smiled. A little.

Then, unexpectedly, Rorden leaned closer to Ria and said in a low voice, "I have twenty gold pieces for you if you catch one."

Ria looked at him in shock. Was he serious? His eyes twinkled, and his dimples flashed irresistibly. This was revenge for calling him "Rory." She would have to back down to his challenge and would no longer have the upper hand. Unless…

"Twenty?" she said, lifting her chin. "I would have done it for ten."

She immediately began unlacing her boots.

"My lady!" Biren protested.

Rorden's laugh came out as a short burst. "I didn't mean it! Stop, Your Highness, please!"

Ria removed her stockings and handed them to Biren. "You had best get your money ready, Rory. If you try and cheat me, I'll have you hanged." Then she slipped between the rails of the fence into the pen.

Twenty-Six

M erek watched, stunned, unable to make sense of what he was seeing. What was Rorden thinking, issuing such a challenge to the Crown Princess? And why in all the kingdoms was Ria obeying it? He felt as if he were frozen in a strange dream as he watched her step gingerly into the corral, her gown lifted daintily out of the mud.

The cheers of the crowd quieted and turned to murmurs of dismay. All eyes outside the pen were fixed on the princess. But inside, the children were oblivious to the addition to their group, intent only on the squealing piglets.

Not ten seconds after entering the corral, a boy plowed into the princess and knocked her to the ground.

The crowd gasped.

Just like that, the dreamlike feeling ended. Merek jumped forward, imagining the worst—stitches tearing and her wound reopening—but before he could lift a leg over the fence, Ria rolled over onto her back. She was clutching her side, and she was shaking with laughter.

The crowd's sigh of relief echoed his own. As Ria came up to stand in her mud-caked dress and offered a slight curtsy in their direction, the villagers erupted in laughter. A piglet headed straight toward the princess, but she ignored it, choosing instead to tackle the same blond boy—*was that the cobbler's son?*—who had knocked her flat. The villagers whooped their approval, and several other boys jumped into the fray. Soon all the children piled onto them, leaving the swine forgotten.

It was the most inane thing that Merek had ever seen: the princess's bare feet protruded from the bottom of a muddy mess of children who squirmed and writhed as they all tried to reach the top of the pile. Biren gripped the fence with a horrified expression, but Rorden had collapsed into such a fit of laughter that he had to hold the fence himself for support. Seeing his young clerk, Merek could no longer hold in his own laughter.

Biren looked at him sharply, but her mouth twitched in a suppressed smile. "I believe my lady may be in distress, sir," she said pointedly.

Merek took a deep breath and wiped at the moisture in his eyes. He stepped into the pen and began pulling muddy children off the top of the pile, holding them at arm's length to keep them from soiling his uniform.

As the pile dwindled, Ria saw him and called out breathlessly, "Strong! Did you come to join us? I'm afraid if one more person jumps on I will have all the life squeezed out of me."

Merek spoke loudly so that she could hear over the sound of squealing pigs and children. "I wish you'd told me the royal treasury was in such peril. Next time, I'll lend you a few coins."

Ria laughed as he helped her to her feet. Mud covered most of her, turning her skin dark and dulling the sheen of her violet gown, but her eyes were bright and beautiful. "Twenty gold pieces? For a soldier, that sum is practically a fortune! How could I resist?" She waved to the crowd, giving dramatic curtsies to those who cheered and hollered with the most energy, before ducking through the rails again to where Biren waited in silent reproof.

Merek paused before crossing the fence and shook his head. "Do you ever get tired of being so…" He searched for a word but couldn't find one that quite fit. "…*you?*"

"Now wouldn't that be a frightful day," she said, then reached over the fence and patted him deliberately on the cheek with a hand caked with mud.

A few villagers laughed, and Merek thought he heard Rorden's voice with them. But he paid them no heed, his head still swimming. Just when he thought she could do nothing else to surprise him, she had managed it. Again.

"She's an extraordinary young woman." Sigrid's voice sounded at his side as she pressed a wet cloth into his hand. "Careful. Before it drips onto your coat."

"Thank you, Mor," he said, wiping the mud off his face and hands as he watched Biren and Ria disappear into the darkness.

"Is she always like this?" Sigrid asked. "Or is it a show for our benefit?"

"No, she is who she is and doesn't pretend otherwise."

"I would have expected more…something. Dignity perhaps?"

"Her playfulness is what endears her to many. But when you know her better, you find that not only is she clever, but she has a strong sense of duty mixed with the kindest of hearts."

"Oh, you don't need to defend her to me, Merek. I quite enjoyed our afternoon together. If she is much like her father, I can see why you became such friends."

The villagers were moving back toward the square, and Merek's mother took him by the arm and followed. The musicians struck up a lively tune to call the couples to dance.

"She does remind me a lot of her father, though she has the beauty of her mother. Sindal was never as handsome."

"Ah, I'd wondered if you'd noticed."

"Noticed what?"

"That she's a very beautiful woman," Sigrid said meaningfully.

Merek snorted. "I'm not blind."

"No. Clearly you are not. I can see why you admire her so. I'm glad."

Something in her tone made him stop and wait as a large family passed them, the father carrying a sleeping infant in his arms. When they had a measure of privacy, he continued, but at a slower pace so that they lagged behind the crowd forming in the square.

"I'm not sure what you mean, Mor, but in case you have hopes of me forming an attachment, rest assured that I respect the princess, but nothing more."

"Nonsense. You may convince others, but not your own mother. I've seen the way you look at her. It's the same way your father used to look at me."

Merek felt himself reddening and was grateful for the darkness. "That's absurd," he scoffed. "The festival spirit has gone to your head."

She squinted at him. "I see. You're resisting the truth. Well, I suppose that's understandable. But someday you'll have to face it, my dear. It's not good for you to keep such strong feelings locked away."

Her words pricked something deep within him. He wanted to deny what she said, but couldn't quite form the words. Instead, he pulled her deeper into the shadows of the trees lining the square. The dancing was in full swing now, and all eyes were fixed on the couples in the center of the ring of firelight. Large bonfires burned around the edges, illuminating the dancers in the square, while casting the night beyond into darker shadows.

Keeping an eye on the people nearest them to avoid being over-heard, Merek asked in a pained whisper, "If you're right—and I'm not saying that you are—but what could I possibly do about it? There's no future for a man like me with a woman like her."

"Why not? She is fond of you, I can see that. Why couldn't you have a future together?"

"She's no more fond of me than she is the tailor who sews her clothing. You don't understand, she treats everyone that way."

"I understand more than you think. Talk to her about your feelings. You may be surprised."

The very thought made Merek's palms sweat. "Never. She's the heir to the throne. One simply doesn't make overtures of courtship without being invited."

"Speak to her father then, as one man to another. He would be able to tell you if such a suit would be acceptable or not."

"I've seen the kind of men she's considering for marriage. She would never issue such an invitation to me. She's young and life holds uncountable prospects for her. She's more likely to be happy with a man like…like Rorden, even, than someone like me."

"Rorden?" Sigrid wrinkled her nose. "A man like him could never hold her interest for long. You underestimate her, I think."

"Or perhaps you overestimate me. Even if she were free of the crown, what do I have to offer her? I'm what, a dozen years her senior?"

"An accident of birth," Sigrid said dismissively. "Easily overcome."

Merek continued as if he hadn't heard her. "I have no fortune, and no noble family name. If she could hear us now, she would laugh at me. Or worse, pity me."

"Or perhaps she would know, as I do, that you are of like minds and hearts and nothing else matters. When I left my family's wealthy life to join your father here in the north, it didn't matter that he didn't have the connections and wealth my family had always hoped for me. We belonged together, and nothing else was more important than becoming his wife."

Merek had never heard his mother speak about the life she had given up to marry his father. There was no bitterness in her tone, in spite of the heartache that such a life had brought her. It moved him but also saddened him, because there could be no such ending for him and Ria.

"I'm afraid it's not the same, but thank you for thinking so highly of me." He squeezed Sigrid's hand affectionately. She opened her mouth, as if to protest, but he stopped her. "No, Mor, what you suggest is impossible. We'll go our separate ways and that's how it should be. Please, don't mention this to me again."

Sigrid nodded sadly. "If that's what you wish. But if I may, there's something else I need to tell you. Some years ago—after

Marga married and she and Halth took over the farm—I began setting aside the money you sent. At first I thought, 'We don't need it now, so I'll keep it safe until someday when our crops fail or the winter is particularly harsh.' But that day never came, and now I want to return it to you."

Merek just shook his head. "Mor, you're too worried about me. I have no use for it. You need it more than I."

Sigrid lifted her chin in defiance. "You just told me how you can't hope to win the woman you love because you have no fortune. What I'm trying to tell you is that you *do*. It's not large, but it's more than anyone in the entire Dimm Forest has ever seen. Do with it what you will, but it belongs to you."

"I don't think that will win me the hand of a princess," he said, but he was touched nonetheless.

His mother smiled. "Well, as for winning a princess, the rest is up to you."

"And if I refuse?"

"Then I'll simply dump it in the river. Oh!" Sigrid beamed. "Look at your princess!"

Merek followed her gaze. Ria had returned. She and Biren were on the opposite side of the square visiting with the musicians, and from the way she cocked her head and gestured he could almost hear Ria complimenting their playing.

The sight of her stunned him. She had changed her clothing into one of the traditional dresses of the native forest women. The full skirt in red and blue was far less sophisticated than her previous gown, but the waistcoat of deep green still emphasized her shapely figure. Her hair was no longer bound tightly to her head, but now flowed freely down her back to mimic the style of the forest maidens. She'd been beautiful before, but now, as Biren slipped white wildflowers into her hair while she chatted with the musicians, he thought he had never seen anyone more lovely.

Sigrid looked at his struck expression and smiled. "You see, you don't know everything you think you do about this young woman."

Merek glanced at his mother. "You can't put her in a different dress and think that will change anything."

"Ah, but she asked for it. This afternoon while you were away. And that's not all she asked, but I won't give away her surprise."

"Surprise?" he asked. But Ria had seen him and was making her way toward him eagerly.

"Surely it means something," his mother whispered, then gently pushed him forward toward the light.

"Strong!" Ria called gleefully. "I should have known I would find you skulking in shadows when there was dancing to be done." She winked at Sigrid and grabbed Merek's hand. "I've asked them to play the *Amola*. Hurry, they're waiting for us!"

Merek didn't move, trying to make sense of her words.

"Come!" she urged. "We mustn't keep them waiting!"

"You can't be serious," he said, noticing the other couples watching them expectantly.

"You promised me a dance."

"I never promised any such thing! You said you wanted to see dancing. That's not the same thing."

"Close enough. I don't want to watch. I want to dance."

Merek allowed her to pull him toward the ring of dancers. He was acutely aware of the many people watching with interest, elbowing their companions to draw attention to the princess and the captain entering the ring of firelight.

"It's been a dozen years at least," he warned Ria in a low tone. "I'll humiliate us both."

"Then we are well matched," she said brightly. "Because I only learned the steps this afternoon. But take courage, Marga tells me this is the easiest reel to learn."

"Marga! My sister taught you to dance?"

"Of course! You didn't expect me to ask your mother, did you? Though she did a lovely job finding me an appropriate costume, don't you think?" She twirled her skirt flirtatiously and skipped ahead of him.

Merek couldn't answer because they had reached the center of the square, and Ria left to join the ring of women facing outward toward their partners.

Merek stood with the men a short distance away, feeling conspicuous in his officer's uniform next to their brightly colored waistcoats. In the final moments before the music started, he removed his coat and tossed it to the crowd. This drew a hoot of appreciation from some of Stefan's soldiers, and Merek relaxed a little. He might humiliate himself, but he would at least do it in front of people who would love him all the more for it.

The *Amola* reel, like so many other favored village dances, told a tale of courtship and romance. The women began by moving clockwise in a small circle, while the men clapped in rhythm to their steps and kicks. Ria had practiced this part well, and quickly recovered from any mistakes. The women nearest her smiled with approval.

When it was the men's turn, they were less kind to Merek. His feet were slow to remember the steps of his youth, and his mistakes were met with gibes and even laughter when he once turned the wrong way.

Eventually, the men stepped forward to claim their partners. Merek hooked his arm around Ria's waist gingerly, far from the gusto with which the other men grabbed their partners.

"Smile, Captain, or it will look as though you're not enjoying yourself," Ria chided, her cheeks flushed with the energy of the dance.

"But I'm not enjoying myself," he grumbled, swinging her from left to right and back again. "I would rather face down a dozen Delth invaders unarmed than make a fool of myself this way."

"Nonsense. I can see it's coming back to you. You just need to relax. Hold me tighter, that will help."

"But your stitches—I don't want to hurt you," he protested.

"They are nearer my ribs than my waist," she said dismissively. "So as long as your hands don't wander…" She raised one eyebrow suggestively. Merek reddened and she laughed in satisfaction.

The drums changed their pattern, signaling a transition in the dance. Ria put both hands on his shoulders, and he grabbed her waist, swinging her into a high lift. She seemed surprised at the height and came down in a breathless giggle.

Merek smiled and as they began the second circuit, the music and the movement chipped away at the anxiety he'd been feeling all night. His worries began to shrink as he moved, focusing only on the steps and moving in harmony with Ria. It wasn't quite as effective as a good skirmish on the practice field, but he was surprised at how much it mimicked the effect, loosening his tension and easing his mind.

By the third circuit, Ria and Merek were moving through the sequence almost flawlessly. The crowd clapped in rhythm to the music, and some of the young men stomped their feet in appreciation. The energy was intoxicating, and Merek grinned. When the music ended with each of the women wrapped in the arms of her partner, the crowd cheered.

"Kiss her!" some of the young men cried. With an exuberant laugh, many of the couples complied.

Ria looked up at Merek, her eyes alight with the dance and the firelight. And challenge.

"Kiss her!" the soldiers from Stefan's company called, and Merek knew they meant it for him. The swine.

Instead, he spun her away from him and turned her to face the crowd, then gave a deep bow. She joined him, adding flourish with an elaborate curtsy. Then, in a flash, she turned and swiftly kissed him on the cheek.

The crowd roared with delight, though a few groaned loudly in disappointment. They clapped energetically as Merek and Ria exited the square.

"Thank you, Strong," she said to him as he escorted her toward the nearest bonfire. "That was most invigorating! All that I'd hoped it would be. If you'll excuse me, I need to thank the musicians."

Before he could think of something to say in response, she was gone, and the night suddenly seemed more dim without her.

"Well done, sir!" Rorden grinned broadly as he held out Merek's uniform coat.

Biren smiled warmly. "I confess that when I heard her plan to get you to dance, I didn't believe she could do it. But I'm happy to be wrong, and even happier to have seen it!"

"Her plan?"

"Oh yes, she was plotting all afternoon with your mother and sister. I don't know why, but she insisted that she dance with you and no one else tonight."

Merek thought about his mother's words. She had known about Ria's scheme. Is that why she had said what she did? Had she misinterpreted what the princess likely intended only as a lark?

"Probably just because she knew it would needle me so," he said.

"She does have a gift for it," Rorden agreed. "I'm just glad I was here to see it. I can't wait to tell Captain Eldar!"

"You'll do no such thing if you know what's good for you, Sergeant," Merek warned. "Or should I call you Rory?"

"Fair enough!" Rorden laughed, raising his hands in surrender. "I won't say a word. It's a great shame, though."

Biren glanced over her shoulder and spoke apologetically to Rorden. "I mustn't stray too far from the princess in case she needs me." She nodded to Merek in parting and slipped away.

"Be careful with her, Rorden," Merek said, as they watched the young maid depart. "I quite like her and wouldn't want to see her hurt."

"There's nothing to worry about, sir. She's too tied to the princess to have a serious suitor. Which is unfortunate. She is remarkable," he said wistfully.

Merek snorted. "Of course she is. Do you think the princess

would have chosen her otherwise? But I don't think her Highness would take kindly to you stealing her away."

"Perhaps not," Rorden said grimly. After a pause, he added, "But it may be fun to try, don't you think?" With a cheeky grin, Rorden turned and hurried to catch up with the young woman.

Merek followed their path to where Ria stood talking to the musicians. One handed her his long wooden flute deferentially. Ria took it and examined it with great care.

The surrounding crowd was growing noisy and restless waiting for another round of dancing. When the princess blew into the flute, however, the people closest turned and quieted. She played a few more notes, their tone heavy with warmth that sounded mournful to Merek's ears.

The tune was unfamiliar to him, but as she played even the noisy children grew quiet, listening, eyes fixed on the woman with the flute. The light from the blazing bonfire scattered shadows over her face, adding to the haunting mystery of the melody.

As Merek watched her play, so absorbed in her art that she seemed oblivious to the people around her, he felt the music tug at something deep within him. Something was awakening that was powerful, wondrous, but also dangerous.

He thought of holding her as they were dancing, her exuberant laugh, and the feel of her lips brushing against his cheek. Unbidden, other memories rushed into his thoughts. Standing with her atop a pile of rubble as she challenged him to follow her into enemy country. The sight of her moving like an angel amongst the displaced and suffering. Her haughty anger and her teasing wit. The helpless fear he felt when she collapsed at the inn in Cillith. As these memories filled his mind, an overpowering yearning washed over him.

And then it was over. The song ended in one last, long somber note, and the silence around him erupted into applause and hearty cheers. Ria smiled and curtsied graciously, beaming at the villagers. Then, as she bent to return the flute, she caught Merek's eye. Her dark eyes flashed briefly, and before she turned away, she winked.

In that moment, Merek felt as if the world shifted under him. It took his breath away, and he felt instinctively a need to steady himself.

With it, a stronger emotion flared. Danger. Run.

He stepped further away from the firelight and under the cover of trees. It was as if he stood on a precipice, mere inches from falling into an abyss, and everything warned him to flee. No, he realized, turning his back on the crowd. He wasn't on the edge of the precipice. He was already falling and had been falling for days. Weeks, even. It wasn't just the festival's gaiety and firelight. It was the way the princess regarded the world with brilliant confidence and compassion. Her clever tongue and quick laugh. How she got into his head so that he couldn't think of anything or anyone else when she was around.

He pushed through the forest, searching for the trail he knew was nearby. Yes, he was already falling, but it wasn't too late. With a new sense of purpose, he stepped onto the trail and ran.

The moon was full and bright in the cloudless sky when he reached the wall. He unbuckled his sword belt, stripped off his outer coat, then his boots. He loosened his shirt collar and cravat, already feeling cooler in the night air. And then he climbed.

He didn't scout out a path beforehand, nor did he take his time. He simply moved, attacking the wall with a ferocity that went against the patience and judgment he'd taught Stefan's men. It was just him and the stone, rough and biting under his unprotected hands. He moved so quickly that soon he was breathing heavily and his muscles strained. A part of his mind warned him that he was pushing too hard, but he reveled in the exertion.

He couldn't stop thinking about her, so he didn't try. But as Merek scaled the wall, the world began to right itself under him, and his mind cleared. He'd been careless these past weeks, but so far there was no harm done. In a few days' time, she would return to Albon and he would have no reason to see her again for a very long time.

No harm done.

But the words of his mother snuck into his mind. *Surely it means something.* What if she was right? What if Ria's actions that night were more than just her natural playful spirit? As he opened his mind to these thoughts, more flooded in after them.

What if she weren't a princess? What if she didn't have a throne and a kingdom to consider? What if—and here it really pushed the limits of fancy—she could love him too?

He paused, briefly overcome by an image of Ria as a commoner like him, married and settled together in a humble home in the Dimm Forest. Drained of strength, he closed his eyes as he imagined a different life...a life with her, bringing color and joy to his future. Living with the sound of her laughter as a daily companion. Holding her tenderly out in the yard in the evening twilight, as he'd seen his father hold his mother so many times when he was a child peeking out the window at their silhouettes against the evening sky. Two shadows melded into one, standing in a moment of perfect stillness.

But Merek Strong was not one to pine for that which he could not have.

He opened his eyes, and the image vanished, replaced by the reality of stone. He couldn't change what was, and he'd never been an idle dreamer. She was Honoria Thorodan, daughter of a king, heiress to a throne, and underneath his title and decorated uniform he was just a simple man from the forest. He didn't belong in her world and she belonged even less in his. Even if he could ever win her heart—and the idea was so pitiful it shamed him to think it—he could never ask her to give up who she was to be with him. And in a hundred lifetimes he could never hope to be worthy of a future queen.

Gritting his teeth, he pushed upward again with renewed strength, grasping at the rough stone. He knew what he must do. She must never suspect his feelings. She would probably marry soon—his insides churned at the thought—and the memory of these weeks together would fade. First for her, but eventually for him too. He would keep away from Albon as long as it took to drive her from his mind. By the time they met again, his feelings would be buried so deep they would be unrecognizable even to himself.

It was a good plan. Slowly, as he ascended the wall, it hardened into unyielding resolve.

Ria watched Biren smile at something Rorden had said. She wasn't entirely sure it was a good idea for them to spend much time together. Playful and flirtatious, Rorden didn't seem the type to be constant to a woman. But for one night, she supposed that Biren deserved the attention of a handsome man. This was the most animated Ria had seen Biren since their foreign travels.

The evening had been splendid, and she'd been delighted by the villagers' enthusiastic acceptance of her. The game with the piglet eliminated the mystique surrounding her once and for all, and now they smiled and called to her enthusiastically as she moved among them. But one thing continued to gnaw at her. Captain Strong had disappeared. She'd tried so hard to dispel the cloud hanging over him, and just when it seemed to lift, he'd vanished. She smiled, thinking of his expression when she appeared in the colorful homespun dress. For a time, he seemed to forget his troubles and just be...whoever he was beneath the uniform. She considered it a triumph.

Then it passed, and he'd disappeared. Was it the ever-pressing trees that dampened Ria's mood? In the midst of the friendly crowd of revelers, she suddenly felt keenly alone. She felt an urge to talk to someone she trusted, to hear a familiar voice.

A blond head poked out above a log where a handful of boys played, and she recognized the cobbler's son.

"Finn!" she called, moving toward him.

He saw her and crawled out of a hole in the log. "Oi!" he yelled to one of his fellows. "Give me my cap, Otten, or I'll pound you!"

"Finn, have you seen the captain?" she asked.

"Last I saw him, he was going that way." He pointed vaguely into the darkness of the surrounding trees, then plowed into another boy dancing before him, dangling a cap.

Sensing she would get nothing further from the boy, Ria turned in the direction he'd pointed. The undergrowth made the forest forbidding and dangerous, but the dancing firelight of the bonfire illuminated a small path. On a whim, she grabbed a wine flask and two cups from a passing woman and ducked into the darkness.

Soon the light from the fire and the cheerful music faded behind her. She felt adventurous striking out on her own into the forest, but after a time the night sounds became unnerving. But she was determined. What would cause him to slink away like this in the middle of the festivities? His mother had been so distinguished in her simple way, and his sister was very sweet. But she really didn't understand him sometimes. Just when it seemed he might let his guard down, he would withdraw and keep her at a distance. It was maddening.

At last, a clearing opened up ahead and the gray stone of Danvir's Wall rose before her. She stepped to the edge of the path, frowning in disappointment that there was no sign of the captain. Feeling foolish, she turned to leave when she caught sight of something on the ground.

It was a scabbard attached to a sword belt, and near it were a man's coat, stockings, and boots. Ria was astounded. When she picked up the coat and recognized the captain's insignia, she nearly laughed aloud.

A small sound above her made her look up. She gasped, hand to her lips, and stumbled backward to get a better view. Yes, it was a man. There was a man climbing the wall high above her.

She watched, dumbfounded, as Captain Strong moved one foot to a higher stone, then reached with an arm and pulled himself up.

She held her breath, palms sweating at the thought of him being at that treacherous height with nothing but his own arms and feet preventing him from plummeting to his death.

The full moon made his white shirt shine so brightly that she wondered how she hadn't seen him before. But of course, she would never think to look up. Feeling suddenly giddy, she considered what to do. Her first thought was to call out to him, but she instantly dismissed that notion.

Instead, stifling a laugh, she turned and ran toward the stairs.

When Merek reached the top of the wall, he was sweating and weak with exhaustion. He'd been foolish to push himself so hard at the beginning of the climb and barely had the strength to finish. But it had worked. The exertion had calmed the tempestuous feelings of earlier. His mind was clear. As he heaved himself over the parapet, it was with a great sense of conquering something far more forbidding than a simple climb.

He breathed in the sweet smell of the Dimm Forest with the smoky hint of autumn on the edges of the night. The cool stones relieved the burning of his bare feet. The night was so still, all he could hear was the sound of his own breathing, and even that was slowing to a calm. He breathed deeply and looked up at the full moon above.

A moon like this had power. It could bring babies into the world before their time. It was a moon for lovers, inspiring promises that would shape their futures. Tonight, under its light, it was a witness. A witness that he had confronted what was in his heart and safely locked it away. He had gained strength in his climb, somehow, and he now felt an iron resolve as firm as the stone wall upon which he stood.

"Personally, I find the stairs to be more convenient, but I suppose after so many years perhaps they've become dull."

The familiar voice—*her* voice, teasing, yet firm—was so unexpected, he whirled around in surprise.

Ria sat against the parapet a short distance away, the moon illuminating her round face shining with smug humor. She still wore the native dress of a simple forest girl, but in the moonlight it was drained of its vibrant color.

"You! How—?" he stammered, so many questions fighting to be voiced that they tripped up his tongue. "What are you doing here?"

She waved her hand carelessly. "It seemed a good place to be alone with my thoughts, and I thought you might need a drink after your climb." She held out a cup, and he noticed the wine flask sitting on the stones next to her. "You're welcome."

The incredulity of it all was too much. He laughed, and the last of his tension leaked away. She was unlike any woman he'd ever known, but he no longer feared his feelings for her. He knew their place now, and they would not surprise him again. Shaking his head, he accepted the cup and drained it. When he held it out to be refilled, she smirked.

"Are you sure? It's not watered down, you know. Can your constitution handle it?" she teased as she filled it again.

"This is old Morton's wine. It's so weak it's suitable for children." He looked up at the moon smiling at them overhead and downed the second glass, abating his thirst.

She narrowed her eyes. "I'm not sure what to make of such recklessness, Strong. Please, come and sit with me."

Ria patted the stone next to her. Merek paused, thinking of his decision to distance himself from her. Not even an hour old and it was already being tested. But his mind felt clear and calm, and his resolve was so firm that he might as well have encased his heart in iron. Now that he had identified his affliction, he was impervious to its effects.

He sat, but not next to her where he could feel her warmth. Instead, he sat opposite her a small distance away, stretching his legs out before him with space between him and the princess.

"So," She fixed her dark eyes on his. "Explain."

"Explain what?"

"Explain to me why you left a perfectly agreeable evening of revelry and song and, I might add, exceptional dancing on my part, to risk life and limb climbing a stone wall that must be nearly fifty feet high."

"Not quite," he said. "But close enough. It started as an experiment to see if it was possible. Now it's become a training exercise." *And on a night like this, a singular form of relief.*

"A training exercise? You're teaching others to do it?. That seems a good way of losing soldiers."

"Not at all. Only a select few will learn. If we can stay a step ahead of our enemies, we can be prepared for whatever they might try. This way, we can learn our weaknesses and how we might better guard against this form of an attack." He paused, considering whether or not to tell her of his plans to use Stefan's small squad to attack Endvar's guard. She would certainly be interested, but he wasn't sure if she would be discreet about it when they returned to Endvar.

In the silence, the princess's thoughts appeared to drift.

"Why did you choose your mother to escort me today?"

Merek was surprised at this sudden change in topic. He shrugged. "I just looked to the person I trusted most. Why?"

"Did you consider that choosing her would boost her reputation in the eyes of the other villagers? She's already well-respected, I could see that, but being seen with me today will certainly increase their esteem for her."

"I…" He hadn't thought of that, but of course she was right. "I'm sorry. I didn't mean to capitalize on your position—"

Ria waved a hand to stop him. "I don't mind, Strong, really I don't. Many people far less deserving have gained notoriety by their connection with my family. I wouldn't have blamed you if you had acted with cunning, but it intrigues me that you didn't. Just good instincts, perhaps?"

She smiled as she said it, and he relaxed a little. His body had cooled now in the night air, and he wished for his coat. He was about to suggest that they head back when she spoke again.

"Why didn't you kiss me tonight? When the crowd was chanting, why didn't you do it?"

He looked at her in alarm. But there was no hint of teasing or humor. Her face was open and frankly curious, softened by the moonlight. Was she really asking him *this* of all things?

He grasped for something to say. "I'm not in the habit of letting a crowd make my decisions for me." It came out a little gruffer than he intended.

She laughed softly. "You've never done anything distasteful to please a crowd? I wish I could say the same!"

"I didn't say it was distasteful," he said, hoping she wouldn't see his face redden in the dim light. "But one doesn't simply kiss a princess without invitation."

"Oh, well, thank you for that. I'm glad it wasn't a completely distasteful prospect." She laughed again and tipped her head back to look at the moon, exposing her graceful neck. He had a sudden urge to touch it. Yes, it was definitely time to be heading back.

He stood and offered her his hand. "I'm afraid this conversation is at risk of deteriorating."

"Indeed," she said, taking his proffered hand and drawing her legs beneath her to stand. "I apologize for my questions. The wine and the dancing have made me philosophical tonight. I have badgered you when I should instead be as merry as the good Gathering Witch, granting wishes under the full moon."

She skipped ahead and turned around to face him, bringing him up short. With hands on her hips and a mischievous glint in her eye she said, "Before you pass, Merek Strong, I demand a wish from you. I am the Gathering Witch, and I must know your heart's desire."

Merek nearly choked. His heart's desire? Did she *mean* to torment him? He coughed and instead searched for something safe. "I wish for my father to be alive."

The light in her eyes dimmed and her face fell.

Idiotic fool. Why couldn't he have said something else? Something less…grim. But she recovered quickly and stepped to his side, taking hold of his arm as they walked.

"Do tell me about him," she said kindly. "He must have been a remarkable man."

"I don't know about that. What boy ever truly knows his father? But he was the world to me."

And suddenly, Merek found himself talking about the one person he never spoke about to anyone. He shared memories of his father from his childhood, and Ria listened appreciatively, asking gentle questions to prompt him whenever he fell silent. Whether her manner or the wine had loosened his tongue, he wasn't sure. But he found himself telling her about the horrible night when the bandits attacked.

Merek had never spoken to anyone except his mother about what he'd seen that night. Not Sindal, not even Stefan, who had been his best friend in those days. He shivered involuntarily when he described his errant arrow that failed to stop the bandits from falling upon his father. When he told of the shell of a man his father became, Ria tightened her grip on his arm, rubbing it soothingly in response. By the time he finished, they'd reached the top of the stairs.

He paused before descending. "I always knew my mother loved my father, but the older I get the more I'm in awe at her sacrifice. Caring for him for all those years when he could do little for himself, and she had to take on his labors in addition to her own. Scraping out a life for her two children without the aid of her husband. When I left to join the army, he had just begun to recognize her again, though whether he knew she was his wife or just the woman who fed and bathed him, I don't know."

Ria looked out from the top of the wall into the forest and asked softly, "Did you join the army to escape, then?" There was no condemnation in her tone, but Merek was quick to answer.

"No. Though I suspect that's what most people thought."

"Why, then?" Ria turned to him, her upturned face echoing the pain of his story, but also urgent, searching his own. This mattered to her, though he couldn't imagine why, and he struggled to hold her gaze, looking instead at the stones beneath his feet.

"Mor didn't complain about me leaving, even before I started sending money home to her. She understood. I…" His voice filled unexpectedly with emotion and he cleared his throat before continuing. This was why he never spoke of these things to anyone. Perhaps it would be easier now if he had. Taking a deep breath and looking at a point far in the darkness, he continued. "The money kept Mor and Marga from starving. But the real reason I joined the army is because I never again wanted to be in a position where I couldn't protect those I love. Watching helplessly as the ones I love suffer and not being able to stop it."

He glanced at Ria and saw her look of understanding before she turned away. And something else. Respect. Her voice, when she spoke, was so quiet that if the night hadn't been so still he might not have heard her words clearly.

"I'm sorry for your pain," she said. "But I am also grateful for it because without it you probably would never have ventured away from these forests and into our lives. And what would Rahm be like without our beloved Captain Strong?" She spoke with a hint of wry humor in her words, but he was still moved. He'd never considered how his life may have been different, and it touched him to think she cared. Without another word, and before he said something he would later regret, he led her down the stone steps to the ground below.

Twenty-Seven

Aiya drummed her fingers on the table, trying to focus on the ledger before her. She'd received a letter from Imar the day before detailing his safe arrival in Branvik with lengthy descriptions of the hard, mountainous land and its even harder people. It had taken two weeks for his letter to reach her, and she wanted to report on how business was going when she replied.

But it was difficult to concentrate on the ledger when the afternoon sun was warm and inviting against her neck, and the breeze tossing the curtains was filled with the sharp smell of apples cooking next door. It was a smell Aiya always associated with the advent of fall.

She was getting distracted. Again.

She sat up straighter in her chair and forced herself to focus on the page before her. As she reviewed the sums, she found herself idly humming and realized that she didn't know the words to the tune, but the melody was now familiar to her. The man working outside her back door had been whistling it all morning.

To better protect her in Imar's absence, Sergeant Dan and his squad were building an awning while disguised as simple tradesmen. They were polite and respectful as they worked, never bothering her unnecessarily. Aiya was a little disappointed. A little bother would at least be interesting. She was no longer visiting Hala, and she missed those visits. If she were honest, she missed the danger associated with them almost as much as the idle chatter and friendship.

Closing the ledger with a sigh, Aiya stood and reached for the tea she'd prepared earlier. She snatched a pair of mugs off a shelf, the ceramic clinking as she pushed the door outward.

It stopped short, thudding against a man on the other side.

"*Vakish ta!*" Aiya apologized in Khouri reflexively before switching to Rahmish. "I'm very sorry!"

Sergeant Dan moved out from behind the door, allowing her to push it open fully.

"No matter," he said, rubbing his shoulder. "It serves me right for standing in the way."

Aiya looked up at the frame mounted above her doorway. It stretched the length of the wall, and would eventually form a roof that shaded the entire back side of her house. She sighed with satisfaction.

"You do good work, Sergeant Dan. It will give us shade in the summer and keep us dry during the winter rains."

"It'll do, I suppose." He struggled to meet her eyes when he spoke, though he seemed comfortable enough with his fellow soldiers.

She raised the pot of tea. "I thought you might be thirsty. Do you drink tea? It's cold now, I'm afraid, but I can warm if it you'd like."

Sergeant Dan looked slightly alarmed. He wiped his hands on his coarse brown trousers before reaching for the outstretched mug. "Uh, yes, thank you."

His hands fumbled awkwardly, and Aiya searched for something to say to put him at ease. Of all the soldiers assigned to her, she liked his manner best. The redheaded Jax watched her with too much interest, and she couldn't sort out the others. They looked too much the same, these Rahmish men with their thick beards.

"What is that song you were whistling before?" She hummed a few bars of the tune that had been stuck in her head all morning.

"Was I whistling that?" His fair skin reddened. "My apologies, miss. I didn't realize."

"I don't mind. It's pleasant. Why are you ashamed?"

Sergeant Dan looked at his boots. "It's a drinking song, and not a very nice one, I'm afraid. Not the sort for a lady to hear."

"I didn't hear anything but a nice melody. Now you must sing the words, so I can judge."

He reddened further and gulped down the last of the tea, thrusting the mug toward her. "Thank you for the drink. I'm sorry to disturb you with the whistling."

There was a clear expectation that she was to leave, but Aiya wasn't anxious to return indoors. She placed the pot on a nearby bench and began pulling wilted flowers from the vine that grew up the corner of the house. Dan fidgeted. After a moment, she began singing softly in Khouri. When the tune ended, she turned to Dan with a smile.

"You see, it is not only Rahmish who have drinking songs that are...questionable. This song tells of two lovers who want to run away together, but the woman is already bound to another. On the night they are to leave, the men fight and her lover is killed. She marries the other man but never tells him that her baby is not his." She considered the pale pink flower in her hand before casting it aside. "That was my husband's favorite, but it always made me sad."

"You were married?" Dan asked in surprise.

"Once. But he died many years ago."

"That is a sad story," Dan said, and she wasn't sure if he meant the ballad or the fact that her husband had died. "Is that why you came to Rahm?"

"A fresh beginning is good," she said simply, knowing it was vastly inadequate to describe the pain of starting a new life while torn apart by grief.

"Dan!"

A soldier ran around the corner and skidded to a stop. "They're back, sir. Captain Strong and the rest."

"Where are they? The guard complex?"

"No, not yet," the young man said. "They're in the square. I thought you'd want to know right away."

"Yes, thank you." Dan's green eyes were alight with anticipation.

"I will come with you," Aiya said, removing her apron and draping it over the teapot.

He looked at her in surprise. "You want to meet the princess?"

"I've seen the princess," she said dismissively. "You are anxious to meet your captain, but you cannot leave while I am here. So I will come too."

"Thank you, miss," he said gratefully.

They walked quickly together through the streets of Endvar, the long shadows of evening painting the stone streets black. Shops were closing, but as they neared the square the streets became increasingly crowded. It seemed everyone wanted to see the princess. The pressing crowd separated Aiya from Dan, and she found her way blocked by a wall of men and women packed shoulder to shoulder. Aiya stood on her toes, trying to see where Dan had gone.

A dozen mounted guards dressed in royal green stood motionless in a circle around a carriage. It was not a particularly fine carriage, and the horses looked worn as though they had traveled a great distance. But the woman who emerged from it looked as bright and regal as she had when Aiya had first seen her in the captain's office. Her blue dress complemented the uniform of the man holding out his hand to assist her in stepping down to the street.

It was him.

She knew before he even turned, recognizing his height and black hair. As his face came into view the princess spoke, causing him to smile. In his eyes Aiya caught the briefest expression of something that made her feel like an outsider, a tenderness for the woman whose hand he held that went beyond mere duty and respect.

Aiya's heart sank. She didn't clap with the rest of the crowd as the princess called out a greeting. She didn't listen to her words, feeling instead a distinct distaste for the woman. It was childish, she knew.

The dazzling woman was far more likely to capture the heart of a man like Captain Strong than Aiya ever could. But the knowledge was bitterness to her, and she regretted coming.

Aiya eased forward through the crowd, looking for Dan. He was speaking to one of the royal guards, an older man with an intimidating face that looked as though it had been scarred from the pox. Rorden was there as well, and Aiya's mood lightened to see him. She thought about trying to catch his eye, but just as she did, one of the mounted soldiers shifted slightly and Aiya froze. Across the square, looking out from the crowd, was a familiar face; a dark-skinned man with black hair wearing the colorful layered robes of her people.

Behni.

He looked much older than she remembered, but still had the same rigid jaw and fierceness in his eyes. Hala stood next to him, watching the proceedings with interest. Aiya shrank back into the crowd. Trying not to draw attention, she pushed back the way she'd come.

"Aiya!" a young voice cried out.

Aiya's heart stopped. Finn, the cobbler's young son, waved at her from the square.

"Aiya!" he called again, grinning and waving excitedly.

Aiya glanced at Behni. Had he heard the boy?

She ducked her head and pushed through the crowd, hoping Finn wouldn't call out again. She'd nearly reached the edge of the growing crowd when a commotion bustled through the people next to her, and Finn pushed his way out into the open.

"Aiya!" he complained. "Didn't you see me? Couldn't you hear me calling you?"

"Finn, my sweet boy!" she said, hugging him briefly. "I'm so happy to see you! I'm sorry I could not stop. Did you have a good journey?" She rested one arm around his shoulder, hurrying him down the street.

Finn shrugged, his sandy hair showing the grime of days on the road. "I got to ride on the back of the carriage. I started out with the driver but he said I talked too much, so I rode on the back and talked to the soldiers riding behind us instead."

Aiya tried to smile, but her heart pounded with worry. Had she been seen? Had she left the square before Behni noticed her?

Trying to keep her mind off the danger, she asked Finn questions about his trip in the north. He didn't require much prompting and regaled her with tales that she only listened to half-heartedly.

"Will you be staying with me?" she asked when they arrived at her house.

"No, with Captain Drenall. He's taking me back to Albon with the princess."

Aiya gave him another hug, this time with more warmth. "Come visit again before you go. I've missed you."

The boy darted back down the street, and Aiya sat on the wooden bench near her back door, breathing deeply. She'd known for months that Behni was in the city, but something about seeing him for herself had stirred painful memories.

Aiya closed her eyes as she willed her heart to slow down and her body to relax. It didn't work. Her muscles tensed, and she found herself wanting not to flee, but to fight. It was absurd. As a thief, her skills were to avoid confrontation, not seek it. But still she felt a desire to do something. What had happened to her? For years, she and Imar had survived by staying in the shadows. But now, she felt keenly that just surviving was no longer enough.

The morning air was cool and low clouds obscured their path as Captain Drenall led the mounted party out of Endvar's city gates and through the surrounding settlements. Ria yawned and wished briefly for her traveling cloak. But if the clouds burned off soon, she would be glad she had no more extra weight than her light jacket.

A return to Endvar meant a return to her sidesaddle and fashionable riding gear. After enjoying two days of rest and refreshment at Lord Ogmun's, she felt more presentable than she had in weeks, sitting primly in her crisp riding frock and hat.

But still, something didn't sit right with her. Perhaps it was just the gloomy weather threatening to rain but only succeeding in shrouding the land in a moist blanket of mist. Perhaps it was her worry over seeing her father again.

Or perhaps, she considered, it was the fact that Captain Strong had not come that morning to see her off. She'd even sent him a note the day before, but there had been no sign of him as they made their way through the city. Ria had been prepared for him to be busy in the days since they'd returned to Endvar, but this was just abominably bad manners.

After spending two months together and confiding in him in ways she hadn't to anyone else, she had expected more. Instead, Captain Strong had politely deposited her into the capable hands of Lord and Lady Ogmun and hadn't visited her since. The Ogmuns had been very solicitous, caring for her and their little company and outfitting them for their return to Albon, but Ria was still disappointed.

What did you expect? a part of her scolded. *Would you have him pining after you with tearful farewells?* The idea made her cringe. She pictured that morning in Rellana two years back when Artem had begged her not to leave. His desperation was the most naked emotion she'd ever seen from him and had left her shaken even as she held her ground.

No. That's not what she wanted from Strong. She wasn't quite sure what she wanted, but it wasn't that. In the past weeks, her esteem for him had risen. He'd become a trusted friend whose opinion mattered deeply. She wanted his respect, not his affection. For him to ignore her stung her pride, nothing more.

Feeling satisfied that she'd identified the source of her brooding, she sat up a little straighter in her saddle. After a time, the sun broke through the clouds, revealing a brilliant blue sky. They rode southwest with the sun warming their faces and a gentle breeze blowing patterns in the tall grass around them. Tidy farms were dotted with flocks, and wooden fences surrounded neat cottages with smoke rising from their chimneys.

Ria took a deep breath and exhaled in contentment. The air smelled clean and earthy, washed with recent rain.

"You enjoy the countryside, Your Highness?" Captain Drenall asked beside her. She hadn't noticed him drawing close, so absorbed she'd been in her own thoughts.

She smiled. "It has its charms, Captain. There have been delightful things about each place we've visited, don't you think?"

"I do, my lady. But I am looking forward to going home. I'm not the wanderer that I was in my youth."

"Ah, yes, home," Ria said, trying to sound cheerful. Her last letter from her father had been unusually short and had troubled her. It began normally, but by the end of it she didn't know what to think.

Each day I watch for your return. It feels as though you've been gone an age. I have such a surprise for you. We will finally have the peace I've been seeking. There will never be a reason for you to leave me again.

Ria had puzzled over that final statement, trying to make sense of it. It needled her, and the more she turned it over in her mind, the less she could put it to rest. She didn't know what faced her when she returned, but the excitement she felt about going home was beginning to be tinged with dread.

From the moment Merek rode into the courtyard of Lord Bolen's estate, he was possessed by a distinct feeling of unease. He looked

sharply about him, but there was nothing unusual about the tradesman chatting with the kitchen maid or the young man leading a stallion
in the direction of the stables. Geese honked at a passing cat, and a
shirtless blacksmith pounded the rim of a carriage wheel in rhythmic
strokes. All was as it should be.

And yet, it wasn't.

Was it the guard who left his post at a quick jog? Or the strong
sense of being watched from a curtained upstairs window? Whatever
it was, Merek half expected to be ambushed as he was shown into
a shadowed drawing room. The drapes were drawn against the late
summer light, leaving the air thick and warm.

"Captain Strong. How can I be of service?"

Domar's manner was subservient as he indicated a cushioned settee. Merek remained standing.

"I wish to speak with your master. I assume he received my note."

"Yes, but it wasn't very informative. If you would explain your purpose a little further, then I might be able to help you. Lord Bolen
cannot answer every request for an audience, you understand."

"I'm afraid that this matter requires that I speak with Lord Bolen
directly."

"Of course." Domar nodded smoothly. "My apologies that you
came all this way for nothing. I will send word when his lordship is
available."

He spoke with finality and gestured toward the door.

Merek didn't move.

"If his lordship doesn't want to be arrested for treason, he will
make himself available immediately."

Domar paused. "Treason?"

"Two months ago, Lord Bolen gave warning that the princess was
in danger, yet failed to give adequate information to prevent the attack. If there is even a hint that he's been working with her enemies,
the king will have his head."

Something flickered briefly in Domar's eyes. "Where was this attack?"

"I will share that information with Lord Bolen," Merek said firmly.

Domar bowed slightly. "One moment, please."

When Lord Bolen stormed into the room a few moments later, his face was red with anger. He jabbed a fleshy finger in Merek's direction.

"How dare you threaten me? Arrested for treason! Who do you think you are?"

"My lord, I meant only—"

"I came to you in good faith, and you spurned my warning. Now you come here speaking of treason!"

"If I might speak with you alone, I can explain—"

"You will regret this, Captain, I can promise you. If you think—"

"My lord!" Merek growled in the voice he usually reserved for soldiers. Lord Bolen stopped mid-sentence, his mouth agape. "I mean no offense. But a matter of some urgency has come to my attention and it's imperative that I speak with you alone. Now."

Bolen snapped his mouth shut, fuming. He looked as if he wanted to throw Merek out of his house, but his eyes held an insatiable curiosity.

It was Domar who settled the conflict. He stepped forward obsequiously. "I'm sure the captain will keep his business brief, my lord. I will be just outside the door if you need me."

Bolen nodded and waved his steward away. When he and Merek were alone, he wiped his forehead with a silk handkerchief. "Well then. What do you want? To arrest me and throw me in prison?"

Merek breathed deeply to keep his voice calm. "No. But I must know how you knew there would be an attack on the princess in Cillith."

"Cillith? I know nothing of an attack in Cillith."

Merek paused. "You warned me that the princess was in danger before we left Endvar. While we were in Cillith, a man broke into her rooms and threatened her."

Bolen's expression relaxed into a smug smile. "You think my warning referred to a common rogue?"

Merek shifted his stance, burying the urge to grab Lord Bolen by the scruff of his neck. "So you know nothing of it?"

"This is the first I've heard of it."

"Then what was your warning referring to?"

Lord Bolen's smile turned hard. "I've already told you all I know about the princess, Captain."

"Where did this information come from?"

"Whispers here and there. I have far greater connections than you suppose, Captain. The things I know would turn your beard gray."

"What sort of things?"

"Things that will turn this city on its head."

"How so?"

Lord Bolen's eyes darted to the door. "There's a shift in power coming to Endvar. You would do well to consider carefully your allegiances."

"My allegiance is to the king."

"As is mine," Bolen said pompously. "Which is why I warned you when I learned of a possible threat to the princess's safety."

"Your warning is worth nothing if you refuse to tell me where this threat comes from."

"I tell you, I don't know more than that. But as the princess is well on her way to Albon, perhaps it was no more than idle talk. I'm sure she will be well protected on her journey."

Merek felt a surge of anger at Bolen's condescending tone. "And what of the tunnels?"

Lord Bolen blanched. "Tunnels?"

"Yes. The tunnels beneath the city. Ask your man Domar. He's well acquainted with them."

Merek knew he'd crossed a line, but the look of shock on Bolen's face gave him a perverse sense of satisfaction.

"Domar!" Bolen bellowed. The steward appeared so quickly, Merek was certain he'd heard every word of their conversation. "Captain Strong is finished here." He turned his back, but not before Merek saw his look of fear.

Twenty-Eight

Aiya lay in the darkness listening to the sound of her own breathing and a cricket chorus under her window. The silence of her room pressed in on her ears. She'd had trouble sleeping the past few nights, even with a soldier posted outside her door. Ever since seeing Behni in the square, her nights had been restless and disturbed by vivid dreams. Many hours she spent lying in the dark waiting in vain for sleep to claim her.

Had Behni seen her or heard Finn calling her name? Hala had kept her secret thus far, but if Behni suspected the truth, how long would that last? What would Behni do to her if he found her?

These thoughts tripped over each other until finally she sighed and sat up. She threw off her blanket and went out into the main room. All was dark and still, except for the curtain which moved faintly in the breeze of the open window. It took only a minute to find a clean cloth and dampen it with water from a pitcher. She pressed the cloth against her face, closing her eyes against the soothing coolness.

Then she remembered that the window had been closed when she retired for the night.

She reacted in an instant, dropping the cloth and reaching for the pitcher. She swung, aiming for the head of her hidden assailant, but the shape behind her ducked out of the way easily.

Aiya jumped backward, nimbly dodging a chair, then grabbed a vase from a nearby table and threw it at her attacker. It hit the floor, the crash loud in the darkness. Aiya wondered why the soldier didn't come rushing in, and then realized with a sickening feeling that the intruder would have seen to him first.

She was alone.

Panicked, she grabbed the firebrands kept near the hearth.

"Aiya, please," a voice whispered loudly in the darkness.

She paused. Her attacker was silhouetted against the window, hands raised in a gesture of peace.

She knew that voice.

"Hala?" Aiya breathed in disbelief.

Hala pulled the scarf away from her face and took a step forward, but Aiya raised the fire poker threateningly.

"Please, Aiya. You and I both know that won't do any good." Hala's voice was different somehow, full of an unfamiliar hardness.

"*You* are Behni's Menari warrior? The one who fought the soldiers? All those injuries…"

"It was convenient to let you think Behni beat me, but Behni learned long ago not to touch me. He doesn't need to, does he? Not when he's the father of my children and has power over everything I care about," Hala said bitterly.

"Did Behni send you here?"

"No. But he is coming for you. Not tonight, but soon. I tried to hide your presence here as long as I could, but he saw you in the square. He'll find you soon, but even if he doesn't, you must leave the city. Tonight!"

"Why?" Aiya asked, still trying to make sense of beautiful Hala dressed before her in the traditional black Menari garb of a hired killer. How much she must have hidden from her!

"There are dangerous things taking place here, and I beg you to leave before…Soon it will not be safe for you."

"Before what? What do you know, Hala?"

"It doesn't matter," Hala said dismissively. "I don't know all the details, but Behni is worried that they will be discovered soon. Already they have moved against the princess, a desperate gamble because they are acting sooner than planned. It is a significant risk, and he's angry that his hand is being forced."

"Why are you telling me this now?"

"Because I don't want you to get hurt. When the soldiers come, this will be a dangerous place for anyone, but especially for you. Behni has not forgiven you for Tupin's robbery, but I fear—" Here she glanced at the ceiling. "If Behni learns who lives above you, he will suspect you of greater treachery. There have been obstacles to his plans in this city, and if he has any reason to think you are involved..."

Aiya didn't respond. How had Hala learned all this? One thing was certain. If she'd told Behni what she knew, Aiya would already be dead. Hala had kept Aiya's secrets for herself.

"Please promise me you will leave the city tonight," Hala begged, grasping Aiya's hands in her own and taking the poker from her fingers. Aiya let her, knowing that if Hala really wanted her dead, there was nothing Aiya could do.

But she didn't want her dead. Instead, she was warning her to flee.

"I have nowhere to go," Aiya said.

"You will start again. Just as you did when Imar died."

So, there *were* things Aiya had kept hidden from her. This gave her comfort.

"Thank you, Hala," she said warmly. "You have risked much in coming here tonight."

"Promise me that you will leave," Hala repeated.

"I will do all I can to be safe," Aiya replied. "If that means leaving the city, I will do it."

Hala embraced Aiya, resting her forehead against her own.

"I will pray for your safety. You might go to Ardania. They are still friendly to Khouris, but soon will not be friendly to Rahmish. I hope you are not here to see it."

Hala slipped her scarf over her face again in a smooth motion, and just as fluidly, leaped up to the open window and out onto the pavement below, disappearing without a sound.

Aiya didn't waste a moment. She yanked open the door and ran to the shape motionless on the ground. The soldier's eyes were open, unseeing. Dead.

Aiya growled in frustration and ran inside, trading her slippers for a pair of sturdy shoes and putting on a coat against the cold night air. And then, she ran.

"I still don't believe Lord Bolen is behind it all." Dan said. He sat against the wall in Merek's office, rethreading the laces on his boots.

Rorden snorted with disgust. "Not likely. A cow has more intelligence."

"I don't believe it either," Merek said, rolling up the map of the city where Rorden had sketched out the tunnels according to the kitchen maid's drawing. "He was too eager to gloat, like someone who's been let in on an important secret. I don't think he even realizes that he's Domar's puppet. There must be something Domar gains from Bolen gaining power. Let's look into who Bolen's enemies are and find out what he might gain if they're eliminated."

"Bolen makes enemies wherever he goes. No one in this city likes him," Rorden said.

"No, I mean true enemies. Those who actively resist him or compete with him in trade." Merek leaned back and scratched his neck. The beginning of a headache was forming behind his right temple, likely from lack of sleep and poring over maps by candlelight. It had been dark for hours, and the courtyard had grown quiet, but they were still no closer to deciding what to do about Lord Bolen and his strange servant. He'd gone to Bolen's hoping to gain information and access to the tunnels. Instead, he'd been rebuffed, and in turn revealed too much to the enemy.

"It's a pity I mentioned the tunnels," Merek said, stifling a yawn. "They'll be watching them closely now."

"But you didn't tell him you knew where the entrance was," Dan offered.

"It's true," Rorden said thoughtfully. "We might still be able to get in with Yulda's help."

"No, I don't want to put the girl at risk." Merek said. "It isn't worth—"

A sudden thump made Merek start in surprise. He strode to the door and threw it open, one hand on his long knife.

Aiya stood on the threshold, a wild look in her eyes, her hair loose and unkempt. Under a man's coat she wore her nightdress. A pair of boots peeked out under the hem.

"Hala came to me tonight," she said breathlessly, as if having run a great distance. "To warn me to leave the city before it is too late. Behni knows that you have almost discovered them."

As her tale continued, Dan's expression darkened.

"You're sure Regin is dead?" he asked.

Aiya nodded. "I'm sorry."

Dan spat an ugly curse.

"So you think Behni is working with Ardanians?" Merek asked. "But Ardania has always been friendly with Rahm."

"I'm just telling you what she said. She seemed in earnest. She also said," here she looked meaningfully at Merek, "that there would be an attack on the princess."

"The princess? When?"

"Soon. She didn't say more, except that Behni is acting desperately because you are close to learning the truth."

"Do you trust her?" Rorden asked. "Could it simply be a distraction?"

"I believe she spoke the truth. She risked too much to come to me."

Merek swore and pressed his hands against the desk, his mind racing. If Ria was in danger, he had to do something. But if Behni thought they were close to uncovering his plans, how could they abandon their efforts now?

"We can send out riders to warn Captain Drenall," Rorden suggested, as if reading his thoughts. "It may only be a ruse, but if not, they'll be swift in going to the princess's aid. We're so close, sir. If we can get into the tunnels—"

"If you go to the tunnels tonight, you will certainly face a trap," Aiya interjected. "They will be ready for you."

The room felt suddenly too warm and the air too stuffy. Merek's vision sharpened, the same heightened sensation he felt going into battle. The question was, which battle? He had a duty to protect Endvar. But long before receiving that charge he had sworn an oath to King Sindal. Surely, that oath extended to his daughter as well. The thought of leaving Ria unprotected made his pulse quicken.

Rorden waited expectantly for his decision, but offered nothing more in his anxious expression. But Aiya…in her dark eyes Merek saw understanding. She knew what he would choose, and she approved.

"Alert Captain Eldar that we ride to the princess's aid," he said decisively. "With any luck, we'll reach Drenall in time to warn him, then return as soon as the princess's safety is assured and plan our next steps against Behni. In the meantime, send for Captain Wott. His peacekeepers can watch for suspicious activity in our absence."

Rorden nodded and left at a brisk trot, his footsteps echoing down the stairs at the end of the hallway.

"How can I help, sir?"

Dan's question brought Merek back to the present. His mind had already moved to the miles of hard riding ahead of him. He looked at Dan, standing together with Aiya.

"Make sure Aiya is safe. Get her out of the city. Today, if possible. She has great enemies here and has risked much for us all."

"But sir," he protested. "The woman who did this, we can't just let her go. Regin—"

"Aiya's safety is more important than revenge," Merek interrupted. "Once she's safe, make yourself useful to Captain Wott. You know as much about this threat as anyone. He may need your perspective. Whatever you do, don't go after Hala alone."

Dan nodded stiffly, but didn't look pleased.

Merek laid a hand on Aiya's shoulder, and she looked up at him, dark eyes luminescent. "We all owe you a great debt, Aiya. Thank you. Dan will see you to safety."

"Many thanks, my captain." She hesitated, then said something in her native tongue that sounded rhythmic and musical. Merek had no idea what it meant, but it sounded like a farewell, and Merek briefly wondered if he might never see her again.

Twenty-Nine

"I believe you're quite the horseman now, Edvin," Ria remarked to her father's clerk as he rode up next to her.

He beamed. "Thank you, Your Highness. I f-feel m-more confident now," he said, stuttering slightly.

"You don't sound like it," a young voice piped up. "You sound downright nervous."

Ria turned to the cobbler's son with a retort on her tongue, but Biren was already chastening him. He rode with Biren on her horse, too small and inexperienced a rider to control his own mount.

"You mustn't say such things," Biren said in his ear. "A gentleman knows when to keep hurtful thoughts to himself."

"I'm not going to be a gentleman," Finn grumbled.

"But I'll bet your far knows how to talk to them in their manner," Biren said wisely. "His best manners probably earn him his best customers, am I right?"

Finn huffed in reply.

Ria felt a twinge of jealousy watching her maid. Biren still wore trousers so that she could sit astride her horse, the only practical way to ride if she were sharing her horse with another. Watching Biren reminded Ria of the freedom she'd felt while wearing trousers. She was surprised to find she missed it. A little.

"Do you have anything to eat?" Finn asked Biren.

"We ate no more than an hour ago!"

"I'm still hungry," he complained.

"Patience," Ria said. "Edvin tells me that tonight we will be staying in a proper inn, and you will eat until you cannot fit in one more bite."

"If that's possible," Biren teased.

The road narrowed as they skirted a large rock outcropping which loomed above them on the left. To their right, the ground fell away sharply to the river far below. Edvin moved forward of the women to accommodate the narrow path, and Ria noticed a stain on the back of his shirt that would cause some laundress a headache when they returned home. She wouldn't mention it, of course. Teasing was only for men of the right temperament and rank. A man such as Edvin—reliable and intelligent, but most comfortable unnoticed in his service to the crown—earned no more than bland politeness from the princess.

Ria didn't see the arrow fly until it struck Edvin in the neck. With a choking sound, he slumped in his saddle, loosening his hold on the reins.

Ria gasped as a volley of arrows rained down from above the rock outcropping. Captain Drenall called out in alarm at the front of their company, and the soldiers nearest her shouted commands to each other.

But Ria couldn't tear her eyes away from the ghastly sight of the arrow protruding from Edvin's flesh. She knew he was dead, which meant the archer who had fired the shot was very skilled.

Sluggishly, Ria finally realized she was in danger and felt a surge of panic driving her to flee. But she was trapped. Edvin's horse blocked her way, and by the sounds of conflict around the bend, she knew that Captain Drenall contended with armed men ahead. There would be no escape that way.

"Turn around!" she cried to Biren behind her.

Biren nodded, her face pale, and tried to maneuver her horse back the way they had come. The soldiers nearest them had fallen, leaving their mounts unguided. With the massive rock on one side and the steep drop to the river on the other, the women were wedged in tightly. The

press of men and horses made it impossible to move, and the shouts
from Drenall and his men were growing more insistent.

Ria's mount danced with agitation, and she cursed the sidesaddle
that made her so much more difficult to control. In frustration, Ria
tried to urge her horse closer to the shoulder. It was tricky footing,
but if she could just get turned around—

An arrow struck her horse's withers, and the mare screamed, rear-
ing up on her back legs. Ria clutched at her mane desperately, her
weight pulling hard on the unbalanced saddle. The pommel dug into
her leg as she slid backward. With a terrifying jolt, the animal beneath her stumbled and stepped off the cliff.

The soldiers rode without speaking, nothing but the continuous
drumbeat of hooves filling the air and the smell of sweat and horse
seeping into their clothes. The sun was high in the sky now, and they
moved faster than they had in the dark. But Rorden was beginning
to lag, the sleepless night weighing him down.

Before him, Captains Strong and Eldar rode abreast, leading the
company.

"Sir!" Eldar called out to Strong. "We really should rest the horses."

And ourselves, Rorden thought.

Strong looked at Eldar, his expression hard. Rorden recognized
that intensity and knew it would be hard to distract him from his
purpose. But it was foolish to continue like this without any rest, either for themselves or their horses. If they were completely worn out
by the time they reached the princess, what good would they be to
anyone?

Understanding flickered in the captain's eyes, and he nodded
briefly.

Strong brought the company to a halt on a grassy knoll beside the river. They kept the horses saddled, expecting only a brief respite. The horses moved to the water to satisfy their thirst, and several soldiers stretched out on the ground. Rorden wasn't the only one feeling the effects of the long night.

Captain Strong climb to the top of a nearby hill, scouting the surrounding countryside. Rorden felt a duty to join him, but he also knew that this might be his only chance to rest. If there was a battle ahead of them, they would need all their strength. So he laid down as well, closing his eyes and trying to clear his mind. As much as he was worried about the princess, he worried even more for Biren and Finn. If the situation was dire for the heir to the throne, it would be even worse for her maid who had no value to their captors.

Biren screamed.

Ria reacted as she'd been taught as a girl, standing in the stirrup so she could free her right leg while pushing off the pommel to escape the massive beast. She fell through open air for several terrifying seconds before hitting the ground hard.

The impact knocked the breath from her lungs, and her left shoulder erupted with pain as she tumbled down the embankment through grass and bracken, finally coming to rest in a patch of woody vines that tore her clothing and skin. She lay for a moment, unmoving, the pain in her shoulder drowning out the sounds of battle above her.

Opening her eyes, Ria grimaced at the gray sky and forced herself to breathe. Even breathing was painful, but with effort she pushed the pain away and focused on the rest of her body. She was undoubtedly bruised and scraped, but the rest of her limbs felt sound.

Ria sat up, and with that simple motion her shoulder flared

with pain so excruciating that she yelled out. Quickly, she snapped her mouth shut in a whimper. She couldn't move her arm without blinding pain. Her head swam with it, and she closed her eyes. When she could bear to open them again, she sat for a moment, taking in her surroundings.

A tangle of woody vines had stopped her fall. Her horse lay on the sharp rocks below at the river's edge, twisted and unmoving. Ria squeezed her eyes shut and looked away. Above her, she couldn't see the ridge where Captain Drenall and his men fought for their lives, but she heard sounds of a fierce struggle. Horses whinnied, and men cried out in desperation.

"My lady!"

Off to the left, Biren was climbing up the embankment, the boy Finn following behind her. The leaves and grass in Biren's auburn hair told Ria that theirs hadn't been an easy descent either, but they were in far better shape than Ria.

"You're alive!" Biren scrambled toward her, using the thick vines to pull herself up to where Ria sat. "When I saw you go over the edge, I was so afraid! Are you all right?"

"I seem to be in one piece, but my arm is hurt." Ria's voice was stronger than she felt. That was something.

Biren moved to her injured side. "Shall I look at it?"

But before Ria could respond, a man tumbled down the cliff and landed not ten yards from where they crouched. One of their attackers. He breathed raggedly, pink foam forming around his lips. His eyes flickered toward them, and he croaked a sound like speech.

"We must get away from here," Biren whispered, gesturing to the river. "If we can get around that bend, we'll be able to cross without being seen. Then we can hide in the woods until help comes."

"Your horse..?" Ria asked, but Biren shook her head.

"I had to leave him."

Biren helped her to her feet. Ria bit her lip against the intense pain, panting with the exertion of holding back a cry. It was slow going down the cliff until they got to the river's edge, and every time she slipped the pain in her shoulder intensified. But she forced herself to keep going, feeling helplessly exposed to the ridge above.

Until help comes, Biren had said. But Ria knew that there would be no help coming for several days at least. If Captain Drenall survived, it would be that long before he could return to Endvar for reinforcements. If he didn't, it would be many days more before they were missed in Albon and a search party sent. All that time, they would be on their own.

And hunted.

Thirty

Aiya was grateful that Dan didn't try to talk her out of going to her home before leaving Endvar. He had insisted on waiting until midday when there were crowds in the street and less chance for unexpected danger. He'd spoken to a laundress at the guard complex and borrowed a proper dress so that Aiya wouldn't draw attention in her nightdress and ill-fitting coat.

Dan had also insisted that they bring another soldier.

They found Jax behind the stables, about to lose a knife-throwing contest with three other soldiers. He was happy to cut his defeat short and join them.

"You just saved me from losing my next week's wages," Jax said, grinning at Aiya as he fell into step beside Dan.

"You shouldn't be gambling, Jax," Dan chided. "I'll have to report you if it happens again."

"Come on, Dan. It was just a friendly wager."

Dan glared at him. Aiya sensed that this wasn't the first time they had had such a conversation.

They traveled through the back streets of Endvar, taking an indirect route to Aiya's house. A light rain drizzled steadily, creating striated patterns on the old stone buildings like a giant inkwell had been poured over the city, slowly running down the walls to pool in the streets. The smell of smoke on the air mingling with the scent of rain was one of Aiya's favorite sensations that marked the changing seasons.

As they drew closer to the textile district, the scent of smoke grew stronger. Aiya was about to mention this when Dan stopped them.

"Something's not right," he said. "Stay here." He jogged ahead and turned down a side street.

Aiya hugged herself, looking around the alley where they had stopped. It seemed too quiet, even for a rainy afternoon. And that smell, it didn't smell like a common wood fire. It was more like—

Dan reappeared around the corner, looking stricken. "I'm so sorry, Aiya. Your home. There's nothing left."

Aiya pushed past him and turned down the side street. A pile of smoldering rubble was just visible, and it wasn't until she ran down the street and out into the open that she saw the full extent of the damage. One half wall and a chimney. That was all that remained of her home. They had burned down the entire building. Not just Imar's shop, but the milliner next door and the tailor on the far side as well. She stood in shock, trying to take it all in, until Dan grabbed her by the arm and pulled her back into the shadows.

"They might be watching," he hissed.

Aiya let him pull her away. There was nothing more for her to see. She realized now she should have expected it. If Behni wanted to send her a message, what else would he do? There was a dark irony to it that terrified her.

"We must go. Now," Dan said urgently, his eyes darting in all directions as if expecting to meet an enemy at every corner. It was only when they neared the market that Aiya realized they were headed toward the city gates. "We'll stay close to the market. There will be more people and peacekeepers there. It's less likely they would risk an attack."

But Aiya knew that was an idle wish. Behni had burned down her home with impunity. If he was following her now, he would find a way to attack no matter how many people were watching.

It was as they passed the market—where many vendors were closing early due to the rain—that the screams started. Shouts came from the other end of the street, sounding angry and afraid. Aiya craned her neck around a grocer's cart but couldn't see anything except a few peacekeepers headed in the opposite direction. She suddenly felt very tired and wanted nothing more than to find a place to rest.

"Jax, go see what it is," Dan nodded in the direction of the disturbance. The taller man stepped around the cart and disappeared from sight.

Then, almost as one, the crowd turned and began running toward them. People dropped their wares in their haste, fear and panic written on their faces. The shouts grew louder, and Aiya saw a flash of brown; peacekeeping soldiers engaged in battle. They were losing, falling back toward the crowd.

Aiya was a tumbling rock in a stream of people. They knocked her out of the way as they called out to loved ones, stumbled, snatched up little ones who had gotten free of their grasp. But all Aiya could do was watch, letting them push her wherever they would.

Where was Dan? He was no longer by her side. Had the crowd separated them? Or had he gone to help the soldiers? She couldn't remember if he'd said.

A large man shouldered her out of the way, and she fell, scraping her hands and knees against the paving stones. She tried to stand, but a woman tripped over her and knocked her back to her knees.

Pain pierced the fog in her mind, and Aiya became acutely aware that she was in danger of being trampled. She crawled under a nearby cart, and huddled behind a wheel. Now all she could see of the crowd was a pandemonium of legs and feet. Beyond them, the peacekeepers' numbers were faltering.

As the crowd cleared, Aiya finally got a look at who the soldiers were fighting. It chilled her. There were only a few dozen peacekeepers. But their foe numbered in the hundreds.

Armed men wearing no crest or formal uniform, but skilled soldiers nonetheless. She saw it in their ordered ranks, their effortless stances. They cut down the peacekeepers as though they were saplings beneath the axe. A mix of both dark Khouri and fair Ardanian, the contrast formed something like a scene from a devil's carnival.

The last of the crowd dispersed, and Aiya suddenly realized that she was horribly alone. The peacekeepers were falling fast. Soon there would be nothing between her and the devil army. She scanned the street behind her, then bolted to the nearest alleyway.

She ran down the empty alley and turned a corner. It was a dead end. Aiya hesitated long enough to get her bearings. She was facing east. Leaning against the wall were several stacks of crates towering at different heights. If she could get over the wall, that would bring her closer to the guard complex.

And safety.

Boots sounded down the street, coming at a quick pace. She slipped her feet out of her heavy shoes. The stones beneath her feet were wet with rain, but the wall was still mostly dry.

It had been so long since she'd done this.

Backing away from the wall, she took it at a run, jumping at the last moment to attack the wall in mid-leap. Using her momentum, she bounded off the wall and propelled herself up toward the shortest tower of crates. Pausing only a moment, she leaped to the next, then back up the wall like a lemur, never pausing long enough to put any weight on any one spot.

A shout below told her that she'd been seen. It took her a split second to realize the language had been her own native tongue. That wasn't comforting.

Aiya scrambled over the top of the wall, wishing she were dressed properly for climbing, then scanned the ground beneath her. It was a walled garden with no obvious way in or out. But on the other side was an empty street, and in the distance, an intersection she recognized. The guard complex wasn't far.

Shakily, she pushed herself up to stand. There was a time when balancing on top of a narrow wall such as this was child's play. But those days were long past, and she trembled as she breathed to steady herself.

A small dart whizzed by her ear. Another clattered against the top of the wall. Khouri weapons. Aiya jumped forward, moving at a pace just short of a trot. She followed the wall, then turned when it intersected another, her balance improving as she went.

She left the soldiers behind, trapped in the alley. Unless they had been trained as she had, they would be unable to follow. It would take too long to dismantle and rearrange the crates. The streets around her were emptying quickly. There were sounds of fighting off to her left, though she could see nothing with the height of the buildings towering over her.

Just how many armies were there?

Aiya leaped off the wall into the air, grabbing a tree branch that hung a few feet away. Her momentum swung the branch low, and she dropped to the ground, rubbing her scraped hands against her skirt.

Of course there was more than one force. Endvar had four gates. No attack would succeed without getting control of the gates, preventing the garrison from stopping the attack.

And if they were prepared to handle the garrison, they had certainly prepared for—

Aiya ducked inside a doorway and wiped the rain from her face as a mass of soldiers ran past. They did not wear Rahmish colors, and they were running toward the guard complex.

Aiya cursed softly. There would be no safety there.

She ran the other direction, her bare feet slapping painfully against the wet stones, picking up little pieces of sharp gravel. At the end of the street, she rounded the corner and ran into a man.

She shrieked, but cut it short as she recognized him.

"Aiya!" Dan said with relief. "I've been looking—"

"Soldiers. Behind me!" Aiya panted.

Dan frowned and looked back the way he had come. "There are armed men down that way too. Follow me."

He broke into a run, and Aiya followed as quickly as she could, slowed by her bare feet and awkward skirts. Dan paused at the intersection, waiting for her to catch up while he scouted the street. Debris from the hasty departure of so many citizens littered the road. A dog picked through the contents of an abandoned basket, and a mule waited obediently, still harnessed to a small wagon.

Aiya leaned against the wall, gulping air. Her lungs burned and she felt a metallic taste in the back of her throat. She wasn't as fit as she had once been. Years of quiet shopkeeping had taken their toll.

Dan glanced down. "Where are your shoes?" he asked, incredulously.

Aiya coughed a laugh. "I…lost them," she said. It seemed a silly thing to try to explain.

"We won't be able to go too much farther this way," Dan said. "But if we can find a place to hide for a few hours, we can sneak you out of the city after dark."

Aiya looked around, trying to figure out where they were. She hadn't paid much attention to where they were running, so she was surprised when she realized that they weren't far from her rented room.

Though she hadn't been there in weeks, it was still hers. Hala might not have told Behni about it, since that would reveal that she'd been hiding knowledge of Aiya for all those months. It might be a safe place to hide.

Or hired killers might be waiting for them.

What choice did they have?

"There may be a place," she said to Dan. "Come with me."

Thirty-One

Rorden awoke to find himself being nudged by Captain Strong's boot.

"Riders," he said, nodding at the horizon.

Rorden jumped to his feet, shaking off the groggy feeling from a hard sleep interrupted too soon. Captains Strong and Eldar were already mounting their horses.

A small group of riders was headed their direction, and as they approached, Rorden recognized the green of the Royal Guard.

Four soldiers, each bloodied as though they'd been through battle. Rorden's heart sank. They were too late. One of the soldiers reined his horse to a stop before their group.

"Captain Strong!" the sergeant called out. "I'm glad to see you, sir. We've been attacked, and Captain Drenall sent me for help." He looked around at the company of soldiers with an expression of awed relief.

"Is the princess safe?" Strong asked urgently.

The sergeant's shoulders drooped. "They took her, sir. We would have pursued, but we lost so many men, outnumbered three to one. We're the only ones fit to ride, us and another squad that Captain Drenall sent to Albon. Everyone else is either too wounded or—"

"But she's alive?" Strong interrupted.

"Yes, I think so. No one saw them take her, but her horse was found at the bottom of the ravine. The maid and the boy are both missing too. We searched for any sign of them, but they must have been taken. If they were dead or wounded, I'm sure we would have found them."

"How much farther until we reach the ambush site?" Eldar asked.

"Not far. Perhaps two hours. It's lucky you're here. I expected to have to go all the way to the city before—"

Without waiting for another word, Captain Strong spurred his horse and started down the road at a gallop. Rorden hurried to catch up. The sun was already beginning its descent in the western sky ahead of them, offering only a few more hours of daylight. The thought of the enemy getting away with their captives in the dark filled Rorden with fear.

After a time, the road climbed away from the river, the bank growing ever steeper. Ahead, an outcropping of rock narrowed the road further, and Rorden saw signs of a battle recently fought. Men and horses littered the road, the dirt beneath them stained red. A few shapes moved among them, pausing to look up as they approached. Captain Drenall was the first to step forward, his shoulder bleeding copiously.

"Strong!" Drenall called out, his voice weak. "I'm glad to see you."

Captain Strong dismounted and eyed the man critically. "You're losing too much blood from that shoulder. Rest. Eldar will care for your wounded."

Drenall slumped a little and a nearby corporal rushed to his side to support him.

Strong turned to Eldar. "Tend to the wounded before making camp. The dead can wait."

Eldar nodded grimly. There would be many graves to dig this night.

Among the dead were several men with a foreign look. Fairer than the Rahmish, they had flatter features and widely set eyes.

"Ardanian," Rorden said, bending over one.

"Yes," Strong agreed. "It appears Aiya was right about our friends to the east."

He kicked a fallen spear out of the way, and then stopped abruptly, bending over a man fallen in a crumpled heap. He rolled the man over on his back, revealing sightless brown eyes and a slender arrow protruding from his neck.

"Is that the king's clerk?" Rorden asked in recognition. Seeing the poor unarmed man who hadn't expected death, Rorden's fears for the missing women and young boy intensified.

"Do you think they're still alive, sir?"

"This was a very precise ambush." Strong looked around them at the terrain and the fallen men. "If they wanted them dead, they would be dead. We just have to hope they'll continue to want them alive until we can find them."

He walked to the edge of the ridge and Rorden joined him. The broken corpse of a horse was visible far below on the rocks near the river.

"I don't see any sign of them up here, do you?" Strong said. Then he stepped off the cliff.

Rorden yelped in surprise, watching in awed bemusement as the captain slipped and stumbled down the steep slope but managed to keep his feet. The sergeant glanced at Rorden, unsure whether or not to follow.

Rorden shook his head and sighed. Then he too stepped off the cliff. The embankment was frightfully steep, and he nearly tumbled head first. He slid, grasping at the vegetation to help slow his descent. Soon he reached the bottom near the river and looked up.

"How do you suppose we'll get back up, sir?" he called out to Strong. The sergeant and his men were following, but some of them were having a harder time, spending more time on their backsides than their feet.

Captain Strong was bent over a body on the slope and didn't look up when he answered. "We won't."

He straightened and moved to a patch of bracken nearby. Rorden waited patiently, knowing that whatever the captain was seeing would be lost to his eyes.

At last, Strong turned and bounded down the slope to Rorden's side, joining him on the rocks. "They were here," he announced with satisfaction.

"Yes?" Rorden felt a seed of hope at the captain's expression.

"I don't believe they were taken. I see no signs of struggle. Pursuit, yes, but not capture. If we hurry, we may find them before it's too late."

Captain Strong jumped off the boulder onto the gravel shore and Rorden followed. The sergeant and his men made so much noise splashing in puddles and crunching on loose gravel that there was no need to wonder how far behind they were.

They followed the river around the nearest bend, where Strong stopped. He turned, moved a few paces one direction, then another, then returned to where Rorden stood waiting. He dropped to all fours, then sat back on his heels, frowning and scratching his chin in thought.

"Sir?" Rorden prompted.

As if making a decision, Strong jumped to his feet and stared across the river. "There are multiple trails, but I believe they crossed the river at this point and none of their pursuers did."

"Is that good?"

The captain just grunted. "Rorden, come with me. Sergeant, you and your squad continue to follow that trail along the shore. If you don't find anything before dark, return to camp."

At this time of year the river was running low, and the men walked all the way across, wet almost to the waist by the time they reached the other side.

The opposite bank was much flatter and covered in tall grass. Even Rorden could plainly see where someone had passed not many hours before. The sounds of the soldiers tromping down the other side drifted across the river.

"I trust that you can keep quieter than those fools," Strong growled.

"It would be difficult not to, sir. But what if we meet the enemy instead? We'll wish we had their numbers."

"We won't. At least, I don't think we will. I'm more concerned about scaring off the frightened women by sounding like a herd of wild boars."

The small clearing ended in a dense wood, and there Rorden had to trust to the captain's tracking skills again. They followed the trail until the sun glowed golden through the trees. With the fading light, the captain's urgency increased. If they didn't find them before dark, there might not be another opportunity until daylight.

Captain Strong stopped, posture erect and listening.

"What is it?" Rorden asked, but the captain held up his hand to quiet him.

After a moment, Rorden heard rustling in the brush. His hand moved to his sword hilt.

From the left, two figures broke free from the undergrowth.

"Biren!" Rorden cried.

The young woman was flushed and disheveled, her auburn hair loose and falling about her shoulders, but seemed unharmed. She ran to Rorden, the boy Finn close on her heels. He held them both for a moment, then pulled back as Captain Strong spoke.

"Where is your lady, Biren?" Captain Strong asked urgently. "Where is the princess?"

"She's safe, sir," Biren said. "We found a place to hide—a farmhouse. She's hidden in the hayloft, but she's hurt. Her arm—I think it's out of joint, not broken. She sent me to get help, but I never thought I would find anyone so soon!" She turned back to Rorden, her eyes shining with gratitude.

"Where is this farmhouse?"

"Only a few miles, I should think," Biren said. "I can take you, but I'm afraid it might be too much." Her eyes flitted to Finn, who looked as though he might collapse from exhaustion. She didn't look much better.

Rorden crouched before Finn and looked him in the eyes. "Would you like to ride on my back?" he offered. Finn's bleary eyes lit up, and he nodded once, crawling onto Rorden's back with the agility of a squirrel. Rorden stood, shifting Finn's weight to be more comfortable. The boy was heavier than he looked.

Strong looked back and forth between Rorden and Biren. "Rorden, take them back to the road. Tell Eldar you need half a dozen men and horses to escort you to Valdirk. You won't reach it until after nightfall, but they will be much more comfortable there."

Rorden nodded, understanding. Strong didn't want them lingering at the scene of the battle.

"Wait for me at the inn in Valdirk. If I don't arrive in two days' time, continue on to Albon without me. Don't return to Endvar. It isn't safe anymore." And without another word, Captain Strong disappeared into the trees.

Thirty-Two

"Someday I hope to hear your whole story," Dan said, looking around Aiya's room with a strange expression.

"Perhaps." Aiya smiled, seeing how foreign the room must look to his eyes with its Khouri pottery and colorful textiles. It felt foreign to her too, but for a different reason. It was a stage, a prop for deception. Not a place where she had lived and created history. That place was a smoking heap of rubble.

Aiya's heart clenched, and she pushed the thought away. She found a knapsack and packed it with the few useful things left. When she came across the boy's clothing she'd used as a disguise, she paused. She slipped into the bedroom and quickly changed out of her rain-soaked dress, donning the familiar pants, shirt, and coat of the street urchin. With the cap on her head and boots on her feet, she felt more in control. It was a small thing, but she clung to the feeling.

Aiya had just finished lacing up the last boot, when a sound behind her made her turn. A figure in black stood by the open window of the bedroom.

"What are you doing here?" Hala said fiercely in Khouri. "I told you to leave the city!"

"I'm trying," Aiya said, keeping her voice low to not alert Dan. "We're leaving at nightfall."

"It's too late for that! The gates are sealed now."

Aiya felt a surge of panic. If she couldn't get out of the city, where could she go? How would she hide?

"You should have gone when I warned you," Hala said, and her eyes looked pained. "Behni is on his way here now."

"You told him about this place?"

"I had no choice."

"Then we must leave now. Tell him you never saw us," Aiya said, slinging the knapsack over her shoulder.

At that moment, Dan entered the room. His stiffened when he saw Hala and drew his sword. Hala, too, stared at him with eyes wide.

"Stand back, Aiya!" Dan cried, raising his sword.

Hala threw a knife so quickly that Aiya didn't even see her draw it. Dan ducked so that it just scraped his ear.

"No!" Aiya cried, but neither of them paid her any heed. Dan attacked with a ferocity that left her stunned. She couldn't believe his stocky frame could move so fast. It wasn't elegant or controlled, just angry.

Hala dodged and fended off his blows with the grace of a Menari, but she couldn't get the upper hand. The room was too small and Dan too quick for her to do much more than keep him at bay.

"Stop!" Aiya cried again, throwing a glass jar against the wall. It shattered in a terrific crash near Dan's head, and both he and Hala looked at her in surprise.

"This isn't helping!" Aiya pleaded, then realized she had spoken in Rahmish, a language Hala didn't understand. In the split second Dan paused to listen, Hala leaped onto the bed, and swung Aiya's discarded dress toward Dan's sword, wrapping it around the blade in an expert move that rendered it useless.

She yanked on the dress, but Dan held firm, then released the sword so that Hala's own momentum knocked her against the wall. Dan pounced, tackling Hala in a vicious hold and throwing her to the ground. Hala kicked and squirmed, but Dan was stronger and he pinned her to the floor with one knee deep in her stomach, both hands manacled in one of his own high above her head, and one of her own knives pointed at her neck.

"Stop, Dan!" Aiya cried. "She's here to help."

Dan swore and yanked down the scarf covering Hala's face.

Hala let out a stream of curses of her own, her dark eyes flashing murderously.

"Hala," Aiya said in Khouri. "I've told him not to hurt you. I said you've come here to help us."

"I've come here to kill you!" she spat defiantly. "Behni knows you're alive and won't rest until you're dead. He says it is a matter of family honor. You were a fool not to run when you had the chance!"

"Then let it be true. Let us run. Tell him you couldn't find us. Tell us how to get out of the city, and you will not see us again."

"Does she need convincing?" Dan said menacingly. "I could spill your blood right now you little—"

But Hala had had enough. She brought her head up fast against Dan's nose, making a cracking sound with her skull. He reeled back, letting her go. She scrambled out from beneath him, wiping at the beads of blood on her neck where she'd scraped it against her own knife. Dan moaned, blood seeping between his fingers where he held his nose. Hala breathed in great coughing gasps.

Aiya stepped forward warily. "Will you help us?" she asked Hala in her native tongue.

"You're dead anyway," Hala said, but the fight was gone from her voice. "You can't get out of the city. But even if you could, the Ardani-ans are coming and then all of Rahm will burn. You should have left when you had the chance."

"You must know something. Something that can help. I know you don't want me dead."

Hala's eyes flickered to Dan and back to Aiya, and in that moment Aiya saw something like decision.

"I don't know how much it will help, but there are tunnels below the city. That is where Behni hid the soldiers these past months."

"Yes?" Aiya prompted. "What of them?"

"The tunnels are empty now. Useless. No one else knows of them, but our soldiers don't need them anymore."

"I don't see how this helps us."

"That is how Behni got the men into the city. There are entrances outside the walls."

Ah, at last. "Where?" Aiya demanded.

Hala shook her head. "I don't know. I never went in the tunnels. But I know that there were two entrances outside the walls. In Ardania."

"Ardania!" Aiya exclaimed, and Dan frowned hearing the familiar name. He'd made a makeshift rag out of the discarded dress to staunch the bloodflow from his nose.

"That is no good to us, to send us right to the enemy!" Aiya argued in Khouri.

"I've had enough," Dan said, tossing the rag aside. He looked at his discarded sword but didn't reach for it. Yet.

"Leave her alone," Aiya demanded. "She's trying to help."

"She's distracting us while she waits for reinforcements," Dan insisted, the veins on his neck bulging. "We're better off killing her now while we can still escape with our lives!"

Aiya stepped in front of him. "Don't do this, Dan. She's the only one who can help us."

Behind her, Hala spoke in Khouri. "You said you wanted to get out of the city. That's the only way I know. I know it isn't much, but I swear to you that I will not tell Behni. If you're going to escape, you must go now!"

"Thank you, Hala." Aiya nodded to Dan and said in Rahmish, "She's done all she can. Come. We must go."

"What of her? She killed Regin. We can't trust her."

"She will not hurt us," Aiya said firmly in Rahmish. She looked back at Hala, who sat slumped against the wall, and was struck with a sudden idea. "Come with us, Hala."

"What?" Hala's head snapped up. "Are you mad?"

"I mean it. Come with us. Leave Behni behind forever. He'll have no power over you. You'll be safe with us."

Hala's lips twitched. "Safe? You cannot win this fight. Even if you get out of this city, do you really think the Rahmish will welcome me after all I've done?"

"I will speak for you," Aiya said, kneeling before Hala and grasping her hands in her own. "You do not deserve to be tied to him, always doing his will. Being his weapon. Come with us and be free of him."

"I can't," Hala said, but the wistful look in her eyes said she wished she could. "I cannot leave my children. I am the only hope they have. Would you not do anything to bring Mara back?"

Aiya's protest died, and with it her hope for her friend. She leaned forward and kissed Hala on the forehead. "Thank you. I hope we shall meet again in better days."

Thirty-Three

Ria rested her back against the wall of the hayloft and watched through the gaps between the barn's planks, trying to focus on something to take her mind away from the pain in her shoulder. The setting sun was just visible through the slits, a glorious display of fiery orange with clouds tinged muted pink. The farmer had come in not long before to feed the two cows and chickens. Ria had briefly considered revealing herself, but he was trailed by a young son and daughter who kept up a constant stream of chatter, causing Ria to shrink further into the shadows of the hayloft. Perhaps if he returned without the children, she would try again. But he didn't return.

It was probably for the best. What protection could a single farmer hope to offer against skilled assassins? Not to mention children whose discretion was unreliable at best.

And yet, as the night grew still, Ria missed the cheery sound of their voices. Biren had been reluctant to leave her, but Ria knew that help wouldn't come unless they sought it, and her situation was dire. She no longer had much feeling in her left arm, and her hand was turning a sickly gray color.

Of course, there was another reason she'd sent them away. If the enemy found her, she wanted Biren and Finn to have the best chance to escape. There was no sense in having them die needlessly.

But now, as daylight faded outside and a heavy sense of loneliness settled upon her, Ria regretted sending them away. It was easier to be brave in the light. In the dark, the time passed slowly and the silence was unnerving.

The loft was full from the summer's harvest, and the hay was warm from the day's heat, a welcome comfort as the night's chill crept through the walls. Biren had shaped a spot in the back corner of the haystack where Ria could recline in relative comfort while hidden from the ground below. Climbing the ladder had been difficult, but she had managed it slowly with Biren's help. Ria felt a surge of gratitude for the young woman. Not only had she seen to Ria's safety—rather than panicking uselessly as others might have done—but she also soothed the boy's fears as they traveled through the woods, keeping him quiet so that he didn't alert their pursuers.

Ria could use some calming herself. The lack of feeling in her left arm worried her. She listened to the sounds of the animals quieting for the night and the creak of the rafters above her. The night sounds were mournful to her ears. It wasn't long before full night descended, and the darkness pressed in on her.

Ria tried not to relive the terrifying attack, but to no avail. Images of Edvin, her horse, and the sickening feeling of falling off the cliff cycled through her mind. She tried to focus on something positive to calm herself. Rescue and relief. But into her mind came images of Biren being attacked in the woods, or Ria being discovered helpless and alone.

Exhausted, she slipped into a dreamlike state where she was not quite sleeping but not fully conscious either. When the creak of a door sounded below, her body tensed instinctively, bringing her back into the present even as her mind struggled to be fully awake.

It was not her imagination.

Someone had entered the barn.

All senses heightened as she strained to hear her approaching doom. The sweet smell of summer in the warm hay. The rough wood grain against her back. The scrape of a boot against the wooden ladder. The dim light of night coming through the gaps in the planks.

Against the outer wall of the loft, a shadowy figure loomed in silhouette.

Ria's breath caught, and her right hand flew to her mouth to stifle the scream that rose in her throat. As her heart raced, her mind raced as well, urging her to be still against every instinct that cried out for her to flee. Whoever these men were, they likely wouldn't kill her. And she didn't want to risk alerting the farmer and getting him and his whole family killed.

"Ria? Are you here?"

The voice was so comfortingly familiar, Ria nearly laughed aloud with relief.

"Merek Strong, is that you?" She exhaled in a rush. "Oh, you gave me a fright! Give me a moment to think of something clever to say. My wits are fairly addled."

"Keep talking so I can find you," he said quietly. "It's as dark as the devil's lair up here."

"Well, I thought about lighting a candle, but this is a hayloft, as you can see. Starting a fire didn't seem a good way to stay hidden." She felt almost giddy with relief.

"It sounds like you've recovered your wits all right," he said drily. The floor of the loft creaked under his weight, and when she sensed him close, she reached out her good hand.

"Let me see your arm. Biren said you were hurt."

"Are you a physician now, Captain?" Ria asked, but hope robbed her tone of its playful bite.

Carefully, he knelt at her side and felt for her left arm, moving his fingers up to her shoulder. She tried to bite her lip against the pain, but when he moved her arm, the sharp intake of breath came as a screech, startling them both.

"Shhh," he said soothingly, releasing her arm gently. "Biren was right. It's not broken, but it is out of joint. It's very swollen, and might not return to its socket in the first try. You must try not to scream."

She knew him well enough now to hear the edge of anxiety in his voice.

"Maybe we should wait for a physician," she said, suddenly wary.

"No. Trust me. Waiting will only make it worse. I just wish I had someone else here to help me. It's easier with another pair of hands."

"Wait, you're alone? Where are your troops?"

"It's all right, I can do this." He cleared out the hay to her right, making room for him to kneel next to her.

"So this isn't really a rescue?" she said, panic churning in her stomach. "You're in just as much danger as I?"

"Actually, you could say that I'm in greater danger because whoever's chasing you won't hesitate to kill me, whereas I expect they want you alive. Since my arrival now puts you in much less danger than you were before, your situation has only improved. Whereas the danger for me just increased substantially."

"I'm not sure I appreciate your flippant tone, Captain."

"And I don't appreciate your implication that I can't keep you safe, Princess," he returned. "Now, lean into me and try not to scream. It will hurt at first, but if I do it right, it will be over soon."

"*If?*" Ria asked, her voice shrill.

Kneeling on her right side, Captain Strong wrapped his arms around her and grabbed her left shoulder. She turned her face to his chest and leaned against him, taking comfort in his warmth and the musky smell of outside air mixed with sweat. His humanness in contrast to the dark loneliness she'd felt earlier was unexpectedly soothing. Breathing deeply, she willed herself to be silent. But when he yanked with far greater force than she expected, she couldn't stop the cry of pain, muffled though it was in his shirt.

And then it was over. Her shoulder slipped back into place, and immediately warmth flooded her arm as the blood flowed freely again. In the same instant, the intense pain subsided, leaving behind instead a throbbing ache. Steady, but manageable.

"Oh!" she gasped, laughing weakly. "It worked! That was quite remarkable. Where did you learn to do such a thing?"

Strong released her and sat back on his heels, sighing in satisfaction.

"The battlefield creates physicians of us all. Now, it will take some weeks to heal. We need to immobilize it so that you don't injure it again as we travel." He paused for a moment before continuing. "Forgive me, but unless you have another suggestion for a sling, I'm going to have to ruin your dress."

Ria leaned back against the wall, basking in the lessening of pain. "Do your worst, Strong. It was doomed the moment I tumbled down that cliff."

"You're lucky your horse didn't crush you," Strong said. "I feared the worst when I saw her, poor beast."

Ria felt him fumbling with the hem of her skirt. Despite her cavalier words, she cringed at the sound of tearing cloth. Using strips of fabric torn from her hem, Strong fashioned a sling that held her bent arm close to her body. She was amazed at the difference it made once her injured arm was wrapped, taking the weight off her shoulder.

"I take back what I said about the troops, Strong," Ria said with a contented sigh, shifting her weight to get more comfortable in her makeshift nest. "I feel better than I have in hours. If you're half the soldier that you are physician, I suppose I'm in good hands."

Strong snorted. "I hope I'm a far better soldier than physician. But with any luck, that claim won't be tested. Now, get some rest. Once you've recovered your strength, we'll leave."

Ria thought about scolding him for giving orders so freely, but she didn't have the strength to argue. So, settling back she closed her eyes and soon sleep claimed her.

Ria awoke in the darkness with a finger on her lips and Captain Strong's voice low in her ear.

"Don't speak. Don't move. Don't make any sound. Do you understand?"

She nodded, and any memory of sleep vanished. She must not have slept long because it was still the deep of night, and she sensed rather than saw the captain move away.

Careful not to make any noise, Ria slowly pushed herself up to a seated position with her good arm. Yes, there were people moving down below in the barn. By their attempts at stealth, she knew it wasn't the farmer out on a midnight errand.

How many were there? Where had Strong gone? What if there were more than he could handle? Should she try to sneak away undiscovered? She tried to gather her legs under her in case she had to bolt.

A quiet thrum sounded not far away, so soft and still she felt its vibration rather than heard it. It was followed by another, and another, and another. Below them, a man groaned, and another choked off a cry.

Arrows. She counted six total. Strong was firing arrows in the dark, and hitting his mark!

It was over in less than a minute.

"It's all right." Strong's voice sounded calm in the darkness. "You're safe."

Ria hurried to her feet, astonished. "But how—? In the dark—?" She struggled to find the words to express her amazement.

There was a pause, and when he spoke again he sounded uncomfortable. Embarrassed, even. "It was quiet," he said, as if that were reason enough. "I listened for them moving, breathing..."

"You found them in the dark because of their breathing?" Ria was incredulous. She picked her way carefully around the hay until she bumped into him. When she did, she groped in the darkness to find his face.

"What—?" He knocked her hand away. "What are you doing?" he demanded in a loud whisper.

"Checking to make sure you are really my Captain Strong and not some woodland sprite who's borrowed his voice."

He chuckled. "No, I'm afraid you're stuck with me. And please, keep your voice down. There might be others outside. We can't wait until first light. Are you rested enough to travel?"

Before Ria could answer, a scream split the air. They both jumped, and Ria clutched at his sleeve with her good hand.

"The farmer's family! You must do something."

"My first duty is to protect you," he said, but his voice was full of indecision.

"Then I will go, and you can follow. But I will not have those people come to harm because I sheltered in their barn without their knowledge."

As she expected, Strong didn't need much persuasion.

"Stay here," he commanded. "Hide if you must, but don't leave. I don't want to have to find you again."

He crept away and Ria could just make out the faint outline of the outer door opening. For the second time in one night, she was left alone in the hayloft.

Sitting and waiting was torturous. Ria peered through the gaps between the outer planks, but the farmhouse wasn't visible from that side of the barn. When she heard a man's shout, she could take it no longer. Carefully, she made her way down the ladder one handed, easier now that her injured arm was safely bound, but still a slow and deliberate process.

When she got to the bottom, Ria tripped over a man lying on the floor of the barn. Belatedly, she remembered the bodies of the men Strong had shot some minutes earlier. She scrambled away from the man, repulsed, and picked her way more cautiously to the door.

If she'd remembered those men lying in their warm blood earlier, she wouldn't have stayed in the loft as long as she did. The thought made her shudder, and she felt momentarily weak. *Don't think about it,* she told herself, gulping the cool night air to clear her head.

When her legs felt sure beneath her, she ventured around the barn to the house. A dim light flickered in the closest window. As she

crept nearer, she heard the thumping sounds of a scuffle and a child's
cry in the distance, coming from the dark forest behind her. A chill
crept up her neck, and she hurried to the house.

The window was small and dirty, the only illumination coming
from a clouded oil lamp that lit the room with a meager brown light.
Two men held Captain Strong against the wall, while a third raised a
heavy club. Blood oozing from a cut at Strong's temple looked black
in the dim light as it ran down his cheek.

Aghast, Ria ran to the door and flung it open.

"Stop!" she yelled. She rushed into the room and grabbed the first
weapon she could find—a pair of knitting sticks with coarse gray
yarn still attached.

All four men looked at her in surprise, but Strong recovered the
fastest. He twisted out of the grip of one of the men, and brought his
head hard against the face of the other. Then he turned and struck the
first with his free fist.

Ria saw nothing more, however, for the man with the club had
started for her. She ran for the door, then stopped short. A man
stood there, looking as if he'd materialized out of the night air. His
clean-shaven face was sallow in the lamplight, with a coldness in his
eyes that pricked her heart with dread.

"Princess," he said. "We have looked long for you. Come with me
now, and you will not be harmed."

Ria looked back and forth between him and the man with the
club. There was no escape, and her knitting sticks were no match
for that club. Behind her, the sounds of fighting continued over the
throbbing of her pulse in her ears.

"What do you want from me?" Her quavering voice betrayed her
fear. "What grievance would lead you to commit such a heinous
crime against your king?"

The pale man's lips parted in a sneer, baring teeth. "My crimes
have nothing to do with any king."

A mercenary then.

She swallowed and tried again to speak without a tremor. "I deserve to know why you would attack my guard and threaten me. Who do you work for?"

The man with the club inched closer, and Ria backed away, knocking her ankle painfully against a wooden stool.

"You will know in time," the pale man said dispassionately, stepping over the threshold and into the cottage.

A body slammed into the table next to Ria and she started, jumping out of the way as the man fell to the floor, a long knife deep in his chest.

In the moment Ria looked away, the man with the club sprang. He grabbed her roughly, wresting the sticks from her hand and pulling her tightly against him, pinning her good arm. Her left shoulder flared with pain, and she screamed out in spite of herself. When he pressed a knife to her throat, she stilled.

The pale man smiled. "Well done, Tesh. My master will reward you well for your work tonight."

Ria's head spun. The pale man had spoken in Ardanian.

"Who are you?" she rasped, tears of pain pricking her eyes. She struggled to get free, but the man's large arms tightened around her. She couldn't think straight. Her vision blurred at the edges.

"His name is Domar." Captain Strong stepped around the table and pulled the knife from the dead man's chest. Ria looked away from the gore, feeling suddenly ill. Now was not the time to succumb to her weakness. She focused on Strong instead. He breathed heavily from exertion but spoke with measured calm. He wiped blood out of his eye, and it smeared across his cheek. "He's an Ardanian who's been living in Endvar for some months now, claiming to be Rahmish so he could worm his way into noble society. Apparently with you as his target."

Why would an Ardanian mercenary abduct a Rahmish princess? Ria wanted to ask. But with a blade pressed against her neck, she could only manage, "We're…allies." She thought of Artem and his sister,

Tollana. Even Idan, the new king whom she didn't know as well, would be outraged at this treatment of her by one of his subjects.

But Artem and Idan weren't here.

"Allies today, enemies tomorrow. It's all the same to me," Domar said, stepping further into the room and tossing his cloak over one shoulder, revealing the hilt of a broadsword at his hip. But he didn't draw it. The room was small, and a long sword would be an encumbrance. Still, the warning was clear.

"You said you wouldn't hurt her." Strong's eyes hardened like flint as he glanced at Tesh's knife pressed against Ria's throat.

"I don't intend to hurt her," Domar replied. "But my instructions were only to take her alive. If we're followed, she will suffer for it."

Instructions? But who?... Why?

"You know I won't let you take her," Strong said, still looking at Tesh. "Six of your friends lie dead at my hand tonight, and you think I'll just let you walk away? Let her go now, and you may have a chance to live. Make me work for it, and you'll join them." Despite his calm tone, his eyes looked more fierce than she'd ever seen them. Deadly.

Domar smirked. "Again you prove yourself an annoyance, Captain Strong, turning up uninvited at the wrong moment. But with no real power to stop us." He jerked his head toward the open door. "Take the princess out and bind her well," he instructed in Ardanian. "I'll deal with the captain, but don't wait for me. Take her to the boat. If I don't follow, inform the prince directly. He'll think it was a fair enough trade."

A boat. They were taking her to the river.

The Ardanian man pulled Ria backward toward the door, and she moaned with pain. Every movement jostled her wounded arm. Her helplessness was terrifying. Why didn't Strong act?

"Merek." She tried to speak, but the blade stung her skin. His eyes flickered to her, and she screamed in her mind, *Do something!*

As Tesh pulled her out into the night, Strong nodded slightly. Ria only had a moment to wonder what it meant before she heard a sickening crunch and felt her captor shudder with the reverberation of a heavy blow. The Ardanian man's grip slackened, and she quickly pulled away from his weight as he fell forward. Behind her stood the farmer, one eye swollen shut and a pickaxe in his hands.

Ria stood frozen in shock, swaying on her feet. She was vaguely aware of Domar growling and leaping toward her, only to be knocked aside by Merek as he plowed into him. But she couldn't look away from the man at her feet.

His crushed skull was a mess of darkness against fair hair. Blood dark as shadows trickled down his neck and pooled against his collar. She looked up desperately at the farmer, her throat tight and eyes wide. The end of the pickaxe held a clump of matted hair.

It was too much. Ria stumbled away from the house into the darkness but only made it a few steps before she collapsed to her knees onto the hard-packed earth. The edges of her vision darkened, and her head pressed with the wooly sensation that preceded a fainting spell. She breathed deeply, trying to keep it at bay. She didn't have time for this.

Ardanians. They were looking for her. She needed to run.

Instructions. What did he want with her?

Prince.

No, it couldn't be. He wouldn't—

As if from a great distance, she heard Strong's voice. "Ria, listen to me. Listen to my voice. Just breathe. Feel the night wind. Think about that wind. Let it fill your lungs. In and out. Each breath clean. In. Out."

The imagery and the calm sound of his voice helped. After a few minutes, Ria's vision cleared and she found herself kneeling on the ground outside the farmer's house with Strong at her side.

"I'm all right," she said. Then, with a sudden rush, she vomited the meager contents of her stomach onto the ground.

"Well," Merek said, patting her awkwardly on the back as he stood. "It's progress."

Thirty-Four

The streets of Endvar were eerily quiet as Aiya scurried to the doorway of a brassworker's shop. The roof's overhang sheltered her from the rain. She retrieved two long hairpins to ease open the door's lock. She hadn't done this in many years, but it was a familiar enough act that even in the darkness it didn't take her long.

Aiya cringed as the door scraped noisily against the floor. The shop was quiet and empty. Pots, lamps, buckles, and curios stood abandoned on shelves and tables. The owner must have left before the troops attacked, leaving his shop swept and tidied for the day. She just hoped he wouldn't return to check on things once night fell.

Carefully, Aiya felt her way through the darkness, moving further into the back of the shop. As she neared the far corner, a shape leaped out of the darkness, knocking over a tin that clattered to the floor. Aiya jumped in alarm, her heart pounding. The size and swiftness of the creature suggested a cat, but in the dark she couldn't be sure. She paused for a moment to let her pulse settle, listening to the creature's frantic flight into the shadows.

At the back of the room, a door led into a cramped workroom dimly lit by a small window. She passed the workbench littered with scraps, found the outer door, lifted the heavy bar, and pulled the door open.

Sergeant Dan slipped into the room. Aiya had instructed him to wait there in the back alley while she scouted out the interior. If the shop had been occupied, she would have been much less likely to raise an alarm as a solitary woman rather than in the company of an armed soldier. Dan had argued that it was a foolish risk but had conceded in order to make a thorough search of the back alley and surroundings.

"Your hair is too light. Even in the dark I can see it," Aiya said to Dan as she closed the back door and replaced the bar. "The shopkeeper may have left a cap or hood."

She scratched at her head under her own cap. Despite the itching, she was grateful for the extra warmth. As night had descended, it brought a chilly mist with it.

Dan grunted in annoyance, but he dutifully searched through the shelves and boxes on the floor. Aiya went back to the front room, looking for the stairs. She climbed them slowly, ears straining for any noise indicating that they weren't alone.

Upstairs was a large room used for storage. Stacks of pots and pans created a maze that made it difficult for Aiya to pass through noiselessly. The further she went into the room, the more diverse the items became. Books, broken furniture, and even a pile of moth-eaten blankets blocked her way to the back window. She slipped carefully between the precarious piles until she wedged herself up against the dirty pane. She sat perfectly still on the wide sill, listening to muffled footsteps in the room on the other side of the wall.

Below, a high wall marked the border of Lord Bolen's garden. From this view, she could see over the fruit trees to the back side of the estate, where bulky shapes indicated buildings. Lit windows showed shadows passing back and forth, and a few fires in the courtyard illuminated small groups of soldiers. Unlike the rest of the quiet city, Lord Bolen's estate was alive with activity.

"Aiya?" Dan whispered loudly from the doorway.

"I'm here," she responded softly.

A moment later, a terrific crash rang through the room, the sound of pots falling to the floor.

Aiya cursed under her breath, jumping up and easing her way out of her hiding place. "Are you trying to wake the dead?" she scolded, when the last lid finally lay still.

She worked her way back through the maze, tripping over a pot that now lay in her path.

"I'm not used to skulking about like a burglar," Dan growled.

When Aiya reached him, she placed his hand on her shoulder.

"Here, follow me. Quietly," she whispered. With Aiya as his guide, Dan managed to reach her alcove near the window. He knelt, taking in the scene with a frown.

Aiya watched him with a critical eye. How well could she trust this man? He had been a solid companion as yet—searching for her when they were separated and following her lead when her experience surpassed his. But she didn't know him well, and it took more than a handful of interactions to forge a trusting partnership.

There was something else that bothered her.

Creeping up beside him, she spoke softly into the darkness. "Dan?"

"Hmm," he replied, his eyes fixed on the courtyard below the window.

"If I had not stopped you, would you have hurt Hala?" she asked.

He glanced at her, surprised. "Before I knew she would help us? Yes, I suppose."

"But even after that, you were so angry. I thought you might hurt her still."

Dan shook his head. "She needed convincing, and I'm very good at pretending."

Her skepticism must have been plain because he smiled, and his stern expression softened. "My brothers were members of a traveling theater troupe when I was young. Still are, in fact. I did it for a time, but it wasn't…well, let's just say it didn't suit me."

"Why not?" Aiya asked, curious at this unexpected revelation.

Dan grimaced. "Do you promise not to laugh?"

"Of course."

"As the smallest and youngest, I always had to play the women characters."

"The women?" Aiya was astounded by the thought of this burly man impersonating a woman.

"I was young," he said defensively, "and shorter than the rest of them. But after a heated disagreement I left and joined the army. Thought I'd give it a try and come back if I grew tired of it. No one was more surprised than I to find it suited me. Better yet, I could grow a beard and no one could call me Irpa any longer."

"Irpa?"

"The old queen, Danvir's wife. Because my parents gave me this ridiculous name. My brothers liked to say they gave me the wrong one. Got many a laugh over it."

Aiya hid a smile. She couldn't imagine someone mocking this man. True, he wasn't as tall as other Rahmish men, but he was still a formidable opponent. But she supposed brothers didn't always see each other in the best light.

He didn't seem interested in saying more, so Aiya tucked her legs under her, reaching for one of the musty blankets. She spread it over her for warmth, coughing as dust clouded her nose. There was no reason not to believe Dan's story, but a skilled actor was also a skilled liar, wasn't he? What would stop him from turning against her if things went wrong?

Stop this, Aiya scolded herself. *He is not like Tupin. Captain Strong wouldn't trust him if he wasn't a man of honor.*

"You say these tunnels are reached through the kitchen?" she asked, looking out at the shadowy building with lights flickering in patterns against the courtyard.

"That's the only entrance I know of, which makes it pretty impossible to reach now that there are soldiers everywhere. I wonder what happened to Lord Bolen," Dan mused. "Is he conspiring with the Ardanians? Or is he a hostage?"

Aiya didn't respond. She had no fondness for the cross man who had struck her the last time she came close to his gates. But she felt a twinge of pity for him all the same, and even more for his unwitting household.

After a few silent moments, Dan spoke again. "You should probably try to sleep. I want to watch for a few hours, to get a sense of their movements. If there's any chance of sneaking in, it will be in the middle of the night."

Aiya didn't argue, but she had no intention of sleeping. Their situation was too precarious, and she wasn't in the habit of sleeping in the company of someone she didn't fully trust. Loyalty could be short lived when tested.

Nevertheless, as she watched the shadows moving in the courtyard below, her eyelids became heavy, and she vaguely realized how exhausted she was. She'd been awake for nearly twenty-four hours. Despite her efforts to keep herself upright, she surrendered to sleep.

Thirty-Five

Ria sat on an overturned milk pail while Strong conversed in low tones with the farmer. She rested her head against the barn's rough wooden siding and closed her eyes, weaker now that the danger—and her near-fainting episode—had passed. She was grateful to the farmer who had seen his family to safety and returned in time to save her. But she didn't care to relive the events in conversation with the man.

Strong left the farmer with a warning to leave the area for a few days in case Domar returned. The Ardanian had escaped, though he bore a knife wound that should prevent him from following them until he'd seen a surgeon. By then, they would be long gone.

Merek reached for Ria's good hand to help her stand.

"I thought I told you to stay in the barn," Strong said, as he led her into the woods.

"Did you? If I had stayed in the barn, who would have stopped you from being pummeled by that club?" After all she'd been through that night, Ria didn't think she deserved censure.

"Better that than put you at risk. You're lucky the farmer returned when he did. Who knows how far that man could have taken you in the time it took me to best Domar?"

"Is this all the thanks I get for saving your life?"

"I would have been fine. But even if I wasn't, my life isn't worth as much as yours."

Ria had no answer to this, so she changed the subject. "How do you know this Domar?"

"He's been connected with recent criminal activity in Endvar. But I don't know who he's working for and what he wants with you." Strong's voice held an undercurrent of frustration.

Artem, she opened her mouth to say. But the words didn't come. Domar had spoken of a prince, and Ria feared he meant Artem. But to accuse him outright? For what purpose would Artem threaten her? They'd had a falling out, it was true, but she was sure he had loved her once. Why would he wish her harm? Her mind burned with questions, and the last thing she wanted to do was have to explain herself to Strong. For all she knew, the prince Domar had spoken of wasn't even Ardanian.

She didn't speak her fears aloud, but they cycled through her mind all the same as she walked. There was no path that she could see in the darkness, but Strong led the way with confidence. She clung to his hand, and more than once he stopped her from falling to the ground after tripping over a rock or large root.

After a time, they stopped before a massive tree trunk. It stood taller than their heads, black and twisted by a lightning strike of ages past. The inside was hollow, with an opening at the base large enough to crawl through.

Ria swayed unsteadily on her feet as Strong inspected it.

"This will do nicely," he said, satisfied. "There's even room for you to lay down, if you don't mind sleeping on the ground."

"We're stopping?" she asked weakly. She was torn between her exhaustion and longing for a proper bed.

"I'm unfamiliar with these woods, and it's difficult to know what direction we're heading."

"Are you saying we're lost?" Ria's voice rose in panic.

"No, not lost. Merely unsure of our current location." His voice held a smile, and Ria glowered at him, knowing it was lost in the dark. "Do not fear, Princess. Dawn is only a few hours away. With daylight,

I'll be able to get our bearings easily enough. But for now, you need rest.

Ria crawled inside the hollow tree awkwardly, her injured arm strapped against her in the makeshift sling. She was pleased to find a thick, springy layer of pine needles inside. The air was a little warmer too, sheltered as she was. But it was still a cold night for early autumn, and now that she wasn't moving, her body cooled quickly.

Captain Strong sat on the ground outside, his back covering the entrance and sending her into deeper darkness.

"Are you going to sit out there all night?" Her voice was loud inside the hollow tree.

"Don't worry about me. Get some rest."

"There's room in here for two," she said, shivering.

He didn't answer.

Ria tried to relax, but when she closed her eyes, all she could see were the horrors of the past day. The mournful cry of a wolf sounded in the distance, and she closed her eyes tighter, trying to ignore it. But when an insect skittered in the shadows near her, she sat up, heart pounding.

"Merek, please!" she begged. "Your sense of propriety does you credit, but after today's events, I'm only a breath away from completely unraveling. Please don't make me spend the night alone in this hole!"

Her desperation finally evoked a response.

She sensed a shifting in the darkness as Merek crawled inside. "Forgive me," he said. "I should have realized. Of course you shouldn't be alone now."

Ria was so relieved that he didn't laugh, and so comforted by the presence of another human being, that she reacted in the most unlikely way possible.

She burst into tears.

In no time at all, he gathered her gently into his arms, careful to avoid moving her injured arm.

"It's all right," he murmured.

"I don't know why I'm crying," she gasped between great gulping sobs. She buried her face in his chest and leaned into him, trying to stifle the sobs even as her body shook from the effort.

"Let it out, don't fight it. You've been through a great shock today, but it will pass. I've seen it many times with soldiers."

"Really?" she asked, pulling her wet face away from his shirt.

"Really. Let it go, and you'll feel much better when you're through."

It was some time before the tears stopped, but he just held her, stroking her hair and speaking in soft, soothing tones. She couldn't remember a time when she had ever felt so vulnerable, and her heart swelled with gratitude at his tenderness. But she wasn't sure if she felt better when she was finished because sleep claimed her first.

Aiya sat up with a start. At first she felt alarmed and instantly collected her senses to see if she were in any danger. Slowly, alarm gave way to curiosity. She was alone in the upper room of the brassworker's shop. Where had Dan gone? Why hadn't she heard him leave? More importantly, would he be coming back?

For a moment, she considered the possibility that he had abandoned her. That wouldn't be so bad, she decided. Going their separate ways might give them both the best chance of survival.

A fly buzzed near her ear, and she swatted it away. Her mouth was parched. Dan or no Dan, she needed to find some water. She searched the shop first, looking for a bucket or pitcher of water. But there was nothing.

The workroom was a little more fruitful, with a half empty jug of ale sitting on the back of a dusty shelf. Aiya removed the cork and sniffed, wrinkling her nose at the smell. She would have preferred a steaming cup of tea, or even plain water. But her thirst told her this was not the time to be picky, and she obeyed, coughing against the taste.

The back door opened, and Aiya stepped out of sight into the shadow of a cabinet, hand on her knife. But it was only Dan who slipped inside, a bundle tucked under his arm. He paused, eyeing the jug of ale she'd left on the worktable.

"Don't forget to bar the door," she chided, stepping out from behind the cabinet.

Dan whirled in surprise, dropping his bundle and reaching for his sword. He relaxed when he saw her, muttering, "I swear, Aiya, you're as quiet as a thief."

Aiya picked up the bundle. Men's clothing. Something clattered to the floor and she picked it up. A long straight razor.

"What is this?"

He shrugged sheepishly. "You got me thinking last night. I'm not as light as an Ardanian, but maybe with the right clothes and no beard I could pass for one. At a glance."

"Do you speak their language?"

"Not more than a few phrases, no. But I don't intend on sharing a drink with them in The Seven Moons."

"I don't speak their language well, but I understand it. Mostly. I should be the one sneaking around their camp."

"Right," Dan scoffed. "Because you would blend in so well. Aiya, relax. I know what I'm doing." He began unbuttoning his shirt and Aiya looked away, her face growing warm.

She moved past him to the door. "I'm going to look for water. There is none in the shop. Only that old jug of ale, but that won't help you with a shave."

Dan just grunted as Aiya grabbed an ornate urn and slipped out the back. She scurried down the narrow alley, padding lightly over the wet leaves that had piled up in the recent storm.

When she reached the street, she paused. This was the same avenue where she had followed Domar some months before. Now the trees were brilliant shades of red and gold, their fallen leaves forming a colorful carpet on the street below. A door creaked somewhere to her left, but no one appeared.

The whole city was deathly still.

Waiting.

A small distance away and across the street, a large rain barrel sat beneath the gutter of a jeweler's shop. With the recent rain, it would certainly hold water, but it would also bring her in view of Lord Bolen's gates where Khouri soldiers stood guard.

Scanning the empty street one last time, Aiya darted forward to the opposite alley. She circled around the shop and approached the rain barrel at a crouch, out of sight of the guards. Bolen's main gate was just visible through a small gap between the barrel and the wall of the building. The Khouri soldiers fidgeted with anticipation, their postures alert.

Knowing that she was so close to water only intensified Aiya's thirst, making her throat burn. She clutched the brass urn to her chest, trying to decide how to best dip it into the water barrel without drawing attention to herself.

The grinding sound of wheels against stone made her look up. Following a group of soldiers, a horse-drawn wagon approached, driven by an Ardanian man. In the wagon bed sat a group of Rahmish citizens. Their fine clothing indicated they were members of the noble class; their beleaguered expressions marked them as captives. Aiya's breath stilled as the wagon passed. Two small children sat in the back, their chestnut brown hair barely visible above the side as they leaned against a woman who must surely be their mother. At the sight of those two children—likely going to their deaths, or at least soon to become orphans—Aiya shrank further into the shadows.

The soldiers at the gate sprang to open the heavy wooden doors, heaving them wide on squealing hinges. Gathering her courage, Aiya stood, dipping the urn soundlessly into the rain barrel. The barrel wasn't even halfway full, so she had to reach far into its depths and felt horribly exposed to the enemy soldiers.

It only took a moment, and when she stood again and glanced at the gate, no one appeared to have noticed. Then Aiya realized with a start that the soldiers bringing up the rear weren't Khouri or Ardanian. They wore the dark blue uniforms of Captain Strong's Wall Guard. These were a bedraggled lot; wounded and, in some cases, half dragging each other when one of their fellows couldn't walk on his own. Aiya spotted a familiar redheaded soldier supporting the weight of another as the man's right foot dragged uselessly beside him.

Her heart leaped into her throat. Jax was alive, and so were others of Captain Strong's men.

She needed to tell Dan. Immediately.

Thirty-Six

When Ria awoke, she was lying alone on the ground with Strong's coat over her. It was difficult to tell the time, but the day was bright outside the hollow tree and her empty stomach told her it had been many hours since her last meal. She felt remarkably rested, though her injured arm still ached. She would need to ask Merek to adjust her sling so that it didn't rub her skin raw.

At the thought of the captain, she burned with shame over the previous night. What had gotten into her? It wasn't like her to be so emotional. She shivered in self-disgust. He had treated her with kindness, but she felt humiliated all the same.

Well, there was nothing for it now but to make sure it never happened again. She was a princess and would act with dignity.

Ria crawled out of the tree and awkwardly brushed the pine needles from her dress. Seeing it in daylight made her cringe. The fabric was soiled and stained, the hem torn raggedly almost to the top of her boots.

Hoping to be a little less unkempt by the time Strong returned, Ria stepped on the edge of her skirt and with her one good hand tore another section of fabric. She soaked it in the collected dew from a plant with elephantine leaves, then used it to wipe her face clean. Everything was difficult one-handed, and she was more bruised and sore from her fall than she had realized the day before. But she felt mildly refreshed when she was through.

Ria had succeeded in unpinning her hair and was trying in vain to comb out the tangles with her fingers when a voice behind her startled her.

"I'm no lady's maid, but I do have two hands if that helps."

She whirled around as Merek stepped through the undergrowth carrying a knapsack over his shoulder.

"Good heavens!" she blurted, straightening up at the sight of him. Now that it was light, she saw clearly the wound over his eye that had bled so freely the previous night, and the dark bruising that had settled around it.

He grimaced at her reaction. "Does it look that bad?"

"It looks—hmm, on your knees so I can see." She tugged on his sleeve until he reluctantly knelt on the ground. Using her makeshift cloth, she tried to clean away the dried blood.

"Are you a physician now?" he asked wryly.

She smirked. "Yes, so hold still." It made her weak to look directly at the wound, so she focused instead on the surrounding area. "What was it?"

"A pot, I think. Some piece of crockery? It was a little difficult to see at that point, but whatever it was, I—" He broke off as he looked at her. "Ria? Are you well? You look pale."

She wished he'd pretended not to notice. She'd been trying to ignore the staining of her makeshift rag, but at his words she suddenly became aware that her hand was stained as well, and had picked up the metallic smell of blood. Looking down, she dropped the cloth and felt suddenly ill.

"Well, I'm no substitute for a physician, but I hope that helped."

She walked quickly away, wiping her hand on her skirt. She looked up at the forest canopy overhead, trying not to make it obvious that she was breathing deeply. It was so ridiculous, this weakness of hers.

"Here." Merek held out a waterskin. "Let me help." He poured a little water into her palm, then used his own hands to massage it into her fingers and clean away the signs of blood.

"You must think me very childish," she said, chagrined.

"For this?" He fought a smile. "No."

She narrowed her eyes. "But for other things…?"

He just shrugged and walked away, picking up the knapsack where he'd left it on the ground.

"What's in the sack?" she asked, resuming her earlier task of picking at the tangles in her hair.

"Breakfast." He dropped it to the ground at her feet.

Her stomach rejoiced, and Ria felt like a street urchin scrabbling after a few crumbs from the baker's cart the way she crouched and tore open the sack with fervor. Inside was bread, cheese, dark purple grapes, and an assortment of nuts.

"Where did you get this?" She tore off a piece of bread and devoured it with gusto. A part of her sighed inwardly. Dignity would apparently have to wait until her belly was full.

"The farmer last night mentioned neighbors. There are several farms just on the edge of these woods near the river. I tried not to take enough from any one family to be noticed."

Ria stopped chewing and swallowed hard. "You stole it?"

He raised an eyebrow. "You didn't expect me to knock on the door and ask for food to feed Princess Honoria, did you? 'And by the way, if some ruffians come looking for her, forget I was here.'"

"I guess not." But she felt less enthused about her meal now that she knew others might go hungry for missing it.

"Ria," he said with exasperation. "I don't like it either, but under the circumstances we have no other choice. Once I've delivered you home safely, you can send compensation and elaborate thanks to everyone we inconvenience on our journey." He crouched and helped himself to some of the food.

Ria ignored his sarcasm. "We're going to Albon? I thought we were going to join your soldiers."

Strong offered her the waterskin, and she took it gratefully, amazed at how thirsty she was.

"They'll be delayed for days caring for Drenall's wounded. It's best if we continue on to the city. If all went well, Rorden and Biren are waiting for us at Valdirk with a small group of soldiers to escort us to Albon."

When she returned the waterskin, he slung it and the knapsack over his shoulder, then began walking back the way he had come. He didn't offer to hold her hand now that it was light, and she didn't ask. But that meant she followed a little more slowly as she picked her way through the brush, and occasionally he had to pause and wait for her to catch up.

"How did you come to find me so quickly?" Ria asked, realizing for the first time that it should have taken much longer for word of the ambush to reach Endvar.

"I received word from a trusted friend that there was an attack planned. We left immediately, hoping to reach you in time to warn Drenall to change course."

"Who's your friend? I must find a way to thank him."

"She's a Khouri woman who came to Rahm to escape a dangerous past, but it seems intent on following her. Fortunately for us, she's used those connections to gain valuable information. It was she who first alerted us to Domar's activities."

She? This surprised Ria, but what really unsettled her was the respect she heard in Strong's voice when he spoke of her. He had called her his friend. Was there more to their relationship than that? Suddenly her memory made a connection. "Oh! I believe I've met her! Is she that lovely woman who was with you when I first arrived in Endvar?" Ria spared a glance up at him for some kind of a reaction, but his back was to her.

"Yes, that would have been her. Her name is Aiya, and she and her brother own a little textile shop. I've rented their upper room for the past few years."

It was a simple enough statement, but something about his tone seemed…guarded. Ria wished that she could see his face to better judge what was being left unsaid. It seemed that there shouldn't be secrets between the two of them, and it saddened her that there were. They'd been bound together these past months. Ria was sure Merek felt it as she did. In some ways it wasn't even a surprise that he had found her first when she was hiding alone and afraid in the hayloft. Looking back now, she should have expected it.

"Merek," she said, her eyes fixed on her feet as she stepped over a large root protruding from the damp earth. "I haven't properly thanked you. I shudder to think what would have become of me if you hadn't found me last night. And...I'm glad it was you." It was one of the most honest things she'd ever said, and she felt naked not couching it in wit. With her eyes on the ground, she didn't notice that he had stopped until she nearly ran into him.

She tensed reflexively to catch herself and winced at the pain it set off in her shoulder. Merek reached out an arm to steady her, frowning with concern. Ria thought about her emotional outburst of the previous night and tried not to blush as she met his eyes.

He regarded her steadily, one hand scratching at his beard.

"Do you think you could get on a horse?" he said finally.

"Do I—what?" she said, drawing back in astonishment.

"If you had assistance, do you think you could ride? Could you manage the movement, do you think?"

"Perhaps," she said, flustered. "But did you even hear what I said? That's not an appropriate response!"

He grinned, kindling a lively spark in his eyes. It was such a welcome sight that it took the edge off her irritation. "Oh yes, your words were very fine. But a little premature. Save your thanks until you're in your father's arms. That will happen sooner if we can get you on a horse."

He turned his back on her and resumed walking through the forest. Ria sighed and stomped after him. It was slow going without a proper path. Strong said they were following a wolf trail, but she couldn't see it. Her torn skirt regularly caught on brambles, and she had to step carefully to avoid tripping on the uneven ground. Merek wanted to avoid the road until they got closer to Valdirk, so they kept to the trees for hour after hour. By the time they reached the village, the sight of chimney smoke rising from the trees was the most welcome sight Ria had ever seen.

She pushed forward toward the road, but Merek held out a hand to stop her. "The inn isn't far from here. Let me scout ahead and see if Rorden is there. I would hate to get this close and find a trap waiting for you."

Disappointed at the delay, Ria waited in the trees until he returned some time later with four soldiers at his side. She stood at the sight of them, suddenly aware of how disheveled she must look in her torn dress, with her hair loose, and her skin surely as filthy as her clothing. In spite of her appearance, the men bowed with respect, then positioned themselves around her in a guard formation to escort her to the village.

"This is almost as good as a parade," Ria said cheerfully. "Give me your arm, Strong. Let's make it a proper procession."

He humphed, but obeyed.

As the inn yard came into view, the cobbler's son jumped from his fencepost perch. He ran up the steps of the inn, but before he could even reach the door, it thumped opened and Rorden bounded down the steps.

"They're here!" Finn shouted inside, and a crowd of people burst out of the door behind Rorden.

Ria scarcely took in the sight of a homely woman grinning a gaptoothed smile and Biren rushing down the steps before she was engulfed in Rorden's exuberant hug.

Taken aback, she was momentarily speechless.

She wasn't the only one.

"Soldier!" Merek sputtered beside her. "Remember yourself!"

"Oh it's quite all right, Strong," Ria grinned, patting Rorden awkwardly with her good hand. "Only do mind the shoulder, Rorden."

"Yes, of course, Your Highness." Rorden stepped back apologetically, his face beaming. "Sorry for taking liberties, my lady. We've just been so worried."

He pulled away so that Biren could step forward. Emboldened by Rorden's example, she too embraced Ria. Ria held her tightly, no words adequate to express the gratitude she felt.

The gap-toothed woman greeted Ria with an awkward bow that seemed better suited to addressing a milk cow.

"I'm Tatti, Your Highness. If you'll come inside, I think you'll find we are quite prepared to see to your every comfort."

Ria nodded graciously and followed her up the steps to the inn, listening as Biren explained in low tones what she might expect from the establishment. No proper bath, but Biren had procured a change of clothes and the mattress tick had been newly stuffed, although the two of them would have to share, and would she rather eat first or rest?

"Food first," Ria said decisively. "If I lie down in this state, you might as well find a burial shroud."

Rorden was in high spirits and nearly toppled Merek's cup as he reached to spear another boiled potato with his fork. Merek caught the cup before it tipped and moved it further away from the offending elbow, but Rorden didn't seem to notice. He was too busy teasing the soldier next to him.

"What do they teach you in the Royal Guard, eh? Do you wear bells on your boots to announce to all the Hall that you're coming? That couldn't be any louder than the noise you made crashing through the forest."

The soldier next to him guffawed. "This from the man who got lost—twice, even!—trying to find Valdirk?"

The banter continued as Rorden regaled the women with tales of their hasty pursuit while the other soldiers shouted him down with their own version of events. The inn's common room had only one long table with backless benches on either side, so those who weren't fortunate to squeeze in with the others were stuck sitting on the bare floor or grabbing an overturned barrel for a stool. A cauldron of thick stew hung over the nearby fire, and Tatti's daughters brought fresh bread faster than the soldiers could eat it.

Merek leaned against the wall and closed his eyes, exhaustion descending on him as a heavy weight. He hadn't slept much the night before, resuming his vigil outside the hollow tree as soon as Ria had quieted into sleep. Partly it was out of fear that enemies roamed the woods searching for the princess, but more than anything it was to escape the princess herself. The warmth and weight of her against him taunted his resolve, and the quarters were far too close to comfortably spend the night without assuming a level of familiarity that was far beyond his right.

So he had spent the night listening to her soft snoring while sitting on the hard ground outside in the cold, having surrendered his coat to aid her comfort. In truth, there were worse ways to spend a night. He probably would have slept if his mind would have allowed him. But every time he started to doze, he was transported back to the previous night in the farmer's cottage when, for a few terrifying moments, Ria had been in the enemy's hands. The fear in her eyes had ignited something primal in him, and it was only with great effort that he'd stayed calm instead of rushing headlong to wrest the knife away from her throat.

He shuddered inwardly just thinking about it.

But she was safe now. Or...almost. With her shoulder injured as it was, riding would be difficult. Valdirk was only a small village with no residents wealthy enough to own a carriage, and in any case, Merek preferred the speed and flexibility of a horse. A carriage would slow them down and limit them to a predictable route, which could be a costly mistake if Domar and his men still pursued them.

Merek's thoughts drifted to the strange Ardanian man who was so pale that he'd looked like an apparition when he appeared in the farmer's doorway. He was the key to this whole plot, and Merek had almost had him. But when Ria collapsed outside the cottage, Domar had taken advantage of the distraction to slip away into the night.

You're getting too attached, a part of Merek warned. *You're making costly mistakes to protect her. You could have had Domar and learned his plan for Endvar, but instead, you rushed to her side at the first sign of distress and let him escape. Fool.*

Finn's high pitched laugh brought Merek back to the moment. "Tell 'em how you fell off the cliff, Your Highness!" he cried. "I've never seen anything like it! I thought you were dead for sure!"

Merek's eyes snapped open and he stood at once. The soldiers quieted in response, and the room grew still. "That's a tale for another time, I'm afraid," Merek said, casting a warning look at the boy. "The princess needs rest, and we all need to be prepared for an early start tomorrow."

Finn moaned in disappointment, but Ria flashed Merek a look of gratitude that made his heart swell.

Idiot.

He turned away from her under the guise of needing to assign sleeping and guard duties to his men. The sooner he could deliver Ria safely to Albon, the better. But he couldn't help attuning his ears to her voice as she and Biren moved toward the staircase.

"I do hope to hear more of how you've spent your time, Biren," Ria said lightheartedly. "What could possibly have put Sergeant Rorden in such a fine mood tonight?" The sound of her laughter as they left the common room made Merek feel mournful, like the last rays of autumn sunlight before the winter chill set in. Yes, the sooner he put distance between them, the better.

Thirty-Seven

The stillness of the night was broken by a woman's shriek. Ria woke with a start, her heart racing. She was in an unfamiliar bed in a strange room, and it took a moment before she remembered that she was in Tatti's inn in Valdirk.

Next to her on the hard straw mattress, Biren was panting.

Ria sat up. "Biren, are you all right?"

"Yes, my lady," came the breathless answer. "It was only a dream. I'm sorry to wake you."

A knock sounded, and the door opened. "Is everything in order, Your Highness?" a man asked.

Ria quickly adjusted the blankets in the shaft of light that came from the hallway.

"We're quite well," she said, squinting at the soldier's silhouette. "Thank you for your attentiveness."

He closed the door, leaving them again in darkness. Ria's breathing slowed, but her limbs still tingled, ready for action. She leaned back against her pillow and closed her eyes, but sleep had fled from her.

Biren sniffed and Ria recognized the soft sound of someone trying to hide their tears. She sat up and laid a hand on her maid's shoulder. "We're safe now. There's no need to worry."

Biren wiped at her face with her sleeve. "I'm so sorry, my lady. I don't mean to be childish."

"Childish?" Ria exclaimed. "Biren, I owe you my life! Without your courage and quick thinking, I would even now be in enemy hands. I've never been more indebted to you!"

"Is this courage?" Biren asked, sitting up and wiping again at her face. "I'm shaking like an old grandmother. Where do you find your strength, my lady? How do you stay so calm even after...after everything?"

Ria chuckled. "You didn't see me last night when I was a sobbing fool. I was like a leaking dike—the more I tried to hold it in, the more it burst."

Biren gave a choked laugh. "You don't mean that."

"It's true! You can ask Captain Strong. Actually, I'd rather you didn't. It wasn't my proudest moment."

"What did he do?"

"He just held me and said it was perfectly normal under the circumstances. He said even soldiers will break down like that sometimes."

"He *held* you?" Biren straightened with interest. "That sounds... romantic."

Ria swatted her playfully on the arm. "It wasn't like that. It was just...comforting. In a fatherly sort of way."

"Fatherly?" Biren snorted in disbelief. It was a most unusual sound to hear from the taciturn young woman. "There are many words I would use to describe Captain Strong, but 'fatherly' isn't one of them."

Biren's words surprised Ria. Not just the words themselves, but the openness with which she spoke them.

"Just how would you describe him, then?" she asked, amused.

"Well, I—" Biren hesitated. "I'm sorry, my lady, I spoke out of turn."

"Not at all. Please, go on."

"I don't really think—"

"I insist."

"Please, I—"

"Come Biren, out with it!"

Biren sighed in submission. She pulled her legs beneath her and knelt up on the mattress. The moonlight coming in the window washed her copper-colored hair and freckled skin in a silvery light.

"He's not like other men, of course. Not like Rorden whose brilliant smile and dimples make me melt right here," she said, striking her heart. "Or like…well, like other men who can dazzle a girl into forgetting her own name. But Captain Strong, he's like…a fierce storm. You can't take your eyes away, but it terrifies you all the same."

"I can't say I've ever found Captain Strong terrifying!" Ria laughed, then cut it short, glancing at the door. She didn't want *this* conversation overheard by the guard in the hall.

"It's not that *he* is so terrifying," Biren whispered. "It's all that feeling he carries within him. Have you really not noticed? He's a man of passion, but he controls it with such strength! It would be thrilling to be loved by a man like that. But also terrifying, don't you think?" Her voice was tinged with awe.

Ria was speechless. It was as though Biren were describing a completely different man. She'd always thought of Merek as serious and respectable, with a clever streak that prevented him from being completely dull. But never passionate.

Although, maybe Biren's words weren't that misplaced after all. There had been moments over the past few weeks when Ria had been stirred by…something. Perhaps even the very feelings Biren was describing.

Biren took her silence as agreement. "Of course, I could never be with a man like that. He would intimidate me, and I'm afraid I would bore him. But when you speak of him holding you in the dark, there's a part of me that thinks it's the most romantic thing I have ever heard."

Ria blushed in spite of herself. "Then I'm glad you weren't there last night to swoon. As it is, I'm afraid I will have a hard time looking him in the eye tomorrow!"

Biren giggled. "You mean to tell me you didn't swoon even a little?"

"No! I was too busy sobbing like a child! I assure you there was nothing about it that felt..." Ria paused thoughtfully. "I've never really thought of him that way. He's always been just a friend, like family. I've never thought of him as a man a woman might swoon over, which is really for the best."

"How do you mean?"

Ria hesitated. The darkness was loosening her tongue. But it felt good to unburden herself in this way. Is this what it would have been like to have a sister? Biren wasn't her sister, of course, and this confidence would end in daylight. But that was hours away still, and after the things they had been through together, Ria felt driven to speak.

"Biren, what would you say if I told you I was going to marry Captain Strong?"

Biren gasped. "You do love him! Oh, I knew it!"

"Love him? Don't be absurd!"

"But—"

"I'm going to marry him because he's the finest man I know and will make an exceptional king. Just the sort of man whom I want to rule by my side."

"Is that all?"

"What else matters? I'm a princess. It's my duty to marry a king, not a lover," she said firmly.

Biren's enthusiasm dimmed. "Does he know that you don't care for him?"

"He knows nothing about it. I haven't spoken to him yet, and I trust you will say nothing. I want to seek my father's counsel first. Surely in light of this, they'll be able to put aside their differences. I'll make a public announcement of our betrothal at the celebration commemorating twenty years of my father's reign and plan the wedding for next summer. After the ceremony in Albon, we'll hold a special celebration in Endvar since it's been Merek's home for so long." She thought this was a particularly generous idea, throwing a party for the elite of Endvar to honor Merek. The Ogmuns would be thrilled to help, and Merek would be…well, not thrilled exactly, but he would manage.

Biren stretched out again on the mattress and was quiet for a moment. "Does this," she asked hesitantly, "have anything to do with a certain fair-haired prince?"

In a heartbeat the room seemed to grow colder. "I can assure you it does not," Ria snapped.

"Forgive me, I don't mean to be impertinent."

Ria suppressed a shudder. She considered sharing with Biren what she'd heard Domar say and her suspicions about Artem, but with Biren's cries so fresh in her mind, she thought it best not to distress her further.

Softening her tone, she explained. "Prince Artem has no claim on my heart. I count myself blessed that I came to my senses when I did."

"It was for the best that you refused him," Biren agreed, sounding relieved. "But I noticed that there was an unpleasant tension between you when we passed through Rellana on our way home. I wondered if perhaps you still had feelings for him."

"No, his bride is welcome to him. Though I expect she will regret her fate someday." Ria was anxious to leave the subject of Artem behind and quickly steered the conversation back to safer ground. "But you see how the heart can lead you astray? There's no place for it in the business of choosing a husband. If I had taken a fancy to Merek, I couldn't trust my own judgment. How could I be sure that I was making the right choice?"

"If you say so, my lady. It just seems a shame to me that you don't care for the man you hope to make your husband."

Ria smiled at her wistful tone. "I do care for him, in a way. Merek and I have something better than love. We respect and trust each other. That will give us far greater success than any passing fancy that fades with time. And someday, if love grows from it, it will be more enduring than mere affection."

"Do you think he'll agree?"

"Of course!" Ria laughed. "Why wouldn't he?"

Biren didn't respond, and Ria sensed condemnation in her silence.

"I know it may not seem very romantic, but it's better this way," Ria insisted. "I can trust reason and sound judgment, but love is a fickle thing, polluting the mind and driving me into the first pair of strong arms that come along."

"I don't know," Biren said slyly, turning over onto her side. "The captain's arms seem quite strong to me."

Ria felt her cheeks grow warm, thinking of the previous night in the hollow tree. For as much as she said otherwise, it was nothing like being held by her father.

She cleared her throat, banishing the thought. "There's far more at stake in this decision than something as fleeting as fancy clouding my judgment. I made that mistake with Artem and will not do that again. Don't you think the people of Rahm would rather know that I made my choice based on Merek's merits and not my youthful passions?"

"Perhaps," Biren conceded. "Though passion makes a better story."

She giggled and, in spite of herself, Ria giggled in return.

Ria turned away from her maid and pulled the blankets up to her chin, settling into the stiff pillow. She envied Biren's simple view of marriage. For all her talk, Ria wished that she desired Merek in some way. But she didn't feel that heady surge of giddiness that signified she was in love. She had felt that for Artem, and it had only brought her sorrow. That wasn't how she felt about Captain Strong. Respect, honor, friendship…but not the intoxicating feeling of desire that made her feel like she was no longer chained to the earth when he was around.

Ria had spoken honestly. Love was the least of her concerns. But as stillness settled around her and she relaxed, her thoughts relaxed as well. It would be nice, she admitted, if she could look forward to the union with eagerness instead of duty. She was amenable to the idea, but a part of her whispered that it was a poor substitute for true affection.

Thirty-Eight

"Got any more of them fancy candlesticks? I've got a buyer if you do." The broad woman scratched at the dirty scarf tied around her hair and made a sucking sound through her large front teeth.

Aiya shook her head, trying to hide her revulsion. "Just these." She held up the ornate buckles, a matched pair taken from the brass-worker's shop.

The woman glanced down the alley toward the main street. "You know they've sealed the gates. No one in or out. Buckles and candle-sticks won't do nobody any good if they can't eat."

It was the problem that was driving the citizens of Endvar to finally venture out of doors after three days of hiding behind their shutters. With the gates closed to farmers and merchants outside the city, how long could the citizens go without new sources of food?

"I will try someone else, then," Aiya said, sensing that the woman was wasting her time.

"I know his mark, you know. The brassworker you're stealing from. I can't sell these to anyone else who would recognize it." The woman sniffed and rubbed her nose.

Aiya froze. The woman chuckled at her expression.

"I'm not going to tell him, don't worry. He's no friend of mine. Doesn't live around here anyways, and I doubt he'll be showing his face anytime soon. Everyone knows this is where they're, you know…" She glanced over her shoulder in the direction of Lord Bolen's estate and drew her finger across her throat.

Although enemy troops were few, rumors of soldiers torturing
the noble class had kept the citizens of Endvar cowering in fear. Aiya
wondered why no larger force had yet arrived. A part of her was frustrated that the citizenry didn't act to take back their city before it was
too late. But she was trying to escape attention herself. It wasn't fair
to blame them for doing the same.

"If you can't help me…" Aiya began, but the woman stopped her.

"I'll get you the oil, but I want double payment."

"When?" Aiya asked, handing over the buckles.

"Tomorrow morning."

"Not good enough. I need it tonight."

"Fine. Meet me back here at nightfall. And bring something a
little more interesting than these trinkets," the woman said, coughing
as she tucked them into her filthy bodice.

Back at the shop, Aiya found Dan at his typical place before the
upper window. He'd cleared away some of the piles of detritus and
found a low footstool upon which to sit while he watched the movements on Lord Bolen's estate. This is where he spent the daylight
hours. At night, he snuck onto the estate to look for his friends. But
so far he'd learned nothing about the soldiers Aiya had seen.

As Aiya entered the storage room, Dan turned. The pale light
from the dirty window illuminated his features, and Aiya was struck
by how handsome he was without his beard. His features were fine
and delicate, almost in the way of a Khouri man, though his fair col-
oring was a striking contrast from her native people. She understood
why in his youth he would have been picked for the woman roles in
his brothers' theater troupe. But she wouldn't tell him this. He would
see it only as an insult, while she would have meant it as a compliment.

"Any luck with your flea-ridden friend?" Dan greeted.

"She pretended not to like the buckles, but she'll get us the oil. We
can leave tonight if you think you'll—"

The creak of the door opening downstairs cut her off. She looked at Dan in horror.

"Did you bar the door?" he hissed, drawing his sword.

"I—" she started to say, but Dan was already moving to the stairs. Aiya followed close behind, marveling at how quickly Dan was learning to move with stealth.

In the back workroom, a young woman leaned against the door, panting.

"Oi! Who are you?" Dan exclaimed.

The girl jumped and reached for a long file from the nearby workbench.

"Stay back!" she cried, raising the tool high. Its end was sharp, but it wasn't much of a weapon. The girl watched Dan's drawn sword with a terrified look in her eyes.

"Calm down," Aiya said, stepping forward. "We will not hurt you."

The girl's eyes darted back and forth between Aiya and Dan. She was dressed like a servant, and her hands were red and chafed. Her features were narrow and sharp, but it was her hair that was most shocking. The tangled light brown curls were cut short in a brutal fashion, as though someone had hacked her hair off with a knife. In places, patches of skin were visible, the scalp matted with dried blood.

"What are you doing here?" Aiya asked.

"I followed you," the girl said, her eyes flitting to Aiya and then back to Dan. "All the other doors were locked."

"Is someone chasing you?" Dan asked, taking a step toward her.

"I said stay back!" the girl screamed in a panic, jabbing the file toward Dan's face. He caught it easily, twisting it out of her grip and dropping it to the floor. The girl gaped, blinking in surprise.

"If someone is looking for you, screaming is not the wisest choice," Aiya said flatly. "Come away from the door so Dan can bar it properly."

The girl hesitated, looking as though she wanted to bolt. But whatever danger had driven her inside, she wasn't anxious to face it

again. She sidled along the wall, keeping as much distance between
her and Dan as possible.

After Dan replaced the bar, he turned to the girl and folded his
arms. "Now, who are you and what sent you barreling into this room
like the devil and his legions are after you?"

"Why should I tell you anything? You don't belong here any more
than I do."

Dan glanced at Aiya and the corners of the girl's mouth twitched
into a smug expression.

"What? You think I don't know what a brassworker looks like?
This isn't your shop, and you aren't Ardanian even if you are dressed
like one. And you—" She looked over Aiya's boyish clothing. "Well,
I don't know what you're up to, but some of those soldiers have skin
like yours—"

She paused and her eyes widened. "You're the one they're looking
for! The foreign woman!" Her eyes flickered to the door, but Dan was
too fast. He jumped forward, cutting off her escape, his hand on his
hilt. She froze, fear in her eyes.

"What do you know of these things? Who are you?" he growled
threateningly.

"My name is Yulda," she gulped, her fair skin flushing pink. "I
heard Master Domar talking to a strange man—a dark man…foreign,
like her—dressed in strange clothes." She jerked her head toward
Aiya, but didn't take her eyes from Dan's face.

Behni, Aiya thought, feeling sick. They had stayed in this shop too
long, and now they'd been discovered.

"So you thought you'd run to him and tell him you'd found her, is
that it?"

Her eyes widened in alarm. "No! I wouldn't! I'm trying to get as
far away from him as possible! He'll kill me if he finds me. But if he's
looking for her, I can't stay here either."

"How do you know this Domar? Why would he want to kill you?"
Aiya asked.

Dan's brow furrowed in thought. "Yulda. Why does that name sound familiar?"

The girl gasped as a dark shadow passed in front of the window. Aiya slipped behind the tall cabinet, and Dan, nearest the window, grabbed Yulda and yanked her to the floor. They all held perfectly still, barely daring to breathe. The shadow moved on but was followed by three more. In the silence, they heard the low murmur of men's voices in the alley outside.

After the last shadow passed, Dan gestured to Yulda to follow him. Together, they crept into the dark of the front shop, out of sight from the back window.

"Were you followed here?" Aiya asked the girl in a low whisper.

"No. That is, not at first. But they'll be looking for me now."

"Wait," Dan said. "Do you work for Lord Bolen? His cook or something?"

Yulda stiffened. "I was his scullery maid, but after the soldiers came and killed everyone, Master Domar made me his cook."

"Ah! This is a piece of luck!" Dan's expression brightened. "Rorden says she's been in the tunnels. She might know a way—"

"Rorden?" Yulda asked suspiciously. "You're friends of Rorden?"

"Yes," Aiya nodded. "Do you know him?"

The girl's face relaxed into an unexpected grin. "Confound my stars. It figures when I run into trouble he's involved somehow."

Yulda's suspicions melted away, and as they did, her story unfolded. She'd been working in the kitchen days earlier when half a dozen armed men had appeared out of nowhere. They were dark and foreign, and she suspected they'd come through the passage in the larder. But in the noisy kitchen she and Cook had heard no sound to alert them. They cut down Cook and the other maids without a moment's hesitation. But their backs were to Yulda, who had been searching in a lower cupboard. Before they could turn, she climbed into the cupboard and sat, trembling, waiting for the men to be gone.

More soldiers followed, and Yulda heard terrifying screams throughout the house. Covering her ears didn't help, and anyway she wanted to know what was happening so that she might know when it was safe to come out. In the end, she judged wrong.

"I climbed out of the cupboard and there he was, watching me. Master Domar, the devil himself with his cold eyes and white skin. Two soldiers grabbed me, and these ones were pale like him. He spoke to them in another language and then smiled at me in a ghastly way. Said I wasn't to die just yet." She shivered.

"Why?" Aiya asked. "Why would he spare your life?"

"I don't know. He made me cook for him and the soldiers, always with two or three soldiers in the kitchen with me. Then last night, when the soldiers left—"

"What do you mean, 'left'?" Dan demanded.

"They were sent away; I don't know why. Something to do with prisoners. It was the first time I was left alone since they came. I saw my chance and took it. I figured I was going to die either way. If I got away, maybe I'd have a chance."

Aiya wanted to ask her about her hair, but restrained herself. Whatever this girl had been through, it was more than just cooking for an enemy army. "What about Lord Bolen?" she asked.

"Dead," Yulda answered, hugging herself. "All of them. They made us watch."

"There were others who survived?"

"A few other servants like me. No one very important."

"Any soldiers?" Dan asked. "You mentioned they had prisoners."

"I didn't see them," Yulda clarified. "But I overheard Master Domar say they would be useful as prisoners."

Hope kindled on Dan's face. If some of the soldiers had survived, maybe his friends were among them. Aiya laid a hand on his arm in warning. "We must try to get out of the city," she reminded him in a low whisper. "We're not strong enough to rescue anyone else. I'm not sure we can even save ourselves."

Dan's lips pressed into a thin line, but he nodded. "Yulda," he asked, fixing her with a hard stare. "How well do you know the tunnels?"

The girl blanched and shook her head, backing against the wall. "No. No way." Her voice was thick with fear. "I'm not going back to that place. You can't make—" Yulda knocked into a shelf and a bowl clattered to the floor.

Aiya winced. "No one is going to make you do anything, child. But with the gates sealed shut, the tunnels are the only way out of the city. If you come with us, we'll protect you."

"If they find me—"

"They won't find you. I swear it. You will be safe with us."

Aiya held Yulda's gaze, hoping to project confidence and kindness. The girl was terrified and had no reason to trust two strangers, but Aiya hoped Yulda would accept her lie. Of course, they couldn't guarantee her safety. But neither would she find safety alone on the streets of Endvar.

Yulda looked back and forth between Aiya and Dan. "Just how well do you know Rorden?"

This time it was Dan who answered. "Well enough to know that he thought you were the only maid of real intelligence among the lot."

Yulda raised her eyebrows. "He said that?"

Dan nodded.

"Well, maybe he wasn't as useless as he seemed." Yulda sighed hopelessly. "Very well. I'll do it."

Albon came into view as Ria and her small group of riders crested the final hill before descending into the valley. The faint yellow stone of the city reflected sunlight in a hazy glow that gave Ria a comfortable sense of homecoming.

She thought back to the last time she had seen this view, after returning from her foreign tour more than six months earlier. How different this homecoming was by comparison! Bruised and injured in body, filthy and weary from hard travel with no respite, and with the memory of recent danger so fresh in her mind, she nevertheless felt more...whole. Yes, she was worried about Domar and the intrigue brewing in Endvar, but she felt stronger and more certain of herself and her future. With Merek's help, she would be able to make things right for her father and her people.

Ria breathed a sigh of contentment.

Merek chuckled behind her in the saddle. "What's the matter, Princess? You haven't enjoyed the accommodations?"

"I don't know, Captain," she replied drily. "I suppose there's a certain charm in sleeping in grottos and abandoned outbuildings, and being soaked to the bone from two days of rain is always delightful."

"Always so difficult to please," he responded, urging the horse forward.

As the group descended the final hill, the view of the city was lost among trees. Merek and Ria rode together on the sturdy mount they'd procured in Valdirk. Biren had protested privately to Ria about their riding arrangements, suggesting that the two women should ride together and Finn could ride with Rorden. It was improper for an unmarried man and woman to ride together, she reminded her delicately. But as humiliating as it was to not be able to lead her own horse, it would be doubly so to ride with a woman much smaller than herself. To be partnered with a large man like Captain Strong, however, wouldn't make her feel so oafish. And when deciding between propriety and pride, there was no question. Ria's pride came first.

In any case, it couldn't be nearly as improper if she planned to marry the man, could it? Ria had to admit she rather liked the feeling of Merek's warmth behind her. But if she ever forgot herself momentarily and began to relax and lean against him, a pointed look from Biren was all it took to help her straighten up in embarrassment.

It really put a damper on things.

They passed through an open meadow with their escort of soldiers, and Ria knew that just ahead was a bend in the road where the trees would part, allowing their first view of Thorodan Hall. She watched for it eagerly.

"Just think," she sighed dreamily. "Tonight there will be a soft bed, a warm fire, a hot meal, and a nice long bath."

"The longer the better," Merek said with a pointed sniff. "The smell of goats is not becoming."

"How dare you!" she exclaimed, blushing. She glanced up, but Rorden and Biren were talking animatedly and oblivious to the pair behind them. Ria lowered her voice. "It's this cursed cloak, and you're entirely to blame for that. Imagine, making me wear refuse from an abandoned barn!"

Her indignation was rewarded with a low chuckle. "It's kept you dry, hasn't it? So much complaining."

"Hmph. Again you show your true character, Captain. No one else would dare address me in such a manner, no matter how poorly I smelled."

Leaning forward, he whispered in her ear. "That's only because no one else has heard how you snore."

That was too much, even for her. Ria laughed freely, drawing a curious glance from the nearest soldiers. "That is not the sort of thing a gentleman says to a lady!" she whispered, elbowing him with her good arm.

He laughed too. "Ah, but you should know by now that I'm no gentleman." He nudged her back playfully. "If it makes you feel better, you're nowhere near as bad as Rorden."

"That's not saying much. Rorden's snoring is what I imagine the Mirwyrm sounds like."

"The what?"

"The Mirwyrm. It's a mythical beast the Branvik people believe lives beneath the mountains. They say that its roar is like the anguished cry of—"

She broke off because the trees parted and her home came into view, but something was wrong.

"Stop! Please, stop!" she cried.

Merek pulled hard on the reins, bringing the horse to a sudden stop. The soldiers stopped too, alert. Rorden and Biren looked at her in alarm.

Thorodan Hall looked as stately as ever with its polished timbers and steep gables. But where the king's garden should have been was instead a large stone structure. From this distance it was difficult to make out any details, but it appeared to be unfinished and yet already reached higher than the Hall's peaked roof.

"What is that?" Ria said, recoiling at the ugly dark intrusion where so much beauty should have been. "Has he built a silo where the garden used to be?"

"It looks more like a tower fortress. Might it be a watch tower?" Merek mused. "Though it's wider than any watch tower I've seen."

"But in the garden? His own mother planted that garden, and he cares for it more than the Hall itself. Why would he bring it to such ruin?" Ria lamented. At the sight of the tower, her confidence shied away. What had become of her father these past months? She didn't have the last letter he'd written—it was lost in her saddlebags during the ambush—but she remembered his portentous words, and as she considered them her newfound strength cracked like a veneer cooled too quickly.

The party grew silent as they moved on, and the view of Thorodan Hall disappeared again with the changing landscape. A sense of dread settled into the pit of Ria's stomach. She'd been away too long, and now she would learn the cost of her absence.

Pain of Betrayal preview

As trust grows, so does the risk of betrayal.

Enjoy the first chapter of
Pain of Betrayal (The *Wallkeeper* trilogy, Book Two).

Pain of Betrayal
Chapter One

"I can't believe I let you talk me into this," Yulda grumbled. "I was trying to get away from this place!"

Aiya could barely make out the girl's outline in the darkness. With her hood pulled low over her ruined hair and a scarf wrapped around her neck and chin, Yulda's fair skin was well hidden. She was almost indistinguishable from the bulky shape of the woodpile where they crouched, hidden from the open courtyard of Lord Bolen's estate. Once the home of a disagreeable nobleman with criminal connections, it now housed enemy soldiers who had overrun the city of Endvar.

A gentle rain fell around them, and the Ardanians moving in the direction of the grand house hurried to get out of the damp as quickly as possible, their wet boots slapping against stone.

A few of the men were small and dark—Khouri mercenaries—and Aiya tensed when they passed. It was absurd, since their fate would be the same if they were discovered by an Ardanian soldier, but she couldn't help the instinctive response to flee. These were her countrymen, and Yulda said they had been searching for Aiya. Behni knew she was in the city, and he wanted her dead.

"If I had known it would take this long, I would have picked a better position," Yulda muttered, shifting slightly.

"Be still," Aiya whispered, as a gong sounded from deep within the house. "Must you always complain so?"

Yulda sniffed indignantly but fell silent. Over the next few minutes, the traffic in the courtyard slowed, and the night grew still. Another gong sounded, and Aiya idly wondered about the nature of the meeting taking place inside. What secrets might be discussed mere yards away?

But they weren't after secrets, not tonight. When the enemy soldiers sealed Endvar's gates, cutting off help from the nearby garrison, Aiya had been trapped with no hope of escape. Her only companion was Dan, a soldier under Captain Strong who had been charged with taking her to safety. Until they discovered Yulda—Lord Bolen's former scullery maid who had not only been in the tunnels underneath the estate, but had even mapped them out for Rorden. She was their only hope in finding a way out of the city.

A door slammed close by and two shapes suddenly loomed in the darkness before them. Yulda gasped, and Aiya clutched her arm, willing her to be silent. If she didn't move or speak, they shouldn't be noticed here in the shadows.

The voice that spoke was unfamiliar to Aiya, but Yulda stiffened with recognition. "You have not yet been released from your contract. It is dangerous to speak to your men of home when you are needed here."

Another voice responded, and a chill crept up Aiya's neck. She knew that voice. It haunted her memories—memories of fire and death and holding her daughter in her arms as her blood spilled black in the night. Aiya shivered.

"You have your city as we agreed," Behni said in heavily accented Ardanian, his tone full of disdain. "There is nothing further to discuss. It is time for us to look toward home and leave you to clean up your own mess."

"Need I remind you that it was the sloppiness of your men that attracted Strong's attention in the first place? Had you not brought soldiers down upon us, we wouldn't have needed to act before we received confirmation from my master. You will stay and help us hold the city until we receive reinforcements. And you will hope that it will be enough and that he won't hold you personally responsible for nearly unraveling his plans."

Behni spat out a curse in Khouri before returning to Aradanian. "Don't think I will listen to your threats. You who couldn't even manage to take the princess when she practically delivered herself into your hands. Oh yes, I know what happened out there with your bungled ambush. If you want to speak of sloppiness, then I have tales of my own to share with your master. *If* he ever shows his face in this city. I'm beginning to wonder if his secret army exists or if he's as impotent as you are."

The other man stepped forward, and light from a nearby window fell across his profile. Aiya recognized Domar who had infiltrated Lord Bolen's staff as his steward. He looked even paler than usual and moved stiffly as if nursing a wound. "He will come; make no mistake. And when he does, he will reward you if you've served him well. You don't want to risk his wrath."

Behni's posture was aggressive, despite standing more than a full head shorter than Domar. "I am not a fool," he growled. "This is not what we agreed to. I will not wait here until the people of this city grow restless and revolt. My men and I leave in the morning."

He turned and started to walk back toward the door, but the other man's voice stopped him.

"Timar. Rosin," Domar said mildly. "And sweet little Fey."

Behni turned stiffly, his face now illuminated by the lit window. His expression was as hard as steel, but there was a hint of fear in his eyes.

"You may have hidden them from your wife, but my master knows their names. Their ages. And where their mother lives." Domar stepped closer, standing over the Khouri man. "Now, go into that room and explain to your men why they'll be staying in Endvar until our troops come."

Behni knew he was caught. Aiya saw it on his face. He narrowed his eyes and spoke in a harsh whisper that Aiya couldn't hear. But Domar merely smiled a thin, cold smile, and Behni turned on his heel toward the house.

When Domar followed, Aiya let out a sigh of relief. She realized suddenly that she was still clutching Yulda's arm, and it was trembling.

"Oh, poor thing," she said soothingly, wrapping her arms around the girl and hugging her close. "You're all right; he's gone."

"I shouldn't be here," Yulda shuddered. "I should be far away from here."

"If you want to get away, you must come with us," Aiya said firmly. "When the army gets here, this city will be even more dangerous."

"Army? What army?"

Of course. The men hadn't been speaking Rahmish. Yulda wouldn't have understood a word. "That's what those men were speaking of. There's an army coming."

"When?"

"I don't know. That seems to be a matter of disagreement between the two. But Yulda, if any of us is going to escape, we must do it together."

A movement to the side startled her. Dan crept closer in a crouch, lifting his hood slightly to reveal his face. Aiya was struck by how pleasing his features were without a beard. She smiled a little in greeting, while Yulda sighed in exasperation.

"Did you stop for a drink along the way? What took you so long?"

Dan rolled his eyes at her. "I couldn't find them. Not even a sign that they've been here."

"I told you," Yulda said smugly. "There aren't any soldiers being kept here."

"But I know what I saw," Aiya protested. "They were men of Captain Strong's Wall Guard. Jax was there; I'm sure of it! Perhaps they moved them to another place in the city."

"So, what do we do now?" Yulda asked.

Dan blew into his hands to warm them. "Let's go back to the shop. Tomorrow I'll go out into the city and see if anyone has seen or heard anything useful."

"You'll go out into the city looking like an Ardanian soldier?" Yulda scoffed. "You'll have lots of success, won't you? The people will practically flock to you to tell you all their secrets."

Aiya looked back and forth between the two of them. "None of us can go out and not be noticed. Dan looks too Ardanian without his beard, and I am clearly too foreign. Yulda might be able to manage it if she wore a scarf and hood—"

"—and kept her tongue under control," Dan interjected.

Yulda scowled, and Aiya tried not to smile.

"I'm not sure it matters, though," Aiya continued. She recounted to Dan the conversation she'd heard between Behni and Domar. "If there are more troops coming to the city, this may be our only chance to escape. It would be foolish to delay."

Dan considered this. "If there are more troops coming, this may be our only chance to reclaim the city. Just think of it, Aiya. If we can free Jax and the others, we could mount an assault on one of the gates. We'd just need to seize control long enough for the garrison to enter."

"And somehow get a message to the garrison," Aiya pointed out. "How will we do that without someone on the outside of the city? We still need to find a way out. Besides, those men were not whole enough to mount an assault. Many of them couldn't even stand without help."

Dan tugged his hood forward again, and his face was lost in shadow. Aiya recognized his need for a quiet moment to think.

Yulda did not.

"I'm half soaked in this rain," she complained. "Can we please make a decision and get inside?"

"Just how old are you, child?" Aiya asked her. "Fifteen? Sixteen?"

Yulda's head snapped up. "I'll be eighteen next spring!"

"Ah, a proper woman then. I was married at your age with a child on the way. That is certainly old enough to have learned how to keep unpleasantness to yourself, don't you think?"

Yulda glared in return and fell silent.

"We need you, Yulda," Aiya continued. "You've been in the tunnels. If there is any chance of finding a way out, it will be because of you. But *you* also need *us*. We can help each other, but you have to stop treating us like we're the enemy. Do you think you can try?"

Yulda shot her a hostile glance, but after a moment, she nodded.

Dan shifted, prepared to rise. "All right, Yulda. Let's see if we can get into these tunnels without running into any of your friends."

Revisit the rich world of *Wallkeeper* today!

Acknowledgments

This book began back in 2013 with—aptly enough—building a wall. When my sister, Carli, was looking for original fairy tales for a class project, I was in the middle of building a retaining wall from locally quarried stone. It was physically and mentally grueling, and I'd end each day with my arms and legs peppered with bruises. Not surprisingly, my fairy tale featured a stone wall as a major plot point. That short story became a very loose outline for what would later become the *Wallkeeper* trilogy.

Crystal Brinkerhoff deserves a shout out for getting me back into writing after so many years away from it. She and Rachel Stauffer provided critical feedback as alpha readers. Cori Hatch was the first person to read the finished draft and her enthusiasm gave me the courage to share it with others. Other beta readers include Carli Schofield, Joan Schofield, Cindy Schofield, Chris Schofield (surreptitiously, I might add), Jenny Hahn, Sara Epling, Julie Whipple, and Renae Southwick. All of your feedback and support was tremendously helpful! Rachel Pickett provided invaluable editing skills, and deserves extra props for working her magic under a scandalously tight deadline.

And of course, I couldn't have done it without the support of my partner in crime, Andrew. Not only does his encouragement carry me through, but his sweet design skills translate my vague ideas and shoulder-shrugging into something amazing.

About the author

Photo by Rachel Pickett

Caren Hahn writes relationship dramas in a variety of genres (fantasy, contemporary mystery, and historical to date). She also manages Verso.ink, a new fiction-sharing site to connect discerning readers with the best emerging fiction. Caren is blessed to live in the most beautiful place on the planet (i.e. the Pacific Northwest), with her husband and six brilliant children.

You can connect with her on Facebook and at her website, carenhahn.com.